The Book of
Lost & Found

Lucy Foley studied English Literature at Durham and UCL universities. She then worked for several years as a fiction editor in the publishing industry – during which time she also wrote *The Book of Lost and Found*. Lucy now writes full-time, and is busy travelling (for research, naturally) and working on her next novel.

To find out more about Lucy, visit her on Facebook, Twitter and Instagram.

www.facebook.com/LucyFoleyAuthor
@lucyfoleytweets
Instagram @lucy_foley_author

lucy foley

The Book of
Lost & Found

HARPER

Harper
An imprint of HarperCollins*Publishers*
The News Building
1 London Bridge Street
London SE1 9GF

www.harpercollins.co.uk

This edition published by *Harper* 2015
1

First published by HarperCollins*Publishers* 2015

A catalogue record for this book is available from the British Library

ISBN: 9780007575350

Set in Sabon LT Std by Palimpsest Book Production Ltd, Falkirk, Stirlingshire

Printed and bound in Great Britain by Clays Ltd, St Ives plc

MIX
Paper from
responsible sources
FSC www.fsc.org   FSC™ C007454

FSC™ is a non-profit international organisation established to promote
the responsible management of the world's forests. Products carrying the
FSC label are independently certified to assure consumers that they come
from forests that are managed to meet the social, economic and
ecological needs of present and future generations,
and other controlled sources.

Find out more about HarperCollins and the environment at
www.harpercollins.co.uk/green

To my grandmothers

sleek as cat's fur. She sits awkwardly, the pose of a moment held for eternity. Her eyes squint slightly, shielded by her hand from an invisible sun of once-hot. She smiles, in the drawing, just as here.

The Portrait

She hangs in the National Portrait Gallery now. Her smile has not faltered through the years, and her hair still falls just above her jaw, as sleek as cat's fur. She sits awkwardly: the pose of a moment held for eternity. Her eyes squint slightly, shielded from an invisible sun by her hand.

Who is she? The drawing bears no clue, nor the little square of text beside it.

A friend of the artist's, circa 1929, pen and ink.

Friend is a difficult word – it can conceal so much. Who was she, really, to the young man who sat down and

1

sketched her one afternoon, with the spoils of their picnic beside them? Even this most gifted of artists is restricted by his medium to work only in the realm of the visible. Some things must be lost to time.

PART ONE

The Work of a Master

1

Already the gardens are thrumming with life. The air is scented with expectation; people are here to do reckless things, stupid things that they might later regret, though the point of it all is in not regretting. For the idea of the party is youth. Not all of the guests are young, but that does not matter – youth can easily be faked with the right attitude. It is this attitude that counts. It is there in the pale knees that flash beneath hemlines, the clink and spill of champagne, the jungle beat of the drums. Most of all it is in the dancing – fast, too fast to identify each of the individual movements, so that all one can make out is a sort of hysterical blur, seething, sweat-sheened.

Tom is not a dancer. Or, at least, not until he has

had three or more glasses of champagne, the first of which he is drinking thirstily. The spindly stem and the wide saucer with its fragile glass lip were not designed for hasty gulping, and he manages to pour a good deal of it down the front of his shirt, where the material now sticks translucently to his skin.

Tom is somewhat out of his depth. He has never been to this kind of event before. It is the sort one reads about in the society columns: drunken, wealthy youths performing outrageous stunts; the Bright Young People. The press love and hate them – they celebrate them, they vilify them, and they know full well that they would not shift nearly so many papers without them. There are men with cameras stalking the shadowy perimeters of the grounds. Tom spotted a couple planted by the bushes as they came in, though no flashbulb flares were wasted on his entrance. He is here as a 'plus one' – the guest of his well-connected Oxford acquaintance, Roddy. They have both been up there for a year now, and Tom is not quite convinced that the friendship will see them through to Finals. Tom is a couple of years older – his university career having been delayed by his father's ill health – and they seem to have practically nothing in common, but, nevertheless, here they are together. 'You're pretty,' Roddy explained, 'so you'll attract the gals, and I'll swoop in and snare them.'

The theme for the evening is Arabian Nights. Tom wears a fez and tabard, embellished with pieces of mirror and coloured beads. He found them both in an antique shop in Islington. They smelt of mothballs and insidious damp, but he was proud of his discovery, though concerned that they might be too much.

He needn't have worried: the other guests are apparently competing to be too much. Roddy pointed out the hostess herself as they entered – Lady Middlesford, swathed in scarlet chiffon, beringed and bejewelled with the treasures of the Orient, veiled with a scarf of the same red from which a thousand metal ornaments dangle and clink together with the chime of tiny bells. A woman smiles up at him, sooty rings of kohl around incongruously pale blue eyes. By the doors that open on to the garden stands an odalisque, her stomach bare save for the adornment of a winking ruby.

Roddy left Tom as soon as they stepped out into the garden, promising to go in search of drinks, but it has been nearly an hour now, and there hasn't been any sign of him since.

A woman approaches. 'Have you a light, darling?' Her accent is regally, glassily precise, the very apotheosis of Englishness, though her outfit of ballooning silk pantaloons and tight fuchsia jerkin is pure Scheherazade. An imp's face – not pretty, too pinched about the eyes, the front teeth too long – but interesting, all the same. An androgynous sparrow's body and hair, shingled below the ears, of an unfeasibly lurid apricot hue. Then suddenly he recognizes her. He doesn't read the *Mail* as a rule, but you'd have to be a hermit not to know of this particular Bright Young Person. Babe Makepeace: 'twenty-one and lives for fun'. Lives, if the rumours are true, on a pitiful allowance begrudgingly bestowed by her disapproving old pa. Subsists, apparently, on a diet of nuts and Prairie Oysters, to keep that boy's body so fashionably slender in a flapper's shift.

He reaches into his pocket and pulls out his lighter. She lifts the cigarette to her lips, pinching her funny little face together in a deep inhalation.

'You're a jewel.' She gives him a playful knock on the arm. 'What's your name?'

'It's Thomas. Thomas Stafford.'

'Well, Thomas . . . Tommie . . . will you join me for a dance?' She peers up at him expectantly through the jewelled loops of her headdress.

'That would be lovely . . . but perhaps later? I'm not much of a dancer.'

'Suit yourself, Tommie.' Before either of them can say another word she is grasped about the waist by some hearty and hauled off into the throng on the dance floor. Tom doesn't much mind. He's perfectly happy, in fact, to stand back and take in the exotic strangeness of the scene before him. Down on the lake, a small boat has left the bank. In it are three figures, two men, sitting, and a woman who stands between them, laughing and dribbling champagne into their open mouths straight from the bottle. One of the men pulls her down into his lap. She shrieks and the small craft rocks crazily upon the dark water.

He turns his attention back to the seething group of dancers again. He'd like to see Babe Makepeace dance: apparently it's quite something. Right in the middle of the crowd he spies a familiar gingery head: Roddy. So that's where he got to. And then he sees her. The way she dances makes him think of the movement of a swan, the energy and activity beneath the surface, the smooth glide above. She rides the music, she moves within it, above it. The bare skin of her arms is pale and bright in the lantern light and her hair is dark, bobbed beneath her ears. Even from a distance he feels sure that where it meets her neck the shorn part would be as soft and dense as a cat's fur. She is, quite simply, mesmerizing. There is something else, too – something more than the mere spectacle of her. She seems . . . what? *Familiar*. Yet the sense of recognition refuses to reveal itself fully to him.

He strives for a proper look at her face. His sightings of her are snatched and incomplete. Finally, the band tinkles and grinds to a halt, and a new, slower melody begins. Dancers pour away towards the bar, slick with sweat, glassy-eyed and flushed with enjoyment. And she is leaving too, smiling at Roddy and politely shaking off the red hand he has landed on her upper arm. She is moving in Tom's direction, towards the house. Tom breathes out, unsteadily. Is he going to talk to her? He isn't talented at speaking to women. Having sisters

Lucy Foley

should have been some sort of initiation, but being the youngest of the three, and therefore picked upon by the others, has merely given him the impression of women as intimidating, quixotic beings.

As she moves closer, he sees that her beauty is charmingly flawed. Her mouth is slightly too large for her delicate face with its small, narrow nose and sloe eyes. She is taller than most of the women around her, and on the thin side – 'scrawny', his sister Rosa might say.

She is a mere few feet away, and he knows he is staring – she will notice him any second and he will look like an idiot. Just in time, he drops his gaze. His heartbeat pounds in his ears. She is passing him, passing right by, and the silvery stuff of her dress brushes against his leg. It is the slightest of sensations, yet every nerve ending in his body sings.

'Tom?'

He is sure he's imagined it at first, and doesn't look up.

'But it *is* you, isn't it? Tom Stafford?'

When he raises his head, she is right there in front of him, her face level with his own. There is the faintest trail of freckles across her nose, and her eyes are the most unusual colour, not dark, after all, but a strange quicksilver grey.

He clears his throat. 'Yes . . . that's right.' His voice sounds odd to him, like an instrument playing in the wrong key. 'If you don't mind my asking, how . . .?'

'Oh, Tom, I can't believe it!' Her smile is wide,

delighted. Suddenly the feeling of recognition that has bothered him unfurls into understanding. Alice.

'Alice?'

*

Tom last saw Alice Eversley in 1913. She was six years old, a scant couple of months younger than he. Her legs were too long for her body, stork-thin, scuff-kneed, and her hair was an urchin's mop, black as onyx. Not what people expected to find in the daughter of the divine Lady Georgina Eversley, blonde goddess of society. Or of the polar explorer Lord Robert Eversley who was, in England, always close-shaven and sharply tailored – though he appeared in expedition photographs with a beard greased with whale fat.

That summer, Tom's parents had decided that the family would holiday in Cornwall. Mrs Stafford had read an article about the importance of bracing sea air for children's health, and her younger girl, Caro, was still recovering from a case of whooping cough.

Mrs Stafford and the children would stay for two months in Winnard Cove, not far from the fishing town of Fowey. Mr Stafford, a solicitor, would remain with them as long as his work would allow. Tom's mother had found the advertisement in her magazine: *Eyrie House, available for family parties. A picturesque, secluded setting in an idyllic, sandy cove*. It was just the place for them. It faced out to sea: small, weather-aged and salt-sprayed but indomitable. As promised, below the cottage was the long stretch of beach, strewn with pieces of interesting jetsam and sheltered from the wind by the encircling cliffs.

The only detail in which they had been slightly misled was in the promise of seclusion. The cove would have been their own were it not overlooked on the other side by a vast Elizabethan manor of dun-coloured stone, partially hidden by a dense thicket of wych elm. *This*, their elderly landlady informed them proudly, was Eversley Hall: owned by the same family for hundreds of years.

On the third day of the holiday, Mr Stafford returned from a sortie in the dinghy soaked through and pink-faced with cold and exhilaration. His wife and children, taking their tea in the garden, had looked up in curiosity at the spectacle.

'You won't believe who I met today. Lord Eversley: the man himself. Here in Cornwall. I can't believe I didn't make the connection before . . . it all makes sense. The Hall is his.'

Gradually, the story unfolded. It transpired that Mr Stafford had managed to capsize his dinghy as he had crossed the path of a beautiful day yacht, causing chaos in the process. To make matters worse, after plummeting into the water he'd got his life jacket hooked on to his trailing mainsheet, and could not seem to get free.

He had heard a shout and had suddenly become aware of another body in the water beside him. The helmsman of the dayboat had dived in, leaving his crew to manage the craft.

'Just like that, didn't even hesitate – jumped right in and yanked me free. It was him: Lord Robert Eversley. One of the nicest men I think I've ever met.' He beamed at them all. 'He's invited us for supper – all of us, the children too.'

And so, that evening, the Staffords made their way across the sand and up a long flight of steps that had been bowed and worn by ancestral Eversley foot-prints, to be met at the front door by a liveried butler. Within, the Hall had the chilly elegance of a cathedral: dark wood, antique glass, ancient stone. Their foot-steps echoed, and they found themselves awed and intimidated by their surroundings. It was difficult to ignore the feeling that they did not belong in such a place.

Robert Eversley, however, was all affability, as was his golden-haired son, Archie. Even the strange, pale-faced daughter gave them a crooked smile. Each one, it seemed, was making their own effort to make the guests feel welcome to the house as equals.

All, that was, save Lord Robert's wife. As Mrs Stafford would later remark, the beautiful Lady Eversley treated them as if they were the servants, being given a Boxing Day treat, bound to return to their rightful posts in the morning. She had shown no sign of interest or fellow feeling towards them, and even the children had recog-nized the slight. There had been a cold smile as Mr Stafford described his profession, a raised eyebrow at Mrs Stafford's mention of the house in Parsons Green.

'She's a frightful snob,' Tom's mother complained at break-fast the next day. 'She thinks we're not worth her time, and she saw to it that we knew it. I gave up trying with her after the first half-hour: it was simply too exhausting. One gets rather tired of being made to feel so inferior.'

Lady Eversley's *froideur* had been the sole blight on an evening that was otherwise enjoyed by all. Tom's parents had spent the evening enthralled by Eversley's tales of moving ice that could crush a ship, let alone a man, in its giant fist; of ice blue and hard as the sapphires in Lady Eversley's necklace; of ice that yawned, black and treacherous, swallowing men to their doom.

Rosa and Caro – fourteen and ten – had been perfectly happy to spend their evening mooning over Archie who, at seventeen, was tall and broad-shouldered as a man; the lucky inheritor of both his father's heroic good looks and his mother's flaxen hair.

And then there was the daughter, Alice. Tom's sisters quickly rejected the strange tomboyish girl with the terrible hair, who seemed almost a different species from her much older brother. But Tom – Tom had found a kindred spirit in Alice. She, too, was convinced that she had seen pirates from her bedroom window, and smug-glers flashing their lights in communication with the shore. And she'd amassed an impressive collection of curios gleaned from hours perusing the tideline: a parasol; a pair of spectacles; a strange, slightly curved knife that Tom had to admit did look remarkably like a miniature cutlass.

While the adults continued with their dinner, Alice and Tom escaped outside and across the dew-wet grass under cover of darkness, to where they could watch the shore for any signs of activity upon the sea. Alice had a platform that her father had built her in a tree, which formed an excellent lookout post. There they had stayed until Sir Robert, under instructions from his wife, had made his way through the garden to them and, with a smile in his voice, summoned them back inside.

For those eight weeks in Winnard Cove, Tom and Alice were inseparable. They spied for pirates, hunted crabs, built shelters from driftwood and braved the crashing cold surf to swim in the calmer waters beyond, beneath the anxious watch of Tom's mother and Alice's nanny. Alice was small for her age, and almost unnaturally pale – but she was strong, and fearless, braver than anyone Tom had met before. She told him that she wanted to be an adventurer like her father, the first-ever female explorer – and Tom was in no doubt that she would accomplish it. Even now he could imagine that sharp face blackened with whale fat, those small feet shod in fur-lined boots.

As is always the case with the truest childhood friendships, it seemed that they should never be parted. And Tom's parents promised – as eager themselves to return – that they would come back the following year to Winnard Cove.

*

But one October morning later that year, Mr Stafford's teacup fell from his hand.

EVERSLEY PERISHES IN THE FROZEN SOUTH

ran the headline. Lord Robert had plummeted to his death, falling into a crevasse hidden beneath a false surface of thin ice and snow. The body could not be recovered.

The Eversleys never returned to Winnard Cove. Neither did the Staffords. The war came. Mr Stafford, a proud patriot, signed himself up to fight in France and returned a very different man. But he was luckier than some. Archie Eversley was killed at Ypres, on one of the first days of fighting.

2

Kate

How should I describe my mother?

She was small, but very strong. Strong in a way that meant she could dance for hours on end, with faultless grace and precision, even as every muscle in her body must have burned with pain, as the blood from her poor crushed toes seeped into the wooden blocks that supported them, even as she was flung, and spun and blinded by the bright stage lights. Strong in a way that meant she was able to accept her position in the world – abandoned, parentless – and make it a part of her strength, the essential element in the June Darling fairy tale. I don't want to describe the things that only I knew about her. Because they're what I have left, what I can cherish. Besides, people aren't interested in that much beyond the dancing, and the fairy tale.

You'll have heard of my mother, I'm sure. Even people who don't know ballet know her name – she'd attained that level of universal renown when she died. And when she died, that night when the plane spiralled out of the sky as though it were made of paper and lollipop sticks, those few left who had not known her came to hear of her. June Darling, the little dancing girl who through sheer talent had managed to escape the meagre path laid out for her.

My mother used to ridicule what she called the myth of her background. She never had it that bad, she would say. She was never neglected or maltreated, and though she may have started out with no natural family to call her own, she soon had Evie, and then me, and we were a perfect three, a tight triangle of love.

Or at least, that's certainly how it appeared. In my more secret, shameful moments, I wondered whether Evie did in fact resent me for complicating things – for disturbing the sanctity of that bond between herself and my mother. Did I have any proof of this? Not specifically. Though I do not think it would be unfair to say that Evie never spoke to me in the way she did my mother: and with me she could be sharp, impatient, as I suspected she never had been with Mum.

I became rather obsessed with the idea of grandparents – of the sort that my school friend Georgina visited at weekends. The sort who would read to you, and make cakes with you, and take you to exhibitions. That wasn't the relationship that Evie and I had. I didn't call her Granny or anything like that. I called her Evie, and we spoke to one another like adults. Looking back, I am sure that she did love me, but next to all she had felt for my mother what she felt for me paled in comparison. My mother had been her saviour as much as she had been my mother's, you see, and I think that Evie simply could not have cared for anyone as deeply.

Perhaps, too, she disliked the evidence she saw in me of my father, who she seemed to credit with having derailed Mum's career via the pregnancy – notwithstanding the fact that Mum was old, in ballet terms, when she had me. My father had played the part of the villain well, disappearing off at the first sign of trouble. But there are two ways of looking at this. If you asked Mum, she would have told you that my father had meant little to her other than the fact that he helped to bring about me. We didn't need him in our lives: we had one another.

My mother was christened June by the nuns who ran the institution in which she had lived from infancy. I always thought that her name had a curiously American ring to it, but – as she explained to me – it related to the month in which she had arrived. It was a good job that she turned up when she did, when the weather was balmy; if she had been left on the doorstep in February her story might well have gone no further.

Orphanages tend to get a bad write-up, but this wasn't the Dickensian sort, and 'institution' suggests a level of deprivation that my mother always insisted was absent from her experience. True, there wasn't much in the way of food or entertainment, but there were three modest-sized meals a day, there were lessons and musical sessions and excursions in the park. In comparison to some children's experience it wasn't a bad deal. It was also all my mother had ever known.

A couple of the older girls claimed to remember a woman. The velvet purr of an engine beneath the dormitory window had woken them in the early hours of the morning. They had clambered up to look out and had seen her approach the building carrying the bundle, and return minutes after without it. The doorbell had not rung. She had been, they would say later, as sleek and expensive-looking as the car that had driven her away, though they couldn't agree on particulars – the colour of the hair beneath the hat, her height, her age. Yet both had been left with the impression of a great and peculiar beauty.

I once asked my mother if she had loved the nuns. She admitted that she couldn't remember all of them individually – other than as a benevolent, omnipresent abstract, rather like the impression of God that the sisters had furnished her with. The one exception to this was Sister Rose, who didn't stand out for any particular quirk of personality, but because she became an agent in the shaping of my mother's future. She was the sister in charge of music lessons, which didn't entail much beyond an elderly set of instruments, donated by various patrons and kept in a wooden chest in the gymnasium. Every Friday afternoon they would be removed and distributed with precise fairness for the girls to play on in their untutored way.

Then something rather unusual happened. When my mother was about six years old a new scheme was introduced. It was the brainchild of a wealthy patron – an anonymous philanthropist had an idea to set up a programme by which the girls might learn the joys of song and dance.

If my mother had been born a few years later, her life would have turned out very differently. Such a project could not have continued as German bombs rained fire upon the city. As it was, she got her chance.

The ballet teacher – and, as it transpired, the daughter of the philanthropist who had devised the initiative – was a woman named Evelyn Darling.

The Tale of Evelyn Darling

Evelyn Darling was born into the sort of life in which most things could be guaranteed. Her father, Bertram, had inherited his father's metallurgical business, and had seen business boom during the First World War. As his only child, Evelyn stood assured of a large inheritance and a cosseted future. However it soon became clear that she wasn't to be satisfied by the sort of life that heiresses normally lead. She had more ambitious and unusual plans for her future.

As a girl, Evelyn had gone several times to the ballet with her parents, and she had never seen anything as beautiful, as magical, as the creatures that flitted back and forth before her on the stage. It became her wish to learn to dance like them, and her father, unable to refuse her in anything, paid for her to have lessons – as many lessons as she could endure. He wasn't sure about letting her perform: it didn't seem to be quite the thing for girls of the sort of class to which he aspired. Eventually, though, he permitted her to dance in a small way at private gatherings.

Evelyn became rather good. Not, perhaps, of the highest calibre, but talented enough by nineteen to catch the eye of one young gentleman in particular. She might not have been conventionally pretty, Evelyn, but she had a way of moving – like a wood nymph – and a voice like the high clear ringing of a bell.

In 1935 Evelyn and Harry were engaged to be married. Evelyn would take up dancing again after they wed, but she would probably never perform again: it wasn't fitting for a married woman to do so, and, besides, Harry was the love of her life now.

A scant couple of months before the date that had been set for the ceremony, Harry took Evelyn for a drive in the Sussex countryside in the new car that Bertram had bought them as an early wedding present. It was a glorious day, full of the promise of summer, the air filled with sunlight, the roads dry, so no one could be quite sure what it was that caused the tyres to skid. What could be established, however, was that the car was travelling at great speed, far too fast for Harry to have righted their course before they ploughed into one of the beech trees that lined the roadside. Evie was lucky. She lost the baby that she had not even known that she had been carrying, and her right leg was fractured in seven places, forever after to be held together by an ingenious framework of metal pins and bands. Harry was not so fortunate: he was killed outright.

Evelyn, for all the overabundance of her youth, was possessed of an innate toughness of character. She knew that she would never dance again, professionally or otherwise, that she would never again bear children, and that she could probably never love another man in the way she had Harry. And yet she took to the rehabilitation programme devised for her with great determination. Every day she would make the journey to Battersea Park – just across the bridge from her father's townhouse – to perform her strengthening exercises in the green surrounds. It was here that she saw the troupe of orphanage girls in their maroon smocks taking their walk, with two of the sisters at helm and aft. In that moment the idea was born.

I don't think it would be untrue to say that in my mother Evie found the daughter that she had never been able to bear, along with, perhaps, the story of success that could never have been hers. She taught her everything she knew. A year after Mum first crossed the threshold of the ballet studio, Evie had adopted her as her own.

In 1938, my eight-year-old mother won a scholarship to the Sadler's Wells Ballet School and Company. The rest, as they say, is history. The orphanage, the hand-me-down costume that she'd first worn to train in – these became part of my mother's fairy tale.

Fairy tales, however, do not always end happily – in fact, quite often it's the opposite, despite what modern retellings may ask you to believe. That was a difficult lesson to learn; perhaps I am learning it still. The fourteenth of April 1985. I tried to think, later, of what I was doing at the time, the exact time when the crash happened. Did I know, at that moment, in some fundamental part of my being? I have a terrible suspicion that I was buying a round for some of my old art-school friends at the Goodge Street pub we met in: blithely going about my day with no idea of how my life had suddenly changed.

After the plane crash I moved back into the house in Battersea where the three of us had lived: a big, cluttered Victorian conversion on one of those streets leading away from the park. It was only me there now. A couple of years before, Evie had gone into a home, diagnosed with progressive dementia. For a long time, Mum had refused to consider the possibility of moving

24

her into care. Her work as a choreographer had seen her travelling frequently, but she said that she would downsize and find work closer to home so she could spend more time looking after Evie. Yet Evie's behaviour became increasingly confused and erratic. When she was found on the other side of the borough with a broken elbow and no knowledge of how she'd got so far from home, it became clear that she didn't simply need more extensive care, she needed it round-the-clock. Mum couldn't afford to stop working completely, and I had to be at the Slade, where I was taking my degree in Fine Art.

'It would be better', said the social worker at St George's, who had an illustrated-textbook turn of phrase, 'for her to have the company of others – which can be achieved with at-home visits, but is far more easily accomplished in a nursing home, where she can have a social life, too.'

I can see why my mother found the decision such a difficult one to make. This was the woman who had cared for her from infancy, without whose love and influence she would never have had the life she did. I know she suffered over it, felt that she was committing a terrible form of betrayal. There was the added complication that Evie didn't always seem in a particularly bad way – she could have moments of sudden and startling lucidity, and there were whole days when it would appear that nothing at all was amiss. But the bad days were very bad, and the possibilities of what could happen in the hours Evie might be alone were frightening. In the end, Mum had accepted that there was no alternative.

3

It was a year after Mum had died when it all happened. I had just about managed to convince myself that I was all right. Looking back, I can see that I wasn't. I was twenty-seven, and my days tended to consist of an unvarying routine: work, and visiting Evie. But I was managing to present to the outside world a promising enough impression of surviving. It helps that after the first three months people tend to stop asking how you're coping, and, if there isn't strong evidence to the contrary, feel you must be getting on with life.

I saw hardly anything of my old art-school friends. It hadn't been a conscious thing, but I can see now how I distanced myself from them incrementally. I began to decline the invitations to parties and exhibitions – even to the weekly gatherings at our pub. I had realized that my grief alienated me from them, understood the gulf it created between my life and theirs. Even if I had wanted to talk about Mum – which I didn't – I could not have done so with them. Conversation revolved around mild gossip, who was sleeping with who, who had 'sold out' to a big-time collector . . . the many, minor intrigues of our small, incestuous world. The thought of bringing death into that happy, frivolous mix was inconceivable.

Until recently I had been one of them: young, carefree and ever so slightly selfish, in the most harmless way. I could not help feeling that my presence was a souring influence. I know that they would have been mortified to hear this was how I felt – and I saw that they went out of their way to treat me as though I were unchanged.

Despite my withdrawal from my friends and that old world, I did feel the need to keep busy. Busy meant that I didn't have to spend too much time in the house in Battersea, where the quiet and emptiness had a peculiar, terrible weight. I spent more time than ever wandering the city with my camera – especially on those mornings when I woke in the small hours to the roar of silence that surrounded me, and understood that there could be no more sleep. The concentration necessary to taking a good photograph – the careful assessment of the light, the important decisions about exposure, the framing and focusing of the shot – was the only thing equal to forcing all other thought away.

Then there was the sanctuary of the darkroom afterwards. Mum had had it made for me in the Victorian cellar beneath the house as an eighteenth-birthday present. She'd had it installed in the week I was away on a school art trip to Rome and when I came back there it all was: two huge work surfaces, the enlarger, for projecting the film, a red-lensed safelight, the developing trays, and two shelves stocked with all the other equipment I might need. She had even got me my own set of specialist overalls. To use it was now an excuse to seal myself in that hermetic space for a few hours, and try to forget about the empty rooms gathering dust above my head.

I also spent more time than ever at work. This was in a camera shop off the King's Road, which had seemed, when I applied, the next best thing to becoming a professional photographer. It was one of those shops run for love, not money, though my boss, Nick, had once been quite big in the industry. He'd taken iconic shots of people like Veruschka, Bianca Jagger, the Stones, and even my mother. He told me once that my mother was probably the most naturally beautiful woman he'd ever shot. 'Because she was so at ease with herself,' he'd said, 'so graceful, so at one with her body.'

Many of the photos he took are common currency now – constantly dredged up for articles – even if the photographer's name is not. Nick left it all behind, and that world quickly forgot about him. He left because he'd been rather too much a part of it all: had been at the same parties, taken the same drugs, suffered the same comedowns. He'd had what he called the three-year hangover, which nearly destroyed him. So he'd dusted himself off and found a new, simpler life.

Sometimes, when business was slow, Nick would give it up as a bad job, shut the shop and we'd go off on 'tutorials'. We'd head down to the river and take photos from Albert Bridge, or try surreptitiously to snap the punkish kids – faint echoes of their seventies predecessors – who gathered on the benches near the fire station. Sometimes we'd get in Nick's car and drive east to take photographs of old industry, à la Steven Siegel.

I first got into photography when I sat in Mum's choreography sessions after school and tried to capture the ballerinas stretching, leaping, even making mistakes. I had discovered early that I would never make a good dancer. I lacked the discipline, the instinctive grace – and, perhaps most important of all, I was no performer. To have my mother watch me put through my paces at the barre was agony enough, let alone anyone else. I pretended to enjoy myself, for her sake – but Mum quickly saw through it, and suggested I might want to try a new hobby. That was just like her. Another parent might have pushed, desperate for their child to share their interest, but Mum sought for honesty between us above all else.

Oh, but I loved to *watch* people dance, especially

her. One weekend, she took me to an exhibition by the photographer Barbara Morgan: black-and-white images of dancers, starkly lit and caught mid-step and mid-leap. To this day I am still in awe of her work: how the fixedness of the medium – the inevitable permanence of the snapshot – serves to enhance the sense of movement. When I saw them for the first time, saw how she had captured the power and the gravity-defying athleticism of those dancers – had achieved the impossible and frozen a moment in time – I was electrified.

On Christmas day of that year, I unwrapped a new Nikon for Christmas – my own camera, with a special wooden box Mum had found and packed full of film. An interest became an obsession, a whole new way of looking at the world. Some of those first photographs, even those Mum had let me take of her dancing barefoot about our kitchen, made their way into my application portfolio for the Slade.

When Mum died, Nick was great. He was very gentle with me: didn't push me to speak about it, though he intimated that he'd be ready to talk if I wanted to. Which I didn't especially – he was my boss, after all, and though at times he felt more like a friend there was always a certain degree of professional distance that I was wary of traversing. More than anything I wanted him to view me as a promising photographer, not someone who needed his pity.

Nick had suggested at first that I might want to take

some sort of sabbatical, but I think he soon understood that to be away from work – free to think about everything – was the worst thing that could happen to me. It would have been the excuse I needed to seal myself off from the world completely.

And there was Evie too, of course. The nursing home was a few minutes' cycle ride from the shop, down towards World's End, and I'd go almost every day after work to have a cup of tea and some increasingly surreal conversation. She'd deteriorated quickly after the crash: grief, it seemed, had hastened the progress of the dementia. Sometimes she'd talk about Mum as though she were still alive. When she then learned otherwise it was as though she had suddenly discovered the fact. This was terrible for both of us.

On that spring afternoon the day went much as normal. I bought some *cannelés de Bordeaux* – Evie's favourite – from the French patisserie opposite the shop and cycled down to the home. Miriam, one of the carers, was waiting in the entrance hall.

'She's been asking for you all day.'

'Really?' If Evie asked for anyone, it was usually Mum.

'Yes. I kept telling her, "She'll be coming later, dear, same as usual." She'll be pleased to see you.'

'I brought her some new photographs.'

These were of my mother. I collected them for her – and there were quite a number to be discovered in old magazines and performance programmes . . . some of them I had even taken myself. Evie craved them, and they seemed to have a positive effect on her. I found the process of discovering them at once soothing and painful, a strange combination.

'She'll like that. I should warn you though . . . she does seem a bit agitated.'

'Worse than normal?'

'Well, that's the thing. She's much better, in a sense – she doesn't seem nearly so confused as she has been of late. It isn't that, no. It's as if something's troubling her.'

I knew that something was different as soon as I entered the room: I felt it. The air was as close and dry as ever but it was charged with some foreign element, a sharper savour. Evie was waiting for me in her armchair, white-faced. She looked up at me with an expression that I didn't identify at first because it was so unexpected. It wasn't benign ignorance, or wrenching grief – the two states between which she veered. It took me some long moments to recognize it for what it was: fear.

'Evie,' I said, 'are you all right?'

She didn't answer me at first, but she slumped down lower in the seat and her gaze dropped towards her clasped hands. I stood there impotently as the seconds of silence dragged on. And when I noticed she had begun to tremble slightly I panicked, thinking she might be having some kind of seizure. I went to hold her shoulders but she shrugged my hands away, shaking her head, and I stepped back, alarmed.

'Evie, please, tell me what it is.'

'I never told her.' She spoke so quietly, almost to

herself. I wasn't sure if I'd heard correctly at first, and had to ask her to repeat it.

'I don't understand, Evie. Are you talking about Mum?' I'd play along with this delusion, I thought – that was generally better than trying to set her right and only confuse things further. 'What didn't you tell her?'

'I lied to her.'

I prickled with unease. There was, as Miriam had said, an odd clarity to her speech – a distinct lack of the usual confused rambling. Whatever it was she was trying to say, I suddenly wasn't sure I wanted to hear it. I sat down next to her and tried to take her hand. She moved it away, drawing into herself.

'Evie, you're upset. I'm sure whatever it was, well, it can't matter now.'

'It matters more. I should have told her, and now she's gone, and she never knew.'

'But I think—'

'No.' Her tone was sharp, so different to her usual whisper, so alarmingly unlike the docile, childlike person I had become accustomed to. I wondered if this was some volatile new stage of the degeneration. But when she spoke next it was again with that unusual lucidity.

'No. It needs to be said. I should have said something . . . a long time ago, but I loved her so much, I couldn't do it.' She looked at me, imploring, and I saw that her eyes had filled with tears. 'It was a terrible, selfish thing.'

34

My unease had evolved into something more like dread. 'Please, Evie, tell me: what are you talking about?'

'Her mother. She came looking.'

I stared at her, stupidly. 'Whose mother?'

'June's. She came looking for her, and June never knew.'

Mum's birth parents had never had any presence – even as an absence – in our lives. We simply never spoke of them, with perhaps one exception. I can still remember, quite clearly, the one and only time I had asked Mum about her birth parents. It was my twenty-first birthday, and Mum had taken me for supper at the Café de Paris, just the two of us.

I'd felt very grown up, in a beautiful black crêpe de Chine dress Mum had lent me, and I'd had too much excitement, and far too much champagne. It seemed to me the right moment to ask, now that I had become an adult. Was she curious? I asked. Had she ever thought about looking for them? She didn't seem affronted by the question – I think she must have been expecting me to ask one day. Her answer was unequivocal. 'If they wanted me, they'd have come looking, so why should I go after them? I have you, and Evie. You're all the family I need. I don't need to know anything more about someone who chose to leave a baby on a doorstep.'

And that was it: there was clearly to be no further discussion of the issue. I supposed I had to be satisfied. I didn't forget about them, these unknown grandparents who were – or at least had once been – out there in the world somewhere, but to me they were creatures of myth: several shades removed from reality, reserved for the realm of imagination and fantasy.

Evie had covered her face with her hands and as I reached forward to try to comfort her, she let out a terrifying sound, a sort of howl. She looked up at me through her spread fingers, and were it not for the awful circumstances she would have appeared comic – an octogenarian playing a child's game of hide-and-seek. As it was, it frightened me. There was a long pause while I tried to think of something I could say, or do. Then she gave a great, rattling sigh, which seemed to steel her enough to speak. Quiet, and slow, but precise:

'When June was twenty years old, I had a letter. The woman who wrote it, she claimed to be her mother. It was . . . so strange, coming out of the blue like that. She said that if we met she would explain everything.'

'Did you meet with her?'

Evie looked up at me, miserably, and I could already guess the answer. 'Never. I couldn't, do you understand? I was too afraid. I was too afraid that she might be telling the truth. I tried to convince myself then that there was no chance of it. Your mother was getting famous . . . we had mail from all sorts of strange people, people wanting to be a part of her life, wanting things from her.'

'So, you thought it could have been from a crazed fan?'

'That's what I told myself, yes. But she sent me something else. It was then I knew she was telling the truth, only I couldn't say anything. I was terrified – even more so than before. It has never gone away. It has been with me, every day . . . like . . . something crouched on my shoulder.' She folded down into herself, as though feeling the weight of it there now.

'Evie,' I said, taking one of her knotted hands in mine. 'You did the right thing, I'm sure.' I was picking my words carefully. 'This woman, she could have been anyone, a real psycho for all we know.'

She gave a frightened smile and shook her head. 'When I saw the picture she sent a few days later I knew she was telling the truth.'

'What picture?'

Evie heaved herself up and shuffled across to her bureau. It was a varnished Art Deco piece, the only thing she'd wanted to bring with her from the house. Atop it, as it had ever done, sat the framed photograph of a beautiful young man: her husband-to-be who never was.

She reached for the set of keys she still wore eccentrically at her waist on a rope belt – as though she were the chatelaine of some vast property – and bent stiffly to unlock the bottom drawer. It always made me sad to watch her move, she who would once have used her body with such grace: the awkward movements of the shoulder blades that jutted from the curved ridge of her back like small, mismatched wing-stumps, where once they would have framed a strong, straight spine.

The envelope she passed me was light and very old, the brown paper as dry and fragile as a leaf skeleton. The pressure of my thumb was enough to render a slight fissure in its surface. I looked down at it, bemused by the fact that something so insubstantial could be the cause of such crippling anxiety.

'I want you to take it away, to look at it alone,' Evie told me. 'I want you to see what's inside for yourself.'

I stared at her, and she gave a tiny nod. 'Please, take it.'

Back at home, I went straight to my old den. The house was one of those old flights of fancy with squares of rainbow-coloured glass in the half-moon window above the front door, and a singular, rather lost-looking turret feature – the townhouse equivalent of the folly. I had been drawn to it as a child, this strange piece of magical realism, and for years the small round space inside the turret had been my reading place. Mum had even had a window seat installed for me. It was there that I decided to retreat with my envelope – the big empty house echoing around me.

I upended the delicate package with care, and let the contents slide out on to the seat-cushion. Two sheets of paper, tissue-thin as the envelope, faded with age. One, the letter, written in an interesting hand – calligraphic, with something of a flourish to it.

Dear Ms Darling,

I understand that this letter will come as something of a shock, for both yourself and June. I'm not quite sure, I'm afraid, of how to go on without coming straight to the point, so please accept my apologies for the lack of preamble. You see, I am June's mother. I gave birth to her twenty years ago almost to this day.

I know how this will probably appear: that I abandoned my child in a moment of selfishness, and that, all this time later, I have had a change of heart. Yet that is not how it happened. If you would allow me a chance to explain myself to you both, I think you will understand that I had no choice in the matter.

It is difficult to explain everything in a letter, and I am aware that if I were to write the whole sad tale down it would hardly seem credible. As such, I beg you – and June – to meet with me. If you choose to do so, I will be waiting for you, in my rooms at Claridge's Hotel, every afternoon next week. Please ask downstairs for Célia, and you will be directed to me. I do not make any demands – I know that I have no right to do so. I ask only that you give me this chance to meet with my daughter, and to have her understand that I never abandoned her.

Yours faithfully,
Célia

I sat back and looked out of the window, to where I could make out the embroidered arch of Albert Bridge. This Célia, this woman who claimed to be my grandmother, had languished in that hotel for a week, waiting, anxious, perhaps scanning the faces of those passing beneath her window for the one she sought: the face of her own daughter. Perhaps she had waited for longer than a week. If you were desperate it would be easy to convince yourself that the letter had been delayed, or that its recipient needed time to decide to come. She had said she would make no demands. Had Evie had the right to be so cruel? But that was not the way to think about this. I knew nothing of this person, and I had known Evie my entire life and she was good, and moral, and she had loved Mum more than anything. It was not my place to judge her.

I picked up the other piece of paper. It was stiffer, a fine card, one side blank. I turned it over, and forgot to breathe. A line drawing in pen and ink, exquisitely done. It was my mother. She was seated on what appeared to be a picnic rug, with the vague suggestion of a body of water – a river, or a lake perhaps – behind her. She gazed straight out at me, half smiling.

By a slow process of realization, I came to understand that it wasn't my mother after all. It couldn't be, even had the hair not been wrong, had the clothes not been strange and antique, not like anything I'd ever seen Mum wear. For the date, written above the signature, was 1929.

Now I knew who she must be. Now I could understand Evie's wretchedness, her terrible sense of guilt at what she'd done.

When I studied the piece again, later, I was able to view it with greater objectivity, to note the artist's skill, the lightness of touch. It was a study in economy, the whole image described with a few fluid strokes of the pen. Yet it was also finely observed, the sitter's expression somewhere between a smile and a grimace, as though she weren't comfortable with finding herself the subject of a portrait.

I picked up my wallet and drew out the photograph of my mother – my favourite one of her, because it was exactly how I had always thought of her. In it she was perhaps around my own age and wore her 'off-duty' uniform of black Capri trousers and a white T-shirt. She was inimitably chic and beautiful to me in this image. Which journalist was it that had described her as 'a combination of the two Hepburns in appearance'? Her black hair had an almost celluloid gleam to it – obediently straight, drawn back at the nape of her neck. How I had longed for that hair as a child.

I could see that the woman in the drawing had my mother's innate, artless elegance: it was evident even in the slightly awkward, temporary nature of the pose. That smile, though, was absolutely her own. It was a da Vinci smile – a not-quite smile – enigmatic and complex.

This was a work of no common talent. I doubted

that I could ever take a shot that so strongly evinced the character of the sitter. I looked at the signature that sat beneath the date. I could make out two characters, intertwined. An S and a T. Or a T and S. It meant nothing to me, but I stared at it, as though it were some hieroglyph that might reveal the drawing's secret.

Evie died a couple of days later. It was a massive stroke, they told me. It shames me to say that I had not visited her since our meeting. I had not been able to face her guilt, or, indeed, my own confused feelings about what she had told me. I had convinced myself that it would be best for both of us to have a few days apart. I should have known by then that a life can be altered irrevocably in far less time than that. I had lost my chance to tell her that I understood.

The funeral confirmed how completely my mother and I had been her whole sphere of existence: the small church was less than half-full. That old secret feeling that I had always harboured, that feeling that we weren't as close as we could be, was nullified by the tide that surged over me and drew me down for several weeks into some dark, blind chamber of grief. Only when it was too late, only through the loss of her, was I able to understand how much I had loved her.

I went into the shop every morning, but my days had no shape and purpose to them now. Evie's company, however unpredictable, had been so much more to me than I had realized. Above all, she had been my last link to Mum. This was a new loneliness, such as I had never known or imagined possible.

4

A few days after the funeral Evie's things had been returned to the house in Battersea. For a time I could not bear to look at them. The sight filled me with a confused sense of grief and guilt: guilt that I perhaps had not been the granddaughter I could have been to her, busy as I was selfishly wanting Mum all for my own. So for several weeks everything sat in the drawing room, untouched. It was a space we had seldom used and, now that it was only me, I never entered.

Though Evie had not lived there for some time the house seemed even quieter with her gone. Sometimes now I began to wonder if I, too, was gradually becoming a ghost. My meagre presence in the place seemed to make no mark upon it. However much I cleaned – I gave up after a while – the dust seemed determined to settle. I avoided looking in mirrors . . . I did not like what they revealed to me of myself. But I was most afraid that one day I might not see anything at all.

Over the weeks, my curiosity about Evie's things grew. I began to wonder whether that room might harbour something that would further illuminate the secret. Perhaps there was more, I started to think, more that she had not had time to show me.

The room began to exert a pull upon me. Eventually, in the early hours of one morning, I made my way there with the fixed yet unconscious purpose of a sleepwalker, pushing open the door to reveal the dark mound of possessions in the centre of the rug – smaller than might be expected, but no less significant for that.

For someone who had been born into money, Evie had not surrounded herself with much, never one for jewellery or expensive clothing or any of those other accoutrements of wealth. But there were treasures of another order to discover here: an inventory of memories. A small pair of silk ballet slippers, hopelessly battered and worn: the blush pink faded to a sullen grey. Made for tiny feet, I realized, those of a child. Possibly, considering the size and age, my mother's first-ever pair. I found myself gripping them, holding them to my chest like a magical talisman, as though they might still exude some essence of her.

There were programme brochures from what might

have been every performance Mum had ever danced in, the earliest among them already desiccated with age. There were photographs, too, and I took my time looking through these, suspended somewhere between pleasure and pain. One thing that gave me pause was the number of photos there were of me, and not only those in which I appeared alongside Mum. There I was in my primary school uniform on my first day, a look of ill-concealed terror on my face – I was a painfully shy child. Then one of me as a teenager, dressed in T-shirt and shorts in Battersea Park, in what seemed from the seared grass in the background to be midsummer, my camera slung about my neck. Another of me on my twenty-first birthday, in the black crêpe de Chine I wore for supper with my mother. I felt a pang then, because I remembered how pleased I had been that it would only be the two of us . . . that Evie wasn't coming. And she had kept the photograph here for all these years, along with her most treasured memories of Mum.

I came to the letters next. There were hundreds – maybe even thousands – each stack tied neatly together with string. Seeing that vast number, collected here, I could understand how tempting it might have been for Evie to tell herself that the letter had merely come from another fan. There were so many that it was hard to believe that each represented a person who had sat down and written a letter to my mother, to tell her how her performance had affected them. But that was Mum

for you, I suppose. That was how talented she was –
although it had often seemed something greater than
talent, almost a magical power.

I did not know exactly what I hoped to achieve,
when I untied the string on the nearest bundle. I read
the first few letters from start to finish and would have
carried on like this, had I not realized that I would be
there for days if I did. So I began to sift through them,
instead – my gaze catching on those phrases that
demanded to be read: . . . *the most exquisite thing
I have ever seen . . . I will remember you as long as I
live . . .*

A small part of me felt a kind of indignant posses-
siveness as I read the most recent ones, those letters that
had flooded in after her death. I knew it was irrational,
but it felt as though these people – these *strangers* – were
clamouring for a part of her to keep for themselves. Did
they not understand that the memory of her was a
precious, finite quantity, not one upon which they could
stake their claim?

I left these, and moved instead to the letters that were
faded and frail with age, some so delicate that they had
to be handled with great care, making it a painstaking
process.

Then I found it, what I had been hoping – and fearing
– to discover. It was the handwriting that I noticed first:
so distinctive as to be unmistakable, though it could
not be definitive proof on its own. But there was the
name, too.

I read it through, quickly, in such a state of nervous excitement that I didn't take any of it in. Then a second time, forcing myself to go more slowly. If I had been hoping for something revelatory this was not it. In many ways it read like any another fan letter, remarkable only for its brevity. What made it special was the fact that it was from her, Célia:

---

16 November 1956

Dear June,
I came to the performance last night and watched you dance as Giselle. You made me believe so strongly that you <u>were</u> that little peasant girl, lifted and then cruelly broken by love, that the ending was, in a word, shattering. It was perhaps the most beautiful thing I have ever seen . . . and the most tragic.
Yours,
Célia

I went back to my pile, fingers trembling as I sifted carefully through brittle leaves of paper. After a few minutes of searching I found another. The same hand-writing, another short note . . . and then that name. It struck me then as an unusual name. It could have been ordinary, English – save for that accent on the 'e', which made it instantly foreign. Italian, possibly, or French.

Quickly, taking less time to be delicate now, I began to hunt through the other piles . . . just in case. What I discovered was far greater than I could have imagined. A letter, it appeared, for every year that my mum had been performing. I laid them all out together, and they covered the entire rug. I sat back on my heels and stared at them, the blood beating loud in my head with excitement and something not unlike fear. Had Evie seen these? She must have done. Mum, too, must have seen them, though she had never remarked on them. Then again, there was nothing exceptional in the fact of the letters themselves. Many particularly avid fans might write again and again. Only when placed in the context of that first, all-important letter did they attain a new significance.

Suddenly it looked like the evidence of an obsession: decades of the sender's life devoted to this one-sided communication. The breathtaking futility of it. But perhaps she – this Célia – had not thought it futile. Maybe she had believed it would eventually bring Mum to her. What did that say about her . . . about the state of her mind?

This secret that Evie had forced me to acknowledge had suddenly become all the more compelling. At the same time, I perceived a danger in it that I had not been aware of before. Possibly, even when she had believed her reasons to be selfish, Evie truly *had* been protecting Mum from her past. Perhaps it was enough that she had been able to unburden herself of her secret, without my needing to explore any further. What good could come of it? It was all so long ago, and if the woman who had written the letter were Evie's age, she might also now be gone.

I went back to my room, and took the drawing out of its envelope. Once again I was transfixed by it – by this woman who was so similar in appearance to my mother that I, her own daughter, had at first been convinced it was her. Every time I saw it, it stole my breath from me. How could a mere few strokes of pen do that, exert such a pull of memory and emotion? I had no doubt that it was the work of a master – and I knew, too, that I could not rest until I had found out more.

5

'I was wondering whether you could take a look at it?'

'Well, of course, sweetheart, but I can't promise anything.'

'Charlie. If anyone can find something out about this drawing, it's you.'

Charlie was a friend of mine from the Slade. He had also been my boyfriend, briefly, though I generally chose to forget that part. I had at one time thought myself in love with him – hardly able to believe that someone like him, so confident and so talented, would be interested in me. Yet it transpired that he wasn't well suited to monogamy. When it ended I had thought that what

51

I felt was heartbreak. It was only after Mum's death, when I knew the true meaning of that word, that I understood it had not been so. It had been an infatuation, and my hurt and embarrassment, while terrible, had not been the true symptoms of a broken heart.

Perhaps further proof of this was the fact that our friendship had survived the break-up. The only thing it hadn't survived, ultimately, was Mum's death – and this was entirely my own fault. Or at least, I thought it had not survived. Now I was surprised at how ordinary it felt to chat to him, almost as though only a few days had passed without our talking – rather than a good six months or so. I had expected formality or even coldness, but he sounded, if anything, pleased to hear from me.

Charlie had been one of the few of us who had been able to make a career from his work – which was well deserved, as he was phenomenally talented. He also boasted an almost encyclopedic knowledge of the art world. It's my experience that most artists tend to go either way in their attitude to the artistic canon. Either they decide to reject knowledge of everything that has gone before, wanting to create 'freely', without the weight this awareness would bring, or they know the art world and its history inside out. Charlie was of the latter school. He'd told me once that he couldn't engage with subjects that didn't interest him – hence his limping away from his school years with a bare handful of O Levels – but when it came to things that did, such as his chosen field, he was astonishingly knowledgeable.

He seemed pleased by my flattery, as I had guessed he would be. 'All right. I'll give it a glance. Over dinner? I could cook for you.'

This was dangerous. I wasn't flattering myself – given an opportunity to seduce anyone, anything, Charlie would probably take it.

'I don't want to put you to any trouble over it. Why don't we meet somewhere in your neighbourhood? My treat.'

We ate at a cheap, workaday Italian where Charlie seemed known to the staff, though it was unclear whether they treated every customer, regular or otherwise, with the same ersatz bonhomie. When I got up to use the ladies' I saw one of the waiters lurking outside the back door, cigarette in hand, scowling at the pavement, and I felt myself blush, as though I'd witnessed him in a state of undress.

We ordered two vast buttery plates of linguine vongole and some cheap red wine. It was Charlie who brought up the subject of the drawing.

'Well, let's see it then.' He wiped his mouth with his napkin and sat back in his chair, prepared, I thought, to be unimpressed.

I drew the envelope out of my bag, suddenly nervous, my fingers clumsy and my heart thudding. Though it was the purpose of our meeting, I think I had been subconsciously putting off this part. I had a moment of hesitation: did I definitely want to show him? I had convinced myself that it was in some way exceptional. If it was, to do so could be to set something in motion – something over which I might have no control. Though perhaps even worse than that would be to hear that it was nothing special after all, that I had been mistaken.

I slid the drawing out and saw her face again. That geometric hair, those arching eyebrows like two elegant parentheses, and the softness of the other features that contrasted with them: the full lips, the quizzical, intelligent gaze. It was a simple sketch, as I have said, perhaps a study for a more permanent work. Yet each time I looked I saw something in it that I had not noticed before. This time it was the fingernails on the elegant hand, the one held to her neck. They were bitten down, like a child's. The detail convinced me that the artist knew the subject well. In a more considered study there would have been time to notice and incorporate such a feature. In a quick sketch, the work of a moment such as this, the artist would have to have known of it already.

Charlie was silent for a long time as he studied it. His face, usually so mobile, was rigid with concentration, his eyebrows drawn together. He moved the paper closer and closer to his face until his nose almost touched its surface, and it would have made me laugh had I not felt so anxious. I sat there for several excruciating minutes, as the chatter of the room washed over me and a siren blared past along the road outside. Finally, he looked up. His expression was impossible to read.

'Kate.' It was only then I became aware of his excitement, heard the tremor of it in his voice.

'Yes?'

'I think – I mean, I'm almost certain . . . that you might have something rather interesting here.'

I leaned forward, ready with my questions. He put out a hand, and shook his head.

'I don't want to get your hopes up before I've checked it out.'

'But you recognize the signature? You know who it's by?'

'Well, that's the thing – I might do, but I need to make sure. I'll need to borrow it for a couple of days.'

'No! You can't, I'm sorry.' I reached to take it from him.

'Look, trust me, please. I'll treat it as carefully as gold dust, I promise. If I'm right, it practically is gold dust. Better, in fact.'

'That's not why I—'

He put up his palms. 'I know, I know, but as I say, I have to check. I have someone who will be able to tell me, unequivocally, either way.' He looked at me beseechingly.

'Fine.' I couldn't quite believe I'd said it. 'But you must promise—'

'I promise.' He covered my hand with his. 'I'll guard it with my life.'

I returned home excited and anxious – trying not to remember that time Charlie had lost the portfolio for his final degree piece in Waterloo station. And I didn't sleep well the next couple of nights, envisaging terrifying scenarios in which he'd left the drawing on the tube or set fire to it accidentally. It came as a huge relief when, three days later, he finally called with directions to a private gallery in Islington. I was to meet him there at seven, after they'd closed to visitors for the day.

When I got there, five minutes early, Charlie was already sitting on the step outside, drawing hungrily on the remains of a cigarette, his foot tapping. When he saw me he dropped the butt and jumped up, launching himself towards me. He was vibrating with excitement, I could tell, though I tried not to infer too much from the sight of it. He took my arm. 'Come and meet Agnes.'

Agnes was Swiss-German, in her fifties, with a hand-some face framed by large round spectacles, grey hair drawn into a utilitarian topknot. I suppressed a smile. I'd assumed, knowing Charlie, that she would be some ravishing young ingénue with hair to her waist. She treated me to a firm handshake, and ushered us into an immaculate office behind the exhibition space. The only colour came from the jewel-coloured spines of books on a shelf behind the desk, and a vast canvas of riotous, tessellated watercolour squares on the opposite wall that I recognized as a Paul Klee.

Agnes was eager to get straight to business. She reached into the drawer of her desk and removed the drawing carefully, placing it between us with, it seemed, a certain reverence. Against the lacquered black wood of the desk, in a pristine new dustsheet, it looked decidedly small, old and grubby.

'So.' Agnes leaned forward and fixed me with pale blue eyes surreally magnified by her lenses. 'Kate – remind me where you came across this work, please.'

'Well . . . it's difficult to explain.' I searched for the best way of putting it. 'It's been in the family for a while, and it's recently come into my possession.'

Agnes nodded. 'The reason I ask is that I believe you have something extremely precious here. You had a suspicion of this before?'

'I – I didn't know, to be honest. I've no eye for these things, not like Charlie, say, but it did seem good to me. I suppose I hoped it might be special.'

'Indeed. Tell me,' she peered at me, 'are you aware of an artist named Thomas Stafford?'

I laughed. 'Well, yes – of course I am.' You didn't have to be an art historian to have heard of the man: he had achieved the distinction of becoming a national treasure. There had been a big retrospective of his work only a few months previously at the Tate, and I'd seen the poster for it on tube platforms. It had stayed with me particularly, that image, because it had been in such contrast to the rain-sodden April weather we had at the time. It showed a view out across a sun-bleached window shelf: a blue wedge of sea, the white triangles of sails stark against it.

'But the drawing doesn't look like anything I've seen of his.' Yet even as I said it I was thinking of those initials. S and T, T and S. Could it be?

'No,' said Agnes, patiently, 'it certainly doesn't look like his recent work . . . or, indeed, most of the work for which he is known.'

Charlie cut in: 'But you're something of an expert on his work, aren't you, Agnes?'

Agnes gave a modest nod. 'I've had to be. I wrote my thesis on him.' She looked fondly down at the drawing. 'This is, in fact, similar to other early works I've seen in style, execution – even the materials used. He favoured pen and ink or charcoal in the early years, you see . . . perhaps before he'd got fully confident with using some of the more complex mediums. And, I think, because they were quick. He could get the effect of spontaneity that you see here. It was his later works, after the war, that got him noticed in a big way.' She smiled. 'Several of his biggest fans, myself included, think that the earlier works have their own quiet brilliance, but this' – her voice trembled with excitement – 'is the earliest piece I have seen – by a few years. The other earliest known works are from the thirties.' She stroked the dust jacket. 'This is perhaps the best I've seen: the most fluent, the most true.'

I leaned forward. 'So you're sure? That it's by him?'

She nodded her head, adamant. 'I'd bet quite a sum on it being his.' I watched as her finger traced the lines of the subject's face. 'Do you know who this woman is, though? I'm curious about her.'

A thrill went through me. 'I think she might be my relative.'

Agnes raised her eyebrows. 'Well, it seems a very . . .' she searched for the right word, 'familiar, almost intimate piece.'

I nodded. 'I thought so too.'

'But she doesn't appear later on, as far as I can recall. So perhaps not.'

'That's why I'm interested in the picture,' I said, 'because of her. Oh, it's a long story, but I didn't know until recently that she existed.'

'The best person to ask,' Agnes said, ruminatively, 'would be the artist himself.'

'But he's a recluse,' Charlie said, unhelpfully. 'He doesn't even live in the country.'

Agnes nodded. 'It's true. No one's seen much of him since his wife died. It's driven some of the collectors mad. He's always been prolific, and I think they imagine that he's sitting there, producing pieces that no one can get their hands on. He's never seemed especially interested in money, you see, so I suppose he has no real reason to show them to anyone, if he doesn't want to.'

'How should I contact him?'

Agnes sighed. 'That's the thing. It won't be easy. Let me think on it.'

So I went home, trying to convince myself that this was progress. In truth, it was immensely disheartening to have this new lead, yet no apparent way of investigating it further. Agnes, too, had looked rather downcast when I left – though that might have been as much to do with the fact that I was taking the drawing with me.

To make matters worse, the shop was even quieter than usual that week. The weather was terrible – despite it being early summer. The sky was an ominous, lowering steel grey, and the light had a greyish, dirty quality to it, too. It was hardly surprising that people did not feel compelled to think about their cameras.

It also meant that my normal means of distraction – my own photography – was not an option. It was too wet most of the time for me to want to risk getting my camera out. It was old now – and prone to fail. I knew that rainwater could be just the thing to finish it off. I knew, too, that I could easily replace it – Nick would have given me a big discount on anything in the store. Yet I held on to it, stubbornly, for what I suppose were superstitious reasons. This was the camera with which I had taken picture after picture of Mum – and I had convinced myself that it held some final imprint of her inside its compact black body. Besides, it felt right in my hands, as though it had moulded itself to them – or I to it, a strange transmutation.

I needed a new way to distract myself. One day, almost without realizing what I was doing, I took the tube to Green Park, and walked into the Royal Academy. Only when I stood in the foyer, blinking in the bright light that was in such contrast to the mizzling day without, did I understand why I was there. I had come to look at the work of the artist who had suddenly become so uniquely important to me.

I was impressed by what I found. I had peripherally been aware of Stafford's work – and I think I could, with confidence, have picked out one of his pieces in a room. One of the more recent ones, at least. But here were older works – works that were far darker and more subversive than I would have imagined, as well as those of humour and great serenity. There was a vast range evident here – he favoured charcoal and ink for sketches, and oil for paint – but there were also pastels, watercolours, collages. Perhaps what linked them together was the confidence and fluidity of line, and the emotional punch that almost every work delivered. I couldn't pinpoint what the New York street scene made me feel, exactly – perhaps because it stirred a complicated mixture of emotions. Pity, for the drunk or homeless men slumped along the sidewalk. A certain excitement, stimulated by the purplish suggestion of twilight, the cleverly rendered pinpoints of light that suggested a new night falling upon the city, charged with possibility for the men and women that strode in their finery past the sorry spectacle of the others. I could not decide if I liked it; it made one uncomfortable. No doubt that was the point – another mark of the artist's skill.

And the view out across a placid sea – the Mediterranean, I was certain. Viewed one way, it spoke of heavenly solitude. Viewed another, that solitude transformed: became melancholic. Perhaps, after all, it depended on what one made of it, what one brought of oneself to it.

The next day I went to the library and got out a few books about Thomas Stafford. It purported to be an illustrated biography, but the text was disappointingly meagre. The 'early years' section was sketchy, and there was only a brief mention of the artist's time at Oxford University, where he had, apparently, joined a student Art Society. To my frustration I could find nothing about a woman called Célia – nothing about any other women, in fact, until the section on his marriage to a Corsican woman named Elodia. The next book yielded little more. There was, however, one paragraph that gave me pause:

There are thought to be a number of works unaccounted for from the early years, when the artist was still a student at Oxford University. Rumour has it that these are the product of a particularly pivotal time emotionally and creatively in Stafford's life – but none of these works, if they exist, are in the public domain. The earliest works on record date from the mid-1930s, though it is likely that Stafford was already prolific before this period. At the time of publication, we can only hope that these suspected earliest works may one day surface and shed further light on the creative beginnings of this extraordinary artistic career.

The earliest works on record date from the mid-1930s. Now I could understand why Agnes had been so excited. The drawing I had in my possession was dated 1929 – half a decade before. Yet it wasn't so much excitement I felt at this realization as something more like dread. Could the absence of these pieces suggest that someone simply didn't want them to be found?

The spell of bad weather broke, finally, on the Saturday of that week. It was my day off, so I took up my camera and cycled the Thames Path as far as Richmond, but it was a limp, misty day and I knew that the photographs I took would be second rate at best. Frustrated, I made for home.

There was a voicemail blinking on the machine when I got in. I listened – my heartbeat suddenly loud in my ears, almost deafening me. It was Agnes. 'I may have found a way,' she said, cryptically.

I called her back.

'Oh good,' she said, as soon as she heard my voice. 'I've been waiting by the phone all morning.' She paused. 'I shouldn't do this. It's completely unprofessional, you understand, but in the circumstances . . .' she dropped her voice, conspiratorially. 'I can get you the address of his sister. She is the founder of a charity that awards art scholarships to offenders: a friend of mine exhibited some of the winners at his gallery, and has given me the details.' She gave a short, rather wild laugh. 'I let him believe that I needed to get in touch with her about a new project – no doubt he wouldn't have given them to me otherwise. So you mustn't reveal how you came by them if you can help it.' She read out the address for me. 'No phone number, so you'll have to go to her and explain.'

'Just turn up?'

'Yes, I think so. She's your best hope, if you want to get to him directly. If you go via the collector route – and in doing so alert someone else to the fact that you have this piece – you'll only get tied up in paperwork and financials.'

Here it was, I thought, as I hung up the phone: an end to my impotence, my opportunity to act. But with it the doubt returned. It wasn't as though I would be helping Mum in any way by following this path. More to the point, would Mum have *wanted* me to follow it? That one time we had spoken on the subject she had been adamant that she had no interest in her real parents.

Yet the idea of giving up now was inconceivable. I think I was mostly driven by the hope of finding something that would make me feel less alone. For one with no family left to speak of, the prospect of discovering something about this woman – and the shared history she had been a part of – was irresistible.

And so I went to see Stafford's sister, Mrs Delaney, where she lived in a Victorian building off Upper Street. Such a long wait followed my knock on the door that I began to wonder if no one was at home, but, as I turned to go, it opened.

'I'm sorry,' she told me, 'I've been watching a film with my grandchildren, and we had it up rather loud. It took me a while to realize that the sound hadn't come from the television.'

'My name's Kate,' I told her. 'I'm here to ask for your help. It's about a picture—'

'All right,' she said, to my amazement, and, just like that, beckoned me through.

I was so surprised by this easy acceptance that I wavered on the doorstep for several seconds in confusion. I had spent the journey to Islington rehearsing exactly what I would say, thinking of ways to mask Agnes's part in the process, how precisely to lead up to the main crux of things . . . only to find it all superfluous.

Mrs Delaney led me straight through to the kitchen at the back of the house. The two grandchildren were apparently watching their film in the sitting room, off the main corridor. Noise and teenage laughter surged over me in a great wave as I entered and involuntarily I steeled myself against it. I had become so used to the silence of the house in Battersea, you see, that it felt almost like an assault.

Mrs Delaney was vital and upright despite her years, with the sort of handsome looks that are improved by age – undiminished, certainly, by the intricate atlas of lines that mapped her skin. The eyes were her most striking feature: blue as a wolf's, but with a softness to them that was unmistakably kind. Even so, I quailed slightly beneath her gaze. She saw too much, I felt.

'So,' she said, 'how can I help you?'

I had deliberated beforehand as to how much I should tell her, especially as I myself knew so little. 'I need to get in touch with your brother,' I started, and then stopped. No – that wasn't quite how I had planned it. I tried again: 'I'm trying to find out about someone your brother once knew.' Mrs Delaney waited, patiently, as I searched for a way to continue.

In the end I simply removed the drawing from my bag. I showed it to her, and saw her give a start when she saw it properly, as she took in the initials in the lower corner. 'How did you come by this?' she asked, softly.

'It's been in my family for a long time.' I hoped that would be enough. To my relief she seemed to accept it. She took it from me wordlessly, and the kitchen clock counted out a full two minutes as she studied it. Eventually, slightly unnerved, I spoke into the silence. 'I'm trying to find out something about her, the woman it depicts.'

'Well,' she said, still studying the drawing, as though

unable to tear her eyes from it, 'this is . . . rather surprising. I have to admit that I wasn't expecting it to be about my brother's work. Not many people connect us, because we don't share the same surname. I had actually thought it would be something to do with Beyond the Canvas – the charity I work for.' She looked at me then. 'I imagine that's how you got my address, though . . . through someone there?' It wasn't spoken as an accusation, but I felt my cheeks grow hot with embarrassment, all the same. I nodded.

'Anyway,' she said, waving a hand to show it didn't matter, 'however it came about, I do think I see how important this is to you. And my answer is yes.'

'Excuse me?' I asked, rather stupidly.

'I mean to say that yes, I will help you to contact him. That was what you asked, I think?'

'Oh . . . well, thank you. I—'

'You should write to him,' she told me. 'And I think you must include this drawing.'

'No – I can't.' It came out more fiercely than I had expected, and it seemed impertinent – it was her brother's work, after all. I tried to explain: 'Sorry,' I said, 'but I couldn't bear the thought of losing it.'

She nodded. 'All right, a photocopy then – I forget there are these modern alternatives. But, if I know my brother, it is this drawing that will make him take notice.'

She saw me out. 'Goodbye then, Kate Darling.' She gave me a quick smile. 'Good luck.'

*

Sitting on the tube on my way back, I thought of what it could mean, having Thomas Stafford's address. Did I want to follow this thread, not knowing where it might lead? Again, I had that feeling that had been with me since Evie had first unburdened herself – that she might almost unwittingly have been protecting Mum from her own history. I thought of the sight that the girls in the orphanage had described – the woman who had left the baby on the doorstep without a backward glance, without even stopping to ring the doorbell. What sort of person would do that to their child? What if the truth I uncovered was a terrible thing, something that once unleashed could not again be hidden or forgotten?

But then a rebellious voice spoke to me from the edge of thought. *It's up to you*, it whispered. *You're the only one left to decide.*

By the time I got home I had made my decision. I would write my letter and I would do the closest thing to sending the drawing: photograph it, and send that instead. I took several versions in the kitchen where the light was good, and developed them meticulously in the darkroom. They all came out rather well, but I chose the one in which the expression on her face had been best retained: that wry smile, the slight quirk of the eyebrow.

I tried to keep the note that I would send with it short, to the point, resisting the temptation to steep it in my anxiety and hope.

Dear Mr Stafford,

Please accept my apologies for writing to you directly in this manner, but I obtained your address from your sister, Mrs Delaney, and am hoping you may be able to help me with something very close to my heart. I enclose a photograph of a drawing that I believe may be your own work. It recently came into my possession along with a letter, sent thirty-odd years ago, by a woman claiming to have given birth to my mother. This was addressed to my adoptive grandmother, and signed, simply, 'Célia'. Célia asked to meet with my mother – a request that was never granted. My mother, the ballerina June Darling, died last year without knowing anything of this.

If the drawing is indeed your own work, perhaps you know something of the woman it depicts? The resemblance to my mother is uncanny and, I have come to believe, speaks for the truth of the letter's claim. I am desperate to learn of all you might know or remember. I think you may be the only person who can help me, who may be able to tell me anything of who she was.

Yours faithfully,
Kate Darling

I gave the address of the house, and the number. As I fed the envelope into the mouth of the postbox my hands shook.

For a couple of weeks, there was nothing. I was extremely vigilant. My hope – a quiet, desperate hope – was strong within me. Every day, as soon as the post arrived I would hurl myself down the stairs and watch as the letters spilled through the door – catching them, sometimes, before they touched the mat.

Nick knew that something was up: I was listless and distracted at work. Even a trip to the nearby Cadogan Arms for a 'medicinal' glass of wine didn't help. He asked me if there was anything I might want to chat about – he knew about Evie, and probably thought it related to that. I didn't want to talk. For one thing, I didn't want to explain that there was anything besides the loss of Evie occupying my thoughts. And I felt a superstition, however foolish, that to speak of it would be to jinx it.

I think it often happens like this. You wait, and hope, until eventually the hoping seems in vain and the thing you wish for begins to seem impossible. You try to forget, to move on. And sometimes, once you have gone through this painful process, by some peculiar alchemy, it happens.

The reply came: just like that. For once, I hadn't even heard the soft drop of the letters as they hit the floor – I wasn't even in the house, having gone out to buy milk and the papers. When I returned, there it sat.

A small white envelope addressed in an unfamiliar hand, a foreign postage stamp. My fingers were clumsy as I opened it.

Dear Kate (if I may)
Please forgive my delay in replying to you. The post takes an extraordinarily long while to arrive here – the house is rather remote, you see. It has also taken me some time to organize my thoughts sufficiently to sit down and write. I will be honest and tell you now that your letter and photograph have disturbed me somewhat. I never thought I would see that drawing again.

I think you should come to Corsica. Can you spare the time? I feel we have much to discuss, of the sort that can't be addressed in a mere letter.

Please know that, if you decide to come out, you need not concern yourself about accommodation: you would be my guest here at the Maison du Vent. We aren't particularly smart, but I'd like to think you would be comfortable.

I hope the enclosed will help. It will, I think, be sufficient to cover the price of a flight to the island. An odd conceit, perhaps, but we do not have a telephone here. So if you are inclined to accept my offer (though I appreciate that it may be difficult to find enough time for a visit) please send word of when you expect to arrive, and we will make sure that someone is there to meet you at the airport.

If you are not bound by a schedule, my advice would be to book a single flight and decide once you are here on when to book the return. I feel that what we have to discuss may take us some time. I await your reply, Kate, and I hope – more than hope – that you will choose to come and visit us as soon as you are able.

Yours truly,

Thomas Stafford

When the cheque fell into my hand I sat down hard on the sofa and stared at it in bewilderment. It was for a thousand pounds.

PART TWO

The Logic of a Fairy Tale

6

Corsica, August 1986

The heat was heavy, tangible, and the air shimmered above the dry earth through the windows of the arrivals lounge. As I'd stepped from the plane I had experienced an almost instantaneous prickling of sweat on my face and between my shoulder blades. The Corsican sky was exactly as it had appeared on that tube poster: a flawless blue that stretched like a spinnaker to the pale horizon. The scent of the island was everywhere, even inside the airport: herbal, resinous, heady. I thought of the unseasonably sodden London that I had left behind, the metallic smell of wet tarmac, and the lowering monochrome sky. And yet most of me wanted to run back up the steps into the plane's cabin and beg them to let me return home.

Stafford had explained in his letter that someone would be there to meet me, but hadn't said whom I should expect. A thin line of waiting taxi drivers and family members straggled along the barrier, and I peered at the signs but couldn't see my own name anywhere. I realized in that moment that I hadn't even got a number to call if nobody showed for me. Merely the name of a house, somewhere on the island. The absurdity of the whole situation struck me anew. What if this were all some expensive prank on Stafford's part, and I was to be left here interminably? It would be less of a stretch of the imagination to believe that than to believe that he, the world-famous artist, had invited me to stay in his house.

Then a voice said, 'Kate Darling?'

I turned. A tall man stood there, at a guess not much older than myself, with black hair of that unusual hue that bears no relation to brown – the blue-black of a raven's feather.

'I'm Oliver,' he said, by way of a greeting, and took up my bags without exactly looking happy to do so. Then he gestured through the glass doors. 'I'm parked out that way.'

His accent intrigued me. It was impeccable, almost antique – which, oddly enough, gave it a foreign sound. I trailed behind him to the car park, realizing that he had offered no explanation of who he was . . . and didn't feel that I was invited to ask. This was a bad start. I had hoped that once in Corsica my doubts would miraculously retreat – that I would be filled with new confidence and purpose. Now, with this less-than-friendly welcome, my apprehension had increased.

The car was an elderly 2CV in mint-green, speckled like an old apple with rust. The man, Oliver, appeared incongruous beside it: too tall and solemn for such a small, jaunty-looking vehicle, and had I not been so preoccupied by nerves I think the contrast would have made me smile.

The long, low buildings beyond the airport were quickly lost to new surroundings: steep and arid, the road a dusty ribbon hedged on either side with dry and thorny shrub. We were driving across the spine of Corsica, Oliver explained, a ridge of mountains that ran the length of the island. The car barrelled along at what felt like a dangerous speed, clouds of dust foaming behind us. We saw no sign of civilization for a long stretch. Suddenly, as if from nowhere, a man appeared over the top of the next incline, running towards us along the other side of the road. He was shirtless, his chest burnt to a deep mahogany by the sun, his skin slick with sweat. We had to be some way from the previous town. I watched him pass, craning round in astonishment to see him start on the steep incline that the car had clattered its way down.

'Corsicans are tough people,' Oliver said, with an unmistakable note of pride. Was he Corsican? I wondered again about his connection to Stafford. Was he a member of staff, perhaps, a protégé . . . a lover, even? I knew that Stafford had had a wife, but that didn't mean anything. I studied his profile, pondering this.

Just then he turned his head and caught me looking, and I looked quickly away. I concentrated resolutely on the view from the window, letting the false breeze created by the movement of the car tickle the damp hair away from my forehead and cool my hot skin.

Suddenly the sea emerged before us on the horizon: a strip of brilliant metallic blue between the sentinel peaks of two mountains, appearing at first like a trick of the eye. So majestic was this view that my hands itched for my camera – now buried deep in my rucksack – and if I had been braver I would have asked him to stop.

The arid landscape gave way gradually to vineyards, stretching as far as the eye could see. The scent of the herbs grew stronger, and there was salt in the air. I wondered whether one might be able to taste it in the wine produced from the crop that grew about us. The view of the coast was uninterrupted and I could see to where the great lump of grey rock that was the island sheared away in steep cliffs, atop which a sprawl of buildings clung like a white growth of lichen.

'Bonifacio,' said Oliver.

I craned to take it all in. From here it seemed that the whole town was about to plunge headfirst over the edge into the Mediterranean. 'There must be incredible views.'

He shrugged. 'The view from the house is better.'

We drove for another thirty minutes or so to a fork in the road, where we bumped and clanked our slow way along a potholed track for twenty minutes. Finally, just as I had begun to wonder whether I could stand one more minute of the bone-jolting movement, we arrived.

The Maison du Vent crowned the promontory of rock that it sat upon like a citadel, high above the deep, placid blue of the Mediterranean Sea. Below was a square of gravel where Oliver parked the car next to an even more decrepit vehicle – a three-wheeler truck of almost toy-like proportions. A flight of steps, carved into the rock, climbed erratically up from the roadside. Rosemary grew at intervals from cracks in the stone.

'That's Gerard's car,' said Oliver, gesturing to the van. 'He's the groundsman here. His wife is the housekeeper, Marie.'

As if invoked, a small, dark, broad woman appeared at the top of the steps and shouted something incomprehensible back at the house before hurrying down to us. She wore a dress of a stiff calico, spotlessly white against her sun-browned skin. As she drew closer, I saw that she was older than she'd appeared from afar, perhaps sixty or more, but everything about her – the powerful hands and plump arms, the skein of coarse black hair wound upon her head – suggested the strength and vitality of a much younger woman.

'Welcome, welcome.' She spoke with such a heavy accent that at first I thought the words had been in another language. She insisted on taking one of my bags from the car, hefting it from the roof rack and grasping it beneath her arm as if it weighed nothing. Then she turned and took to the stairs again. Oliver carried the other, leaving me to walk up the steps feeling rather useless, my arms swinging free.

We came up around one wall on to a terrace formed from the same lump of stone as the house itself. I saw immediately that the villa, a low-slung, flat-roofed building, was not the point. The point was the view. It was like looking down from the lofty eyrie of some cliff-dwelling bird: an impossible perspective. I could make out a boat in the distance as a tiny white crumb, tracking its slow progress across the still blue carpet of water. It wasn't difficult to see why Stafford had chosen to make his home here, nor why he hardly ever left. The three of us stood gazing out to sea for a moment, and even Marie, who I would have supposed inured to it by now, appeared to take pause. Perhaps you never quite get used to a sight like that. Then the door opened behind us, and Thomas Stafford stepped out into the sun.

I had seen pictures of him, naturally, but even I can admit that photographs are not always enough to convey the true presence of a person. I think I had expected that he would be more eccentric in appearance, perhaps even the cliché of the artistic figure – paint-splattered, wild-haired. Stafford, however, was tall and elegant in pale linen. His hair, white and still thick, was combed back from his brow. His expression, as he came towards me, was perhaps the only discomposed thing about him. I have never felt under such scrutiny as I did then beneath the unblinking intensity of his gaze.

'Good God.' He whispered it so quietly that at first

I couldn't be sure whether I'd imagined it. But as he moved closer he spoke again. 'Extraordinary,' he said, '. . . uncanny.' When I saw that there were tears in his eyes I looked away, completely discomfited. After a long pause he gathered himself. 'I'm sorry,' he said, in a steadier voice, 'I seem to have forgotten myself. It is just that for a second I could have sworn . . .' He shook his head, and gave a careful smile. 'I don't know what came over me. Please, forgive a foolish old man. And welcome, Miss Darling.' In an instant, the frail person I had briefly glimpsed had disappeared, and Stafford had taken charge of himself once more. 'You have met Marie,' he gestured, 'and Oliver, who . . . ah . . . who appears to have vanished.' Oliver was indeed nowhere to be seen.

'Please, call me Kate,' I said, and wasn't able to manage much more. Something rose up inside me and I felt suddenly overwhelmed. I don't know what it was: the strangeness of the situation, perhaps, or of Stafford's reaction to me. I swayed where I stood and shut my eyes, trying to regain my composure.

Stafford looked concerned. 'Are you all right?'

I shook my head, feeling foolish. 'It's the heat,' I said, 'and – I didn't sleep well last night. It's been a bit of a shock, all of this.' I gestured about me, lamely.

'I think,' said Stafford, 'we should both sit down for a few minutes.' He led me to an ironwork table and drew out a chair for me. I sank into it gratefully, and he took a seat opposite me. I hadn't even noticed Marie

81

leave us, but she returned in a couple of minutes bearing tea. It was, despite the heat of the day, strangely refreshing – and comforting too, a taste of normality. Stafford studied me thoughtfully. 'You must have been through so much in the last year,' he said, 'and now this. Kate – I want to say how sorry I was to hear of your mother's death. I saw her dance, you know, as Juliet. I confess I'd never seen the point of ballet before that – I'd always been much more interested in opera – but she danced her part so beautifully, with such grace, that I was close to tears in the final scene.' He smiled gently. 'I know that the memory of an old man cannot mean much to you, but . . . I felt that I should tell you, all the same. She was exquisite.'

His kindness was disabling. I felt something rend within me and panicked, thinking I might be about to cry. It was with a great surge of effort that I managed to regain control. I sipped my tea carefully, watching the incremental progress of that distant boat across the horizon, and gradually felt myself retreat from the edge.

When he seemed satisfied that I had recovered sufficiently, Stafford offered to show me about. The earliest part of the house, he explained, had belonged to a Genoese noble some three hundred years ago. It had been a retreat for the man and his family, modelled on a simple peasant dwelling – but several times the size. The building had been in a state of complete disrepair when Stafford and his late wife, Elodia, had happened upon it during a walk along this part of the coast. Back then, it had been nearly impossible to gain access through the thick growths of ivy and bramble that had wrapped themselves about the structure like a noose, completely obscuring the stone steps that were the only way of gaining entrance.

'It's an ongoing project,' Stafford said. 'Every year there's some other bit of decrepit plaster to patch, stone wall to repair . . . safeguards to stop the whole thing toppling into the sea. I'm probably getting too old for it now, but I can't help myself – I'm in love. It almost looks like it wants to fall, don't you think? That's what I've always liked about this place, the drama, the audacity of it. Elodia thought I was mad when I set my heart on it – though ultimately she came to care for it even more than I did. Her people were Corsicans through and through – they could trace their ancestry right back to the days of Genoese rule of the island. So, for her, living here was a way of being further connected to her homeland, to her past.'

At the far end, I noticed, the sun-bleached old building had grown an extraordinary appendage: a structure made from glass and chrome, and yet, through the genius of the architect, not at odds with the old stone it annexed. Stafford explained that this was his new studio. 'Oliver built it for me. He's an architect.'

'It's astonishing.'

'It has become his trademark, you could say, marrying the old and new. A delicate art, knitting the two together.'

'Did you commission it from him?'

'No,' he gave me a quizzical glance, 'it was a little less formal than that.'

'Oh, I see.' Except I didn't.

Stafford looked at me. Then he laughed. It was a sound that had not aged with the rest of him, that was still young and vigorous. 'Oliver's my grandson.'

I must have shown my surprise because Stafford laughed again and shook his head. 'I take it he didn't choose to tell you that much.'

'No.'

'Ah, well, that's Oliver for you. He has always been a man of few words.'

'He doesn't look like you.'

'No, indeed,' Stafford said.

I was embarrassed, having realized too late how rude it sounded, and looked for something else to say. 'Does he live here?'

'Not usually. He's based in Paris. He only qualified a couple of years ago, but he's already had a number of commissions. His aesthetic is popular – he seems to have struck a balance somewhere between the commercial and avant-garde.'

I quashed the uncharitable thought that having a grandfather who occupied the position Stafford did in the art world could not have hurt Oliver's career.

'So he's here on holiday?'

There was a pause, slightly too long. 'Yes,' Stafford said. 'Yes, of a sort.' I waited, to see if he would say more, but that was, apparently, the end of it.

He asked me then about my visit to Mrs Delaney. 'She wrote to me, you know,' he said.

'She did?'

'Her letter arrived only a couple of days after yours. That is absolutely like Rosa, you understand, feeling she had to make sure I did the right thing – not convinced that I would do it on my own.' He smiled. 'She is at once the best sister imaginable, and the most infuriating. But then she is the elder sister, and I am the younger brother – the baby of the family – and that is how it will always be.'

We continued with the tour. Below the courtyard where we stood, a flight of stone steps led down to a swimming pool – of which, leaning forward, I could make out one blue corner.

'It's far from grand, and rather cold, I'm afraid: the water comes from within the rock. There was a well there before. It used to worry me, the thought of water in the very cliff my house was built on, trickling through, perhaps undermining the structure, but it's been that way for centuries, so why should it have to change now? An old man has no business worrying about such things.'

Beyond that, another series of steps led down to a private cove. 'Ah,' Stafford said, as a figure emerged at the top of them: small and wiry, of indeterminate age, with a thin, sun-browned face and a cap affixed to his head. 'Hello, Gerard.' The man waved and grinned, then carried on past us to wherever he had been headed.

'There's a rust-bucket of a fishing boat down there that you're welcome to use if she's watertight – it's been Gerard's pet project recently to make her seaworthy. Perhaps Oliver could show you around. He's been taking her out since he was a boy, so he knows some of the best spots – places that can only be accessed by sea.'

The idea of spending more time alone with Oliver, taciturn and monosyllabic, was less than appealing. 'But, of course,' Stafford said then, to my relief. 'That is not why you are here.'

7

It was Stafford and I for dinner. Oliver sometimes came back to the house late, Stafford explained, if he'd gone off with his camera – his other passion, besides architecture, being photography. I wondered, curiously, what sort of photographs he would take, how his architect's eye might inform the shot.

'He tends to get wrapped up in it and forget he needs to eat until he's practically collapsing with hunger,' Stafford said, 'especially when the light's this good. The best time for taking photographs, he says, is first or last thing, when the shadows are longer and the colours richer.'

'He's right,' I said. 'That's what I do, photography.' He looked at me with interest, just as Marie placed our supper before us: baked fish scented with thyme atop a pile of sautéed potatoes. Stafford poured the wine. It was Corsican – and it did, I thought, taste a little of salt and herbs.

Then Stafford asked about my work. I found myself going into more detail than I'd intended. Something in his manner – interested, but undemanding – drew me out. 'I do enjoy working in the shop,' I said, 'and I like my boss. I know I'm lucky, being able to work, well, at least tangentially to what I'd actually like to do, but I'm twenty-seven – I think I hoped I'd be doing more by now, setting the world alight, or something. When . . . well, when Mum was my age, she'd been a prima ballerina for eight years.' I told him then of my secret fear that I perhaps wasn't good enough, would never be good enough to make it in any real way.

I expected Stafford to laugh and tell me I was still young, that I must wait my turn: the stock response of those who have accomplished in life what they want to – to whom, with the perspective their success lends them, the path looks easy. But he considered it seriously. 'I know it's difficult,' he said. 'Believe me, I've been where you are now. The most important thing is to continue to do the thing you want to, to keep battling on. That, in my opinion, is the main part of the struggle. Most give up when it seems too difficult.'

Then, without warning, he stood and disappeared inside the house. When he returned, I saw that he was clutching something, but I didn't realize until he placed it on the table between us that it was the photograph I had sent him.

'Do you have it with you?' he asked. 'The original?'

I took the envelope from my bag and handed it to him. He drew the paper out and placed it carefully before him. Very slowly, his finger traced the image and I watched, riveted, feeling in some strange way that I was witnessing something I shouldn't.

'When I drew this,' he said, eventually, 'I wasn't yet where you are now. I knew that I loved art – and yes, I suppose I knew that I was good at it. But I wasn't brave enough to have decided that it was something I would actually try to make my life.' He smiled. 'I was lucky, though. I had someone who believed in my ability with far greater conviction than I.' He turned the drawing to face me. 'Kate Darling, meet Alice Eversley.'

I stared into that quixotic gaze I had come to know so well, those inkblot pupils. 'But her name is Célia.'

'No, it isn't. Or, perhaps it is both. I suspect there are aspects to all of this that I don't fully understand myself. What I can tell you is that this woman is – or was once – a girl called Alice.' He smiled then, as if at a private joke. 'But *of course.*'

'What is it?'

'I've been thinking about it ever since your letter – trying to puzzle it out, and I have just understood it. It is the letters of her name, merely rearranged. That is so like Alice, too. We used to write each other messages in code when we were children – and she was always particularly fond of anagrams.'

'Oh.' I realized, spelling it out in my head, that he was right.

Stafford's attention was on the drawing once more. 'Firstly,' he said, 'I need to ask how you came by this.' There was no challenge in his words, but he spoke with an intensity that unnerved me.

'There isn't much more than what I wrote in my letter.' And I described that dreadful day in the nursing home – Evie and her terrible guilt.

'It was an unforgivable thing, in many ways, what she did,' Stafford said. 'However much she may have loved your mother, it wasn't her secret to keep.' I was about to interject, suddenly filled with a powerful need to defend her, when he said, 'It is understandable, though, don't you think? She had built her life around being a parent. I imagine she was very frightened by that note. Her whole purpose, suddenly, could have been stripped away.'

I nodded. 'She had an excuse to ignore it, for a while,' I said. 'My mother was already quite famous by that stage. So I think, at first, it was easy for Evie to convince herself that the person who wrote it was merely a fan, lying in the hope of getting close to my mother. It was never a secret that Mum was an orphan, you see.'

'Then the drawing arrived,' Stafford said.

'Yes. And my mother and this woman in the picture . . . they could almost be the same person. When Evie got it, when Mum was twenty, I think it would have been even more obvious.'

Stafford regarded me thoughtfully. 'I've seen photographs of your mother. And, yes, I can see it now – though, interestingly, I never would have made the connection before. When I saw you, it was different. You are – how can I put this? – the image of Alice as I remember her. That is why I was so taken aback when you walked up those steps. It was a strange moment for me.' He sighed. 'I do not want to make you uncomfortable in any way. I am an old man now, and it all happened many years ago. But when you appeared at the top of those steps, I thought I was seeing a ghost. It nearly brought me to my knees. You see, she was the love of my life.'

Hertfordshire, August 1928

It is her: Alice. Unmistakable now that he has made the connection. The band has started up again, another fast number, but neither of them moves. He can feel himself smiling at her, stupidly. He must look like a fool, with his inane grin – and wearing this ridiculous fez. But she smiles back, and is suddenly transformed into the girl he knew, all those years ago.

They do not part again all night. It is like being drunk, Tom thinks briefly, this feeling of only being able to focus on one thing, on one person, though the effects of the champagne must have worn off by now. It is, then, perhaps, the feeling of finding again that one soul that speaks clearly to his own.

Alice is no longer that girl he met in Winnard Cove – she is a grown woman, beautiful and refined. Yet beneath this new exterior she seems, in the essentials, unchanged. Tom finds in this Alice the same yearning for adventure, the same love of the unconventional, the same fey intelligence that he knew in her six-year-old self.

He follows her as she leads him through the dark dew-wet grass, towards a stone folly hidden in the trees on the far side of the lake. Like that time, long ago, when he would have followed her anywhere.

They sit on the stone seat together and as he looks at her pale face, at once familiar and strange, he is flooded with memories that he had lost – subsumed within the vague, nostalgic haze of early childhood. It is as though the very presence of her has provided him with the lost key to that past.

Now, with astonishing clarity, he remembers how she showed him all of her favourite parts of Winnard Cove, how she introduced him to its secrets. The cliffs that one could enter at low water by climbing around the sharp promontory of rocks that fringed the beach on one side. He recalls them now: dark and dank, and with the sounds of wind and water echoing strangely within them – sometimes giving out a long moan, like the sound of an animal in pain . . . or worse, the last cry of a dying man.

Alice, he remembers, had always planned meticulously for their visits to those caves, knowing precisely when her nanny would be at her least vigilant: after tea, when the woman was digesting the walnut cake of which she was so fond, and, most likely, falling asleep in her chair. A handful of unlucky times they had been caught and severely reprimanded, but the experience was never painful enough to outdo the enduring lure of those dark caverns and the possibilities – boundless and terrifying – that they encompassed.

And the cellars of Eversley Hall, he thinks, with a thrill of surprise as the memory reveals itself to him. The approach to these was fraught with another danger: Lady Eversley. Tom had known with a child's keen instinct that his presence in the Hall would not be approved of. But again the enticement was too great to ignore. The cellar of the Staffords' house in Parsons Green was a simple cavity beneath the drawing room of the house – half the height of a man, dark as pitch, disappointingly small. The cellars beneath Eversley Hall had been of a different order. There were rooms and corridors, a warren-like configuration that seemed almost as large as the structure above. The first space was taken up with Lord Eversley's extensive wine collection. It was here, for the first time ever, that Tom had sampled the bitter but strangely alluring drink: a Burgundy from before he had been born, when the old queen had still been alive. A few draughts of this had been more than enough for the world to begin to reshape itself. The two of them had torn through the labyrinth, hallucinating shapes from the shadows.

Tom recalls his desperate hope that when Alice began

her exploring in earnest, she might consider him for a member of her crew. In each of their expeditions he strove to prove to her his courage in the face of adversity. He could be useful in other ways, too. Alice had generously praised his proficiency at map drawing. He made her a map of the beach and the caves, and another of that subterranean world beneath the house – and another, more imaginatively, of the possible smuggling routes between Winnard Cove and France. Alice had him sign each with his initials – lest, she said, he ever became a famous cartographer.

'I still have the maps,' she tells him now, with that familiar conspirator's way of hers. And she smiles, but he sees from that smile that the memories are coloured with sadness for her, too. It is the awareness that that past is only to be viewed as a halcyon, barely believable time – a lost paradise. After it, everything had changed – for them both, for the world.

'My mother remarried,' Alice tells Tom, when he asks about her family, 'not long after the war ended. It was as if she'd had my father to look after her, and then Archie . . . and when they'd both gone she needed a new protector. I wonder sometimes if she can actually love him, the new one.' She glances over at Tom, her face in shadow.

'What is he like, your stepfather?'

'He's . . . ambitious, you could say. Carving out something for himself in politics.'

He and Lady Eversley, thinks Tom, sound rather well suited to one another. 'And you have a stepbrother?'

'Yes. Matthew. A facsimile of the Wicked Stepfather . . . only less charismatic. It's bad of me to say that, I know, but according to him I waste my time with fairies and degenerates, so I would say the feeling is mutual.' She does not seem inclined to say more.

Then Alice speaks of her childhood grief for her real father and brother: her disbelief that they could both have been taken so quickly from her. She tells Tom of her banishment to a convent school in Switzerland some years later. 'Which was funny, as it was when they died that I decided I didn't believe in God.'

Tom talks about his father. He tells Alice that which he has never told anyone, of Mr Stafford's erratic behaviour – the nightmares that end with him screaming the whole household awake. He talks about his mother's hope that he will follow his father's footsteps into the law and his desperation whenever he contemplates the possibility. And, with a reckless plunge, he tells Alice of his secret desire to become an artist.

They sit like this for a long time. They watch the lights of the party on the opposite shore, the numbers dwindling through the small hours of the morning as revellers leave in search of sleep, until the first glow of a new day appears in the sky and turns the silver surface of the lake rose pink.

Corsica, August 1986

The sky had lost the last light of the day now, and we depended on the candles for illumination. Something strange had happened to Stafford's appearance: perhaps it was the chiaroscuro effect of the candle flame – though it might have been something more complicated than that. According to this illusion, his hair looked not white but fair, and the surface of his skin softened, so that, if only for a moment, I was able to believe that I was looking at a much younger man. For those scant few seconds, I thought I saw young Tom Stafford, in love.

Then he spoke again and the spell was broken. 'It felt like a miracle, to find her again. So much had happened in between that 1913 seemed like another age. Fifteen years is a long time – particularly when one is young – but back then it was the difference between two worlds: the Before and the After. My father had gone to war and came back quite changed. He was undamaged physically, which was a miracle, considering the state in which so many returned. He was never again right in his mind, though. Nowadays he would be diagnosed with shellshock, but it was unidentified at the time, and all the more frightening for it. My mother suffered terribly.

'The world had changed. It must feel like that after every war, but to me, because it coincided with my leaving childhood behind, it was the loss of innocence – only magnified on a vast scale. All those men, coming back physically and emotionally maimed. Men far younger than my father, who had already grown old through what they had experienced. And there were those who never returned, like Alice's brother.

'Far more had changed in Alice's life than it had in mine. She and her mother now lived with the stepfather and his son. Not a nice man, Lord Hexford.'

I tried to think why the name sounded familiar to me. 'Not—'

'Yes,' said Stafford, guessing what it was I searched for, 'the Fascist. One of Mosley's cronies.'

Now I remembered. 'He was disgraced, I thought?'

He nodded. 'Churchill had him imprisoned in 1941, and Alice's mother was detained soon afterwards – though only for a brief time. After the war she seemed to disappear from Society completely, probably to escape the mortification of it all. And she *would* have been mortified by it. If I know anything of the sort of person she was, I'd imagine that to have her husband brought down like that would have almost destroyed her.'

'What was she like, Alice's mother?'

'All I have to go on are my memories from when I was a boy. But I do believe that when you are young your impressions of character are often more true, because they are based on instinct alone, on pure feeling.

'When I first saw her, I was still young enough to associate beauty with goodness. Though some people, perhaps, never relinquish that idea.' He smiled. 'Artists, in particular, have to be wary of making that mistake.

And Lady Eversley was particularly exquisite – one of the great beauties of her time. She looked like the illustration of an angel in a children's book.

'I think my child's mind found it difficult to understand how it was that someone who looked the way she did could be so cold – even to her own child. Alice, that is, not Archie. She loved Archie – he could do no wrong in her eyes. But Alice she barely acknowledged.'

'Poor Alice.'

'Yes. I think her mother hoped that sending her to that school in Switzerland would refine her. She had no doubt succeeded in part. Yet Alice was still the girl I'd known in 1913. That was what I loved about her: her trueness to herself, a particular kind of courage.'

I wanted to hear more, to press Stafford for further details about her, but we were interrupted by the distinctive cough of the 2CV's engine from the road. A few moments later, Oliver appeared at the top of the steps, camera slung about his neck: a heavy, professional-looking Canon. He sat down between us, but did not seem particularly inclined to talk, even after he'd finished the plate of food Marie had brought him. With him there at the table, it was impossible for Stafford and I to continue our own conversation.

Suddenly I was almost overcome with weariness – it had been a long day. Stafford, with a sensitivity that I already understood was characteristic of him, noticed this and asked Marie to show me to my room.

I said goodnight to them both. As I did, Oliver raised his head and I saw the dark gleam of his eyes reflected in the candlelight. I could feel that hostile, dark gaze upon me as I left, and my skin prickled.

When I saw the girl for the first time my old heart nearly stopped. There she was, to all intents and purposes Alice: almost exactly as I remembered her. She was dressed in the garb of her generation. Denim jeans cut off above the knee, a pastel-coloured T-shirt. My first thought was that such clothes would have been anathema to Alice; as different from anything she would have worn as the dress of a Red Indian. Then I remembered the loose men's shirts and those dark trousers I had seen her wear in Paris and I realized perhaps not.

The hair was different – worn long, with a curl to it – but her face was so similar. The shape of the mouth: the top lip fuller than the lower, the straight nose with its unexpected tilt, the pointed chin. But all of these things were as naught to the eyes, which were Alice's exactly. The resemblance had thrown me. It was – and it strikes me that this is absolutely the word for it – uncanny.

I was forced to face another fact, perhaps even more disheartening than the first – that even were Alice to walk up those steps, she would not be the woman I recalled. Time would have worked its distortions upon her, too: within as much as without. Would I know her still for the person I had loved all those years ago? The thought disturbed me.

When the girl's letter had arrived, with its extraordinary photograph, I had not known what to do. Some part of me had been prepared to believe that it was a hoax, that the drawing the photograph showed was a fake, that I should not pursue it. But I knew that it was real.

I had told the girl in my reply that everything had been delayed by the Corsican postal system. That was only half the truth. I had spent a full week with her letter in my possession, trying to decide what to do: veering between excitement and dread. Surely, I thought, in my more sensible moods, no good could come of it. It would only mean bringing difficult memories to the fore, exhuming them from where they had long stayed buried.

The hold the past had on me turned out to be even stronger than I had realized. I could not sleep at night for thinking about it. Or, when I did sleep, my dreams were of long ago, so astonishingly vivid that when I woke reality itself seemed false, and I could not understand where I was – how I had come to be trapped in this old man's body, on an island in the middle of the Mediterranean Sea. Thus through the girl's letter the past called to me, staked its claim once more upon me. And the lure of revisiting that time – both the good and bad of it – was, in the end, irresistible.

I had not explained the presence of the girl to Oliver, not properly. I'd told him simply that she had come to talk to me about a drawing of mine – one that I had long thought missing. I had chosen not to explain anything of the history and meaning behind that work.

Oliver had arrived only a few days before she did, unexpectedly. Paris was too quiet, he told me. And, I am sure, too loud with memories as a result, filled with the spectre of his former life there.

He had come down several months before, too, when it had all finally come to an end. Marie had been quite tearful when she first saw him, and I admit that every time I had glanced at him it gave me a shock. For an attractive man he had looked, in a word, terrible. He had lost weight, and it showed in his face most of all, the bones sharp beneath the skin. I had not seen him like it for years – not since he was a boy, after all the horror he had endured. How relieved Elodia and I had both been when, finally, he appeared to be shedding the grief and guilt, when we began to see him smile occasionally. I had hoped, vainly, that in the future I would be able to protect him, so that he would never have to feel such pain again. But then that boy became a man who had to make his own choices, and his own mistakes.

It was some comfort to see that he was no longer so gaunt, and to hear that his life had resumed once more.

He had talked to me about his work – his upcoming project, a hotel – with a new energy. Still, if I had known beforehand that he had planned to come down I might have tried to postpone the girl's visit. Alas, there had not been time – and for once I had rued the lack of a telephone at the house.

As it was, I knew that the Maison du Vent had always been a place of refuge for Oliver and I did not want that to change, nor did I wish to burden him with the knowledge of what I would be discussing with the girl. Perhaps I was wrong not to, but I flinched from the thought of hurting him. He had loved Elodia so fiercely, and the existence of the drawing – if properly explained – might have seemed to him like a betrayal.

8

I did not sleep well that night. I was tired, but my thoughts were too agitated. My mind was too full of all that Stafford had told me – of this past that had suddenly become a part of my own story, where before there had been only a blank.

I feared now that Stafford might decide he did not want to continue. Even as he seemed to take some pleasure in recounting them, it had been clear that the memories pained him, too. Perhaps he would feel that it was not worth that pain. If he did, could I simply return to London and carry on as though nothing had happened? I did not want to contemplate it.

I rose gratefully as the first suggestion of the day began to show itself through the window, dressed in my swimming costume and cut-offs, slung my Nikon around my neck and crept from the bedroom into the hallway without.

I padded through the sleeping house, looking about me with furtive curiosity. I had expected to see Stafford's work everywhere, but save for a small landscape study in my room there was none in evidence. This spoke to me of the modesty of the man. Instead, there were photographs. Many of them were of a solemn child who I realized, with a shock of recognition, had to be Oliver. His black hair and sharp chin lent him a fey appearance. There he was with Stafford in a dinghy, a smile transforming his face; with a dark, smiling older woman, who I assumed was Stafford's wife, and another woman who was much younger – beautiful, I supposed, in a poised, heavily coiffed way. She rested one small white hand on the child's shoulder but otherwise stood apart from him. This had to be Oliver's mother: they shared the same eyes: almond-shaped, heavy-lidded. There was something odd about her. I couldn't put my finger on it precisely, but it was to do with the way she seemed to gaze out of the frame to a point beyond your shoulder, as though scoping her escape.

When I stepped outside the air was cool, though the cloudless sky suggested that it would be another searingly hot day. The moon was still visible, way up in the violet reaches: a pale sickle-shaped sliver.

The sea, too, looked purplish at this hour, deep and dark: less benign than it had seemed in the full light of day. I lifted my camera and framed the scene, but felt unusually frustrated by the limitations of my art. I wanted to capture it all: the scent of herbs, the hush of the breeze, the tentative warmth of the newly risen sun on my bare shoulders. I wondered if this was something Stafford might experience, too, when he sat down to try and render it in paint.

I'd go for a swim, I decided – it was early enough that I could hope to have the pool to myself. I picked my way down the steps Stafford had indicated. The stone was coarse as pumice beneath my soles, and desiccated in places, falling away before me in miniature avalanches of scree.

When I reached the pool, I saw that it was a modest size but quite deep. The very fact of its creation gave cause for wonder: it had been carved out of the steel-grey rock of the cliff itself, which fell away on the far side towards the cove. There was no diving board and no stepladder, merely an unembellished tank of – I dipped a cautious toe in – ice-cold water.

I shrugged off my shorts and laid them down several metres away with my camera and towel. Gooseflesh washed my skin as I stood poised in indecision on the edge. Then, before I had any more time to think about it, I jumped. There was a shock, the smack of the surface, a rush of frigid water around my ears and my feet touched the slick bottom. I shot back up, gasping and laughing to myself stupidly, my heart racing from the cold, my breath high in my chest so I felt I couldn't draw enough air into my lungs. But almost immediately I started to acclimatize, and the temperature began to seem bearable. I dived and surfaced, shook my head like a dog, revelling in it.

'Good morning.'

I spluttered and blinked, disorientated. Water was dripping from my lashes, blinding me, but gradually a dark figure took shape at the top of the steps that led up from the beach.

It was Oliver, I realized. I saw that he carried his camera around his neck.

'Oh, hello,' I said, making an effort to be friendly. 'Have you been down on the beach?'

'Yes.' That was clearly all I was going to get. The other questions I had intended to ask – about the photographs he had taken down there – died on my lips. Then he gestured to the water. 'Aren't you cold?'

'No,' I said with some bravado. 'It's fine once you're in.' I was starting to cool down though, I realized, and began to tread water to get my blood moving again.

'Your lips are going blue.'

'All right,' I conceded. 'It's freezing. In fact, come to think of it, I'm refreshed enough. Would you mind passing me my towel?'

Oliver picked it up and held it to his chest. I reached for it, but he stepped back. 'You need to concentrate on getting out first. Here—' he put out his arm, apparently suggesting I take hold of it. 'I keep telling Grand-père that he has to put some steps in.'

'Oh, don't worry – I'll be fine.' Rather stubbornly I decided that I did not want to accept his help. But when I surveyed the side, the small cliff of stone seemed suddenly intimidating and much steeper than I had realized.

Eventually, accepting defeat, I relented and took Oliver's outstretched hand. He gave a haul and I pushed with my spare palm against the stone lip, feeling the water suck lovingly at my legs and belly before it released me with a rush, leaving me sprawling at his feet. I thanked him pertly, making quick efforts to stand, but he merely pulled me up with another easy yank.

My swimming costume was school-regulation chaste, a robust black fabric with a modest neckline. In terms of the amount it concealed, it was not so different from those suits worn by Victorian bathers, merely less flamboyant. All the same, I felt exposed before him, pale and scrawny. I looked down and realized that, despite its thickness, the material was doing a poor job of concealing my nipples, painfully erect with the cold. The whole experience was humiliating. It was as though an Olympian had stepped off his perch to offer a floundering mortal his divine assistance. I thought of the boy in the photographs with that sombre dark gaze. Could they really, I thought, be one and the same?

'Why are you here?'

His question was so unexpected that it threw me for a moment. There was an element of challenge in it, and suspicion.

'What do you mean?' I asked, stalling for time. I retrieved my towel and wrapped it about me – an inadequate suit of armour.

'My grandfather is a very private man.' It sounded like an accusation.

'Well,' I said, 'he did invite—'

'People will try anything,' he said, cutting me off. 'Absolutely anything at all to get in touch with him. It's ironic – the more he has tried to get away from people, the more eager they are to seek him out. You're an art student, aren't you?'

I suddenly understood what he was accusing me of. 'You think I'm some sort of . . . groupie,' I said. And then I laughed – because it was so ridiculous.

He went to say something, but this time I got in first. 'You're wrong,' I told him. 'It isn't anything like that.'

'What is it, then?'

I gestured down at myself, at my sodden towel and goose-pimpling skin. 'I'm not sure this is the time to talk about it.' He did not have to know that I had no intention of discussing it with him. Anyway, I decided, if Stafford had not felt it necessary to explain everything, it probably wasn't my place to do so.

I looked up at him, and saw that he was not convinced.

'One thing I can promise you,' I said. 'This is about something important, something very close to my heart. And, I think, your grandfather's too.' As I spoke I held his gaze, and felt triumphant when he was the first to look away.

After he had gone I realized that I was trembling slightly, and not merely from the cold. I was appalled that I had managed to incite such dislike in him – and so quickly. I told myself not to take it personally. Yet no matter how much I tried to convince myself otherwise, it felt personal.

'I salute you,' said Stafford to me at breakfast. 'I've only ever gone in in the heat of the day, when the water has had a chance to warm up. You are clearly made of sterner stuff.'

We were eating at the table by the pool and it glimmered before us, its depths once more inviting, now that I was warm and dry. Marie had navigated her way expertly down the stone staircase with a laden tray, batting away my rather futile attempt at assistance, and unloading a cornucopia of delights: hot rolls, fresh figs, coffee, a luminous golden pat of butter. Stafford and I talked while Oliver sat gazing out to sea, apparently lost in thought – making no effort to join our conversation. Every so often Stafford would glance in his direction, though whether these were looks of concern or irritation, I could not tell. It was amazing: here was a man who was, at a guess, in his early thirties, behaving like a sullen teenager. A temperament more different from Stafford's could not have been conceived – clear evidence, I decided, for the prevalence of nature over nurture.

'Kate,' said Stafford, leaning across to refill my coffee

cup, 'I had hoped that you and I might carry on our discussion after breakfast.'

'Yes, please, I'd like that.' So he did want to continue, I thought, in relief.

'Good. I thought that we could sit in the studio, to avoid the heat. And I have an idea I'd like to put to you. I'll explain when we're there.'

Oliver had turned to watch us now. It irritated him, I was sure, that his grandfather and I had something together from which he was excluded, and I could not help but feel a sort of childish triumph at this.

The studio, rather like Stafford himself, was unexpectedly devoid of eccentricity and creative disarray. It was a cool white space, filled with light. The vast windows prevented any sense of sterility, however, for they let the outside in – the sea and sky felt immediate and present.

I looked about me. 'What a wonderful room.'

Stafford smiled. 'My grandson is very talented. It was one of the first projects he undertook after he'd qualified. It's another signature of his, I think you could say, making the enclosed space the point, not that which encloses it – so that the structure is simply incidental, a frame. You'll have to tell him you like it.'

I nodded vaguely.

Several large canvases were stacked against the far wall, but their board backs faced outwards so that no paint was visible. Stafford explained that these were works in progress, but that he didn't like to have them turned around unless he specifically chose to look at them, 'or they clamour at me, and I see all their mistakes – it makes me want to throw everything away and start again.' Perhaps, I thought, a certain well-concealed eccentricity was present here after all. There were two chairs in the room – one was clearly the artist's, with a contraption like a small easel fixed to an arm. The other chair faced it, as though in conversation.

'I should explain my idea to you,' said Stafford. 'Feel free to say no, but I thought that you might be prepared to let me make a study of you, while we talk. I find I think and speak more freely while I'm working. It's always been that way.'

Thomas Stafford, internationally renowned artist, was asking me to sit for him. The fact that he felt the need to ask for my approval was almost laughable. I didn't especially like the idea of it – I knew that I would no doubt disappoint as a sitter. But, more than anything, I was reassured. It seemed further proof that Stafford assumed I would be staying.

'I'd be honoured,' I said. 'Though I should warn you that I doubt I'll make a good subject. I've been told I don't take a good photo because I fidget, and I never know what to do with my face – I can't seem to hold an expression. I'm always happier to be on the other side of the lens, as it were.'

'None of that matters,' Stafford said. 'If anything, I prefer it. A bit of movement translates well into a sketch – it helps to give the sense of strong, visible character.

Alice was such a model – incapable of sitting still for any length of time. You can see it in the drawing that brought you here. It's my favourite thing about that work: the sense that it's an expression of a moment in time, that she is about to stand, to turn and jump into the water.'

So I let myself relax into my chair as best as I was able, and Stafford picked up a stick of charcoal. I heard him describe long strokes on to the paper in front of him – once, twice, three times. And then he began to talk.

'After the party I was terrified of losing her again. I was going back up to Oxford, you see. I gave her my address at Magdalen and she promised to write, but I'm not sure I believed her. I wasn't sure she would welcome my friendship. Inside she might be the Alice that I remembered, but she was also a beauty: elegant, cultured and fiercely intelligent. She would have real men, men of experience, vying for her company, while I was still just a boy. How could I hope to compete with that?'

9

Oxford, October 1928

Tom unfolds the letter with fingers made suddenly clumsy. He felt sure it was from her as soon as he saw the unfamiliar hand on the envelope. Green ink. Beautifully shaped, calligraphic lettering: a mark of that expensive Swiss education. But a subversive quality to the style, too: a certain flamboyance that is unmistakably hers alone.

He had given up hope of hearing. Over a month has passed since he saw her, and nothing. Now, miraculously, here it is. Word from Alice.

If he had expected to find a long letter, he is to be disappointed. A couple of lines, merely:

Dearest T,
Staying with Aunt Margaret in Oxfordshire. She
has a car, and she's going to get her man to teach
me how to drive it. Apparently there's nothing to
it! Perhaps I shall come and visit? Still a few weeks
left for picnics, I think . . .
A

No date to look forward to, no confirmation that she will come. Yet this makes the possibility of it all the more thrilling.

Three days later, Tom walks outside to find that something is happening in front of the building. There is an electric hum of excitement in the air, and a cluster of students stand in the street, intent upon some spectacle as yet invisible to him. He steps through the arched entrance and then he can see it. There, almost too large and modern to look quite real next to the antique building before it, is an enormous car, chrome body gleaming expensively in the autumn sunshine. In the front seat sits a woman from a *Vogue* illustration – a fantasy – emerald cloche pulled low above a pale face framed by the soft, dark suggestion of her hair. Alice has come to Oxford.

'I thought it would be fun to look the part,' she tells him, as they fly along the lanes that have led them ever deeper into the countryside outside the city. The hands that grip the leather steering wheel before her are clad in gloves of soft, close-fitting kid, and she wears a jacket of the same rich green as her hat. The same hat that, when they rounded the bend in the road from the college, she pulled off impatiently so that she could let the dark mop of her hair whip across her face. 'It's a bit much for picnicking, but it seemed worth it. A bit of pantomime.'

Tom thinks of the surge of pride he felt, climbing in beside her before his watching peers – a feeling that had only a little to do with the spectacular car.

It is unusually warm for October, though it feels odd to be picnicking on ground carpeted with dead and rotting leaves. They unpack the things they bought in a grocer's shop en route. A rustic meal: bread, a lump of wax-sealed cheese, a couple of bottles of cheap red wine. 'The lunch of a French peasant,' Alice says delightedly. She has a smear of engine grease across her flushed cheek that Tom can't quite bring himself to point out. 'The best sort of meal,' she declares. 'Who in their right mind wouldn't prefer this to one of those interminable dinners with six courses of tiny portions, all lukewarm from the fussing and stalling before they get to the table?' Tom nods, although he hasn't had much in the way of that sort of dinner, in all honesty. He tends to live on sandwiches in his rooms, punctuated by the odd supper in the college dining room, when he manages to get to it. This is the gulf between them – the one that she has always been so wonderfully ignorant of.

They eat their lunch, and lie back on the rug – full,

content, warmed by the wine, so that neither notices the air growing cooler or the shadows lengthening. They are both slightly to the wrong side of tipsy, and the time has come for the sort of confidences best made in this state.

'Do you know,' says Alice, 'I always thought your sisters rather hated me.'

'Oh no, not hated. I think they didn't quite understand you. They didn't see why you wanted to get all grubby on the beach like a boy while they played clean, dull games with their dolls.'

'I never had much time for that sort of thing – to my mother's despair. What are they like now, your sisters?'

'Not quite so fond of dolls. My oldest sister—'

'Rosa?'

'Yes, Rosa – she's recently had her second child.'

'Oh, how marvellous. I'm not surprised – she was always a caring type. I could see it in the way she looked after you. And . . .'

'Caro?'

'Yes. She was such a beauty, even then. Do you know, I think Ma would have exchanged us two, if she could.'

Tom isn't sure this is quite true. Yes, Alice's mother did seem to feel the horror of having produced such an unfeminine child, but he doubted that Lady Eversley ever paid much attention to the Stafford children, except, perhaps, to disapprove of them as acquaintances for her own.

'You know, Archie was fond of Rosa, I remember.'

'Oh, I think *she* was fond of him.' He feels slightly disloyal, even now, but the wine has loosened his tongue. 'I think she was rather in love with him – as much as a fourteen-year-old could be. She'd draw pictures of them together in her sketchbook: their marriage, their children. I found it . . . she was terribly cross.'

'Poor Rosa.' But Alice's tone has lost its levity. 'Poor Archie.'

Tom nods, thinking of the war. 'It must have been awful for you. He was so young—'

She turns to him. 'Oh, you think I mean about him dying.'

He looks at her in surprise. 'Well – yes.'

'I do mean that, but I was thinking of something else, too.' She frowns. 'I wish, every day, that he was still here. But it would have been hard for him if he'd lived, you know.'

'What do you mean?' Tom asks, thinking of the affable golden person he had been so in awe of. Everything must have been easy for him. Archie Eversley had seemed to excel in anything he chose to do.

Alice rolls on to a forearm. Her cheeks are rosy from the wine – two livid points of colour in her pale face – and her hair falls across her brow. He remembers her lying beside him in this way in the tree house, sharing secrets.

'Tom, I know I can say this to you because I'm certain you won't speak of it to anyone else.'

He shakes his head. 'I won't.'

'I know.' She pauses. 'Do you remember that friend, Ralph, the one who came down halfway through the summer to stay with us? There was some trouble with his parents: a separation, I think.'

Tom nods. He recalls the slight, dark young man with the face that seemed that of a far older person, someone who had seen much, who knew things. Such an odd friend for Archie, he'd thought at the time. The two of them so different: Archie radiating energy and athleticism whilst Ralph was watchful and withdrawn, a classic introvert.

'I followed them, once. I was cross with Archie, for always going off and leaving us.' She smiles up at him. 'Not that I wasn't satisfied with you for company, but I didn't like the idea that Archie thought himself too good, too old, for Winnard Cove. He and Ralph were always disappearing off on their bicycles for a whole day at a time, never asking us if we'd like to come along. There was something else, too . . . something I couldn't work out.'

Tom feels a prickle of apprehension, without quite knowing why.

'I followed them out to the paddock and saw them go into the stables. At first I thought they were going to reappear with one of the ponies, but then I realized they'd gone into the empty stall at the end, which was being kept ready for the new mare. I waited for several minutes, and when they didn't reappear I decided they must have made themselves a hideaway there, like the one we had in the tree house.

'It was quite exciting – it became a mission, of sorts. I knew that there was a window high up in the back, to let a bit of light in when both doors were bolted. I climbed up to it, stealthy as I could. I remember my shoe got caught in a nick in the wood and I had to wriggle it free – but managed it without a sound and was proud of myself.

'At first I could barely make them out – only vague shapes. I rubbed the glass until it was clearer, and they were . . . embracing. Not in the way that friends might, but as I understood a man and woman might. And I saw them kiss: it was almost violent.

'I was so shocked my arms forgot to hold me up, and I fell down, my leg catching a loose nail on the way. I couldn't feel any pain but it began to bleed almost immediately – it was that thin skin over the shinbone. Blood, quite a bit of it, running down my leg and into my sock. I ran as fast as I could for the copse behind the paddock, and I thought I had done it in time. A moment later, they came out, Archie first, followed by Ralph, and I watched them from behind my tree.

'They looked up and down the paddock for a couple of seconds and seemed to decide it must have been nothing. Archie began to walk away, back in the direction of the house, and Ralph made as though to follow him, but then he turned, suddenly, and looked straight across at the tree. Even if he couldn't actually see me, he knew I was there.

'When I next saw Archie, at tea, he was careful around me. I was desperate for him to tease me, as he always did. Instead he treated me like a stranger: enquiring politely about my leg . . . but not with the affection he normally would. He was like that, more or less, until he went away to the front.'

'I'm sorry,' Tom says.

'Don't be. It can't be helped. I only wish that he could have trusted me enough to understand that he didn't need to be careful, that I would never have told, that I would have kept his secret for him.'

Tom wakes – without remembering falling asleep – to discover that the sky is beginning to lose its light. Alice lies on her side, eyes closed. Her face is close, just beneath his own. He can see the constellation of faint freckles, a surprise against her pale skin, across the bridge of her nose and cheeks. He can study the shape of her mouth, the sharp indentation above her upper lip that gives the impression that her lips, when they are not smiling, are set in a slight pout. He sighs.

Alice returns two days later, causing a sensation once more at the gates. She wears dun riding breeches, a short tweed jacket, men's brogues. Her hat this time is a red cloche, pulled rakishly down over her forehead.

They stream along country roads strewn with fallen

leaves. The fields beyond the hedgerows are hazy and golden with that peculiarly rich early autumn sunlight. They pass men bringing in the last of the harvest who turn to gaze at them. There are engine-powered tractors now, but here the farmhands load sheaves on to a trailer harnessed to a carthorse. They stare at Tom and Alice as though they are visitors from the future.

They break for tea in a nearby village. The exhilaration of the drive has left them both hungry, and they order food: a plate of ham sandwiches, a vast golden seed cake.

'So tell me about Oxford.' In the muted light of the tearoom Alice's hair appears black as ink, and she has tucked it behind her ears. The effect is charmingly austere.

'It's all right.'

She looks outraged. 'Only all right? Tom, if you knew how much I envied you, you wouldn't dare say something like that.'

'I think you'd make a much better student than me. I always loved History at school, and it's interesting enough, but I can't make it *mean* anything. It would help if we were studying, say, recent history, rather than French revolutionaries, but the War seems to be out of bounds. More time needs to pass, perhaps, before it can be considered safe territory.'

Alice nods, and considers him. 'So what does mean something to you?'

'Painting.'

'I remember that about you, you know. You had such

121

a gift. Those maps. Even the drawings you would make in the sand . . . the castles you'd build on the beach. Is it what you'd really want to do?'

He laughs. 'In an ideal world, yes.'

'Well, why don't you?'

'I don't think it's as easy as all that. For one, I don't know if I'm good enough. Besides, I'm meant to build a career. My parents have always expected it.'

Alice smiles and moves her fingertips across the tablecloth, so they are touching his own. He looks down, seeing how small and clean her hand appears next to his own, where flecks of paint cling stubbornly to the skin. 'I don't think it can be a shameful thing,' she says, 'to follow the thing you love.'

They fly back to Oxford along new roads. Alice accelerates and Tom feels the engine roil and thrum beneath him. His eyes stream in the wind as though he is weeping, and perhaps he *is*, from sheer exhilaration. He looks over at Alice. Her dark hair is whipping in a silken mass about her head: a mad, glorious dance. She turns to him, laughing. Her cheeks are brilliant with colour, and the tip of her nose is pink. He has seen this look on her face before, he realizes. He remembers a day when the two of them jumped white horses – huge waves funnelled into the cove by the wind, both of them crazed with a violent mixture of exhilaration and terror. And he recalls Alice urging him on, moving further and further out to sea until her terrified nanny screeched at her to return to shallower waters.

So this is it, Tom thinks to himself. This is what it is to be young: this is what people mean when they talk about the freedom and folly of youth, the reckless glamour of it. It is the purest sort of intoxication, this flying over rough ground so that the breath is knocked out of you, whizzing through the world with such power and grace and danger.

Tom sits labouring at a study of a nude woman. He has joined the college Art Society: a haphazard group run by a decadent postgraduate who wears rouge and suits of printed Chinese silk, a self-styled patron of culture.

Some of those about him are intent on their work, but others talk in murmurs, make lewd comments to one another, as though this isn't an artistic endeavour but some Soho establishment. Tom feels alone and exposed. He is struggling, as perhaps many of them are, even the jokers, to project a façade of unconcern – as though this isn't the first woman he has seen without her clothes.

Tom has not had much in the way of experience with women. He was never one of those boys at school who preferred experimenting with each other to nothing at all. He has kissed two girls in total, which doesn't count; snatched opportunities that were nothing compared to what he feels, *knows*, a proper kiss could be.

He glances surreptitiously at the faces around him. He is sure that he can't be the only virgin. Truth be told, it's quite difficult not to be. It isn't as though the few girls of his acquaintance would be willing to besmirch themselves in any way. Besides, as Tom's college friend Henry has pointed out on more than one occasion, 'English women are impossible.'

Henry lives with his French mother in Paris in the holidays and has – allegedly – had plenty of success. If Tom were a Frenchman, he feels, there is no doubt that he would now be a lover of Casanovian experience and ability. He knows that some of his peers have made trips down to London, in order to meet a more willing sort of woman there. And yet this has never appealed to him, despite his awareness that matters are getting fairly desperate.

Tom knows that he should be concerned only with his craft – thinking as a painter, not as a sex-starved young man. Surely the artists that he admires most are able to gaze upon a naked model and see form alone, to empty their minds of baser concerns.

He looks at the woman prostrate before him and thinks, unwisely, of Alice. The model's limbs are compactly voluptuous and the skin is mottled, pinkish in places where touched by the warmth of the gas heater, which makes for an excellent study in skin tone. But Alice's – he thinks of the almost translucent skin of her neck and shoulders – would be luminous and pale. Her legs, much longer than the model's, would reach beyond the end of the ottoman. This woman's breasts are large, slightly pendulous, with brown, shilling-sized areolas. Alice's, he has no doubt, would be as small and as beautifully shaped as those parts of her body he is familiar with: the gentle shell curves of her ear lobes, the charming slight retroussé of her nose.

He'd better stop.

In fact, he'd better concentrate on the task at hand. He looks at what he has so far. He can already tell it isn't going to be perfect. The proportions are not exactly right. The limbs are exaggerated, the hands a fraction too small. All the same, it has life in it, perhaps more than he has ever managed to instil a painting with before. This could be his greatest success to date with the medium. Oils still intimidate him – he finds them heavy, unwieldy, and it is difficult to prevent the colours from muddying one another. This time, though, they seem to have yielded to him, accepted his mastery. The flesh tones are vivid, and he has managed to capture even the faint flush to the lower belly and the tops of the thighs. The hair, too, is right; the coppery mass falling across the dimpled shoulder and full breast as in life.

The face he is finding more of a struggle, and this is what he is working on now. The model's eyes are wide and round, with irises of an uncomplicated blue. They shouldn't be difficult to depict. As eyes go they are fairly unchallenging, devoid of any expression other than a gentle sleepiness.

Why then the trouble? The problem is that the eyes Tom has painted are not the eyes of the woman before him. Where they should be round, they are almond-shaped.

And they are not blue but defiantly grey – a strange, silvery grey. The expression in them is also wrong: too animated, too bold.

They are the eyes of Alice Eversley. He has managed to paint Alice's eyes into this other woman's face. Despite the red hair, the ripe curves of the pink-and-white body, it is Alice who stares out at him, who drapes herself nude and languorous across his canvas.

Eventually, the painting given up for the day as a bad job, he cycles back to college. The sky is darkening to purple, and the air has a crispness to it that wasn't there a week ago. It seems that the Indian summer might finally be coming to an end.

10

Corsica, August 1986

We broke for a late lunch shortly after three o'clock. I could see that Stafford was tired by the morning and ready to finish for the day. As he worked, he had told me of those afternoons spent in Oxford with Alice. Already, I felt that I was beginning to form a sense of the person she might have been.

The meal set out for us on the terrace was a simple affair: bread and cheese, a bottle of dusky wine. It was oddly reminiscent of the picnic that Stafford had described eating with Alice in the Oxfordshire countryside. I wonder if he noticed too. Here the cheese was a pungent Corsican variety, herby and friable, made from the milk of the island's goats. And our bread was a loose-grained white baguette of the sort that doesn't exist in England.

I looked at Stafford and once more experienced that strange double vision. I was certain in that instant that I could again see both Thomas Staffords before me, as in one of those Victorian composite photographs where many faces are layered to form one visage. I could see the elderly man – the famous artist who had spent the morning looking back upon his life – and I could see the young man, too, still really a boy, who had not yet made his mark in the world and was unsure whether he ever would.

When we'd finished eating, Stafford disappeared inside for his afternoon rest. I decided to go for a walk, taking my Nikon with me, though I knew I wouldn't get any very good shots in the fierce light. At four o'clock the sun was barely weaker than at midday, and it wasn't the most sensible idea to head off in such heat – pale-skinned and ill-adjusted to the Corsican climate as I was. But after spending the morning indoors I felt the need to explore, to re-engage with the present.

I headed further down the track that ran past the Maison du Vent. I soon discovered that as it continued the way became even less defined. Stafford's house was apparently the last mainstay of civilization before the land took over once more.

The path was covered in dust a couple of inches thick, fine as flour and bone-white. There couldn't have been rain for weeks. The heat pressed down upon me, but I began to enjoy its fierce embrace. On either side of me the vegetation was alive with the rapid-fire staccato of cricket song. It gave off the most tremendous aroma, this shrubbery – complex, warm, by turns sweet and savoury. This was the scent of the Corsican maquis, a native tangle of herbs, wild fig and bracken. 'When Napoleon was in his prison on Elba,' Stafford had told me, 'he claimed he could smell it, carried across the water on the wind – the scent of his homeland.'

I followed the road around and away from the sea, inhaling deeply to draw the perfumed air into my lungs. I stretched my arms up above me and out to the side in windmills, feeling slightly foolish and glad of my solitude.

Gradually the bush thinned and the land opened out on either side to reveal rows of pale olives, nets spread out beneath them to catch the fallen fruit. There was an oddly temporary look to the scene, though for all I knew olives had been grown here for millennia. It was as if the island had permitted the clearing of the natural vegetation and the taming of the rocky soil, but with the proviso that it could claim back the land whenever it wanted without warning.

I heard a mewing, high above, and saw a bird of prey plummet from the blue – as true and deadly as an arrowhead. I watched, transfixed as prey, as it swooped close to the earth, claws raking the ground. As it rose, moving away from me towards the purple shadow of the mountains, I saw that some small creature wriggled in its grasp.

Corsica was a wild place, I thought. I had never been anywhere quite like it. Mum and I had always travelled to cities – Rome, Paris, Berlin – because that was where her work took her. Yet I knew she would have loved it here. She loved anything in its untamed state. At the time of her death she had still been performing, though it wasn't technically ballet. The best thing about her success, she explained to me once, was that it had given her licence to experiment. She had begun to perform improvisations, barefoot, which proved a liberation for her point-battered feet. These dances were beautiful but raw – her movements remarkable not for their choreographed precision but for their instinctual animal grace. It was, you could say, what free jazz is to a piano recital. Some of the purists turned their backs on her then, but I believe it was at this time in her career that she was at her happiest – and most exceptional. It was how she danced for me, when as a child I had asked her to, following her about the room on stumpy legs.

The memory became an ache in the centre of my chest, as though it had opened up some cavity there. I knew that I could not allow the pain to take over, lest it split me in two. So I took my camera from its case and flipped off the lens cap, training it upon the wheeling black arc that was the bird soaring with purpose towards the distant mountains. It would be a terrible photo, undoubtedly – the light was too harsh, and would wash all detail out. But the act of finding the shot, bringing it into focus, breathing my way through that all-important click: it was the best way of forgetting that I knew.

When I returned to the house, labouring my way up the – I counted them – eighty-five steps, Oliver was standing on the terrace with his back to me, looking out to sea. He was quite still. I was tempted to try and sneak behind him into the house, to avoid having to make any awkward pleasantries. But I would be my braver, better self, I decided.

'Hello,' I said.

He gave a tiny start and turned. In that unguarded moment I thought I saw something in his face that I recognized. Akin to loneliness, though altogether more complex than that. Then it vanished without trace, and I wondered if I had imagined it completely.

Now he gazed back at me, impassive as ever. 'Does that hurt?' he asked.

I followed the direction of his gaze – saw that the loop of skin above my T-shirt was a raw and flaming red. So too, no doubt, was my face. Now that I was aware of it, the skin felt tight and painful. I'd thought, in my foolhardy English way, that the sun cream I'd applied first thing in the morning would suffice.

'Oh,' I said, gazing down at the burnt skin in horrified fascination. 'I'd better—'

He cut me off. 'How long are you staying?'

'I . . .' his question had ambushed me – and I was thrown for a moment. 'I don't actually know.'

'Well,' he said, 'I should tell you something, while you're here. I know that Grand-père will be too polite to ever say it, but he gets tired. It is one of the reasons that he rarely has guests. And the few times he has had them, it is only for a day or two. Never longer.'

The message was clear: don't overstay your welcome.

'Thank you,' I said, as civilly as I could, unable to believe his rudeness. 'I will bear it in mind.'

Once within the sanctuary of my room I went to the mirror, and saw that it was as bad as I had suspected. I was angry, humiliated, thinking of how foolish I must have looked to Oliver. I drew closer to the glass to inspect the damage, and jumped at a knock on the door. For an awful second I thought it might be him, having decided he wasn't quite finished with me.

It was Marie. She had a white tube, which she held towards me. I read the label: aloe vera lotion.

'You put it . . .' She gestured to my chest and face.

'Oh – thank you.'

'He tell me,' she said.

'Who?' I asked. 'Mr Stafford?'

She shook her head. 'Ollie.'

It took me a couple of seconds to realize who she meant – that it must be her name for him. 'Oh,' I said again, quite stupidly.

When Marie was gone I slathered the stuff all over the burn. It was cool and immediately soothing, with an unusual marine scent.

I was mystified. After his words on the terrace, it seemed bizarre, almost perversely so, that Oliver had then chosen to do something that could only be construed as kind. Still, I thought, not too kind. It wasn't as though he had deigned to bring it to me himself. And perhaps he was merely trying to spare his grandfather the unpleasantness of having to look at my raw face over his easel.

I woke early the next morning. My sunburn was hot and uncomfortable, and there was a clamour of thoughts in my head. My immediate thought on waking was of Mum. Even now, in those first few moments of consciousness I had to re-remember that she was gone, that it had not all been a bad dream, that I would never see her again. As always, there was some stubborn part of me that refused to believe it.

Now these thoughts were joined by all that Thomas Stafford had told me the day before. Even if he had not told me he loved her, the woman named Alice, I would have been able to hear it from the way he first spoke her name. But it was more than that, I felt. He loved her still.

I knew I was not going to go back to sleep now, so I resolved to head outside and feel the cool morning air on my raw skin. I slipped from my bed and padded out into the corridor. I was making for the front door, but the pictures that hung in the hallway drew me back to them again – inevitably, as though they exerted some invisible pull upon me.

This time, when I looked at the photograph of Oliver and his mother, I realized something. That same look, that one I thought I had glimpsed the previous afternoon, was there in his face. Fascinated, I unhinged the picture from the wall so I could examine it more closely. I studied her – haughtily beautiful and immaculate, her slender white arms exposed by the sleeveless black shift, her hair upswept to reveal the two delicate drop earrings. I was struck anew by the way her hand on his shoulder seemed to hold him away from her body – not at all the caress that it pretended to be.

I was so absorbed that I didn't hear anything – no door opening, no approaching footsteps – until the sound of his voice, loud and very near, sent shock exploding through me.

'What are you doing?'

I spun around. There wasn't time to do anything other than drop the hand holding the picture, in an attempt to shield it from sight with my body. It was a vain effort: his eyes went straight to the empty space on the wall where it had hung. I don't know if it was his intention, but I felt that he had caught me stealing, or spying. Which wasn't, in fact, so far from the truth.

'Oh – I was looking at something.'

'That?' Oliver pointed behind me, to where my concealed right hand clutched the photo. Slowly, I brought it into sight.

'Yes,' I said, and heard my voice waver, guiltily.

'Have you seen everything you wanted?'

'I didn't—' I began. 'I mean, I was on my way outside, and I spotted this. It's you, isn't it?' It seemed best to be frank about it. 'And your mother?'

He nodded.

'She was beautiful.'

'She died.' He said it impassively, a simple statement of fact.

I stared up at him, shocked by his bluntness. 'I'm . . . sorry.'

'Don't upset yourself about it,' he said, almost viciously.

Then he moved past me, out on to the terrace, while I stood there clutching the photograph to myself. Slowly, I turned back to the wall to rehang it, trying to ignore how my hands shook as I did.

11

'It's looking much better today,' said Stafford, peering over his easel at me after breakfast. Oliver – to my relief – had not appeared for the meal. 'Less painful. A potent thing, the Corsican sun . . . and deceptive when there's a breeze. I've had it much worse than you – I remember spending a day out on the water with Elodia, and because the wind made it feel cooler than it was I had no idea I'd been fried to a crisp until it was too late. Elodia found my sunburn hilarious.'

'Marie gave me some lotion to put on it – aloe vera.' I didn't mention Oliver's part in it; it made even less sense to me now. Every time I thought about the photograph I was suffused with embarrassment.

136

'Ah, yes – she learned that from my wife. Elodia was always good with anything botanical. With Gerard's help she even managed to make something of the garden, though the soil is so poor. Oliver helped too, when he came to live here – he had his own herb garden, which he looked after with great care.

'We all used to joke that Elodia had witch's powers – and I think Oliver always secretly believed that it was true. She would tell us stories of the island, the history – Napoleon and all of the great Corsican men and women who had come before him, but also the folk tales of mountain creatures, magical animals, elves . . .'

I thought of Oliver as he was now, and found it hard to imagine that he had ever believed in fairy tales. But then I remembered that he had once been that boy in the photographs who had looked rather like a faerie creature himself.

Something Stafford had said had intrigued me, and despite my better judgement I decided to ask him about it. 'I was wondering – you mentioned Oliver coming to live here. Why did he?'

Stafford's expression closed, instantly, and I realized that he was not going to tell me. For someone who was prepared to be so free with his own history it seemed that his grandson's past was a different matter.

'Sorry,' I said quickly, 'I shouldn't have asked.'

'It's fine,' Stafford said, 'and you shouldn't feel you have to apologize for asking. But it was a difficult time for all of us, especially Oliver. So I'd prefer not to discuss it.'

I nodded, relieved that I did not seem to have offended him.

'Tell me,' he said then, in a clear effort to change the subject, 'about your walk yesterday.' He smiled. 'I do hope it was worth the price you paid for it in sunburn.'

'I didn't go far,' I told him, 'a short way down the track, down to where the olive groves begin.'

'Did you get any photographs?'

'Quite a few – mainly of the olive trees, with the mountains in the background.'

He nodded. 'I'm sure you'll have more luck at capturing the olives than I have done. I have tried and tried to get the perfect shade for the foliage – that unique silver green – and to properly depict the way the sunlight comes through the branches . . . but it has all eluded me. Every effort has come out looking lumpen, wrong. It is terribly frustrating. Cézanne – or Matisse, undoubtedly – would have known exactly what to do.' He smiled at me. 'Will you show me your photographs, at some point? I should like to see them.'

'Yes,' I said, flattered by his interest, 'though I don't have any with me, and the ones I've taken here will need to be developed.'

Stafford looked rueful. 'More proof that I must have a dark room installed, as Oliver keeps suggesting. But if you were to come back, perhaps?'

'Of course,' I told him, buoyed by the suggestion – vague though it was – that I might be welcome to return.

All was quiet for a few minutes, as Stafford went back to working in earnest at his easel. It struck me that the silence was not tense or weighted, as it so often is with a stranger – a gap that must be quickly filled with words. The brief moments of awkwardness that had followed my question had completely dispelled, and now it felt natural: the sort of silence you might expect to have with an old friend. I wondered whether this could be due to some artist's trick of putting the sitter at ease, but dismissed the idea. It was simply how Stafford was – a mark of his calmness, his confidence.

Before I met him I had viewed Stafford merely as a conduit to the woman in his drawing, a means of discovering more about her. I had presumed that he would turn out to be the difficult, reclusive type that his lifestyle suggested, and had never anticipated that I might feel such a strong liking for the man himself.

I watched him now – he seemed entirely lost in thought. And when he spoke his words seemed to come from some hidden well of feeling: 'Often, when I wake, I forget that I am an old man. In those first few moments I can sometimes believe that I am back in England, lying in my room at Oxford and hoping for a letter from Alice.'

He gestured out of the window. 'That view, out there, it's the same as it has been for centuries, perhaps even

139

millennia, give or take a couple of the boats. When you are confronted with the permanence of other things in that way . . .' He paused. 'Well, it heightens the sense of one's own short span here. I know that I'm lucky to have lived so long, and seen so much – luckier than Elodia, luckier than many people. That doesn't make it any easier to see this old man's face in the mirror when I'm not expecting it.'

I looked for something to say. 'But your work has permanence.'

'You're kind. Yes, I suppose it does – in the most literal sense, at least. It will continue, hopefully, to exist when I am gone. But will it have relevance?' He shrugged. 'That cannot be known.' He shook his head, as though chastising himself. 'I'm sorry, Kate, I don't know what has come over me. I woke up in a strange mood this morning . . . I can only think it is this travelling into the past. It's all so vivid that something in me refuses to believe that so much time has gone by.' Then he smiled. 'She was the first person to see my work, properly, you know. She was the first person to believe in me too – as an artist, not a boy with a fantasy.'

'Who?' I said, rather stupidly. 'Elodia?'

He shook his head. 'No. Alice, of course.'

12

Tom has returned to London for the Easter holidays, and he has found himself a studio: the boathouse in Putney that has belonged to his family since he was a boy. They used to keep a dinghy in it for outings on the Thames, but the place was abandoned after Tom's father came back from the front, when it became clear that he was no longer the sort of man who went on boating trips.

The boathouse should have been sold along with the dinghy, but Tom's mother cannot quite bring herself to believe that there will never be another trip on the river. To sell it would be irrevocable confirmation of that. So it has remained, virtually untouched, for over a decade.

It is a large space, made hazardous by old sailing paraphernalia. There is a roll of ancient sailcloth in one corner and a precarious stack of life jackets on a high shelf to the back. A couple of mildewed oars lean tiredly against the wall, and tangled heaps of ropes, toggles and pieces of old material litter the floor. It is perfectly serviceable, though, and as Tom isn't the tidiest person when he's working anyway, it suits him. Everything has a slightly paint-splattered effect now, which is rather cheering – it looks a less desolate place than before. There is more light than one might expect, from a large, shell-shaped window above the tall double doors.

Mrs Stafford thinks that Tom is using the space to revise for the end-of-year exams, and he hasn't said anything to disabuse her of this. The pieces that he has worked on over the last couple of weeks are stacked facing the walls. Tom finds that to have his work visible while he is painting is intolerable. Either it depresses him – he has days when it seems that everything he has produced is completely execrable – or it intimidates him, if, say, there are a couple of works on display in which he feels, by some fluke, he has reached a peak that he may never attain again. It is better not to have to look at them.

Sometimes he flings open the doors so that he can gaze at the stretch of water visible through them, and attempt to capture the scene. His presence is a source of some curiosity for the other boathouse users. Several rowing teams train on the river, and they treat him with a slightly bullying camaraderie. The third building down from his is owned by a rather glamorous Italian family, who always come down with their own skipper, fully attired in nautical whites and blues. Before Alice came back into his life he had thought himself rather in love with the eldest daughter, with her sloe-dark eyes and fall of thick black hair.

Alice is coming to the studio this afternoon. Lord and Lady Hexford are out of the country on political business of her stepfather's, and Alice has seized the opportunity for an excursion that she knows would otherwise be illicit. Lady Hexford isn't one to forbid, exactly, but she has her delicate ways, the power to make things difficult for her daughter if she goes against her wishes.

For Tom, the occasion could not be more momentous. He is going to show his work to another person, and it will mean the exposure of his innermost self. Alice is the only person close to him that he can trust to deliver the truth. His mother, in her love for him, would be unable to be objective. He knows that anything would be, to her, a work of genius. His Oxford friends – unthinkable. Alice will be candid, but she won't ridicule him, at least.

It is a leaden day for spring, with rain coming in sideways, so the doors are shut, and Tom has had to light all the lamps because it is as dark as twilight outside. These preparations will keep him dry, but they also mean that he won't see Alice coming, won't have time to prepare himself. He bought a cheap bottle of wine on the way here for them to share when she arrives, though he has already drunk a large glass to steady his nerves.

Shortly after three p.m., there is a bang on the door. 'Open up! It's a monsoon out here!'

He takes a swift gulp of wine and swings the doors wide. A bedraggled figure stands before him, water cascading from the brim of a heavy-duty sou'wester, a bicycle propped against one hip. Tom stares. The figure laughs, lays the bicycle down and rushes at him, enveloping him in a sodden embrace.

Once inside, Alice pushes back her hood. Her nose is red and her eyes are wet from exhilaration and the unseasonably bitter wind. The fine fronds of her damp hair are black as liquorice and wild above the turned-up lapels of the coat.

He ushers her in. Would she like to take off the coat, or perhaps keep it on until she's warmed up? Would she like a glass of wine, a biscuit?

She laughs. 'I'm fine. Stop fussing. It's nice and warm here.' She peers about her.

'Where did you get the bicycle?'

'It belongs to William, one of our footmen. He hardly ever uses it – only when he makes the trip to his mother in Hackney. Thank goodness Ma is away with the evil stepfather. I think it's safe to assume she wouldn't approve of me cycling round London wearing a cricket sweater and men's breeches.' Alice shrugs off the coat to reveal the outfit. She looks like a beautiful boy.

She moves about the room, studying the paraphernalia. 'Do you enjoy having all of this about you?'

He grins. 'When it isn't trying to kill me, yes, I suppose I do. But it's more that it doesn't have anywhere else to go.'

Then she spots the canvases. 'Why are they all turned that way round? I can't see any of them.'

'I prefer them like that. I'm not . . . used to showing my work to people. You're the first, actually. I'm worried it might be a bit . . . well, pointless – you making this trip specially.'

'What do you mean?'

'It might not be any good. I don't want to waste your time.'

She stares at him. 'What *utter* nonsense. Tom, I asked to see them – you didn't drag me here. I think the least you can do, now I've nearly drowned myself getting here, is to satisfy my rude curiosity.'

'All right.' Where to begin? Can he show her the most recent work, the one he is most proud of? It is the oil of the redhead – and while he has reworked the eyes meticulously he can't be certain that Alice won't glimpse her own eyes behind them, through the layers of paint. Tom studies the blank backs of the canvases in their ugly wooden frames – he knows each without having to turn them. Finally, he decides. It is a small charcoal of Rosa, his second favourite. The essence of his sister is there, even if the chin isn't quite right. But the shape of the brow and nose is nearly perfect and the expression, too, is Rosa's. It is her 'older sister' look: appraising, amused.

Alice turns, notices him clasping the small frame. 'Can I?' He hands it to her. She studies it and he watches her. There is a tiny mole – a freckle, really – on the back of her left hand, near the base of her little finger. He stares. How can something so trifling hold such charm?

It seems an eternity before she speaks, though it is only a matter of moments. Then, simply, 'It's wonderful.' He looks up at her in surprise. 'I mean it. This is Rosa . . . the Rosa I remember.' She laughs. 'Well, not exactly – she was fourteen when I last saw her. But she has the same expression *precisely*. I remember it so clearly.'

'Thank you.' Even in his vainer moments, he had not anticipated this. He feels hope bloom.

By the end of the afternoon, all the pieces have been turned around – even those Tom vowed he would never show to another soul. The room is ablaze with colour now, in defiance of the miserable weather without. Alice has studied each work in turn, minutely. When she reaches his study of Winnard Cove, constructed from memories still vivid through the telescope of the years, she turns to him and her eyes are wet with tears.

'Tom,' she says, fiercely, 'this is what you must do.

I'm certain of it. I know I haven't any expertise what-soever, but you don't have to have it to be moved by something, to understand . . . to *feel* how good it is, how unique.' Alice thinks. 'You should meet my aunt Margaret. She isn't an artist, but she is an expert of sorts.' She is speaking rapidly, excited, and she reels off a series of names – artists whom her aunt has apparently advised – a list that includes several of Tom's personal heroes. He sits forward in his seat, tense with excitement.

'I'd love to meet her.'

Alice nods. 'You'd like her. She's Pa's sister. She's similar to him, in many ways. Pa was famous for his bravery, but Aunt M. has been just as adventurous, just as courageous, in her own way. She was a Suffragist in her youth, you know. She walks with a cane, now, and it's because of that. They caught her scaling the fence at Westminster. One of the policemen hit her knuckles and she fell and crushed her hip. My grandparents were mortified by the disgrace; they were terribly traditional. Funny that their children turned out the way they did.'

'She sounds fascinating.'

'She is. Her marriage caused a fuss, too. Her husband was years older than her, an Italian – and Jewish – which did *not* go down well with my grandparents. He was also enormously rich – though money's never been important to Aunt M, or rather only in so much as it allows her independence.

'Ma has always been fond of making remarks of the "he was the only one who would have her" sort. But I know it's not true. She could have taken her pick. Aunt M. might not be beautiful, like Ma, but she's got such *energy*. She makes me – I can't explain it exactly . . . she makes me want to be something more than what is expected of me.'

Tom nods, understanding.

Lady Margaret's London residence is a Bloomsbury apartment: an exquisite arrangement of rooms and a pair of large French windows leading out on to a delicate roof garden with a view to the buildings on the other side of the square. Tom is surprised that someone of her prodigious wealth lives in a space of such modest size, even if it is a smart address. The apartment is not much larger than the ground floor of his parents' house. Alice explains that this is one of many of her aunt's homes, in the city in which she spends the least time. Three of the others are abroad: in Rome, in Venice and Marrakech.

The red-brick exterior of the building is identical to all of the others in the square. Once inside, Tom finds it easy to forget that he is in England at all. If one chose not to look through those glass doors on to a scene so unmistakably British it could not be anywhere else, one could imagine that *this* was a Moroccan riad. The air, even, seems different to the air outside, where the smell of wet pavements pervades.

He can smell fig, amber and the weighty, exotic scent of frankincense.

Tom first meets Margaret's likeness in an early-Cubist nude that hangs on the opposite wall as they come in. It is done in the *naïf* style, with a fecund circle for a belly and further, smaller circles to represent the breasts. For all the crudity of the shapes and simplicity of the colour palette, it is replete with the personality of the sitter. The style is at once reverential and playful: the woman's gaze challenges her onlooker, but the smiling feline mouth implies amusement. What talent the artist must have, Tom thinks, to convey all of this. How brilliantly he has distilled the essence of the subject into the work.

There are works of art everywhere, from every modern school he knows of – and many that are unknown to him, shocking in their newness and flouting of convention. The very doorknobs here are made from porcelain painted in an earthy pattern of primary colours that seems to him distinctly Bloomsburian. And there is a gorgeous oil of seated women, the colours almost pungent in their vividness. In the style of Gauguin, perhaps Gauguin himself. Anything seems possible here.

His sketchbook is heavy beneath his arm. Why on earth did he allow himself to be persuaded to bring it? He knows the answer: he was swept up in Alice's enthusiasm – intoxicated by it, even, and through her he saw himself as a real artist, worthy of Lady Margaret's attention. Next to these brave, brilliant works, however, his own attempts seem jejune: humiliating in both their hesitance and their pretension.

He is thrown out of his funk by the arrival of Lady Margaret into her sitting room. Alice's aunt is, in a word, astonishing. She wears loose pantaloons in a vivid green silk, far more shocking than the most revealing flapper's skirt. These are topped by what appears to be a man's dress shirt, several sizes too large for her thin frame and tucked in so that it billows extravagantly at the waist. A jewel of the same hue as the trousers flashes at her collarbone. Her limp is prominent, though she carries it well, and she walks with a silver-topped cane of polished ebony. Her hair is wet, smoothed back over the crown of her head, and Tom can see that it is short and very red.

'Alice, my darling.' Her voice, as low as his own, has a gentle roughness to it that speaks of cigarettes and a life well lived. She enfolds Alice in her arms. Then her heavy-lidded gaze moves in his direction, and Tom, too, is clasped in her fragrant and rather bony embrace.

'You must be Tom.' She takes a step back, but keeps a hold of his upper arms, so that she can look at him. 'Delighted,' she murmurs, and he echoes the word to her rather stupidly.

She draws away and surveys them both. 'Have you been waiting for me a terribly long time?'

'No,' begins Tom, but Alice says, playfully, 'Yes, Aunt. Tom's practically grown a beard since we arrived. Luckily, you have all this art about, so we had something to entertain us.'

'I *am* a scoundrel,' Lady Margaret says, confession-ally. 'I told you so specifically four o'clock, but I've developed a fondness for long baths, especially in the afternoon. Once you're in, it's like entering a different world – one tends to lose any sense of time. It rejuven-ates one splendidly for the evening . . . particularly important for we elderly.'

Tom cannot imagine anyone less befitting the label 'elderly' and laughs, despite himself.

Lady Margaret turns to smile at him. Then her gaze falls to the sketchbook beneath his arm. He feels his every muscle tense, his hand gripping the spine of the book involuntarily. Margaret's eyes run over him, and she seems to make a quick calculation. 'First, I think, tea is in order. One cannot discuss art on an empty stomach.'

Tea (mint leaves, stewed in the pot) and cake (spiced, almond-studded pastries specially imported from Turkey) are brought in by the enigmatic Beatrice, Margaret's young housekeeper, who smiles at them dreamily, but doesn't say a single word. Margaret explains that this is because she only speaks Italian, and a Venetian dialect at that. She looks, thinks Tom, like a Modigliani model, with large, rather vague grey eyes in a perfectly oval face and a slender white neck that is bent forward like the stem of a bloom grown too heavy for its support.

Lady Margaret bids Tom pass her his sketchbook. It is as though the strange, delicious tea and the deep purr of her voice have had a soporific effect upon him, for Tom realizes that he no longer feels any anxiety about doing so. He hands the book over.

Lady Margaret pores over it in silence, while Tom and Alice make rather strained small talk, Tom keeping half an eye on his sketchbook. He can't help noticing that Margaret spends far longer on certain pages, and flicks through some as though there were nothing there: clearly their contents are considered beneath her notice. It is a humbling experience.

After an apparent eternity of time Lady Margaret's head snaps up.

'I think you have some way to go,' she says. 'There *is* something here, but you need to work at it, draw it out.'

Tom nods. 'Yes. I need much more experience before I can produce anything—'

'It is not necessarily a matter of experience, though,' Lady Margaret cuts him off. 'It is a matter of confidence. Tell me, if it isn't art, what is it to be?'

'You mean, what shall I do?' She nods. 'Well, law, most likely. My father was – is – a lawyer . . . I know that's what my parents would like to see me doing.' He thinks of boyhood visits to his father's office – the smell of aged paper, the dusty, wasting hours – and feels the familiar panic rise within his chest.

'Do you think of yourself as an artist . . . or a lawyer?'

'I'd certainly like to consider myself a painter one day.'

'No!' Lady Margaret shakes her head emphatically. 'That is not the way to go about it. I have always felt that to be an artist, of the true sort, and therefore the only sort that matters, you must believe in your vocation *absolutely*. To hope is not enough. You cannot go about as a boy with a hobby on the side and produce work of the highest calibre.' She points behind her at the Cubist nude. 'What do you see?'

'It's a fantastic piece,' Tom begins. 'The artist must be extremely talented, the—'

'That is not what I mean,' she admonishes. 'What I find in it is bravery. Courage to go beyond convention, beyond engrained ideas of style and form. You need practice, yes: you must hone your eye, certainly, but that is not what is holding you back. Technically excellent though these may be' – she gestures to the sketchbook – 'there is something almost . . . apologetic about them. To truly create, to innovate, you cannot care about the sensibilities you may offend. You cannot mind that some people – your own mother, perhaps – will violently dislike your work. Do you understand?' Tom nods, and Alice gives him a secret smile of encouragement.

'What I see here' – Lady Margaret taps the open page of the sketchbook with a long finger – 'is potential, but undeveloped. You are handicapped by a lack of self-belief. And that' – she looks up at him – 'is my diagnosis.'

13

It was Alice who gave me confidence and Lady Margaret who pushed me towards new heights. I was rather terrified of her, and a little under her spell, probably. She wasn't beautiful, at least not in the conventional way, as Alice's mother was, but there was in her an innate confidence and strength that was more attractive than any heart-shaped face or mane of golden hair could have been. It was the same strength that was in Alice.

Lady M. was a true maverick. She was *modern*, too. I couldn't believe what I saw when she went to turn the page of my sketchbook. Her sleeve was pulled back slightly by the movement and I glimpsed a tattoo on the inside of her wrist. It was small but extremely dark against the pale skin. Alice explained that it was of a serpent. Her aunt had been bitten by a rattlesnake on a trip to Nicaragua, and nearly died. After she had recovered she had the tattoo done. It was a talisman, a symbol of the force of will that had brought her through it. Such a thing is, even now, a sign of rebellion, of non-conformism, but back then, nobody had tattoos, and especially no one of Lady Margaret's class.

She criticized my work ruthlessly, but when she told me that it had promise, I felt again that hope I'd had when Alice had come to the studio. Only this time there was, perhaps, more foundation to it: Lady Margaret knew art.

Some of the pieces she dismissed outright. I had gone through a Picasso phase, as so many artists of my generation did, in which I didn't so much work under his influence but lifted elements wholesale: a cross-hatching technique here, a colour-blocking effect there. In one sketch I had literally copied the jug from Picasso's *Pitcher and Lemon*, and was embarrassed when Lady M. called me out on it. 'It is a talent of sorts,' she told me, 'to imitate another's work, but it is not the sort that you should pursue. There are dozens of Frenchmen in Montmartre doing precisely that, and much better, for they have had years to hone their skill. Find your own style – and you must be brave, because it takes courage to strike out alone. You must not be afraid of ridicule; indeed, you may want to court it. To be able to illicit a strong reaction of any sort is a powerful thing. God forbid that people should *tolerate* your work.'

You felt that if she believed in you, harnessed you to her, it was impossible that you should fail, and absolutely possible that you might do anything. And while she had been fairly damning about my work in one sense, she was supportive in the way that mattered the most: she urged me to continue. She thought that, even if I hadn't got there yet, I would.

She told me to return, in a year's time, when I had sought out my own style, and had a new portfolio of works to show her. I went back to the studio and tore up half of my work, burned it in the brazier I kept there. Afterwards I felt that I had undergone a form of catharsis. I cannot remember a single one of those paintings, but I have no doubt that, if I could do so, I would not regret that action for an instant. The collectors might feel differently . . . sometimes a painter's first terrible daubs are worth more than his mature work. Presumably they derive excitement from seeing the artist's style in its embryonic state. For me, those works were the artistic equivalent of a teenage diary: full of overblown sentiment and melodrama.

The drawing that Kate had brought me, though, that was different. It was one of the works I'm proudest of. I'm not sure that I would have been capable of ever drawing anything quite like it – and not only because of the way in which my style evolved. There was something in the essence of that sketch which, like my innocence at that age, had to be lost to time. A certain un-selfconsciousness . . . a lack of the cynicism that comes with experience, perhaps. And it was the record of a memory, too, of what I still think of as the happiest day of my life.

Kate

It seemed Stafford was tired of talking, for the next couple of hours passed in relative silence, the only sound the scratching of pencil upon paper. The warm air stilled as the day reached its midday peak and the sea beyond the windows was one uniform expanse of blue, seemingly unruffled by wind or tide. It looked as though it could have been painted on to the glass. I felt my eyelids beginning to droop.

'Time for lunch,' said Stafford suddenly, as if he had guessed that I was tiring.

I shook myself out of my stupor. 'Yes, please.'

'Excellent. I shall call for Marie.'

I spent the afternoon down in the cove, half reading my book, but mainly thinking about all that Stafford told me. At times the past he was describing now felt more real to me than my life back in London, which now seemed insubstantial, far away. I only wished that I could have shared this new discovery. I was sure Mum would have been fascinated by it all, in spite of herself.

The sand was coarse-grained, whitish, and hot to the

touch. The beach was a mere few metres across: a brief gap in the rock that extended along the coast on either side. I waded into the shallows at one point, and discovered that if I stood there long enough, letting my feet sink into the sand, tiny brown fish would dart about my ankles. Until, that is, I wiggled a toe – whereupon they would disappear from sight in the blink of an eye.

Afterwards I lay back on the warm sand, and must have fallen asleep for a while, because I awoke with a start on hearing my name called. I looked about me, bleary-eyed, and saw to my dismay that it was Oliver, standing a few feet away with his hands in his pockets. Instantly I was on my guard, but the hostility that I prepared myself for did not come.

'Marie has put out tea,' he said, and his voice sounded different: not friendly, exactly, but approaching civil. 'I thought I'd come and see if you were hungry.'

'Oh.' I sat up, confused. My first reaction, irrational though it might have been, was: *this must be a trick*. 'Yes,' I said, carefully, 'I am – thank you.'

He turned and disappeared from sight. I waited for a few moments, letting my head clear of sleep – I wanted to be alert for whatever confrontation was to follow – and then followed him up the steps. I realized that it might simply be that Stafford had asked him to fetch me – though that wouldn't quite explain the new, courteous way he'd spoken to me – but when I reached the terrace the artist was nowhere to be seen.

'Grand-père's taking his nap,' Oliver said, catching me looking about for him.

'Ah.'

We sat down at the table together, which had been set with an elegant china pot, two cups with matching saucers, and a large Victoria sponge. There was something quite pleasingly surreal about the sight of it all sitting there, as the distinctly un-British sun beat down on us, and the cicadas chattered in the vegetation all around.

'It's Grand-père's favourite,' Oliver told me, indicating the cake. 'Grand-mère used to make it for us. Marie carried on baking it, after she died.'

I looked at him, curiously. He had spoken quickly, even nervily.

He cut and plated two generous slices, passing one to me. I took it, feeling tense, as though I were readying myself for an interview, still trying to guess what his purpose might be. Maybe, I thought, he was about to give me my marching orders, while his grandfather was conveniently out of sight.

I lifted a small forkful of cake to my mouth. The delicious morsel momentarily distracted me: the lemony airiness of the sponge, the unctuousness of the cream and the tartness of the raspberry jam. I looked up and found that Oliver was watching me.

'It's very good,' I told him, because he seemed to be waiting for me to say something.

There followed a long, tense pause, during which I tentatively ate another bite of cake. Then Oliver shifted, leaning forward in his seat. 'Well . . .' He stopped, looking uncomfortable. 'I'm not quite sure how to say this . . .'

I waited, braced for the sting – whatever it was to be. This time I would be ready to defend myself.

'I wanted to say I'm sorry.'

My surprise made me swallow my mouthful too quickly, and the sponge lodged horribly in my windpipe. I coughed, and barely managed to stop myself from spraying him with crumbs.

'Why?' I asked hoarsely, when I could trust myself to speak again. What I really meant was 'Why now?' He'd shown no sign of being troubled by any qualms only a few short hours before.

'Well,' he said, spreading his palms, 'I realize that I haven't been . . .' he shrugged '. . . the most welcoming I could have been to you.'

'It's fine,' I said. I stared at him, still half wondering if it was a trick.

But then – with a sudden flare of clarity – I understood. 'Is this about my mother?'

I knew immediately that I had found the answer, because I saw it there in his face: pity.

Oliver nodded, shifted in his seat. 'Grand-père told me, this morning,' he said. 'After I bumped into you.'

I saw it now. He must have gone to Stafford to tell him about my 'crime', and Stafford, to exonerate me, had told him. He shouldn't have, I thought – he had no cause to. I had no desire to be pitied, especially not by Oliver. In fact, now that I considered it, it had almost been a relief to have one person who didn't know, who didn't feel they had to treat me as if I might break with rough treatment.

Oliver cleared his throat. 'I read about it, when it happened. I couldn't stop thinking about it – all those people . . .'

I grimaced. I did not want to think about the newspapers, the photographs they had somehow been allowed to print. Sensing this might not be the right tack, Oliver said, 'If I had known, I wouldn't . . .' He stopped. 'I suppose I jumped to conclusions. I thought you were here to pester Grand-père for something. He's explained to me that you're here at his express request – that you've come here as a personal favour to him.'

This last made me uncomfortable – because it wasn't strictly true. Then again, if Stafford had decided to doctor the facts, I was happy not to contradict him.

'He told me about your mother . . .'

'Honestly,' I said, firmly, 'you don't need to worry about it. It happened a while ago.'

'A year,' he said. 'That's not long, not when you've lost someone you love. Grand-mère died several years ago – and I haven't stopped missing her.'

He was staring at me intently, and suddenly I found that I could not hold his gaze. To my horror, I felt my eyes smart ominously. Not now, I told myself, not in front of this stranger, who until moments earlier had been behaving like an enemy. I had preferred him when he was hostile – it was far easier to deal with. I stared down at my plate, forcing the tears into retreat.

That evening and at breakfast the next morning Oliver's new civility continued – which I suppose should have come as no surprise. And yet, given how he had been before, I was thrown by a feeling of unreality. He acted towards me like a polite stranger – a waiter, or a train conductor. I was quite relieved when Stafford asked if I was ready to head to the studio with him.

I was rising to my feet to follow him when Oliver stopped me.

'Kate,' he said.

'Yes?'

'I wanted to ask you something. I'd planned to go to Bonifacio this evening – I always try to visit while I'm here. I wondered if you felt like coming with me.' Again he spoke with that curious new tone – the remote, formal politeness.

'Thank you . . . but no.' The prospect of spending an evening with Oliver acting as though I were an invalid was even worse than spending it with him at his most hostile. I was certain that he was not motivated by a genuine desire for my company. 'I mean,' I said, feeling the need to explain, 'it's kind of you to offer, but I don't want you to feel that you have to . . . babysit me. I'm quite happy to stay here with your grandfather.'

I wondered, in fact, whether this too had been orchestrated by Stafford. The idea that Oliver might be asking me under sufferance of his grandfather's wishes made it even less appealing.

'All right,' Oliver said, 'but that's not why I was suggesting it. I'd like to go, and I know that Grand-père will be too tired to come: he never goes out in the evenings now. And – well, if I can avoid it, I'd prefer not to go by myself.'

I was not convinced. 'Did your grandfather suggest it?'

Oliver looked slightly insulted. 'No,' he said. 'It was my idea.' His annoyance was something of a relief, far more natural than the impeccable courtesy.

'Oh.' I sought for an excuse. 'Surely it would be rude, though, to leave him here?'

'I don't think he'll mind.' No, I thought, he undoubtedly wouldn't. In fact, I suspected that Stafford would be rather pleased if Oliver and I reached an accord.

'Look,' Oliver said, 'I understand why you wouldn't want to, but I will try to be . . . better company from now on, I promise.'

I looked at him, and saw that he meant it. This was his peace offering – and it would be churlish not to accept.

'Fine,' I found myself saying, before I could think further about it. Immediately I regretted it, but told myself that it was only one evening. Hopefully, once he was satisfied that he'd done his duty, he would leave me alone.

'Oliver offered to show me Bonifacio,' I told Stafford, as I took my seat in the studio. 'This evening.'

My suspicion that the invitation was the artist's doing was laid to rest by his delighted surprise.

'Excellent!' he said, beaming at me. 'It is an incredible place – and you could not wish for a better guide.' He seemed especially pleased by the idea, and I hoped he wouldn't set too much store by it. I could not imagine Oliver and I becoming the best of friends. In fact I remained on my guard, awaiting a return to hostility.

'Kate,' he said, 'I know that he feels badly for not having been . . . as friendly as he might have been to you. In his defence, Oliver has had a bad time of it recently – as I think I mentioned. He has not quite been himself.'

Presently, to my relief, we moved on to the subject of Alice.

'After Easter, I went back up to Oxford,' Stafford said, 'and though I hoped she might, Alice did not come to visit again. She told me that she wasn't able to, because she no longer had anywhere to stay in Oxfordshire. Lady M. had left the country for her riad in Marrakech. She used to go there to write, apparently.'

'She was an author?'

'Of sorts. She wrote . . . a certain kind of book . . . of the more risqué variety. It was a hobby rather than a vocation, I think you might say. I can't imagine it endeared her to Lady Hexford – if, indeed, she knew of it. She wrote under a nom de plume: Scheherazade. They aren't badly written, you know – I believe they are now considered classics of their kind, though they are somewhat explicit. Lady Margaret did not do things by halves.

'It was probably a good thing that I didn't see Alice, because I don't think I would have been able to concentrate on my studies if I'd been anticipating her appearance at any moment. And it was exam season.' Stafford smiled. 'Though I don't want to give you the impression that I was a good student. I was too intent on trying to put Lady Margaret's advice into practice: experimenting with different techniques, pushing myself to be more radical in my approach. My room was littered with half-finished canvases, not books.'

'Did you see Alice once you got back to London?'

Stafford nodded. 'That summer was the happiest of my youth . . . perhaps of my life. I have spent many wonderful summers here, but there is nothing to equal the perfection of an English summer, when the weather it at its best, and when one is young and in love. Because I was in love, you see, even if I wasn't quite aware of it then.

'Alice and I were invited to a number of weekend parties in the countryside, at the homes of friends, or almost-friends. I felt something of an interloper, knowing the only reason I'd been invited was my perceived association with Alice.

'Alice was always the first to change into her tennis outfit, to pull on her boots to go for a walk in the grounds. She'd been the same way as a child; forever restless, forever active, impatient to get on the tennis court, attempt a round of golf or croquet . . .

'She looked delicate, but she was a gifted sportswoman. She couldn't compete with someone like Diana

Ruston, who had arms like great haunches of ham and could hit a tennis ball as hard as any man, but Alice was so determined, even fierce at times. Not exactly competitive, at least not in any unpleasant way, but she so enjoyed the game – any game – that she threw herself into it with an incredible vigour. It was an energy that was . . . intoxicating.'

14

Sussex, September 1929

It is the hottest day of the year so far – even hotter than the couple of weeks that have preceded it, which have left the ground cracked and arid, the grass withered, the leaves of the plants curling in desperate thirst. People are beginning to complain: September should not be like this. And yet it is, in a way, rather glorious.

Alice is enjoying it. She bathes in it – stretching out her long pale limbs in almost feline delight, letting the sun beat down upon the delicate skin of her face as she turns the pages of her book. There is already a pinkish stripe across the bridge of her nose, but Tom would never suggest that she move into the shade, for she would only laugh at him. He knows, too, that like many fragile-seeming things, Alice is far stronger than she appears. And except for that stripe, her skin retains the same pallor as the interior of an eggshell, while most of the guests – himself included – have turned ruddy and brown.

They have been at the house for a couple of days now. The building is a spectacular if elderly Palladian affair. It reminds Tom of one of those grand old ladies seen at certain London parties. The noble lines of the façade are drooping slightly with age – a picturesque decadence – and yet the underlying structure stands firm, throwing an important shadow before it, its grandeur less about aesthetics than the simple fact of its impressive longevity.

It would be wrong, however, to assume that the structure of the household within is crumbling along with the stones and mortar of the exterior. The boundaries that exist between above and below stairs are as rigidly defined as ever. Tom has stayed in few houses of this sort, and is bemused by the extreme deference of the staff, and unsettled, when he returns to his room, by the evidence that someone has been there in the interim. He never realized that pyjamas could be quite so impeccably folded. It is as though his every whim is anticipated, and that it is always somebody's absolute pleasure to indulge it.

Tom doesn't know his host and hostess well, and is fairly sure that he has only been invited because of his connection to Alice. He is perfectly prepared to accept this, and has had a pleasant time of it. There is a colourful array of guests in the party. The writer with the girl's name, small and fair and minutely observing everything about him. A young photographer too, increasingly popular among the female Bright Young Things because of his talent when it comes to retouching. He is caustic in his disparagement of painting. Tom decides this is probably because he couldn't draw if his life depended upon it. He tells himself it isn't worth his while to engage with the fellow, yet Alice has other ideas.

'Surely,' she says, 'now that photography can be used to show us things as they are, painting is liberated.'

'I don't quite take your meaning.'

'Well, these days painting can be used to the best, the most noble ends, as interpretations of reality, not direct reflections of it.'

The young man scowls but seems, for once, lost for words.

Roddy is here, too. When he catches sight of Alice and Tom sitting together he raises his eyebrows and mouths something excitedly. Tom decides it is safest to pretend he hasn't noticed, but when he goes outside to take some fresh air Roddy follows him on to the steps.

'So,' he says, hunkering down next to Tom and lighting a cigarette, 'you and the Honourable Miss Eversley, is it?'

'I don't know—'

'I'm happy for you,' says Roddy. 'No need to say more.

Though, I hope you don't mind my saying this' – he peers at Tom – 'wouldn't have seen it coming, personally.'

'Why?' Tom asks, despite himself.

'Thought she'd be the sort to go for an older fellow.' He draws on his cigarette. 'Have you met the stepfather yet?'

'Hexford? No.'

'An interesting fellow, as far as I can tell. Gave a thunderingly boring talk at the Union, got ever so exercised about nationalization of industry, the Jews, degenerate art – that sort of thing. Jolly excitable, for such a serious-looking chap.'

'What about the stepbrother? Do you know him?'

'Matthew? Oh yes. Knew him at Harrow. He was my head of house.' Roddy, for once, seems subdued, and disinclined to say more.

The next morning there is a hunt – following the hosts' outlandish idea to hold a summer fixture – and a party made up of most of the guests will depart at mid-morning to meet up with the rest. Tom, never having learned to ride, has declined. Alice, too, though Tom knows that she is an excellent horsewoman.

'Don't stay on my account,' he says – thinking that he could happily spend his day in solitude, sketching the house and grounds, perhaps taking a cooling dip in the lake he has spied from his bedroom window.

'The thing is,' says Alice, 'I don't see why something

has to die for the sake of sport. I get as much pleasure from unbloodthirsty games. No one has to die in tennis.' She pauses, thoughtfully. 'Though it looked like it might go that way for poor old Roddy in that third set yesterday afternoon. It can't be healthy for anyone to turn that colour.'

The others depart, leaving behind Tom, Alice and the hostess's mother, who claims a sun-induced headache and elects to spend the morning lying in a darkened room with a cold compress, moaning softly to herself. Tom can't help suspecting that her condition may owe more to the great quantities of champagne she was seen to enjoy the night before.

Alice and Tom take themselves off into the day – he with a sketchbook, she armed with a novel. 'Hemingway,' she tells him. 'Something in the way he writes reminds me of the way you paint. The simplicity, the truthfulness of it.'

They make for the lake and throw themselves down in the blue shade of the trees that fringe the water. The spot is absurdly idyllic. At close range, though, the water looks less appealing than it did from a distance: the shallow banks fringed with dried bulrushes, and the surface an opaque, greyish green, disturbed by occasional trails of bubbles rising up from whatever lives within. Dust motes hang in the sunlit air.

Tom begins by sketching the pair of willow trees that hang over the surface of the water, their foremost branches plumbing the depths. He likes the languorous lines of their boughs, the rough and knotty texture of their trunks. They look like two preening women, he thinks, long hair trailing into their reflections.

When he has made his study of them, Tom turns his attentions upon Alice. She is a poor model, if one is looking for stillness in a subject. She seems to find it impossible to sit in one position for more than a few minutes, but in the end it doesn't seem to matter. The movement is there in the drawing itself, in the quick lines of his pen. This, he realizes in excitement, is something new.

After five minutes or so of feverish work he sits back and surveys the sketch. He knows without doubt that it is the best thing he has ever produced. He puts pen to paper again to sketch a suggestion of the water in the background, the picnic basket and rug.

'Have you nearly finished?' Alice asks, craning forward.

He laughs. 'I'd have finished by now if you'd stop fidgeting.'

'I'll try harder, I promise.' Another minute passes, and then Alice turns to look at the water and sighs. 'I can't do it any longer, I'm afraid. It's too hot to stay in one place.'

'All right – I've almost got it now anyway.'

'Good. Then I think we should go swimming.'

'What, in there? No thank you. Look at that water – it's a swamp.'

'Oh, come on . . . where has your sense of adventure

gone? The Tom I know doesn't baulk at a few weeds. It'll be refreshing.'

Alice stands up and, in one fluid motion, pulls her dress over her head. Tom tries desperately not to stare at the pale body revealed beneath, clad in an oyster-silk shift. She enters the water in a shallow dive, her head surfacing on the opposite side, dark and slick as an otter's.

'Come on! It's gorgeous, I promise.'

Tom has never been much good at refusing her in anything. It takes only a moment to shrug off his own clothes and plunge into the pool, far less gracefully. He surfaces, coughs pond-water and tastes the metallic savour of it in his mouth. He feels the spongy, silty bottom give beneath his feet, the slick tendrils of the weeds brushing and curling about his ankles.

Alice swims towards him in an easy crawl. 'See? Not that bad.'

She moves to float on her back and Tom sees the flash of her bare torso through the now translucent fabric of her shift, the surprisingly full breast with the dark shadow, the mere suggestion, of her nipple.

He seeks to distract himself. He swims beneath the fronds of the willow, letting them trail over the bare skin of his back, while Alice makes her way to the centre, diving beneath again and surfacing, tossing the water from her head in a graceful arc.

When they have had enough, they clamber up on to the bank to dry in the sun. Alice is unselfconscious about her near nakedness. Tom strives to keep his eyes from the shadowy impressions of her naked body visible through the slip, and feels himself burn with the effort. If he could have one sign from her, he thinks . . . if there wasn't such a weight of history and friendship between them.

'Alice,' he says, and his voice is low, unfamiliar, not quite his own. He curls his body over hers. He looks down at her upturned face, at the dark eyelashes parted with the weight of the water upon them and those extraordinary eyes, reflecting the sky. And then, as he is making up his mind to do something, common sense be damned, she pushes herself up on to her forearms, rolls out from underneath him and sits.

'I'm starved,' she says, 'shall we eat?'

They open the hamper that has been put together for them in the kitchen of the great house and unpack a cornucopia of food: cold meats and pâté, pies, cheeses, a game terrine.

'I think they must have swapped our lunches in the kitchen,' Alice says gleefully, 'we've got the spread meant for the hunting party, and they've ended up with cheese sandwiches and a couple of apples.' With a delighted cry she unearths a bottle of fragrant white wine and pours them each a glass. Tom, preoccupied by what so nearly just took place, takes generous sips of his.

'One of the sisters at the school liked her wine,' says Alice. 'She had an excellent supply of it. Once, I persuaded another girl to help me take a bottle, and we drank it one afternoon, sitting in the meadow above the school building, looking down over the valley. I was terribly badly behaved, I'm afraid. But then I was bored, so horribly bored. It's ironic, considering Ma sent me there for my refinement.'

Tom laughs. 'Did it work?'

'What do *you* think?'

'Well, I'd say they've done a fairly good job. I hardly recognized you last summer, at the party.'

She smiles wickedly. 'I don't believe it made a bit of difference. I managed to pretend a sufficient impression of polish, so that Ma and the Wicked Stepfather didn't become suspicious. And I was good enough at my classes that the sisters decided against calling for my expulsion.' She sits back against the trunk of the tree behind her and regards him. 'I'm so envious of you.'

'Why?'

'All of it. Knowing what it is you want to do – having such talent only waiting for you to decide how you want to use it.'

'You're being generous. Besides, I'm meant to be concentrating on my studies for the next year at least: not messing around with paint.'

Alice rolls on to her front. 'When do you go back up?'

'October.'

'Are you looking forward to it?'

'Not particularly.' It will be good to see friends, to take possession once again of the austere little room of which he has become fond, and he enjoys the rhythms and rituals of the place, its peculiar strain of magic. But it will mean being away from Alice, being kept from his studio, being forced back into work that he feels has no real bearing upon what he actually wants to do with his life.

Alice is staring at him. 'Do you know,' she says, almost fiercely, 'I would give anything to be in your place? I can't help feeling that . . .'

'What?'

'That if I were allowed to go to university, if I were given a chance to use my brain, I might be able to make something of myself. Girls do, nowadays.'

Alice tells Tom how, in her final year at school, several teachers recommended that she consider further study. The headmistress had gone so far as to suggest that she apply for an exhibition to one of the women's colleges.

'The Wicked Stepfather forbade it outright,' she explains. 'As for Ma, she was horrified by the idea: "So unfeminine . . . so *beneath* you."'

'I'm sorry, Alice.'

She shakes her head. 'Well, I'm going to have an education of another sort instead. I know Italy is hardly the world, but it's a start.'

'What do you mean, Italy?'

'Aunt Margaret has invited me to stay with her in Venice. We leave in a couple of weeks.'

'For how long?'

'A few months. Aunt M. says that Venice is at its best

in the autumn, when the summer tourists have gone. Ma has given it her blessing, which is a surprise. She's usually terrified of letting me out of her sight for too long in case I disgrace myself.' She smiles crookedly. 'Though I'm sure the fact that Aunt Margaret is rich, and may one day wish to leave all of her wealth to someone, is not an insignificant consideration. That way they could wash their hands of me without it looking too bad of them.'

Tom can't explain what it is he feels now, hearing about Alice's trip. It is akin to dread: a disproportionate reaction to such news. He cannot shake the sense that it will force change, disturb in some irrevocable way this happy equilibrium they have found.

It is past midnight. Though he is tired, and though the bed is the softest he's ever known, Tom cannot sleep. It is too hot, and his head is too full of thoughts. The room is bathed in the blue light of the moon that also illuminates the grounds beyond the window, the silver shield of the lake. The sight of the lake conjures immediately for him that image of Alice, of her stepping from the water in her shift, the wet silk clinging lovingly to the naked skin beneath. Tom turns over and presses his face into the pillow but he sees her still. And he recalls finer details: the dark impressions of her nipples, the darker shadow between her legs.

He decides that the best thing would be to get out his sketchbook and try to recreate the image in his head on paper, hoping it may prove some sort of catharsis. No sooner has he stepped out of bed than there is a knock on the door: soft, imperceptible. He stops, listening intently. It comes again: three quick taps.

'Yes?' he whispers, though it sounds like a shout in the absolute silence.

The door swings ajar and it is her, standing there, a small smile on her face. She moves towards him, through the shadows of the room and her body is milk white in the moonlight.

'I wasn't sure – beside the lake today,' she says, as she draws nearer. 'I was worried about our making a mistake, ruining things.'

He can hardly trust himself to speak. 'And now?'

'I think the mistake would be not to.'

15

Corsica, August 1986

It goes without saying that I didn't tell Kate everything about that weekend in the countryside. I did tell her that it was the last time we spent together before Alice left the country and I returned to my final year at Oxford. She realized, when I told her about the picnic by the lake that it was where that drawing was made . . . the one that had led her to me.

As for the rest, well, it is one of those recollections that I only rarely allow myself. I have a theory, you see, that the most precious memories can be damaged with too much handling, as with all delicate objects. And there is something else, too. It is that, when I think about that night, it reopens a wound that even after all these years remains raw, hidden just beneath the thin layer of skin that covers it.

To counter this I focused my attention more intently than ever on the drawing I was making of Kate. It was going well. In fact, something extraordinary had happened. I had recaptured the urgency, the fluidity. Was it having such a face – so reminiscent of another – as my subject? I had resigned myself to settling for tranquillity from here on, but by some miracle my work had flamed into new life.

It made me nervous, this rediscovered thing, for two reasons. First, because it had arrived so suddenly, and with force; one must be suspicious of phenomena of this nature, the changes they may herald. You do not live on an island set dead in the path of the mistral wind and not learn that lesson. Second, because I feared I would wake up tomorrow, or the next day, and it would have fled from me as abruptly as it had come. Yet there it was, every morning as I set pen to the paper, guiding my hand.

I knew she was curious, but I had an almost superstitious fear of her seeing it before it was done. It was as though in doing so she might sap me of my new-found power. The logic of a fairy tale, I know.

It's a funny thing, because in recent years my work had sold for greater sums than ever before. It seemed that no one but myself, and perhaps a handful of the greatest art critics, realized that the fire had begun to dwindle. But now it was as though some new fuel had been introduced, some stirring breath exhaled.

It pleased me to see Oliver being more civil towards the girl. My original decision not to tell him about her background had not endured. In my defence, my hand was forced when he came to me one morning before breakfast, to say that she was not to be trusted.

'She has to go,' he said, furious. 'You are too kind, Grand-père – you are too ready to believe in someone's good character.'

I looked at him and felt a great sadness. *And you are too ready to believe the opposite*, I thought. *When did that happen to you?* He had not always been that way, not even after all that awfulness when he was a small boy. This was a recent phenomenon.

I asked him what her offence had been. 'I found her . . . poking around,' he told me. 'Early, when she probably thought no one would be about.'

Apparently he had discovered her looking at the photographs on the wall in the hallway. Hardly the great crime his tone implied, but it had clearly disturbed him in some fundamental way.

'She'd actually taken one off the wall,' he said. 'She was . . . staring at it.' I guessed immediately which one it was – none of the others would have elicited such a strong reaction in him. It was time for it to come down, I thought. Elodia had wanted it there

– but I knew that it upset Oliver to see it every time he passed.

Oliver needed to know about the girl, I decided. He was at heart a kind man, and I loved him beyond all measure, but recent events had left their mark on him. I had seen the hostility with which he had greeted her arrival – the disdain that he showed towards her at mealtimes. I had to act, to bring it to an end. And so I told him about the girl's tragedy.

'She is suffering too,' I said, 'as much as you are. She has lost the two people she loved – the two people who were her only family, as far as I can discover . . .'

Oliver listened intently as I revealed her story. Though he knew nothing of ballet, he had heard of June Darling and had read about the tragedy. 'I had no idea,' he said, appalled. There was a long silence, and I could see him reconsidering his assumptions about the girl, exposing them to the light of this new knowledge.

'So,' I said, 'a photograph of a mother and child will have interested her in a particular way. I don't think she is a thief, or a snoop – merely lonely. Please,' I entreated him, 'treat her with kindness from now on. It will only be for a short while.'

'I'll talk to her,' he said, clearly ashamed. 'I'll apologize.'

His reaction filled me with pride. Relief, too, because here, suddenly, was the Oliver I remembered. The old Oliver would never have behaved as he had done these last few weeks; he would have welcomed her from the beginning, without needing the knowledge of a tragedy to inform his behaviour.

Kate

It was just Stafford and I at the house for the day. Soon after breakfast Oliver had driven up to Bastia in the north to look at the interior of a cathedral there – as inspiration for the foyer of a new hotel, apparently. This was something of a relief: when Stafford had his nap I knew for once that I had the run of the place, with no chance of an awkward encounter with Oliver. And for most of the afternoon I managed to ignore the looming prospect of the evening ahead.

When I heard the distinctive rasp of the 2CV's engine in the road below I went into the house to change into a linen dress, feeling not unlike a soldier dressing for battle. I studied the result in the mirror. My skin, having recovered from the sunburn, had picked up some colour and my hair appeared darker and glossier than usual against the pale fabric.

I was about to leave the room when I wavered: was the dress, despite its simplicity, too much? This indecision was foreign to me – I had never been one to care particularly about what I wore. This was not the time to start, I decided. Resolutely, I closed the door.

It was seven o'clock when Oliver and I set off for Bonifacio. We resorted to rather forced, formal small talk in the car – faultlessly polite with one another. Oliver felt as awkward as I did, I realized, and that knowledge made me more grateful for the effort he was making on my behalf. Still, it was a relief when we left the slightly oppressive atmosphere of the car for a few minutes, so that I could photograph the majestic Lion of Roccapina: a rock named for its resemblance to a giant version of the beast, gazing out to sea.

Bonifacio was even more astounding at close range: a city from a fantasy. We parked near the marina, and stood among the boats gazing up at the Old Town, where the buildings clung precariously to the top-heavy cliff face. It was hard to imagine how they had maintained their hold throughout the centuries, resisting the urge to plummet into the waves beneath. As if to reinforce the impression of a gravity-defying stunt, many of them were strangely elevated – perhaps five or six stories high, yet only one or two rooms wide.

I framed them with my camera, pleased with the shot. 'They must be fairly impractical, from an architectural viewpoint.'

'Actually, it's the opposite,' Oliver said. 'They were once extremely practical. In a spot like this, your advantage is the view, you prioritize it – especially when your enemy might be lying in wait across the water.' He pointed to the purple shadow on the horizon that was Sardinia. 'There isn't much room on this cliff, so they had no option but to cram tightly together, growing upwards rather than out.'

'Like Manhattan,' I suggested.

'Exactly,' he said, nodding.

'Well, I suppose they've proved their endurance by not plunging off the edge.'

'One did,' he said.

'What?'

'In the sixties, one building slid off into the sea.'

'Did anyone die?'

'I don't know,' he said, without conviction – leaving me immediately certain that he did know but preferred not to say. 'It was a long time ago.'

I tried not to imagine what it would have been like to witness such a thing – the disastrous inevitability of gravity enacted on such a scale. Then, with another sort of inevitability, I thought of Mum's plane. The dark earth below: beckoning, irresistible. I felt that familiar bleakness threaten, and willed it to retreat.

'It hasn't happened since,' said Oliver, firmly. I glanced across and found him watching me, and I wondered what he had seen in my expression.

We made the steep, sweaty climb to the Old Town. My feet slipped in my impractical flip-flops and my breath was tight in my throat. We passed a prostrate family of scrawny tabby cats, almost camouflaged against the stone, who regarded us indolently. As I climbed I continued to force away the old dark thoughts that drifted inexorably towards me.

A couple of metres from the top I stepped clumsily,

and the toes of my right foot shot forward, breaking the thin rubber thong that held the shoe on.

'Shit,' I muttered, pulling it off my foot and inspecting it. 'It's broken.'

'Here—' Oliver made his way back down the steps and took it from me. 'It's not; it's only come through the base. See?' He held it up. 'I'll fix it for you.'

He repaired it in seconds, and I thanked him. For the first time that I could recall, he smiled. It was surely a reflexive thing, so quick that I almost missed it, but not before I noticed that one of his canine teeth was crooked, overlapping its neighbour ever so slightly. Whenever I had looked at him before I had seen an impenetrable mask, a symmetrical arrangement of bone and shadow; I was strangely pleased by my new-found knowledge of this imperfection.

Wiping the sweat from my eyes I looked towards the sea. Beneath the lip of the promontory was a vast squat rock like an overgrown mossy boulder, washed on all sides by the green sea and dwarfing the grandest of the yachts that sailed beside it.

'It's called the Grain de Sable,' Oliver said. 'The best way to see it is by boat. You can't get a sense of its true size from up here.'

'That's an odd choice of name. It looks more like . . . oh, a giant's footstool, I suppose.'

'That's quite good,' he said. 'The domestic and epic together. I prefer "grain of sand" though; I think it must have been someone's idea of a joke. The coastline is dramatic here. There are sea caves, too, that can only be accessed from the water.'

'Perhaps you could take me to them,' I said, suddenly carried away, 'in the fishing boat?'

'Yes,' Oliver said, 'if you'd like.' But he did not seem enthused by the idea. No doubt he viewed this evening as apology enough – a one-off concession that he did not intend to repeat. And why should he? After all, I had told him I did not need babysitting.

Clearly I was not the only one who had been dreading this excursion. I looked quickly away, back out to sea, so that he could not see my embarrassment.

As evening fell, a festival atmosphere began to prevail. A boat in the marina below us was lit, suddenly, with a garland of white lights, and a cheer went up from the people drinking along the waterside. Laughter and talk from the bars and restaurants swam through the streets and somewhere a band began to play – a tinny, tuneless sound from where we stood, but spirited, nonetheless.

'We should go and eat,' Oliver said. 'If we leave it too long there won't be a free seat left in the place.'

The restaurant was in the medieval heart of the Old Town, and the streets we walked through to reach it were serpentine walkways, sunk in shadow. Everywhere one looked there was some detail that caught the eye: a plaque commemorating a famous inhabitant or histor-ical event; buttresses above our heads that created an arbour of stone; shrines to various local saints. It was perhaps a good thing that it was too dark to take any photographs, because I would have lingered there for some time.

'I'm sorry,' Oliver said, when we got to the restaurant, 'it's only pizza – but the best I've ever eaten.'

'Pizza's fine.'

The place was certainly charming: an outdoor eating area overhung with espaliered vines, with a view straight down the cobbled street and on to the sea.

A waiter led us through the throng to our table, bidding us sit down and choose from our laminated menus. Looking about me, I wondered what the other diners would think if they glanced our way. They would see a young couple. The idea disturbed me, but wasn't altogether unpleasant. Oliver certainly wasn't bad looking, especially when his face wasn't twisted by dislike. All the same it was a pointless – not to mention bizarre – line of thought. I looked for some snippet of small talk to distract myself.

'How was Bastia?' I asked, remembering the trip he had made that morning.

'Exactly what I was hoping for,' Oliver said. 'My grandmother took me into Lucciana Cathedral as a child. I was worried I might have remembered it wrong, but it was just as I recalled. There's something almost modern in the cleanness of the lines . . . even though the place was built in the twelfth century.'

'So is that what you intend for this project?' I asked. 'To marry the old and the new?'

'Exactly,' he said. 'There's a tendency nowadays to completely do away with what's gone before, but we can learn a lot from the past.'

'Your grandfather told me that you built his studio for him,' I said. 'You've combined it there – the modern and the historic.'

'That's exactly what I was trying for.'

'Well, I think it's brilliant,' I told him.

'Oh – thank you.' He seemed pleased by this, surprised by the compliment. He cleared his throat, then he added, awkwardly, 'I still feel I owe you some sort of explanation, for how I behaved before.'

'It's fine,' I said. 'You were just being protective of your grandfather.'

He shook his head. 'It wasn't that. If I am completely honest, I could see from the start that Grand-père trusted you. That should have been enough for me. Whatever it is you're talking about, it seems to be good for him. I don't think I've seen him so happy in years.' He sighed. 'It was selfishness. I came here to get away from things . . .'

I nodded.

'I don't know if Grand-père has said anything to you . . .' Even though Stafford had alluded to something, I shook my head. Oliver seemed relieved. Perhaps he, too, hated being pitied.

'Well,' he said, 'the thing is, not so long ago, my marriage fell apart.'

'Oh.' So that was it.

'I came down here after all the paperwork had gone through, hoping to take some time away from it all. Corsica has always been somewhere I could come when things were tough.'

I remembered now my first impression of him – that he looked like someone recovering from an illness. It must have been a bad split.

'We were young when we married,' he said, speaking quickly, as though now that he had started he might as well get it all said, 'and stupid, I suppose. Too young or too stupid, anyway, to recognize infatuation for what it was.' He raked a hand through his hair. The movement revealed a slender meniscus of shockingly pale skin at his hairline that had not been touched by the sun.

If he had come to Corsica to be alone with his grandfather then I had shown up at precisely the wrong time. I could see why he had resented the sudden appearance of a stranger in his place of refuge.

Our pizzas arrived then, and were just as good as Oliver had promised they would be. Suddenly ravenous, I ate mine with great speed. I had also managed to drink a whole glass of wine almost without noticing. Maybe it was the influence of the alcohol that allowed me to give rein to my curiosity, though politeness dictated I should leave the subject alone.

'How long were you married?'

'Six years. I was twenty-four.' He paused. 'I don't know that you could say we were actually together for that long though.'

I expected him to stop there, but to my surprise he went on: 'Looking back, we should never have married in the first place.'

Then he gave a laugh – but not a proper laugh, rather a painful, humourless sound. 'It was my fault.'

'Why?'

'For not having realized sooner that I was with someone exactly like my mother.'

The woman in the photo. I waited for him to go on. Instead he stopped, looking bemused. 'Why am I telling you all this?'

I had wondered too. Especially as, unlike me, Oliver had only had a little to drink. He shook his head, as though to clear it. 'I haven't even spoken to my friends properly about it.'

'Maybe that's it,' I said. 'It's probably easier because you don't know me.'

'Perhaps,' he said. 'But you don't want to hear all that.'

Yet I did want to hear it, I realized. And not merely out of curiosity – I felt a need to discover precisely what had been the cause of the expression I'd glimpsed on his face in that unguarded moment on the terrace.

But then the waiter appeared with our bill, and Oliver stood up as if galvanized by the intrusion of the everyday.

'We should go,' he said. 'There's still quite a lot for you to see.' And just like that, the unexpected, confessional understanding that had existed between us seconds earlier was lost.

We left the restaurant and walked down towards the barrier that overlooked the new town and the inky sea. A family were there with us, the three young children arguing with their parents, tiredly, to let them stay out a while longer.

Suddenly there was a riot of noise and colour . . . the sky was exploding in flame and the stone of the buildings around us flared back, as if alight. I started in alarm before I realized what it had been: a firework. Next to us, the smallest of the children let out an anguished siren of a wail, while the elder two whooped and shrieked with delight.

The dark water below had been completely transformed by the reflection of the sky-borne spectacle. Oliver pointed out the source, a huge yacht moored at the mouth of the harbour. 'Some millionaire having a party,' he shouted.

'And we're getting a free show.'

In between the booms and clashes of sound we could hear the whoops of onlookers from the marina. For the briefest moment I was aware of something unweighting me. It was a kind of euphoric lightness – a pure, brief, childlike exhilaration.

Then I glanced up at Oliver. As he watched the fireworks I studied the proud lines of his brow, nose, chin as they were washed in colour; the reflecting gleam of his dark eye. I wondered, in the light of my new knowledge, what he might be feeling. Remembering standing here with her, perhaps? They must have been happy together once.

16

'I trust the two of you enjoyed yourselves last night?' Stafford looked at me over the easel. I was surprised by the sudden sound of his voice. Rather than launching into the past he had been completely focused on the work before him, and the morning had passed in relative silence. It was almost as if his enthusiasm for the subject had waned. Or perhaps, I thought, he was simply tired.

'Yes,' I said, 'it was fun.' And it had been – or certainly less terrible than I had expected. 'We even got a free firework show from one of the boats.'

'Oh?' Stafford smiled. 'Well, you must come back in July. Bonifacio is famous for its Bastille Day display.'

I tried not to set too much store by the fact that he

had once again mentioned my returning to Corsica. I told myself that it could have been nothing more than a turn of phrase. Yet despite my best efforts, some disobedient part of me chose to hold on to it, and hope.

Stafford got to his feet then, stretching awkwardly, and I saw the stiffness of his first few movements. These moments were rare with him, in which one suddenly remembered that he was elderly, even frail. Most of the time he hid it so well.

He disappeared through the internal door into the main part of the house. The minutes passed, and I began to look about me. It occurred to me that there was nothing stopping me from turning the canvases stacked against the walls to gaze at their painted fronts – to have the first glimpse, perhaps, of new, never-before-seen Staffords, works that people like Agnes dreamed of.

Nor was I prevented from walking around to the other side of the easel and taking a look at the work-in-progress – the portrait of myself. Naturally, I was curious as to how it was developing. Yet I understood that it would be a betrayal of trust, and not something a friend should do. For I had come, I realized, to consider Thomas Stafford a friend.

He returned presently with a plastic wallet that he handed to me carefully.

'These are from Alice,' he said. 'From when she was in Venice.'

I looked at the envelopes within. The paper had yellowed with age, and the colour of the ink had faded markedly. They seemed like ancient relics. How strange for Stafford, I thought, to see that something from his own lifetime – something that he remembered receiving, the ink fresh, the paper stiff and white – had become antique.

He bade me take them away to read in my own time, so I carried them down to the cove with me that afternoon after lunch. I sat on a large rock – flat and sun-warmed, but, by four o'clock, pleasantly shaded by the cliff face behind. I kept the pages in the wallet, for fear of harming them – or worse, losing them to a sudden breeze. The hand was immediately familiar. Sloping, italic, with that slightly debonair flourish. If I had needed any further proof that Tom's Alice was the same woman who had written to Evie, this alone would have convinced me.

I was about to begin reading when I paused, struck by an odd, almost guilty feeling. Stafford had entrusted me with these letters, had invited me to read them, but still the idea of poring over these private words seemed an invasion. I knew how much anything from her must have meant to him and I felt unworthy. So it was with no small hesitation that I started to read.

17

Dearest T,

How are you? Well, I hope. I am now in Venice –
we arrived last night, having taken the train from
Paris after breakfast. We stopped over to visit Aunt
M's favourite furrier – she needs some new coats to
see her through the coldest months in Venice:
apparently the weather can be surprisingly harsh.
Part of me wished we could have spent longer in
Paris, but our tickets were already booked, and
Aunt M. was awaited in Venice. She is extremely
popular here, you see.

I love travelling by train, and Aunt M. does it in
some style. Our cabin was furnished with everything
we could possibly need to sustain us: a hamper

*packed with things from Aunt M's favourite delicatessen
in Paris, at least twenty novels, all of the newspapers
and a backgammon set for good measure. And yet I
was too preoccupied with watching the land speed
by us – watching as France, at some indiscernible
point, became Italy.*

*The passage across the lagoon is a dramatic one.
All one can see, looking out of the window of the
train, is grey-green water on either side. When we
crossed there was a low mist over the water, which
added to the illusion that we were merely floating
across the surface.*

*It was getting dark when we pulled into the
station. There was a boat waiting to take us to
the palazzo, which is off the main canal. Lamps
were being lit all along the banks, making for a
rather eerie play of light and shadow over the
buildings. I've never been anywhere quite like this
city. It's a place preserved intact from another
era, where the modern has hardly been allowed
to intrude at all, so that everything looks
exactly as it must have done several hundred
years ago.*

*When Aunt M. is away the palazzo is kept in
order by a man called Ludovico, who is something
between a butler and a housekeeper – though I
think either label would probably offend him. He is
thin, elegant and has an extraordinarily mobile face
– when he talks, expressions flit across it at an*

astonishing rate. He seemed delighted to see Aunt M. again, kissing her hand in a highly un-butler-like fashion, so it was more like the reunion of good friends than anything else. Then he rushed away, returning with a beautiful girl who bore a tray of drinks that had been made with fresh peach and an Italian sparkling wine that tastes like champagne. Ludovico called them 'Bellinis': the drink of Venice. I noticed that he joined us in drinking them, too, as though we were all equals. Can you imagine such a thing happening in an English household? I rather approve.

The palazzo itself is, Italian architecture aside, quite similar to Aunt M's London home, meaning that it is full of art and various oddments and curiosities from her travels: African fertility statues, Chinese jade carvings, lanterns of Moroccan silver. But it has a unique feel to it too, which I think is something to do with the reflection of the water on the inside walls, so that at times it feels as though one is not inside a house but a large and beautiful boat.

Aunt M. has a great many friends here: some live in Venice permanently, most are staying for a few months, like us. They are writers, musicians and artists – some of whom I met at a dinner here last night. I am sure they were unimpressed by me and my own lack of any special skill.

I wished then that you were here. Perhaps by

being associated with such a promising talent as yours I might raise myself in the opinion of Aunt M's friends.

Anyway, dear T, do write back when you are able. I would so love to hear about how the painting is progressing, though I'm sure it will be difficult to find much time to concentrate on it this year.

Much love,

A x·

Venice is, in many ways, exactly as Alice has imagined it: serene, eternal, slightly macabre. And yet she doesn't quite feel connected to it in the way she expected to. Perhaps it is that while the stones and water themselves represent the city of her imagining, the people don't. Where are the elegant citizens in their jewel-coloured velvets, their flowing cloaks and gowns? Vanished into history, apparently. In their place are flustered English and American tourists with Baedeker guidebooks, huddled in gondolas or buying up everything from one of the curiosity shops in the thoroughfares. Worse, she is only too aware of herself as one of these hapless visitors. She is convinced that there is another life – the life of the true Venetians, hidden behind a veil that is drawn to hide it from curious foreigners. She longs to discover it for herself.

Strange things are afoot here, too, small ripples in

the placid calm of things. Alice and Aunt M. are taking tea in the baroque splendour of Café Florian when a spectacle erupts in St Mark's Square. A phalanx of men appear, as though from stage right, to wheel and march before them to the bellowed orders of their commanding officer. All are dressed in impeccable black serge, their boots buffed to an impossible shine. The scene is at once both comical in its absurdity, and terrible. There is, certainly, more than a little of the ridiculous about such a display of modernity and precision amid these gorgeous but visibly decaying surroundings. At the same time there is something deadly in the intent, in the intrinsic menace of it, that disturbs Alice.

'Very sad,' Aunt Margaret pronounces, taking a sip of her coffee – which she ordered laced with brandy to 'keep out the autumn chill'. 'I fear this country will soon be a changed place. You are visiting it at the right time. You have come, I think, as the tide is turning. Who knows what will emerge in its wake?'

A meagre crowd has gathered to watch. Alice scrutinizes the faces. Most are preoccupied with finding shelter from the sudden shower that has blown in across the lagoon. Many appear apathetic. There are, however, a number who are clearly stirred, even excited, by the display.

Alice takes a draught of her hot chocolate. It is as thick as custard, a tiny, velvet quantity. The taste – older than the café itself, but well known within its gilt-lined walls – of rarefied privilege. A taste from Venice the city-state, Venice the August, the Illustrious.

As she savours the taste she is suddenly aware of the strangest impression: that she and Aunt Margaret are sitting in a different century, looking upon the future from front-row seats.

7 October 1929

Dearest T,

Thank you for your letter. I can't wait to see the new pieces. You sound so excited by them, and I have no doubt they will be even more brilliant than the others I have seen. I'm impressed that you're able to paint or draw at all. I seem to recall that the Awful Stepbrother had a terrible time of it in his last year.

Some rather dramatic weather here of late – great storms sweeping in across the lagoon, and St Mark's Square was under a foot of water for a few days. You had to take a boat to get across it, and there were people wearing boots like fishing waders that came up to mid-thigh. I love it though. Whilst I haven't seen the city in the summer months, I can't imagine I would love it nearly as much as this city of wet and wind. It also means that most of the tourists have disappeared. They prefer this place when it is crowded, sunlit, and perhaps somewhat saccharine, in the way that so many

European cities become in the summer: lunches in the sun and ice cream and gleaming gilt finishes everywhere the eye can see.

Venice in October is quiet and dark, even during the shortening hours of day, for the water, opaquely green, seems to absorb light and sound. At night, it is black as pitch in the less-busy parts, and one can glance off the thoroughfares down any number of inky waterways to where moored boats jostle against their bowlines in the gloom. You can imagine murders and love affairs going on in the shadows – this city is full of hiding places for those who don't want to be seen. I'm getting carried away, I know, but Venice has that effect upon me.

One thing I do find unsettling is the presence of soldiers throughout the city. The black uniforms make their appearance – always sudden, and so incongruous against the background of elegant old streets and squares – all the more sinister. Aunt M. does not care for it at all, and keeps speaking of what she calls a 'great change' in Europe. Apparently these men are the Fascisti. Whatever the reason for it, their presence troubles me too.

I know I have said it already, but I do wish you were here. Aunt M. is marvellous fun, but she is more than double my age, as are most of her friends, and her arthritic hip, which I'm sure is worse in this damp climate (though she refuses to *admit it), means that she is disinclined to walk far or spend much time out of doors.*

I can't help thinking what fun it would be to explore the city together, you and me, the way we did Winnard Cove, discovering its secrets, its hidden wonders. I know there is more to be discovered here: no doubt a grimier, less picturesque and far more exciting place that I have seen nothing of.

Do write soon. I am longing to hear your news. Much love,

A x

From the balcony of her bedroom, Alice can see the busy thoroughfare of the Grand Canal and beyond, out to the distant blue haze of the lagoon itself and the outlines of faraway boats. When she watches these shapes, moving incrementally closer or further away, embarking upon unknowable voyages to other lands, she feels something move and shift inside her, a feeling somewhere between excitement and despair.

While she is here, staying in with her aunt, she can imagine that she is a person with a purpose to call her own, with options beyond those that usually appear available to her, with independence. In reality, she has none of these things.

Coming to Venice, the thrill of this small voyage out of her usual sphere of existence, has shown her how much more she wants to do with her life than would be possible in that confining sphere her mother expects her to enter. She wants to live courageously.

Later, Alice and Lady Margaret attend a party thrown by one of Margaret's illustrious friends. Alice is again out of her depth in this smoke- and talk-filled room, surrounded by the great and important. She feels talentless and uninteresting. That woman over there is, apparently, a famous novelist; and this man here, with the round glasses, is a pre-eminent psychoanalyst whose recent paper has challenged much of the common thinking surrounding the Freudian concept of the hysteric. What does Alice do, they ask? Nothing? *Really?* How on earth does she spend her time, in that case?

Alice seeks refuge in the ruby-coloured drinks that are being passed round. A 'Negroni', the waiter tells her, and after the first sip, she decides she hates it; it is bitter, almost medicinal, and eye-wateringly strong. Yet she perseveres, for it is the only thing available, and everyone else seems to be drinking them without complaint. She is determined not to be shown up further by her immature palate.

By the bottom of the third glass, Negronis are Alice's favourite drink in the world. She could bathe in them. She is also rather drunk, though still in that strange interim stage whereby she is not so inebriated that she is unaware of the fact, and conscious of the need to do something about it. She slips from the room, letting herself out through the glass doors at the side of the room that lead on to the balcony, intent on getting a breath of air inside her lungs, clearing her head of the alcohol and the fug of cigarette smoke.

It is perfect: cool and quiet, save for the secret sound of the gently moving water. On the opposite bank several lanterns hang reflected in the water as glowing orbs of light. In Alice's stupefied state, the subtle movements of these reflections are mesmerizing. She sits down on a stone bench amid the shrubbery and plant pots, then half lies down and presses her hot face against the cold seat. The sensation is deliciously soothing. At some point she must have fallen asleep, because a sudden disturbance has her returning groggily to herself. Alice is at a loss as to what it is that has woken her, until she hears a voice: 'Rather cool for sleeping under the stars,' he says. He walks towards her, picking his way through the greenery.

She sits up, and his face swims into focus. Not a conventionally handsome man, perhaps, though he is rather romantic looking, if such a distinction can be made. His nose is too large for his face, with an odd flatness across the bridge, suggesting that it has once been broken. His lips are too thin – though there is something attractive, purposeful, about the set of them.

He regards Alice inquisitively, as if an answer is expected of her, and she realizes that she must have been staring. 'Sorry,' she says. 'I came out here to clear my head.' Her words stick to her tongue, run together thickly. She feels how she must look to him: a dishevelled, drunken child.

Yet he smiles and nods. 'Me too. Too much hot air in there, most of it provided by the occupants.'

Alice laughs, pleasantly scandalized, feeling the fog of alcohol begin to lift. He takes a couple of steps closer.

'I confess I followed you out here – it looked as though you had found the perfect escape route. I don't want to intrude, though.' His accent is good, but not perfect: there is the tell-tale guttural sound of the 'r', the dropping of the 'h' – a Frenchman, she thinks.

She shakes her head. 'Not at all. It's nice to have company.'

'Was it very bad in there?'

'Mm. Pretty awful. A bit tired of all those . . . writers.' Alice gestures with her hands, vaguely. There is much more that she wants to say on the subject, but she cannot articulate it. She shuffles along the bench to give him space and he sits, letting out a grateful sigh, as though he has travelled far, through the night, to rest here beside her. Aware anew of the chill of the October air, Alice wonders whether it is because it has been thrown into relief by the warmth of his form beside her. She notices too, now that he is so close, that he has beautiful hair – as dark as her own, growing in tight curls. She feels a sudden, almost irresistible urge to place her palm against it, to test the spring of it. She is still trying to make up her mind whether or not to do so, her hand hovering dangerously at her side, when he speaks again.

'So, you must be Alice.'

She stares at him as though he has performed a magic trick. 'How did you guess?'

'Lady Margaret surely does not have more than one beautiful young niece here in Venice?' It could sound caddish, this line, but he pulls it off – something, perhaps, to do with the way he delivers it, the ironic quirk of his mouth. 'I heard that you were visiting from England.'

'Well,' she says, with bravado, 'since you're so well informed about me, may I ask who you are?'

'I'm Julien.'

'How do you know my aunt?'

'One of my friends is an artist who has sold her a couple of pieces,' Julien explains. 'And some of your aunt's acquaintances have sympathies with my own work – including our host, the novelist.' He quirks an eyebrow. 'I confess that I am a writer, too, of sorts – don't crucify me!' he says, holding up his hands as Alice rolls her eyes at him. 'I promise I'm not going to bore you with a long lecture on the Modern style. I don't write novels. My work as a writer is secondary to my work as a man of action. I write about what I believe in, that which I would prefer to act upon than write about, should the opportunity present itself.'

At her blank look he explains: he is a member of Le Parti Communiste Français. 'Several of us have come over to meet with our Italian brothers. To find out how they're faring, with all that's been happening here. Life has become rather complicated for them of late.' He smiles down at her. 'So, tell me. Who is Alice? What does she do?'

'Nothing,' she says, with a shrug. 'At least, nothing worth mentioning. I'm not talented, you see. I was good at lessons when I was at school, but—'

'Alice,' he says, cutting her off, 'how old are you?'

'Twenty-two.'

'Exactly. So tell me, please, how on earth are you supposed to know what your talents are at twenty-two? When I was your age I wasn't half as interesting a person as you are now.'

She looks up at him, and wonders how old he is. She sees, too, in the light thrown from one of the lanterns, that his eyes aren't black as she'd first thought but a dark almost navy blue, fringed with thick lashes. These eyes give him a roguish, slightly piratical look.

'You mustn't let that crowd in there crush you,' he says. 'They may be talented – a few of them, at least – they may be celebrated, but they aren't necessarily interesting in their own right. Most of them are phoneys, through and through. Your Aunt Margaret – she's a good sort, though. Knows the wheat from the chaff.'

His knowledge of this expression emphasizes his fluency. 'Where did you learn to speak English so well?' she asks.

'I do? I'm flattered. I studied at Cambridge, for three years. A long time ago now, but it's stuck with me – it's a beautiful language, not as celebrated as it should be. People talk about the elegance of French, but it's a dusty tongue, antique . . . unevolved.'

He asks her what she has seen of Venice. She lists

the sights and he shakes his head, apparently appalled. 'So you haven't ventured out of San Marco?'

'The square?'

'The *sestiere*. The district of the city that we're in now.'

'No, I don't think so.'

'In that case you've seen barely a sixth of this city.'

'Oh,' she says, stung. 'Well, Aunt Margaret can't go far at the moment, because her hip has got worse. I'm sure if she could she'd take me.'

'I think you need a guide,' Julien says thoughtfully. 'Would your aunt consider me a suitable chaperone? I've been here several times before, you see – I know my way about rather well.'

'I don't think she'd have any objection. In fact, I'm fairly sure she would have let me go off on my own, if I'd asked her. She'd probably think it an excellent idea.'

'Well then, how about the day after next? Tomorrow I have plans, but Thursday can be yours alone.'

Alice finds herself agreeing. Beneath the mist of alcohol that has dulled her senses she feels a bolt of anticipation shoot through her.

'Have you a Baedeker?'

She nods. 'Yes, of course.'

'Throw it away. You won't need it for my tour. I like the parts of a city that are more . . . mixed. You can't find my version of Venice in your tourist manual.'

When Alice asks her aunt over supper, Lady Margaret is as sanguine about the plan as Alice had anticipated.

'How wonderful that you should have the chance to explore the city with someone closer to your age. How old is he, exactly?'

Alice shrugs. 'I didn't ask. He talks as though he's ancient.'

'Excellent,' says Lady Margaret. 'A man of the world is by far the most interesting sort. Well, you will get much more from the experience, I should think, than you get from travelling about with me.' Alice tries to demur, but Lady Margaret holds up a hand. 'You are kind to protest, but I am certain that it is the case.' She takes a thoughtful sip of her wine, which, incidentally, is an almost perfect match for the pigment she has applied to her hooded eyelids.

It is her third, or perhaps fourth, glass to Alice's one, and Alice would be unable to think by this stage had she consumed the same. Yet the alcohol appears to have no effect whatsoever on her relative. Aunt M. is as lucid and eloquent – if anything slightly more so – than ever.

'Julien Arnaud,' she says, thoughtfully. 'I have read some of his work, and he writes well, though I must admit I do not agree with all of his theories, or the sentiment with which they are expressed. That is not to say they don't intrigue me, but there is too much violence in them, when the world is violent enough already.' Then, in the mercurial way that is her wont, she changes topic. 'Have you heard from that friend of yours? The artist . . . the one who adores you?'

Alice feels her face grow hot. How is it that her aunt is always able to get right to the heart of things? 'He doesn't adore me, Aunt M.'

Lady Margaret gives her a look. Alice braces herself for more, but her aunt takes pity on her. 'I was impressed with his work. I know that I was probably on the harsh side, when I critiqued it.'

'Well . . .'

'In a few years' time I would be extremely interested to see how he has progressed.' She shrugs. 'But then it may all come to nothing. Especially if he gives in and goes into . . . what was it?'

'Law.'

'Yes, I remember now.'

'That's what his parents want.'

'Then we must hope that he has the strength to resist. For all our sakes.'

Why was it, Alice thinks, as she makes her way back to her room, that when Aunt M. was talking of Tom she was aware of an odd, unpleasant sensation within her, almost as though something had lodged in her chest? It is there still, in fact. A feeling curiously like guilt. She reminds herself that she has not done anything to harm him, nothing of which she should be ashamed. Not yet, says an inner voice. You haven't yet.

29 October 1929

Dearest T,

I hope you are well – though I am sure I need not ask as it sounds as if things are better than ever. Your letter arrived yesterday with your news about the exhibition. I know you say it's only a few pieces, but I think it's so exciting. I have no doubt that they will far outshine any of the others. Not particularly sportsmanlike of me, perhaps. I only wish I could be there to sing your praises to visitors . . . and to boast about having 'discovered you'. Please don't sell everything – you must have something saved for me to buy when I come home. And especially not that drawing you made by the lake: I think you know the one.

I, too, have exciting news: I have found a partner in crime. He is no Tom Stafford, but still, he is someone to explore the city with. I met him at a party given by a friend of Aunt M. It was rather a dull affair, for me, anyway, as I am getting somewhat tired of being made to feel gauche, untalented and uninteresting. You, as an artist, would have been celebrated no end. I, though, am barely more than a poorly educated schoolgirl to them. And then I met Julien, or perhaps a better way of phrasing it is to say he rescued me.

I do not know much about him, other than that he is French but knows Venice well – and he speaks excellent English, because he spent several

214

years in England. At a guess, I would say he is around thirty. What's more, he's a Red. Imagine what the Wicked Stepfather would do if he knew! Anyway, Julien has offered to show me around the city tomorrow. He calls it 'the alternative tour', because he claims that it would never appear in the pages of a tourist manual, which is, naturally, a good thing. I shall tell you how it goes. One day, perhaps we shall come back to Venice together, you and I, and I will be able to give you the tour myself.

All my love,

A x

18

The final letter was a surprise: a single sheet of paper only.

Dearest Tom,
I had to write and tell you about yesterday. I felt,
for the first time, a real connection with this city.
I saw the Venice I would want to paint, if I had
your talent. I'm sorry this is a short note. I'm ever
so tired from walking for a whole day yesterday,
and perhaps suffering from some wonderful drinks
Julien introduced me to. Tomorrow afternoon, we
shall explore Santa Croce and San Polo: my
Venetian education continues.
   A

I stared at the last letter, trying to discover some meaning that might be hidden behind the words. The carelessness of it astounded me. Could Alice not see how it would have looked to him? I needn't have worried about discovering words of love that were not for my eyes – they were not to be found here. I did not know what I would say to Stafford when he asked me what had I made of them.

I was so lost in my thoughts that it was several seconds before I realized that Oliver had appeared at the bottom of the stone steps.

'Oh,' he said, 'hello.'

He didn't look exactly overjoyed to see me. Perhaps he too had come down here to be alone. Now that I knew his reasons for being at Maison du Vent, I was guiltily conscious that I might have intruded upon his place of sanctuary.

'I had a good time, last night.'

I looked at him, surprised. But it was impossible to tell whether he was sincere or merely being polite.

'So did I,' I said, because I had, despite my misgivings. 'Thank you.'

He gestured. 'What have you got there?'

'Oh,' I said, as casually as I could, 'some letters.' My heartbeat quickened. I was certain that Stafford would not want me to share them.

Something flashed into Oliver's face then: irritation, or – conceivably – hurt. To my relief, he let it go. Instead, he sat down on the sand a few metres away, next to the water's edge, and stared straight out to sea, resting on his forearms, his feet making lazy circles in the shallows. I was pleased that he had decided to stay, that he hadn't seen fit to leave immediately upon finding me there.

'It's a great spot down here,' I said.

'What?' He turned around, and I saw that he had been lost in thought. He looked at me for a few seconds as if he had forgotten I existed. Then, finally, he seemed to register what I had said. 'Oh . . . yes. It's the best beach I know on the whole island.'

'Though of course you may be biased.'

'Yes, I suppose so. I used to come down at the end of the holidays – when I knew it was time to go back to Paris, I'd hide under there—' he gestured to the blue-hulled fishing boat, which had been dragged up the beach and turned over. 'For some reason it took Grand-père hours to find me.'

'Ah,' I said, 'perhaps he didn't want you to go either.'

I gazed out at the scene before me: the colours of the sea and sky so vivid that they were scarcely credible. I admit that I forgot about the letters for a while, and simply sat and enjoyed the feeling of the heat pounding down on the bare skin of my shoulders and legs, pushing my feet into the sand until they met the cold, secret layers deep down that were untouched by the sun.

Mum would have loved this, I thought, automatically. But then I stopped. No, I realized . . . she wouldn't. She'd never been able to be still for long: to simply sit and look at something. That was me, what *I* liked.

Mum, in contrast, needed to be active, constantly occupied. The scant couple of times we had been to the beach together she'd grown bored of sitting on her towel within minutes, and had exhorted me to play catch, or come swimming with her. How could I have forgotten that, if only for a second? It terrified me that I had done so. Because here was the awful feeling again: that she was slipping away from me, that I would lose her bit by bit until there was no more than a shadowy outline.

I glanced up, and realized that Oliver was watching me. Instantly I felt panicky, exposed.

'What is it?' he asked.

'What do you mean?'

'You looked . . . I don't know, upset for a moment.'

I hesitated, deliberating whether or not to tell him. 'It's difficult to explain.'

'Try me.'

'Well . . . I was thinking that my mother would have loved this, sitting here, doing nothing. And then I realized I was completely wrong. She wouldn't: she'd hate it.' I found, with a kind of amazement, that my vision was blurred by tears. I hadn't cried for so long – had managed every time to fight the urge into submission. Now it had taken me by surprise.

To my relief, Oliver didn't remark upon it. He regarded me in silence for a while, then said, 'I think – perhaps – I know what you mean.'

I didn't believe for a moment that he did, but I appreciated the effort.

'You're worried about forgetting her.'

I stared at him. So he did know, after all. For a second, I wondered if he was thinking of his mother, but then he said: 'It was like that when Grand-mère died. I was terrified I'd forget, but things come back to you – things that you probably couldn't even have remembered while they were still alive. Naturally, you have to accept that it's impossible to remember everything, but the memories that are most important – those you'll never lose.'

It was the sort of thing I imagined Stafford would say.

'Thank you,' I said.

'I haven't done anything.' He seemed embarrassed by my thanks.

'No,' I told him, 'you have.'

Oliver left the beach soon afterwards, while I stayed there with the letters and my thoughts for the next couple of hours, wondering what I would say to Stafford when he asked me about what I had read. Through Stafford's accounts of Alice I had come to see why he would have fallen in love with her. The idea that I might have once had a relative like that – brave, rebellious – had excited me. Now I felt . . . rather disappointed in her. I reminded myself that she had been young, and no doubt naïve. Nevertheless, there was no mistaking the fact that she had acted callously.

I broached the subject of the letters that evening, when Stafford and I were alone at the table before supper.

'I've read them all,' I told him.

He nodded. 'Good. So you know about him?'

'Yes. I couldn't help wondering . . . well, how you felt, reading that last one.'

'Rather sorry for myself, in truth. Rather worried. Even though there was nothing concrete in it, I was stuck in Oxford and she was all those hundreds of miles away with that man showing her about, "educating her". I didn't like it at all. It was quite clear to me that he had managed to get his claws into her. I chose to believe that it wasn't anything real, whatever fascination he held for her. It was the allure of the unknown.'

'Were you tempted to go after her?'

'Absolutely. In fact, I had it all planned out: I'd sold my first painting, for what to me was a considerable sum – enough for my passage to Venice, if nothing more.'

'But you never did?'

'No. I never had time to. I got her telegram first: "'Dearest Tom . . .'" he said, quoting from memory, "'returning England end of week latest. Will write soon.'"

19

Corsica, August 1986

That night, I went to bed and slept soundly, until I awoke suddenly in the middle of the night with the sense that something was amiss. And then I became convinced that I was not alone in the room. A bolt of pure fear ran through me, and I thought – though I blush to say it now – of the Genoese noble, hundreds of years dead in his resting place beneath the stones of the house.

I sat up in bed. The sensible thing would have been to turn on the light, but like the helpless heroine in a horror film, it never occurred to me to do so.

The door was ajar. Had I shut it? I was certain I had – I did so every night, before I changed into my pyjamas.

No, it had definitely been closed. Now a sliver of moonlit corridor was visible in the aperture between door and frame.

'Hello?' I whispered, into the still, dark air, feeling a fool as I did. Then again, 'Hello – is anyone there?'

I heard a tiny sound, a crepitation. The claws of a rodent – or the sound of something metallic worried against a surface – the wall or floor. Something gleamed in the moonlight, a few feet off the ground. I was riveted, unable to look away. It was unmistakably an eye, the eye of something crouched beside my bed. I screamed.

There was the sound of quick footsteps, and my door banged back on its support. Oliver stood in the frame, haloed from behind by the hallway light. 'What is it? There was a scream . . .' He peered inside. And then he began to laugh, quietly. It was the first time I had heard him do so.

Napoleon, as I learned the animal was named, was some kind of lurcher-wolfhound mix. Even in the dim light I could tell that he was one of the ugliest dogs I'd ever seen, with a sparse, pockmarked coat and bandy, overlong legs. He had, as if for comic effect, the most uneven set of lower teeth, all pointing in different directions. His tail was a terrible-looking stump.

'Sorry for waking you,' I told Oliver, feeling foolish.

'Don't worry – I wasn't properly asleep anyway.' He stood at the foot of my bed, where I could just about make him out.

I asked where the animal had come from. 'He turned up one day,' he told me. 'Grand-père said he and my grandmother were sitting having lunch on the terrace when the dog appeared at the top of the steps that lead up from the road. The poor thing was in such a state that they didn't have the heart to send him away.' He rubbed at the spot behind Napoleon's ear and the animal lolled against his leg in apparent bliss, tail thwacking on the ground where he sat, gazing up at us with beady dark eyes and grinning through his hideous teeth.

'Why Napoleon?'

'I think it must have been Grand-père's idea of a joke. Poley's the least warlike creature you can imagine. He's lived here for years, but he's still got the mentality of a tramp . . . he'll wander off and won't be seen for weeks, sometimes months, and then suddenly he'll turn up out of the blue, like he did this evening.

'Grand-père was worried the first time he disappeared. He set off in Gerard's van, convinced that he'd been hit by a car. When he eventually turned up unharmed we realized that he'd simply taken off in search of adventure. Though, when my grandmother died, he stayed in the house for a full three months. I imagine it went against his every instinct to do so: that's loyalty for you. He can be excellent company. But right now, old boy, I'm sorry to say you aren't wanted . . .'

'No, I don't mind . . .'

Oliver shook his head. 'He may be lovable, but he's probably ridden with fleas. Come on, Poley.'

He made his way towards the door. The dog gave an odd whinny of love and clambered creakily to his feet, following a few paces behind as though attached by an invisible lead.

78

I did not sleep well that night – even before I heard Kate's scream. My first reaction was to leap from my bed and rush out into the corridor, but I stopped at the sound of voices, followed by laughter. To my astonishment, I recognized it as Oliver's. When he introduced Napoleon I knew that my old friend had returned. Oliver must have sprinted from his bed to get there before me. Rather pleased at the thought, I crept back to my bed.

Though I closed my eyes and hoped for sleep, the thoughts that had been plaguing me returned. If I had dreaded showing Kate the letters, I was looking forward to recounting the next part even less. When I had first invited Kate to stay, I had conveniently managed to forget how painful some details would be to revisit. The temptation of remembering those few blissful months had been too powerful . . . briefly eclipsing the bad.

I could hardly stop now though. Having started, I had no option but to tell her the whole. I had heedlessly released the brakes on a juggernaut that I was now powerless to halt.

I would give myself a day, I decided. In the meantime there was something else I had to do, something just as pressing.

20

Corsica, August 1986

I lingered in bed the next morning, aware that I did not feel as well rested as I should have done, that my sleep had been disturbed, but unable at first to remember how. Then, in a rush, I recalled the surreal night-time arrival of the mangy dog.

When I eventually made my way down to the table by the pool I discovered only Oliver sitting there, with Napoleon dozing a few feet away in a patch of sun. I was confused. Even in the short time I had been here I had come to understand that there was a routine of sorts. Stafford was always there, at nine o'clock prompt, with the papers spread out before him.

'Grand-père's gone into town,' Oliver said, seeing my

confusion. 'He had some business he wanted to attend to. It's not like him to run off on errands – Marie or Gerard always take care of the shopping, and the doctor comes to see him here. Did he mention anything to you?'

I felt his curious gaze upon me. 'No,' I said, 'nothing. I had no idea he was going.'

Oliver seemed unconvinced, and I sensed he had already decided that Stafford's trip was in some way connected to me. 'Well,' he said, 'it means you will miss your time in the studio with him, I suppose.'

At a time, I thought, when it felt as though Stafford was close to telling me something important. I tried to shake my vague feeling of disquiet.

Marie appeared then with the usual fare: steaming rolls and hot pastries, preserves, fresh juice and coffee, and I concentrated on these, my unease giving me a focused appetite.

'Kate,' said Oliver, 'since you're free today, I wondered if you'd like to take a trip to the mountains.'

I was taken aback, having convinced myself that he viewed the trip to Bonifacio as a one-off. Still, the prospect of heading up into the mountains was certainly more appealing than waiting around all day, wondering what Stafford's absence could mean. 'Yes,' I said, 'if you're sure. Thank you.'

'Good. Grand-père thought you would like the idea.'

'Ah.' So it had been Stafford's doing. This knowledge was curiously flattering.

Marie put together a lunch for us of bread, charcuterie and cheese foraged from the fridge, which she handed over solemnly. I had packed my swimming costume, as apparently we would be able to bathe in the mountain pools, and wore a straw hat. We took the steps down to the road and clambered into the 2CV, inside which the temperature seemed – incredibly – several degrees higher than outside. The seats were almost too hot to bear. 'I'll put the roof down,' Oliver said, climbing back out and heaving at the contraption. 'It will be dusty – but we need the air.'

'Tell me about the pools,' I said, when the quiet in the car began to feel oppressive. At some point – perhaps since our conversation on the beach – we had traversed the gap between that earlier, distant courtesy towards something less formal, something friendlier. Even so, I was not yet relaxed in his company and felt the need to fill the silences with words.

'They're one of my favourite things about this whole island,' Oliver said. 'The water is incredibly clear – you can see every pebble on the bottom, even where it's deep.'

The road began to climb, and soon we were among the mountains. The ground sheared away on one side into a rocky gorge beneath, and on the other side were knotted pine trees, the sharp, sweetish scent of their resin filling the warm air.

As I craned to see the bottom of the gorge a rush of air plucked my hat from my head and lifted it away before I had time to clamp my hands down on it. I watched in dismay as it was carried over the roadside barrier, swooping and bucking in the breeze as if it had a life of its own, and then diving down into the deep void below. I swore, and Oliver stopped the car. He wore an odd, strained expression, and at first I assumed that it was irritation. Then, to my surprise, I realized that he was trying not to laugh.

There were no other vehicles to be seen in either direction, so we climbed out and peered down at the scree and rock beneath us. My hat was a pale speck where it had landed in a clump of gorse. 'We could go down and get it,' he said, dubiously. 'But it would take most of the day to make our way down there. Look, it's not elegant, but if you're worried about the sun you can have this.' He indicated the red cap he was wearing – the peak fraying in places so that the plastic beneath showed through, the colour bleached to a pinkish-orange by the sun. He reached over and fitted it on to my head with surprising gentleness, tightening the adjustable strap at the back. I stood very still as he did so. As the calloused pad of his thumb brushed against my temple something happened, something for which I was unprepared. I felt a thrill steal over my skin, as though a current had passed from that tiny patch of flesh and into every part of my being.

It had not been anything real, I told myself as we got under way again. Merely a reflexive response to the unfamiliar touch of a stranger.

The drive took a couple of hours. I hadn't believed it could get any hotter than it had been when we set off, but the temperature had built steadily through the morning. Heat came off the road before us in great shimmering waves, and I relished the slightest of breezes.

The road became increasingly decrepit, until it was barely deserving of the name. We lurched and seesawed over potholes and my face was coated with a fine layer of the grime thrown up by the wheels. I glanced behind us at one point and was astonished to see how high we had come. The Mediterranean from here was so dark it was almost purple: wine-dark. A tiny mote of white was traversing the expanse: a boat, perhaps a vast yacht like the one that had produced the firework display, but from here utterly inconsequential.

I saw the first pool through a cluster of roadside pine and olive trees. It was, as Oliver had promised, unfeasibly green and limpid: a water nymph's retreat. I was ready to throw open my door and leap out, but we creaked our way past and continued further up the road.

'Why not here?' I asked, and again, as we passed another pool a hundred yards further on, then a third.

'Too close to the road,' Oliver answered, and, 'too many people – look, it'll be dirty.' Then, 'it's too shallow, not good for swimming,' and, 'That pool's always swarming with flies. I got badly bitten near it once.'

Eventually we pulled up next to an unassuming clump of gorse and Oliver stepped out. There was no water in sight. I looked at him. 'Have we run out of fuel?'

'No. This is it.' He hefted the picnic bag over his shoulder and strode off into the thick vegetation. Bemused, I followed him, wincing as the razor thorns of a shrub grazed my arm. I felt a vague anger at this unnecessary discomfort. The other pools had looked fine to me. What were a few flies, I thought, compared to wounds inflicted by the Corsican maquis? And there was the hot sand underfoot, working its way between my soles and sandals to burn the skin, forcing me to take quick hopping steps across the surface.

I became aware of a distant rushing, a little like – I fancied – a swarm of angry bees might sound. Ten minutes later we were still walking – or rather crawling – through the undergrowth, with no sign of water. I felt grimy, blistered and exhausted. The noise was following me, and I wondered whether my clumsy progress had disturbed a hornet or wasp nest. An insect sting, I thought, would just about compound my discomfort.

'Really,' I began, 'I don't think—' Then I stopped. I could see something glittering through the pale leaves of the wild olives ahead. He pushed the branches aside and turned back to me with a look of triumph.

'Oh.' I caught up with him, and followed his gaze. Down below us was the pool, and it was perfect. Deep and clear – so clear, I discovered, that even from here you could see every pebble on the bottom. A shoal of tiny fish caught the light and shone as one great silver mass before disappearing into the shadow of the overhanging rocks. There was a small beach of whitish sand and now I could see the source of the noise that had worried me. It was a waterfall – a gleaming spout shot from the high cliff of dark rock at the far end of the pool, foaming noisily where it met the surface.

'This is my favourite of the pools,' Oliver said. 'Hardly anyone knows about it and because of that' – he gestured at the waterfall – 'the water is always fresh and clear. Flies can't stand the spray from the falling water, so there aren't any, apart from a few dragonflies – if you don't mind them.' He looked at me. 'I hope it's worth it?'

I dragged my hand across my grimy brow. 'It is. And I definitely need a swim now.'

We clambered down the rocks on to the beach, the water drawing me towards it, but the sun was merciless, and I was loath to expose my pale English body, now oddly marked by my healing sunburn, beneath its glare.

I wondered if I could simply wade in a little way to cool my feet and legs. But no: I wanted to be submerged in it, to wash away the accumulated grime of the journey. In a rush, I decided I didn't care. Oliver had seen me in my costume before, so why the need for modesty now? Taking a deep breath, I peeled off my clothes. Then I turned, almost reflexively, and found Oliver watching me with an unreadable expression. Perhaps I was imagining it, but I was certain I could feel his gaze, tangible as the brush of a feather, following me, prickling down my naked skin as I walked into the water.

It was surprisingly cold, and the shock of it against my sun-warmed flesh was almost enough to send me rushing out again. But as I grew accustomed to it, it welcomed me, insinuated itself about me. There was the tickle of small fish against my feet.

I glanced back to see if Oliver had followed, but he was nowhere to be seen. Then I heard a call from above and looked up to see him astride the crop of rock above the waterfall, stripped down to a pair of swimming trunks.

Most people are humbled by their nakedness – they seem diminished, fallible. You see all the blemishes, the deficiencies usually concealed. But Oliver, it was now clear, was not made to wear clothes. He had always worn loose shirts and shorts, and I would not have guessed at the grace of him.

Before I had time to grasp what it was he was about to do, he moved away from the edge by a few feet then took a great run towards it, arms and legs pumping, flinging himself over in a swan dive, the water opening to receive him with the barest commotion.

I blinked at him as his head emerged. 'You could have broken your neck.'

He shook his head. 'I've done it before. Grand-père taught me, in fact.'

'I don't believe you.' It was impossible to imagine Stafford, calm and gentle as he was, doing such a thing. But then I remembered the other Stafford I had come to know: young, impetuous – even reckless. They were one and the same, after all.

Oliver turned over to float upon his back, kicking lazily. He was different now, almost joyful: as if the place, the water, had energized him. He was close enough that I could see how the water had separated his eyelashes into glossy spikes, and the way his slicked-back hair had exposed that secret white line of skin beneath his hairline.

I swam some distance away from him and allowed myself to sink beneath the surface. I liked the brief cocoon the water made for me: how it felt to be sheltered from light and sound and air, from everything but the cool press of the water against my skin.

We returned to the beach to eat our lunch. Oliver pulled on a T-shirt and shorts, and it was a relief – and also a disappointment – not to be troubled by my awareness of his unclothed body.

We sat a couple of feet apart on the sand, gazing out over the dazzling surface of the pool.

After a few moments of silent chewing, Oliver spoke. 'Will you tell me, now, why it is that you're here?'

'It's a long story,' I said.

'We have time.' He looked at me, expectant, challenging.

I was trying to come up with an excuse not to tell him when it suddenly occurred to me that it would be easier to simply do so.

Once I had started, I discovered that it was surprisingly easy, that it felt like a release. Oliver sat very still, listening intently to everything I said.

I told him about Evie, about the drawing, the visit to Stafford's sister. When I got to the part about Stafford's involvement, the reason for not telling him suddenly presented itself to me – and I cursed my lack of foresight. His beloved grandmother – the woman he grieved for, still . . . and here I was, about to introduce the fact of Stafford's love for another woman. But I knew, too, that it was too late to stop now that I had started. I could only try to make him understand that Alice had been a part of his grandfather's past, long before – as I assumed – he had met Elodia.

'I know about her,' he said. I looked at him in surprise. 'Grand-père's never spoken to me of her,' he explained, 'but I've seen the drawings.'

'Which drawings?'

'There are quite a few. When I was young I found a

chest of them in his old studio. Like all kids, I was fascinated by anything that was locked – saw it as a challenge. I spent months looking for the key – only to find it in the top drawer of his desk. There were maybe fifty works in there – sketches, watercolours . . .'

'Did he find out?' I asked, thinking that I had to come up with a way to ask Stafford to show them to me.

'Yes. I thought I had been so careful, but I must have left some clue to give myself away, because he knew.'

'Was he angry with you?'

'No – that's not his way. I think he was more concerned that I understood what they meant – that they were a part of his past, not the present he shared with Grand-mère, and with me. He said she had been a very great friend of his. Even then, I knew from the way he said it that he had loved her. He did, didn't he?'

'Well . . .' I said, carefully, feeling that I should be economical with the truth, 'possibly – but it was a long time ago.'

'I thought so,' he said, quietly.

'I think your grandfather might not have told you what we were discussing because it concerned her.'

'Maybe. But he needn't have worried. I lived with him and Grand-mère for most of my childhood, and I know they did love each other. It may not have been the wilder sort of love, and perhaps it was more like friendship, but they were very fond of one other, that much was clear. That seemed to be enough.'

He reached for a peach and bit into it, the juice escaping down his chin. 'So now you want to find out everything about her,' he said.

'Yes, I do. Very much. I have such a strong idea of her – what she was like.'

'Will you try to find her?'

'I – well, I don't even know if she's still alive. From the way he talks about her, I don't think your grand-father has seen her since he was a young man.'

Oliver nodded, thoughtfully, and the conversation lapsed into silence, both of us looking out upon the water before us. After a few minutes, he turned to me again. 'Do you think' – he chose his words carefully – 'that your mother would have wanted you to find her?'

This threw me. It was as if he had spoken aloud my own concern, the one that had travelled with me since I boarded the plane – or even before that, when I had listened to Evie on that terrible afternoon.

'My mother was brave,' I said, 'and determined. It was what made her such a talented ballerina. She never knew anything of Alice, and I can't say for certain that she would have wanted to, but I like to think that she would have wanted me to keep following the thread, once I had discovered it.'

'Then that's what you should do,' he said, with conviction.

I looked at him, gratified. In that moment I could hardly believe that this was the same person who had been so hostile towards me. Yet until a scant couple of days ago I would have assumed that coldness went to the very centre of him.

Stafford was at the house when we returned, the day fading to a blue twilight and the bats beginning to wheel and dart above us. He smiled at us. I can't explain exactly what it was about that smile, but I felt then that he saw more than I would have wanted him to see.

He did not give any explanation for his disappearance that day. At supper he asked a continuous stream of questions about our trip to the pools – even more solicitous and curious than he might usually have been. If I had not known him better, I might have suspected him of guile: of purposefully keeping the subject away from himself and his own excursion.

At eleven o'clock Stafford went to bed. Usually I followed not far behind. Listening, I had discovered, can be strangely exhausting, especially in the case of a history like the one unravelling before me, so vivid that it felt as if I were experiencing it as much as hearing about it.

Tonight, however, I decided to linger a while on the terrace. It was an unusually clear night, more so than the evenings that had preceded it – and there was a delicious texture and savour to the air, cool and smoky.

I wanted to enjoy it for a while longer, so when Stafford said goodnight I remained in my chair.

Oliver remained too. Silently I willed him away. I had been surprised by how much I had enjoyed spending the day in his company, but now I wanted to be on my own, alone with my thoughts. Yet he stayed there on the other side of the table from me, his face drowned in shadow so that I could only make out the barest impression of his features.

'You aren't going to bed?' he asked, and I realized then that he, too, might be wishing to be alone, wishing me gone.

'No,' I said, decisively. 'I thought I'd stay out here for a while.'

'All right,' he said. 'Would you like a drink?'

I saw that my wine glass was empty, but more wine would only make me sleepy, and on this exceptionally clear night that would be a shame. I was about to decline when he said, 'We could have a Corsican drink – a *digestif*?'

My interest was piqued. 'What is it?'

'It's made from myrtle berries – the bushes grow all over the island.'

'All right – I'll try a bit.'

He returned with a bottle, and two tiny glasses, which he filled with the darkish liqueur. I took a sip and immediately felt it warm my mouth and throat – the taste bittersweet, strange, and, I decided, quite delicious.

'Good?' I looked up to find him watching me, waiting for my opinion.

'Yes. Dangerously so.'

He nodded. 'I had my first experience with it when I was eight. I came across it in the drinks cabinet and thought I'd try it – I'd always seen my grandparents having it after supper. I poured myself a whole wine glass of it. I've only recently been able to drink it again.'

I took another sip. Far below us I could make out the splish and plunk of the water spending itself – gently, lazily – against the cliffs.

Then, for something to say, I asked, 'Don't you think the air has an odd feel to it tonight?'

'Yes,' he said. 'It's sometimes like this before the Mistral – exceptionally clear. But it's not always the case; sometimes nothing happens – it turns out to be a false alarm.'

Mistral: the word was vaguely familiar. 'Do you mean the wind?'

'Yes, but it's more than a wind – practically a supernatural force. When it's blowing, you can't think of anything else. Afterwards, the sky is the most beautiful sight you could imagine, incredibly clear and blue.'

I hoped it would come.

'Another?' Oliver gestured at my glass.

Realizing it was empty, I held it out to him. 'Yes, please.'

He filled it up and leaned across to pass it back to me. As he did so I caught the scent of his skin – and it was not unlike the scent of the maquis: complex, warm, savoury. Immediately, without warning, I was confronted by an image of his naked torso – the breadth of it, the soft, secret line of dark hair beneath his navel. I sat back quickly, in alarm, thankful for the darkness that meant he would not be able to see my face – and the colour that had flooded it.

We sat for a few moments in silence, and I tried to quash the image – disturbingly, unprecedentedly arousing – that kept presenting itself to me, like some sort of optical loop.

But Oliver's next words banished it far more effectively. 'I've been thinking about your mother,' he said, and stopped, probably seeing me stiffen. 'Sorry.'

'No,' I told him, 'it's fine – go on.'

'I mean, I don't want to presume to guess how you must be feeling . . . but when Grand-mère died, I was a wreck. I know losing a grandparent is different to losing a mother . . . but to be honest she was more like a parent to me than my own mother was. She and Grand-père were the ones who taught me about the world, how it worked, how to behave in it . . .' He trailed off, apparently feeling that he had spoken too lengthily. 'Anyway,' he said. 'I don't quite know what I meant to say.'

'Thank you,' I said. His awkwardness was rather touching. He wasn't merely offering me platitudes, as so many did.

I took another sip of my drink, feeling it burn a fiery

trail all the way to my stomach. And then, perhaps because he had tried, and because the darkness seemed the place for such confidences, I said, 'She was my best friend. I mean, I had other friends' – I chose not to linger upon my use of the past tense – 'but none of them were like her. I couldn't tell them everything, as I could with her.'

Oliver didn't try to find a solution, which I was grateful for. He simply nodded. Then he fished a pack of cigarettes from his pocket, with a rather surreptitious look. 'Would you like one?'

'No, thanks.'

He took one for himself and lit it. 'I'm trying not to,' he said. 'Grand-père hates it. But every so often . . .' He peered at me. 'You won't tell him, will you?'

I shook my head.

'Thank you.' He inhaled deeply and made a noise of satisfaction, blowing out a cloud of smoke. 'I don't know if this is the wrong thing to say, but in a strange way I'm envious of you. I never had that, with my mother.'

'Oh.' I had never quite considered it like that – that what Mum and I had might be particularly unusual. It had been the best thing in my life, absolutely, but I had rather taken it for granted. I remembered how, greedily, I had for most of my childhood longed for a large family: doting grandparents, siblings and cousins. What at times had seemed a lack now, considering Oliver's words, seemed like a richness.

'But you had your grandmother, Elodia.'

'Yes,' he said, thoughtfully. 'And I had Grand-père. Can I tell you something?'

I nodded.

'He's not actually my grandfather. Not in the biological sense, at least. My mother was born before Grand-mère met him. You've probably noticed we don't look anything like one another. But I love him more than anything – I can't imagine loving anyone more.'

I flushed, remembering my tactless remark to Stafford about how unalike they were. How callous I must have seemed. I thought, too, of how different their relationship was to the one I had with Evie.

'Well, I envy you that,' I said. 'You see I—' I stopped, wondering if I dared go on. 'My adoptive grandmother, Evie—'

'The one who hid the letter?'

I felt the need to defend her. 'Yes – though she was also the one who saved my mother, the one who got her into ballet. I mean, when it came to Mum, she was completely selfless, wonderful . . .'

'But?' Oliver interjected, quietly.

'But . . .' I paused – was I going to tell him? – then, heedlessly, I went on: 'I never actually felt that we were that close.' I waited for Oliver to say something, to condemn me, even, but he remained silent. 'It was only at the end,' I said, 'after she'd died, when I realized how much I missed her. I never expected to. Sometimes

I even wondered whether we liked each other, let alone loved one another.'

I looked over at Oliver now, desperate for a reaction – of any sort.

'Do you think that's terrible?' I asked.

I could just make out the slow shake of his head. 'No,' he said, 'I don't. I think . . . I think it's human.' I hadn't known how much I cared what he thought until I heard him say this. 'And you miss her,' he added. 'Perhaps that tells you everything you need to know.'

'Do you miss your mother?' I asked him.

For a moment I thought he hadn't heard me. Then he said, 'I miss the idea of her, I suppose.'

I wondered what that meant, exactly. 'What was she like?' I asked, shamelessly curious about the woman I had seen in the photograph.

Oliver took a long drag on his cigarette, exhaled slowly. 'Always very busy,' he said, putting a strange emphasis on that last word. 'She was a model, but what she truly wanted was to be an actress.'

'Oh.'

'She wasn't a bad model, I think. She was certainly beautiful.'

Even had I not seen the photographs of her in the hallway, I would have known it from the legacy of beauty I saw in her son, that which had only just been revealed to me.

'She was no actress, though. I saw a film with her in once – she played a sort of femme fatale character. It was a bit part, barely five minutes on screen, but even so it was obvious what a dreadful actress she was. Getting that role had been a bit of a fluke – most of the directors she approached told her to stick with the modelling. The worst part was that she decided they were all wrong, and she kept trying.'

I remembered watching videos of my mother dancing, the gasps and applause from the audience, the hot surge of pride I'd feel in my chest. How terrible, I thought, to bear witness to your parent's failure – to be embarrassed for them in that way.

'Even when she was still alive, I'd often come down to Corsica for the holidays,' Oliver said. 'She wanted to be in Cannes for the summer, you see, and Cannes, she told me, was for adults.'

'So you always spent the summer apart?'

'Yes – not that I minded. In fact I looked forward to coming here. Grand-père would collect me from Paris, and we'd drive all the way down through the country, stopping overnight to break up the journey. Sometimes he would have brought a tent with him and we'd camp somewhere.

'Those weeks down here, staying with my grandparents, were the happiest of my life. I didn't enjoy school much – I'm dyslexic, so I did badly and everyone thought I was stupid. It was an international school, and the other children didn't know what to make of me – thcy were all English and American, civil service parents and that sort of thing. It was all paid for by my grandparents – Maman could never have afforded it. I'd live for those weeks when I got to stay with Grand-père and Grand-mère.'

'Did your mother come, too?'

'No . . . well, rarely. For a week at a time, maximum. She left the island as soon as she could. She was so different from my grandmother, who was – I think the expression is "the salt of the earth"? I'm fairly sure she felt Grand-mère had let her down.'

'For what?'

He stopped, suddenly, and gave a short bark of a laugh. 'You could be an interrogator, you know.'

'Oh,' I said, embarrassed. 'Sorry.'

'No,' he said, 'I don't mean it like that. It's that I find myself telling you things I don't intend to. I have no idea why. Perhaps you were a hypnotist in a previous life.'

He took another long drag of his cigarette, and I watched the tiny, fierce ball of fire created by his breath.

'Anyway,' he went on, 'my real grandfather was an Italian, a soldier. He was one of the Occupiers here during the war. Grand-mère never, *ever* talked about him.'

'I see.'

'But my mother was obsessed with the idea of him. She convinced herself that he must have been someone special, an Italian count, or something. She used to talk about him as if she knew this for a fact, that she wasn't just some Corsican farmer's granddaughter, she had noble blood. She blamed Grand-mère for not being able to hold on to him. Then, when she had me, and my father was nowhere to be seen, she claimed that it was the bad example she'd been shown.' He was silent for a moment. 'The truth is, he's always been my grandfather,' he said, speaking now of Stafford. 'I've tried to use him as my guide, for how I should behave. Even if I haven't necessarily managed it.'

'I think you are like him,' I said, instinctively, wondering as I said it if I truly believed it. But when Oliver thanked me, with real gratitude in his voice, I thought that perhaps it didn't matter either way.

Back in my room I sat on my bed for a while in the half-dark, thinking. I could not believe that I had talked to Oliver about Evie. I had shared one of my most shameful secrets with a man who was still, when all was said and done, barely more than a stranger to me. Much as I would have liked to dismiss it as the influence of the drink, I knew that it couldn't be blamed on that. In fact, I did not feel even remotely drunk now. It was rather the opposite: I felt very sober indeed, peculiarly clear-headed.

It had been some instinct in me, I realized, some feeling that he would not judge me too harshly for it, that he might even understand. And it seemed – to my relief – that he had. I chose not to reflect upon that other thing that had happened: that sudden, *violent* – for there was no other word for it – current of attraction. No good could come of thinking about that.

21

'I forgot to ask,' Stafford said, as we sat in his studio the next morning, 'did you jump from the top of the waterfall?'

'No, I'm afraid not. Oliver did, though. He told me that you taught him.'

Stafford grinned. 'I did.' He seemed inordinately pleased by this. 'Until quite recently I would have been up there doing it myself, but unfortunately as one gets older one has to recognize one's limitations. Annoyingly it isn't the jumping off that has become difficult but the boring part: the climbing up.'

It made me uncomfortable, to hear him speak in this way. It was hard to imagine anything – even old age

– slowing him down, and to hear Stafford himself remark on his increasing frailty was a painful dose of reality. I had grown to like him so much, and the suggestion that he might not be around for ever depressed me. I knew it was irrational, this feeling – it was hardly as though he was on his deathbed – but if the last couple of years had taught me anything it was how short a time you might have left with someone.

'Kate,' Stafford said, surprising me out of my thoughts, 'I have to admit that I'm not looking forward to telling the next part. It isn't a time I would choose to revisit – and I have been a coward in putting it off. You need to know . . . and perhaps it's good for me to speak of it. A catharsis, if you like.' The smile he gave me then, for once, was not a real smile – more of a grimace than anything else.

'After that fourth letter, I had nothing from Alice for months. Complete silence. She'd told me she expected to return in December, and I'd even gone so far as to hope she would want to meet over the holidays, but my weeks back in London passed without any message or sign from her.'

'Didn't you think of going to see her instead?'

'That wasn't how it worked. I know it sounds feeble on my part, but our meetings had always been on her terms. There was the never-spoken understanding that I would not be a welcome caller at Lord and Lady Hexford's house. I was embarrassed, too.'

'Why?'

'Because I'd sent her three letters since that last from her with no reply. I told myself I had to accept the fact that she was tiring of our friendship. That final letter I'd had from her, being so brief and ill thought-out . . . it seemed the likeliest explanation. I was miserable. It didn't help that it was January, with its bleak weather and short days, the distractions of Christmas gone by and only my final exams to look forward to.

'My own misery coincided with a wider depression in spirits. All the news was bad. It had been since October, but by January it was clear that the economy wasn't going to recover quickly, as many had hoped. It was as if we were all suffering from some great tiredness, a malaise.'

22

Oxford, March 1930

Three months into the New Year, and four months since Alice returned to England, and still no word from her. Tom feels his hope dwindling. He thinks of that last afternoon – and of the night that followed. She had been uncharacteristically shy with him the next day, but that was understandable. It was, as she had told him, the first time she'd done 'anything quite like that'. There had been no coolness in her manner afterwards, and yet here it is: the incontrovertible fact that she seems to have forgotten – or chosen to forget – that he exists.

Maybe they did make a mistake that night – though he could never bring himself to see it as such. Or perhaps things could have been different had she not met that self-satisfied Frenchman she wrote about in her letters. Or if Tom had been able to make his way out to Venice, as she had suggested. He is tormented by the idea that his own lack of action may have cost him so much.

The one thing equal to distracting himself from these thoughts is his art. The small exhibition that he wrote to tell Alice about was a success. Where most of those represented had just one piece in the show, Tom, much to his astonishment, had eight. There had been coverage, too: in a couple of local papers and the university journals. It was the first time since that trip to see Lady Margaret that he felt he might have a chance at it.

Tom goes for an early morning stroll along Addison's Walk to clear his mind. At this hour, a month ago, it would have been dark, but this morning the college and its grounds are washed in the thin grey light of dawn. Daffodils, trumpets still furled into tight knots, and primroses with preternaturally bright petals line the path. Spring usually brings thoughts of regeneration, of hope. This year, however, it serves only to remind Tom of how much time has passed without word from her. And of how much closer he is to having to make decisions about his future that he would rather postpone. A little more time, that is all he needs. Time to travel further down that path on which his recent work has taken him. But each month seems to pass more quickly than the one before it. Soon he will be out in the world with his new responsibilities and the weight of his parents' expectations.

Tom likes this route along the Walk because of the sense of his own smallness it inspires; the sense that he is following in the footsteps of men far greater than he could ever hope to be. Usually he would take his time, but the wind is getting up, driving the rain sideways, assaulting him through his thin jacket, so he turns back in the direction of the college building, preparing himself for the daily ritual of asking at the porter's lodge if there are any telegrams. Afterwards, he will head to his cubbyhole to check for the letter that never comes. As he nears the lodge, he thinks, *Perhaps I'll wait. I'll go after breakfast.* Disappointment, even the sort that has become habitual, sits badly on an empty stomach.

Yes, he decides, it can wait. Yet as he passes the lodge he hears his name called from within. 'Mr Stafford – is that you?'

He peers inside.

'Thought it was. There's a message for you. The one day you don't come and ask.'

Tom steps forward. He is careful to appear disinterested. It could, after all, be nothing. A message from his mother, perhaps: always welcome, but no cause for unnecessary excitement.

The man hands him a slip of paper, and he stands in the doorway to read it.

```
Dear  Thomas  STOP  Would  appreciate  your
assistance  in  a  matter  close  to  both  of  our
hearts  STOP  If  you  can  spare  the  time  please
take  train  to  London  immediately  and  all
expenses  will  be  reimbursed  STOP  Yours  M
```

M. It is from Lady Margaret: he is in no doubt.

There is the meeting with his tutor this evening. There is the deadline for the paper at the end of the week. Nevertheless he goes to his room and packs a bag with the few things that present themselves to him as necessary for the trip: his sketchbook and leather pencil case. A couple of books, too, though more out of a sense of duty than any real belief that he will study on his journey down.

On the train, as the waterlogged countryside slides unremarked past his window, he takes the telegram from his pocket and studies it again. It's about Alice, he knows it is. He tries to extract some further meaning. Is Alice in trouble? How, he thinks, could he have been so self-absorbed as to ignore the possibility that something might have happened to her?

Lady Margaret answers the door herself. She is attired no less eccentrically than the last time Tom set eyes on her: a long housecoat in plum velvet with dragons and birds and exotic flora embroidered on the chest and sleeves, a scarf of fuchsia-pink silk about her head in aggressive contrast with her tangerine hair. She uses a different staff today, with a silver jackal's head for a handle, the pointed face peering cheekily from beneath her grasp. He realizes, standing in front of her, that she is not as tall as he had imagined. It is rather the effect of her presence and the etiolated slenderness that lend the impression of height.

'Thomas,' she says, with no reference to the journey he has made, as though his arrival on her doorstep is a given thing. 'Welcome. I need your help.'

She beckons him through to the salon and he sits on an emerald ottoman with feet like the claws of a bird of prey. Beatrice enters immediately, bearing a tall silver flask of coffee, which she pours from an impressive height into two cups.

'Is Alice all right?' Tom asks, unable to bear not knowing any longer.

Lady Margaret reaches behind her, takes a small wooden box from the top of the cabinet and withdraws two slender cigars, proffering one, which Tom declines. She lights the other for herself and draws upon it thoughtfully before she speaks. 'You see, that's the thing. I haven't heard from her since she left Venice. I was rather hoping she might have been in contact with you.' He shakes his head, and she sighs forth a cloud of peat-scented smoke.

'I assumed that she was too . . . well, busy,' he says. 'The last letter I had from her was sent from Venice in late October.'

'Ah, I was hoping you wouldn't say that. So she's had no contact with either of us. I'm afraid there's something strange going on and I feel certain it's Georgina's doing. I have never trusted that woman.'

She draws on the cigar, the tip flaming dangerously, and exhales again. 'My brother was the impulsive sort. Most of his impulses were true, but he cannot have made a worse decision in his life than to marry Georgina. She is a bourgeois, a philistine – and, worst of all, she cannot bear the fact that she has failed to make a daughter in her own dismal image.' She squints at him through the smoke. 'I wonder if anything got back to her.'

'What do you mean?'

'Venice. There was . . .' and here she looks at Tom apologetically, 'someone who took an interest in Alice. He was older, had been around the world a little. I thought it would be good for her to see some of the city with him – an education of sorts.'

'I know,' Tom says, his ears ringing with the concentrated effort of remaining impassive. 'She mentioned him in a letter.'

Lady Margaret nods. 'Once,' she says, 'when Alice had just turned sixteen, I told Georgina that I would arrange to meet her from school at the end of term. Instead of taking her home, I whisked her off to Paris and we spent a long weekend there. Her mother retaliated by sending her to that place in Switzerland for three years.'

'And you think that if she has found out about Venice she might do something similar?'

'I don't know, but I don't like it. I had Jacob drive me to the house the other day, and it all seemed too quiet. I knocked on the door and the butler was very abrupt. No, the family weren't there. Where had they gone? He wouldn't say.' She thinks for a moment. 'Though it might not have been true. Have you seen that house?'

'No.'

'It is like a fortress. If they didn't want anyone coming in or going out they could pull up the drawbridge easily enough. I'm on the blacklist. *On ne passe pas.*' Lady Margaret regards Tom thoughtfully. 'But they don't know *you*, do they?'

Alice's house is exactly as Lady Margaret described it: the modern equivalent of a fortress. The stucco façade is a natural partner for the pewter of the sky, and to Tom it resembles a great plaster cast concealing possible deformities beneath. He stares up at the secret squares of the dark windows, and is reminded irresistibly of the photographs he has seen of Alice's stepfather, with his large square head and the small eyes set slightly too close together in the broad expanse of his skull. For all this, he and the house are handsome: in an order in which handsomeness is equated with a projection of power, authority and utter conviction.

The lofty door, painted dark grey, makes Tom think of drawbridges. He knocks. After several long moments it swings open to reveal an elderly butler. The man insinuates himself into the space between door and frame so as to block the view to within, and peers down at the visitor.

'Can I help you, sir?' he says, but his tone suggests that no assistance will be forthcoming.

'I hope so. I'm a friend of Alice's.'

The butler blinks at him impassively. 'Lady Alice isn't at home, sir.'

'Oh? Where is she, if you don't mind me asking?'

'It isn't my place to say, sir.' But something in Tom's expression goes some way to softening the old man. As though he feels it is against his better judgement, the butler leans forward and murmurs, 'Lady Alice has been unwell. My mistress, Lady Hexford, thought it best that she be removed to the country to recuperate.'

'The country?'

'Indeed, sir.'

'May I ask the nature of Lady Alice's illness?'

'I'm afraid I am not at liberty to say, sir.'

'But . . . is it serious?' Tom thinks of the flu that killed his mother's sister and several cousins in 1918.

'I must insist, sir, on you asking me no more about it. I have told you everything that I—'

A voice comes from within. 'Is this fellow bothering you, Simpson?' The speaker appears: a youngish man, in his thirties perhaps, shorter than Tom but powerfully built, with a large handsome face and a pugnacious set to his jaw. This must be Matthew, the stepbrother.

'Not exactly, sir, he was—'

'You know, old chap,' Matthew says to Tom, 'I think I have something of yours, here.'

'Oh?'

He pulls them from his pocket. It is a moment before Tom recognizes them for what they are, his last letters to Alice.

'As my sister is . . . indisposed, I decided it would best if I attended to her correspondence,' Matthew says, as though it is explanation enough.

'Those were private.'

'Ah, I thought you might say that. I assure you, my sister would understand entirely – no, she'd positively want me to have opened them. We're extremely close, you see.'

Tom turns to go. There is nothing to be done here – and he refuses to waste time on this foul character. The letters have given him new cause for alarm.

'By the way, old chap . . .'

'Yes?' Tom manages to keep his tone civil.

'You know, if I've got one piece of wisdom, it's this.' Matthew glances at the letters, and then up at Tom, a smile playing about his lips. 'I really would advise against all this . . . sentiment. It's not going to work with my sister. If you want to get between her legs, try being less subtle about it. She's a woman of the world, my sister. She'll understand plain speaking far better.'

Tom doesn't stop to think. He turns and lunges for the man, not caring where he is or who he is – not someone brought up to brawl in the streets. All he wants is to inflict the maximum degree of pain possible, preferably a direct hit to that smirking face, but his fist collides with wood instead of flesh, and his knuckles smart with the impact. It takes him a good few seconds to work out that the door has been slammed in his face.

The car is a different vehicle from the one Alice drove on those autumn afternoons in Oxfordshire. It is dark grey and huge – if possible, even larger than the other. It holds, comfortably: the driver, Liverwhaite; a hamper of food 'just in case'; Lady Margaret; Tom, and Lady Margaret's Burmese cat, William, who sits imperiously upon his own cushion between them.

Chebworth is hardly more than a hamlet: a scattering of cottages and an inn, and Chebworth Manor lies a couple of miles from the village. It does not reveal itself until they are directly before it, for the grounds are shrouded with a dark thicket of elm and oak, so that it is impossible to see beyond them to the house. They draw to a halt in front of the ironwork gates that mark the entrance to the drive, and through the opening a vast building can be glimpsed. The car idles. Lady Margaret looks across at Tom.

'You should go in alone.'

Tom is astonished that this fearless woman appears to be showing something like cowardice. As if reading his thoughts, Lady Margaret gives a bark of laughter. 'Oh, I'm not afraid of her, if that's what you think. I'm only concerned that my presence might complicate matters. I seem . . . unable to behave myself, you see, when I'm in her presence. I think it might be safer if it were just you.'

The gates are secured with a padlock and chain, but Tom has been adept since childhood in the scaling of difficult ascents: various species of tree, the low cliffs around Winnard Cove, the drop beneath the dormitory window at school. Lady Margaret, Liverwhaite and William look on as he scrambles his way up and over the wall to drop down into the damp, dark thicket below.

Wet vegetation, branches and leaves claw at him as he fights his way through the undergrowth to the expanse of lawn. The grass is short and soft as green velvet; as immaculate as if it had been clipped with a pair of nail scissors. The gravelled drive stretches away on his right towards the house. The building in the distance looks less like a home than a state building. It is squat and white; for all its pretensions to grandeur it looks like the giant white plinth of some missing statue. The many windows glitter uniformly in the weak sun.

It takes Tom a good fifteen minutes to walk the length of the drive to the front door. The building stares down upon him, impassive yet watchful, like some resting beast. The door creaks open before he has even reached the first step, and another butler emerges: older than Simpson with a shock of white hair, a more pronounced sag to the shoulders.

It is the same story, give or take a few words. Lady Alice is unwell, and not receiving visitors. In what way is she unwell? The butler looks at Tom as if he has committed an act of gross indecency, and informs him that he 'is not at liberty to say, sir'.

'I'm a friend,' Tom says, reasonably, 'and I'm concerned for her . . .'

'Nevertheless, sir . . .' the man begins closing the door, 'nevertheless, I'm afraid that I must ask you to leave.'

'My name is Thomas Stafford' – his voice is almost a shout now, despite his efforts to stay calm – 'will you at least let her know that I called?'

The butler makes a quick motion of his head that could be a shake or nod – impossible to say. Then the door closes, surprisingly quietly for something so large, with a tiny click. Tom stands there, his whole being taut with frustration. In the emerald silence of the grounds, the pounding of his blood in his ears is deafeningly loud. He lingers for a minute or so, considering his options.

As stealthily as possible, Tom makes his way round the side of the house, searching for another entrance. At the back of the building he comes upon a low annexe, which a clamour of metal and belch of savoury steam reveal to be the kitchens. Almost without thinking, he makes for the door. As he reaches it, it swings open and a figure emerges.

'Alice?'

She hurries towards him, pulling her coat about her.

It is a man's trench coat, and her bare knees beneath its hem appear pale and naked in the cold glare of the day. She looks far from ill, Tom thinks. And yet there is a change in her appearance, though it is difficult to determine exactly what. She seems . . . softer. There is an unusual rosiness to her cheeks, too – not, Tom decides, the unhealthy flush of the invalid.

'Let's walk, shall we?' She takes his arm and he feels her warm against his side.

'Look, Alice,' he says, trying to remind himself that he is angry with her, 'what's the game? I haven't heard from you for months. We were worried about you.'

'We?'

'Your aunt and I.'

'I'll explain everything – once we're properly alone.' She leads the way through a gate into the walled kitchen gardens, and they make for a stone love seat at the far end. 'We can't be seen from the house in here,' she says, 'though it may already be too late for that. You made quite a racket, you know.'

'Are you surprised? They said you were ill, but wouldn't say what was wrong or how bad. It was as if you'd been locked away.'

There is sunlight now, though a weak and trembling sort. The stone is cold beneath them, and the dew-wet grass about them exhales a shimmering mist of moisture into the air. Tom looks at Alice, her pink knees, her mussed hair, and forgives her everything: the long silence, the worry she has caused him. Sitting here beside her, in this garden of enchantment, with spring suddenly upon them, it all seems to make sense. Then Alice speaks, in a voice unfamiliar to him.

'The thing is,' she says, quietly and slowly, choosing the words carefully, 'the thing is, I've been rather a fool.' She looks down at her hands, as though she might read her next lines there.

He waits for her to continue. He has never seen Alice like this. In this moment they are so silent and still that a magpie struts its way past their feet, unperturbed by their presence.

Alice twists her fingers together. A slow flush creeps up the side of her face, and she refuses to look up and meet his gaze. Finally she says: 'I don't think there's a way of dressing this up. Oh, Tom. The thing is, you see, I'm going to have a baby.'

He cannot speak.

Alice gives a strange, humourless laugh. It is a shocking sound, in the silence of the garden. The magpie screeches and takes flight.

'Is it . . . was it . . .?' Instantly, Tom is making calculations, weighing options. He'll go into the law after all. He'll make a home for them, support Alice and the child.

But when he looks back up at her, ready to say all of this, he sees that she is shaking her head.

'I don't understand,' he says.

She still won't look at him. 'It wasn't you, Tom. When I was in Venice . . .' She stops when she sees the look on his face. He cannot hear any more. He thinks of the things he could say now, that would leave him anatomized before her.

'It was my maid, in London,' Alice tells him. 'She saw all the signs, even before I did. She must have reported it back to Mother.'

'What are you going to do? You can't want to stay here like this.'

'No,' she says. 'No, I don't.'

'Then why . . .'

'I'm going to play along with her game, Tom. She wants me here, hiding myself away.' She gestures down at herself, and Tom sees now that the curve of her belly is visible beneath the loose folds of the coat. 'I'm in no fit state to do anything at the moment. This is the best place for me . . . until I can work out what to do.'

'You could come and live with me.'

'No, Tom.'

'But I could look after you both.'

She shakes her head again.

'You aren't going to him, surely?'

'To whom?' She looks at him in confusion, and then, understanding: 'Oh. No. No, of course not. I'll do this on my own.'

'Where will you go? How will you live?'

'We'll manage.' Then she smiles, almost like the Alice of old. 'Do you know, I wonder whether that sense I had of needing to do something meaningful, to make something of my life . . . well, I wonder if it was this all along.'

He tries one last time. 'Alice, please let me help you. You can't stay here. Come with your aunt and I. She's waiting in the car at the gate.'

Alice reaches up with her free hand and touches the side of his cheek lightly. He closes his eyes. 'You're so very wonderful, which is why I would never think of coming with you. I will not be your responsibility.'

'But—'

'You should leave, Tom.' She says it gently, but this only makes her words all the more terrible.

'When will I see you?'

She leans over and kisses him on the cheek, and he breathes the familiar scent of her skin. 'Not for a while, I think.'

Returning the way he came, towards the waiting car just visible beyond the gates – Tom turns, once. Alice has disappeared inside. The house stares blindly as before, but then he catches a flutter of movement in one of the upstairs windows. He thinks he glimpses a white face, gazing down upon him. Then a flash – like the scales of a fish turning over in the sunlight – of pale blonde hair.

Back in his room in Oxford, Tom lets his bag fall to the floor. He can feel a great pressure building inside him: pressing itself against his ribcage. A feeling that is more akin to grief than to rage – but easily as powerful and destructive. He looks about him wildly. In the corner of the room he sees the wooden chest, the one in which he keeps all of his painting supplies. As though driven by some influence beyond thought, he strides over to it and unlocks it, begins pulling it all out: paint, brushes, putties and pencils, letting them scatter across the floorboards. A couple of the tins of oils burst their lids and begin to shed their bright contents. Tom doesn't notice – his attention is solely on the task at hand. He pays no heed when he snags the skin of his thumb on a scalpel and the blood begins to flow freely. The sharp pain – so much more manageable than the pain inside – merely aids his single-minded focus. He does not pause until the chest is empty.

The studies of Alice are the only pieces that he has allowed to face outwards – the only works of which he has, up until this point, felt truly proud. This makes them easy to find in the small space, though they are many. Tom takes them up, every one. Into the chest they go, all of them. He forces those that will not fit properly, hearing as he does the crack of wood and the unmistakable sound of ripping canvas. The sound is oddly gratifying. His eyes burn – not with tears, but with the terrible, aching absence of them.

He shuts the chest, wrenching the lid down, and forcing the clasps into place. He takes the key and locks it. Only now does he reach for the whisky kept in his cupboard. He rarely drinks the stuff and the bottle is three-quarters full. It should be enough, he hopes, to take away some of the pain.

*

In the shifting, queasy darkness, Tom wakes from his stupor, and sways across the floor to the chest, lit by the cold, weak light from the quad. He opens it quickly, as though something might escape, and removes the drawing: the one of Alice by the lake. He knows the size and shape of it without looking. He is unable, he realizes, to bear the thought of it shut away in the dark.

Then he rams the lid down, hard.

23

I see now how naïve I was. Before that, I believed that if you willed something to happen with all your being, it could be so. But I had lost Alice, I knew that I had – and there was nothing I could do about it. It was a hard lesson to learn, that one.

Describing it to Kate brought everything back so violently that I could almost feel again the hurt and rage that had carried me up to Oxford and through the weeks that followed. With hindsight, I can see that what I thought of as righteous fury on her behalf was my own unsightly jealousy.

'The baby,' Kate asked me, 'was it my mother?'

I told her that I was as certain as I could be that it

was. She went very quiet at this, but I knew that more questions were taking shape – questions that I knew I couldn't answer to her satisfaction. I admit that I feigned a greater tiredness than I felt in order to escape from these, to buy myself time. Because I simply didn't have the answer to why Alice had chosen to abandon her baby.

24

Corsica, August 1986

Stafford retreated into the cool of the house for the rest of the day. I spent the afternoon lying by the pool, while the shade moved from where it merely grazed my toes to envelop me completely.

Stafford had told me that he was as sure as he could be that the baby was Mum. So, it seemed, my mother had been the Frenchman's daughter.

It was now that I put my secret wish to rest. Since Stafford had first told me of his love for Alice I had harboured some hope that he might, in fact, be my grandfather. I had even – I blushed to think it then – begun to tentatively wonder if my interest in art might after all be something inherent . . . in my genes. I had come to like Stafford so much that I had longed for this to be the thing that strengthened the bond between us so it could not be broken. I had only allowed myself to explore these thoughts in small, furtive bursts, telling myself not to allow the hope to grow too great, as the disappointment would be all the more bitter if it were crushed. In this I had failed.

As for Alice, she had been twenty-two years old, alone and afraid, in a less forgiving era. Was it enough to exonerate her, for giving Mum away? The rational part of me knew that it probably was. But why send the letter, so many years later? Why that desperate, lonely attempt to get back in touch? Could I forgive her that? I wasn't sure.

When Oliver came down to swim lengths I feigned sleep, but it felt as though the top layer of my skin had been removed so that I was aware of his every disturbance of the air between us. I did not want to talk to him. I was oddly certain that if I did I would not be able to stop myself from telling him what I had learned.

I heard him clamber from the pool and pad over to the other chair, where he had left his things.

'Kate?'

I was forced to open my eyes and look up at him.

'Are you all right?'

'Yes,' I said, cautiously. 'I'm fine.'

He reached for his towel and began to dry himself. I tried not to look as he did it, at the expanses of taut skin that were revealed by his movements.

'Gerard and I have spent the morning working on the boat, making sure she's watertight. I was thinking of how – when we were in Bonifacio – you mentioned going out in her . . .'

I nodded, flushing to recall the embarrassment I had felt. It seemed a curiously long time ago, now.

'Perhaps we could take her out later. Would you like to? You could bring your camera, if you wanted.'

'OK then – yes.'

'I don't think we can go as far as the caves – I'm not sure she's ready for such a long journey – but we could take her along the coast here. It's flat out there – it'll be the perfect evening for it.'

So, before supper, we went out in the boat. I did bring my Nikon, and though I'd had misgivings about its safety I was glad that I had. At this time of day the sand of the coves and the rocks that ringed them appeared aflame: a fire that had miraculously found its way across the surface of the water to burn there too.

There was a kind of alchemy to photography back then that has been lost to us in the digital age. Now, we can view a photo on a screen as soon as it has been taken. Then, we were attempting to collect some fragment of what we saw with no guarantee that we would bring back anything of worth. It was akin to a child dangling a fishing net in a rock pool, watching as the life forms seem to swim their way into captivity, only to lift it out and discover that just seaweed remains.

Oliver had brought a tripod with him, and he helped me to fix the Nikon to it. My fingers trembled, ever so slightly, when his hands brushed mine. Then he told me to crouch low in the boat, too, to steady myself.

'The first time I tried to take photographs from the boat they came out like abstracts,' he said, 'blurred shapes and colours – quite beautiful in a way, but not what I had been hoping to achieve.'

I got myself into position, crouching down, thankful that the water was millpond-still. I did not want to risk these photos being ruined. I wanted to get it all exactly as it was. In fact, I felt again that frustration that I could not in some way capture everything else: the marine scent that emanated from the old boat's interior, the warm fingers of the evening breeze. And there was that hush – unlike anything I could ever experience in London – broken only by the call of swifts catching insects near the shore, where they soared and plunged in extraordinary patterns.

'I can tell you're a good photographer,' Oliver said.

'Oh? How did you come to that conclusion?'

'Because of the way you look at things,' he said. 'You're watchful . . .'

I wasn't sure I liked the sound of that – it reminded me, uncomfortably, of how he had caught me looking at the photos. 'Can that be a good thing?' I asked.

'Yes,' he said, intently. 'It's not simply good – it's essential for an artist. I see it in Grand-père too. It has to do with the way you look at everything. An intensity.'

'You must have that too,' I told him, 'to be an architect.'

'No. It's much more prosaic, a matter of mathematics rather than art.'

He was being modest, of course. 'But you take photographs too,' I said.

'Yes, and I enjoy it. But I have never been able to take any I am truly proud of. Mine are just a record of what's in front of me. To make the viewer see something beyond the image – that's a special skill. As different as one of Grand-père's works from a paint-by-numbers. I try – but I won't ever be a great photographer, it's just not there.' He paused. 'It's important to know your limitations. When I was young I thought I could paint, even decided I wanted to be an artist, like Grand-père. It was quite a long and painful process to discover I would never be good enough.'

He said it without any discernible trace of bitterness, though I was sure that the reckoning would have come as a blow at the time.

'Well,' I said, 'it was a short and painful process to discover I couldn't dance. Thank God I found out I could at least do something useful with a camera.'

He smiled at this, and I felt rather pleased – his smiles were a rare commodity.

'I need to stop talking to you and let you concentrate,' he said then. 'You'll lose the light otherwise.'

I realized with alarm that he was right, that the band of brilliant light was slipping down the cliffs, soon to be lost. I put my eye to the viewfinder and took several shots – more than were strictly necessary, just to be sure.

Suddenly a rogue gust of wind whipped my hair across my face, blinding me. Before I could disentangle my hands to sweep it away, Oliver had reached out a hand and done it for me. I turned back to thank him and found him gazing at me with the strangest expression, one that caused the words to stick in my throat. We were trapped by that look, like two animals. It frightened me, the possibility in it, even as excitement quickened in my stomach.

But then Oliver spoke. 'It looks like we're starting to lose the light,' he said, his voice slightly louder than it needed to be. He moved away from me, heading towards the engine – right at the back of the boat. 'We should make for the shore.'

The moment had disintegrated – almost as though it had never existed.

Oliver started the engine. As we sped across the darkening waters, I tried to tell myself that we had avoided something terrible – something that could not have been allowed to happen. He had done the right thing, for both of us.

25

Even all those years later, I couldn't help wondering how things might have turned out if I had acted differently, more decisively. I found myself recollecting what had happened when I told Lady Margaret what Alice asked me to say: that she was all right, that she had a plan, and that for the time being we must not intervene. She disclosed something then that showed Alice's mother to me in a rather different light.

I am trying to remember how she put it exactly. 'She looks young,' she said, 'but she isn't as young as she looks. She was older than my brother when they married, by three or four years. The boy, Archie, was born only seven months after the wedding, and you have never seen such a huge, healthy child. Do you understand what I am telling you?' I nodded, and she went on: 'My parents chose to see it as a young couple's rashness, ill-advised and shaming, but ultimately rectified by the marriage. I wonder now if they saw more than they admitted. You see, my brother only met her the month before they married. I know: I was there that evening to see him lose his head over her.'

I can't quite explain why, but suddenly much about Alice's mother made sense; the way she had doted on Archie and neglected her daughter. The absolute fear she had of scandal of any sort. But it stunned me, too, that she – the apogee of decorum and seemliness – could have been involved in such deceit. Lady Margaret must have seen the expression on my face, because she laughed and said, 'I can see that I have shocked you. Believe me, although there is no love lost between her and I, I do not say this simply to blacken her name. I have a horror of gossip for its own sake. I am telling you because it is worth bearing in mind what she is capable of.'

Kate and Oliver went out on the boat that evening to take photographs of the shore. As soon as they returned for supper, I knew that some new thing had occurred. The silence between them across the table had a weight and texture to it that had not been there before. I was intrigued, but I also felt . . . how to describe it? Not envy, exactly, but some close cousin of it. For I understood then, as I had not before, that I would never again share that particular sort of silence with another person.

I worried for them, too. I reminded myself, firmly, that there was nothing I could do about it. After all, it was exactly what I had secretly begun to hope for. But now that it seemed it might become a possibility, I was all too aware of everything that was at stake.

The next morning, I decided to tell Kate about that last time I saw Alice in England. It was late summer, and I was working in a solicitor's office. I had gained – to everyone's surprise, including my own – a first-class degree from Oxford. I knew instantly that this success would work against me. If I had scraped a Third, I might have been left to my own devices. Instead, I now appeared to be destined for a life of intellectual pursuits.

My father had got much worse, in those last few years before his death. He was still at the firm, but his hours had been greatly reduced: he wasn't well enough to work full time. In truth, he wasn't well enough to work at all, but they kept him on out of loyalty. For more than a decade it had been eating away at him, this disease of the mind, and most of the time he was unrecognizable from the man he had once been. There would have been no question of leaving my mother to cope with him alone, and the responsibility of helping her fell to me. My oldest sister Rosa now lived in

Islington with her young family, and my other sister, Caro, had married in the summer and moved to Nova Scotia. And so I had returned to live in the house in Fulham.

The job was in a solicitor's office in Silk Street – Locke & Proudfoot – and my position was that of a glorified clerk. The work bored me, and the boredom made me stupid, so that I seemed to spend half my time correcting my own blunders. I'm sure that my employer, old Mr Proudfoot, wondered whether the first-class student he had been promised had swapped places with some moron changeling.

The one saving grace was that the hours were good. If I managed to make few enough errors to be able to finish undoing them by six o'clock, I would be home in time to fit in some drawing before supper. That was what I was hoping for the day she came to find me. It was a golden evening, and I was walking home across that small triangle of earth they rather optimistically call the Green. Something about the figure on the bench made me stop in my tracks. I can't explain what it was that drew my eye to her, exactly. Perhaps it was the running dog, returning to its master, that sped through the space between us. Or maybe it was the strange pull she exerted upon me. From that distance I could not have been sure it was her by sight – and yet I knew that it was.

She had fallen asleep, slumped slightly to one side. I remember it so clearly, the way she looked when I stood over her, wondering whether or not to wake her. Her face was thin and drawn. She seemed an entirely different person from the Alice I had seen only a few months previously.

26

London, August 1930

Alice stirs, as though the pressure of his gaze has woken her. She shivers, and blinks in confusion before she comes to an awareness of where she is. Her silver eyes are huge in her face and as she stares up at him she looks strange and fey, rather wild. Then recognition dawns, and she relaxes back into her seat.

'Alice? Are you all right?'

'Tom.' She gives a tired smile. 'I'd almost given up waiting. How embarrassing, to fall asleep.'

'You look exhausted.' He sits down beside her.

'I haven't felt like sleeping much.'

'What are you doing here, Alice? Where . . .' Tom is about to ask after the child, but something stops him.

Looking at her, it is hard to believe that a mere few weeks ago she had been carrying a baby inside her. She is thinner than ever – she looks barely old enough to bear children. Her skin has a yellowish tint to it and her hair is lank, clinging to her skull. He sits down next to her and takes her hand. Her fingers are cold – no doubt from several hours of waiting in the cooling evening air.

'You're freezing. I think we should go inside.' He tries to persuade Alice to come home with him, but she is adamant that she doesn't want to cause any fuss. In the end, lost for inspiration, he ends up taking her to the nearest pub, where the atmosphere is thick with pipe smoke and stale beer, and the men stare at them curiously over their evening pints. Tom isn't even sure that Alice, as a woman, is allowed to be in here. He hurries her to a table in the furthest corner, as far removed from the crowd at the bar as it is possible to be.

She doesn't seem to be aware of her surroundings, or of how incongruous she looks in her well-cut travelling clothes. She takes a tin of cigarettes from her bag and slides two out, offering him one. He reflects that he wasn't even aware before that she smoked. How is it that he didn't know? He accepts one, and she lights them with fingers that betray her agitation with a slight tremble.

'I've left,' she says.

'Oh.' He feels the quickening of excitement – and panic – inside him. What is it that she is telling him?

What does she need of him? His head spins with the possibilities, and he speaks before he has time to think better of it: 'And the baby?'

Alice's expression shutters. She gives the tiniest – almost imperceptible – shake of her head and looks down at the scarred surface of the table. She does not say anything, but she doesn't need to: it is clear what this means. The child could not come too. Perhaps, in the end, she realized she was not up to the challenge of supporting both herself and the child. He understands, too late, that he should not have asked.

Desperate to change the subject, he asks: 'Why don't you stay the night, here, with us?'

'No.' She rests her hand on his wrist. 'I have a hotel. Goodness,' she says, with unconvincing gaiety, 'I do sound independent. I used to find the thought of hotels rather exciting, probably because we so rarely stayed in them. Unfortunately, it isn't that sort of hotel. Nonetheless, it will do. And do you know something? It transpires that hotel rooms are expensive, even the ones with algae-green wallpaper and no soap. But I shan't be there long.'

'Where will you go?'

'Paris.' She smiles and shrugs. 'Where else?'

Tom stiffens. He doesn't ask, because he doesn't want to know the answer, but she watches him curiously, sensing that there is a question. 'What is it?'

'It's him, isn't it? The Frenchman – you're going to stay with him.'

'Oh. No – I hadn't even thought . . . Besides, he doesn't live in Paris, not any more. I want to go because when I think of anywhere I can imagine living, of starting a new life, I think of Paris. It's been like that ever since I went there with Aunt M. as a teenager.'

She tells him that there is a train, early in the morning, to take her to Southampton. Then she'll get herself passage on the first ferry she can.

'Can I visit you?'

She glances at him and her expression is odd, even guilty. 'Perhaps, one day.'

'Or I could come with you.' Yes, he thinks, and feels excitement quicken at the prospect. 'I could get a job, or sell my paintings – the bad ones, the only ones people seem to actually like. There wouldn't be much, but we wouldn't need . . .' He trails off. She is shaking her head, and her eyes have filled with tears.

'I came to say goodbye, Tom. It has to be like this. Do you understand?'

And he understands that he has lost her. The story that started all those years ago in Winnard Cove has finally come to an end.

27

It wasn't the last time I saw her. But I wasn't sure I wanted to tell Kate the rest. Some memories, I have discovered, are too precious – and too painful – to share.

I told her something else. I told her about the postcard. I had gone to Ajaccio to retrieve it, the day Oliver and Kate went to the mountains, because that was where it had been left, in a deposit box at the bank there. I had been worried that to keep it in the house might prompt me, in a weaker moment, to act recklessly.

Like a coward I had not shown it to Kate at once. I had kept it for a couple of days, a vain attempt to play for time. Because I knew that, as soon as she had seen it, everything would change. I would lose her.

The postcard had come with terrible timing. Elodia was dying, then – and it was the worst part of the dying, when she was still fighting against it with all her might. Before she became resigned to it, though the latter is the worst of all, in its way.

I didn't believe it, when it came. My first thought was that it was a hoax. Alice was dead. She had been dead for nearly thirty years.

28

Paris, September 1945

He remembers his way to the square easily, though he has only walked this way once before. There is the building with the small bistro on the first floor.

From a distance, it looks much the same. The fire-engine-red paint, the scattering of ironwork tables and chairs upon the flagstones outside. And there are people, so many people – more, even, than there had been before. It is difficult at first, looking upon this scene, to imagine that these people have experienced war. The same war that has wrung him, torn him, spat him out. Yet, as he draws closer, he sees the chunks of plaster missing from one wall. He sees that the surface of the red paint is chipped and peeling away. His gaze roams thc faces. He feels that at any moment he will see her. It seems impossible that she should not be here. This was how he imagined it every time, crouching beneath the hell overhead. Him, lifting her into his arms, climbing the steep, narrow stairs up to the small attic space. The white bed, the light falling across them. But she is not here. All these people, all these faces, yet not that one he seeks.

He will find the patronne: he remembers her. She will be able to tell him something. It is possible that Alice no longer lives here, but she had loved that room. When he had seen her in it, with her meagre but precious possessions about her, he could not imagine her living anywhere else.

Tom almost doesn't recognize the woman at first. He remembers a strapping Belgesse, ruddy-cheeked, large-bosomed, in the prime of life. He sees, instead, an elderly woman, staggering under the weight of the tray she carries. Something has happened to her face, and her hair, formerly a reddish-blonde, is a shock of bone-white. Her movements between the tables are pinched and arthritic. Tom is fascinated and appalled, frozen for several moments where he stands watching her. What must a person have experienced to undergo such a change?

It could be that his stillness in the midst of the movement and chatter draws her attention, or that she simply feels his gaze upon her. She turns and looks at him, trying to place him, sifting through memory. Then he sees her face change as she recognizes him.

'I'm looking for Alice,' he says. Perhaps his pronunciation is poor, maybe she doesn't hear him properly, because she backs away from him, shaking her head. He follows her across the room. 'Alice? Do you know where she is? I've come to see her.'

The woman told me that Alice had been murdered. They'd taken a group, fifty men and women, into a clearing in the forest and shot them. They were hostages. There'd been an attack on a German soldier on one of the Metro stations, and that was how they did the sums: one German life was paid for in kind by fifty French. The prison had released the list of names in the papers, to warn off others as much as to notify relatives. The woman had paid out of her own pocket for a site in the *cimetière*, though she had nothing to bury there.

Fifty lives. Was it selfish to consider hers more valuable than any of those other lives that had been lost? But to me it was infinitely precious. The irony was that the thought of her had kept me alive. That thought had kept me sane. I had believed in her, in the future we would make together, the way other men believe in God.

I didn't know what to do with myself, after the woman showed me the stone with the dates. And so I went home. I couldn't paint: I think I may have had a breakdown, the quieter sort, the sort that goes largely unremarked. It took me a long time to remember where it was that I'd last been able to paint – where I had last been happy.

It was then I thought of Corsica, the place we had discovered together . . . that time I had not told Kate about. I craved the wind, the sun and salt, the simplicity of the island. I still barely ate or slept, but, gradually, I began to do a little work.

I met Elodia a month after I arrived. There was a daughter – three years old – a product of a wartime liaison. Her family had chosen to despise her, both for having had the relationship with an Italian and then, perhaps more importantly, for not being able to make him stay and marry her. They'd been thrown out, she and her daughter, and left to fend for themselves.

About a week after I moved in she came to my house to ask if I wanted my laundry done, for a small fee. The child clung to her leg. I didn't need anything washed, but I found some anyway. Something about her gave me the impression of survival against the odds, even before I knew the story.

It became a twice-weekly thing. I was perfectly capable of doing my own washing, but I came to look forward to her visits. Eventually, she trusted me enough to explain her situation. In a way she reminded me of Alice: her courage, her tenacity.

We married five months later. I know how it must look, how unforgivable a thing, that less than a year after I discovered the love of my life had been killed, I married another woman. But, you see, in a way it made perfect sense. With her gone, I would never marry for love, that much was certain. The only person for me in that way had been Alice. All the same, I was a young, healthy, whole man – at a time when so many had been maimed or killed. And I was so lonely. When I met this young woman, left all alone with her daughter, I wanted to help her.

Elodia understood that what I was offering was friendship, companionship, support. All the things that should be part of a marriage: all except love. I think that suited her well though. You see, she had known love too, and it had let her down. We did grow to love one another in the way that friends do – though it was a love of a different species entirely to what I had felt, and would continue to feel, for Alice. Elodia and I lived together for more than thirty years in almost total harmony, but unpalatable as it may be, I never stopped mourning Alice and what we could have had.

So when the card came, it seemed an impossible thing. I assumed initially that it might be a cruel hoax, from one who had somehow discovered our story.

> *19 August 1979*
>
> To *my dearest Tom,*
> Would *you consent to a meeting of old friends? I*
> go *by another name now, but I'm still the girl you*
> once *knew.*
>   *A*

She was dead. I had seen the very stone that marked that fact.

But then I turned it over and saw the photograph on the other side of the postcard: *Winnard Cove, Cornwall: watercolour*. The shape of the bay and the wych elms exactly as I remembered, though Eversley Hall had been turned into a hotel, and a phalanx of beach umbrellas bristled the lip of the cliff. The writing was the same – or, almost. And she gave an address: not far from where she had been living before. It couldn't be . . . yet, incredibly, it was. I knew that it was.

29

Corsica, August 1986

My reaction, when Stafford told me about the postcard, surprised me. It was one of anger, of betrayal at the fact that he had kept from me something so vital. I had begun to assume from the way he spoke of her that Alice must be dead. But now, not only was there the strong possibility that she was still alive, there was also an address at which she might – just conceivably – be found.

'Why didn't you tell me? At the beginning?'

'Because you didn't know the full story,' he said. 'I needed to explain all of it to you so that you'd understand. So that you'd understand her, before you went looking.'

Stafford said that before he'd got the postcard, he'd been certain that Alice had died, decades earlier.

That was war, he said, that was the sort of mess it made out of what you thought you knew, out of the life you had imagined yourself having. So the thing seemed, at first, like a message from a ghost.

'Have you seen her since?' Had he kept this from me too?

'No. I never went.'

'Why . . . because of Elodia?'

'Yes. It would have been a terrible disloyalty.'

Was that the whole picture? I think perhaps not. In fact, I am sure there had been fear, too. Fear that he might find Alice changed beyond recognition from the person he had loved: that it would be better to remember her as the young woman she had been. Fear that she might find him terribly changed, too – that she would find him wanting.

'So she lives here now?' I indicated the return address that she had given, in Paris: Rue de Seine.

'I can't say. As there's been no contact since . . .' He made a helpless gesture to indicate the span of years. 'If you went there, though, you might be able to discover something further. A start, at least.'

I glanced down at the postcard. I turned it over, and saw the view it showed: of a sandy beach buffeted by grey waves, and two buildings, one large and historic in aspect, the other nestling in its shadow, a cottage perhaps a tenth of the size. I had the strongest feeling of recognition, as I studied it. And I knew, before I read it, this was Winnard Cove.

30

Corsica, September 1986

I had to leave now, that was clear. I needed to go in search of Alice, but I didn't want to offend Stafford, to whom I owed so much. Any anger I felt at him had ebbed as quickly as it had arrived. I saw how fervently he had wanted to be certain that I understand her before I judged her actions.

When I went to tell him that I planned to go to Paris, Stafford anticipated me. 'I know that you will want to be on your way,' he said, 'it will be so sad to see you go, Kate. Both of us,' he glanced over at Oliver, who sat quite still, gazing out to sea, 'have enjoyed your company enormously.'

I could not see Oliver's expression – and I wasn't

sure that I wanted to. Would it mean anything to him, that I was leaving? It might even be a relief: the removal of a complication. Now he would have the time alone with his grandfather that he had craved.

'You could fly to Paris,' Stafford said, 'or you could take the night ferry across tomorrow and catch a train from Marseilles.'

I was instantly more attracted to the idea of the train. A plane would have been faster, of course, and speed was to be prized. But if I could avoid flying – and the associations it brought with it – I would. I needed time to prepare myself too. A train journey would offer those few necessary hours in which to do so. And it would give me one more day in this place. It was gratifying to see how pleased Stafford looked when I told him of my choice.

Stafford and I talked late into the night, after Oliver had excused himself for bed. It was rare that Stafford stayed up beyond nine, so I understood that to be granted his company at this hour was a great and unusual honour.

He went to pour us both a drink. I never drank whisky, but this one tasted of peat and woodsmoke and I found myself cautiously savouring it. It spoke of adventure and a little of magic.

I looked up at the sky and it was indigo-black. The stars, on this clear evening, astounded me. In London you barely ever see them, and I had always thought of them as a flat canopy stretched over the heavens: a painted surface. Now, studying them properly for the first time since I'd arrived, I saw that they were more like silvery particles sinking through dark water. Was there, just possibly, a coolness to the night air that I had not noticed before? It was the first day of September: no longer summer.

'Do you have anything else to ask me?' Stafford studied me over the rim of his glass.

I did, and the whisky had given me confidence. 'What was it like, when you believed Alice was dead?'

He considered this for a long moment before answering, and I wondered if I had gone beyond the pale, but then he said, 'I couldn't believe, after hearing it, that I could go on living. But you do, you know. Even if some part of you does die in that moment.'

I knew that, well enough.

We had one last breakfast on the terrace the next morning. It was still warm but, overnight, anvil-shaped grey clouds had rolled in from the sea, obscuring the sun and leaving us, after the dazzling glare of previous days, in what felt like a half-light.

Stafford turned to Oliver. 'Would you drive us to the ferry? I'd like to come and see Kate off.'

'Yes,' said Oliver. 'But . . . I was thinking of going too.'

Both Stafford and I stared at him.

'With Kate?' Stafford asked.

He nodded, briskly. 'I have some things I need to be doing in Paris.' He looked to Stafford. 'That is, if you don't mind, Grand-père.'

'Of course not,' Stafford said. 'If that's what you'd like.'

'Kate?' Oliver turned to me. 'Would you mind if I travelled with you?'

That last day was a rather subdued affair. I was depressed by the thought of leaving the house, the island and most of all Stafford himself. I had only known him for a short time but through all that he had told me I felt I knew more about him than one might of one's closest friend. He had been generous, selflessly so, with his own history.

I went for one last swim in the pool, realizing that I would not have the chance to do such a thing for a long while, and wandered down to the beach to drink in the warm briny scent of the sea. I collected a trophy from the maquis itself – a small bouquet of herbs that I hoped would, at least for a while, continue to evoke the island for me once I had left.

I did not see much of Oliver that day. I could not understand why he had asked to join me on the journey to Paris – but I decided that it would do me no good to dwell on it.

After lunch, Stafford called me into his studio. 'It's not quite finished,' he told me, 'but I think it's ready for you to see.'

I followed him round, for the first time, to the other side of the easel. 'Oh.' I could not seem to find anything else to say. It was a work of incredible technical skill, of that characteristic economy of his that allowed for no errant line. Yet it was also at the same time something much more than that. He had found strength of character where I had only seen a lack – had revealed a beauty that I would not have believed existed. Yet it wasn't a lie. It was true – it was me.

Stafford had one last thing to show me. I saw that he had pulled from the corner of the room an old trunk, the leather worn and cracked with age. As he bent, stiffly, to unlock it, I suddenly knew what it was. When he lifted the lid and I saw what was within – what I had hoped would be there – I felt my eyes fill with tears.

31

Oliver and I took the ferry from Ajaccio to Nice. We'd each booked a small cabin, but I knew instantly that I would not be able to sleep: there was too much to think about. Instead, I told him that I planned to remain for a while up on the deck, and he opted to join me.

The clouds that had obscured the sky had finally retreated in the afternoon to reveal a night sky of almost perfect clarity. We found a part of the deck that we could make our own and sat and stared out across the depths towards the lights of the island, receding until they became tiny pinpricks of light, will-o'-the-wisp's lanterns, scarcely real.

'I packed these,' Oliver said, 'just in case.' He produced

303

two beers from the battered rucksack he had brought – the only luggage he seemed to be taking with him. I thanked him as he passed me one, and he gave a quick smile, then looked back out to sea.

I wished that things could be simple between us, now that we had shaken off hostility, then strained formality – all of that. Instead there was this other, complicating element. I was sure I had not imagined the way he had looked at me in the boat the evening before. Yet the idea of acknowledging it, of forcing it to reveal itself, was unthinkable. Now, removed from the island and from Stafford, our aloneness together felt dangerous. Though the boat was crowded with passengers, sitting there in the dark alcove we had found, suspended between the sea and sky, I could believe that we were the only people for miles around.

'I was thinking,' Oliver said then, surprising me, 'I was always so depressed on this journey, back to the mainland, that I never realized how beautiful it is.'

'But coming the other way must have been the opposite?'

'I was generally too excited then to notice.' He took a sip of his beer. 'Mum always hated taking the ferry. She once told me that she thought of it as the passage across the River Styx.'

I tried to imagine how someone might equate the crossing to Corsica, land of light and sea, with a voyage into the underworld.

'For her sake,' he said, 'I hope that it wasn't where she ended up when she died. She'd have hated that, having spent her whole life trying to get away from it.'

I cleared my throat. 'How did she die?' Oliver didn't answer immediately, and my question seemed to echo in the silence. Immediately I felt I had gone too far. But then he said, quietly: 'An overdose.'

'Oh. I'm sorry.'

'Don't be. It happened a long time ago.'

'How old were you?'

'It was the day after I'd turned ten, actually,' he said, his tone slightly too offhand to be truly convincing. 'Mum had this idea that I was now grown up – she had allowed me to come to Cannes for the week – and that we should celebrate in style. It . . . it was the most bizarre day you can imagine. I feel sorry for her, now, when I think about it. She simply didn't have a clue how to be a parent, even though she'd had such a good example from my grandmother.' He shrugged. 'It wasn't in her nature, I suppose.

'She told me that since I was now an adult we'd have a grown-up celebration and go for lunch in the best restaurant. I'd have preferred a cake on the beach, to be honest. Most ten-year-old boys would, probably. Still, she was trying, and I suppose she didn't know what ten-year-old boys liked.

'It was out of town, the restaurant, about half an hour's drive away. My mother told me on the way that it was the place to go – everyone who was anyone would be there. That didn't mean much to me, but she looked very elegant, and I was proud of her when we walked in and people turned to stare. I think she at least seemed like the "somebody" she wanted to be.'

I remembered, as he said this, walking into the smoke-fugged bar of the Groucho Club with Mum, me only as high as her waist at the time. People swarming around her, patting me on the head. There were other beautiful women there, but she was by far the most beautiful, the most interesting, the most talented: I knew this unequivocally. She'd knelt and whispered in my ear, 'We can go as soon as you want to. Tell me when, and we'll leave that very minute.'

'Did you enjoy it?' I asked.

'In a way – it was a new experience, certainly. It was a hot day, but inside the restaurant there was this strange refrigerated cool. You know the sort of place: huge white napkins folded into elaborate shapes, waiters like penguins – a bit old-fashioned now.'

I nodded. He was speaking quickly, as if afraid of stopping, of not getting to the end. I wondered why he had chosen this moment to tell me. Perhaps, I thought, it was to do with the unusual, confessional quality of our spot – the silence and darkness around us like a cloak.

'Maman ordered us champagne,' he continued, 'which I hated, but drank because I didn't want to look like a child. She kept leaning over and whispering to me: "There's so-and-so, there's so-and-so" and making subtle gestures in their direction, which got less and less subtle as she had more to drink. They were mainly men, I think, and to me they all looked old and unremarkable. Judging by her excitement, I imagine they were bigwigs in the film industry: important people.

'Then she said she was going to the bathroom. She was gone for some time, and I began to look about me, because I was bored. Suddenly I spotted her, in the far corner, talking to a man. He was sitting, and there was another man opposite him – and my mother was crouching next to the table to speak to him. I could see, even from that distance, when things changed from being friendly, civil, to something else. She put her hand on his shoulder and he reached up and removed it, very cool, not looking at her. Then she pointed right over at me, and his head came up, and his eyes met mine. I looked away quickly, down into my *blanquette de veau*. I know this may sound far-fetched, and I have no proof other than what I felt . . . but in that moment I knew that man was my father.'

'Oh.'

He took a long drink of his beer. 'When my mother came back to the table I saw that her make-up was smeared – I think she'd been crying. Suddenly she appeared ten, twenty years older than she had before, and drunk. I wish she could have acknowledged that she felt as terrible as she looked. The pretence that we were still having fun was the worst.'

'When she paid, she pulled the notes out of her purse,

like this' – he gestured with his free hand – 'and threw them at the waiters, so they had to scrabble on the floor to pick them up. In the car she forgot to put her driving shoes on at first, so she couldn't work out, when she put her high-heel to the pedal, why it was so difficult to drive.'

'She drove you home?'

'Yes, but she did try to be sensible. She asked me if I wanted to drive instead.'

'She asked *you*?' I tried not to sound as horrified as I felt.

'Yes.' He gave an odd smile. 'It's almost funny, when you think about it.'

'It's lucky you didn't crash.'

'Yes. Although . . .'

'What?'

'I wonder now if that's what she wanted. I mean,' he said quickly, 'don't get me wrong – she definitely wouldn't have meant anything to happen to me. She probably hadn't thought it out to that extent.

'The following morning I waited hours for her to get up. It was hot in the apartment, I was bored. I gathered all our beach things and sat watching the clock. When it was past midday I finally went in to wake her up.'

He didn't say anything else for a while, and I couldn't think, though I tried, of something with which to fill the silence.

*

In Nice we took the TGV to Paris, crammed in with holidaymakers returning to Paris, sunburned families and couples, bags haphazard about them. We just managed to find two seats amid the chaos.

Much of my attention was caught by the warmth of Oliver's body forced against mine on the small seat. Despite myself I could not help but remark the beauty and remarkable size of the sun-browned hands resting in his lap: the curved, dexterous thumbs and elegant fingers. I pressed my head against the window and feigned sleep, watching the countryside rush past through half-closed eyes.

When Oliver fell asleep, his head thrown back against the seat rest to expose the beautiful column of his throat, my sensitivity to his presence beside me waned. Now I was free to think about what lay ahead: all the possibility and terror of it. I thought about Stafford, too. Making another journey all those years ago, through a different France – returning from the front. Both of us in search of the same woman.

It was a balmy afternoon in Paris – a far cry from the scorched and salt-swept bluster of the Corsican climate that I had become accustomed to. As we stepped from the train at Gare de Lyon I looked up at the station clock and found that it was only midday. There was time, I realized – with a stab of apprehension – to make my way across the city, to call at the address.

Echoing my thoughts, Oliver said, 'You could go straight there, I suppose.'

'Oh,' I said, wavering – suddenly drained of all confidence by the prospect. 'I thought I'd drop off my bags first.' I knew that it sounded feeble, a transparent play for time.

When I glanced across at Oliver I saw that he was studying me, and I looked away in case he read my cowardice in my face. 'Where will you stay?' he asked.

'I'll find a hotel.' I'd already decided this. I still had most of the money Stafford had given me, which he had refused to take back.

Oliver seemed to be making up his mind to speak. 'Or,' he said, 'you could stay at the apartment, with me.'

'I don't think so,' I said, too quickly. The idea scared me.

But Oliver was tenacious. 'I know that Grand-père specifically wanted me to ask you.'

I felt fatigue wash over me then. I was too tired to argue the point, I realized, too tired to trawl the city looking for somewhere to stay. The fact that it was Stafford's wish, not Oliver's, made it an easier offer to accept: made the gesture seem less significant.

Oliver's apartment was above a café, of the sort that you see on old postcards of the city – with tables and chairs spilling across the pavement. Now, it was rather subdued – a solitary couple having a quiet drink, but in the morning and during the lunchtime rush, Oliver said, you could faintly hear sounds drifting up through the floors: the thwack and screech of the coffee being made, the murmur of the customers sitting outside.

'I like it though,' he said. 'I love staying with Grandpère, but I don't enjoy silence quite as much as him.'

After the light and space of the Maison du Vent the place seemed on the small side, though I'm sure that it was generous for the city. I could see, too, that it was rather beautiful – with tall windows leading on to a tiny ironwork balcony, and toffee-coloured floorboards. A couple of twin Stafford sketches hung upon one wall: studies of the Maison du Vent from different approaches. There was an antique trunk that served as a coffee table and held a thick stack of architectural digests, and a low-slung sofa. Yet, these elements were far less noticeable than the sparseness that surrounded them: the place was shockingly bare, more like an elegant hotel room than a home. I saw that several cardboard boxes lined the corridor that ran between the rooms.

'I've been having a clear-out,' Oliver said. He didn't elaborate, and I didn't probe, not wanting to know whether any of them contained his wife's remaining possessions. It wasn't hard to understand why he had decided to escape to Corsica.

I looked at him, standing there in his empty flat and felt great pity for him. Whatever had happened between them, they must have loved each other once. The ending, however it had come about, had been a tragedy of sorts. No one entered a marriage anticipating its demise.

311

He showed me to the spare room. 'It's not big,' he said, 'but hopefully it'll be comfortable.'

When he disappeared I sat down on the bed and regarded myself in the mirror opposite. I looked as tired and travel-worn as I felt, but there was something else, too, some barely perceptible change that couldn't be attributed to the colour I had managed to pick up. If it wasn't my imagination I appeared more resolute, more certain of myself. I had begun to avoid looking in mirrors since Mum's death, because the girl I saw reflected in them was not someone I recognized: a spectre, a not-quite person. Now, however, I saw someone with purpose. Was this what Stafford had seen in me, that which I had not known until he had distilled into the portrait?

I returned to the sitting room, where Oliver was waiting. It was odd – he looked awkward in the bare space – out of place – as though he were the guest. But then I recalled how I'd felt rattling around the house in Battersea, feeling like an imposter, a pale imitation of all that had been there before. Perhaps it wasn't so different for him.

'Right,' I said, and my voice sounded loud in the silence. 'I should go now.'

Oliver shifted on his feet. 'I could walk you there, if you'd like? It would be quicker than you having to find your way.'

I hoped, for the sake of my pride, that he could not see the relief on my face.

When I showed him the address from the postcard, and he told me that it wasn't far, my heart began to beat faster. I had been so swept up in the events of the night before that I had almost managed to put it out of my mind. Now my trepidation came flooding back. In that moment, I think I might have preferred if he'd told me that by some misunderstanding we'd ended up in the wrong city. Suddenly I didn't feel ready.

If I had thought I was the only one aware – and only newly aware – of Oliver's beauty, I discovered now that I was not. The sheer brazenness with which people looked at him surprised me. I noticed, even if he did not, the exquisite teenager who treated him to a sliding glance as she passed; the lingering gaze of the middle-aged woman arranging chairs outside a restaurant. Had I been so desensitized, before, that I had been unable to see something that was so obvious to everyone else?

When we eventually came to stand in front of it, I couldn't quite believe that the house existed. The fact of it made it all real – made Alice real. Until this point she had been like a figure from myth, and I had decided, from the off, to expect failure. I think I would have been less surprised to find that the place had collapsed in a cloud of masonry and furniture into some yawning chasm in the ground. It seemed all too easy that I should be able to walk up to Alice's house and simply knock on her door.

It was a beautiful building: soberly elegant, with a lofty grey stone frontage and a graceful symmetry of ironwork balconies through which ivy wended glossy dark stems.

'It's rare to own a whole house here,' Oliver murmured. 'She must be well off.'

This sat oddly with what I thought I knew. Alice was the runaway, the girl who had forsaken a life of plenty for her freedom. I had imagined her scraping by, living a poor, bohemian existence in a grimy backwater, but this was unmistakably the address I'd copied down.

Before I put my finger to the bell, I had what I can only describe as a funny turn. My head felt, suddenly, as though it were filled with helium, my vision swam and my heart beat a tattoo in my chest. As if sensing this, Oliver joined me on the step. 'I could come in with you,' he said, casually.

I looked at him, taken aback by his kindness.

'Are you sure?'

'If you'd like.' He shrugged, offhandedly. 'I don't have anywhere to be today.'

'OK,' I said, 'yes – thank you.' Gradually, I felt my breathing return to normal, my heartbeat slow. I reached out and pressed the bronze button, once, hard.

The door was opened by a woman in her fifties with dark hair cropped close to her head and an austerely beautiful face. She was dressed simply – but not inexpensively – in a dark grey shift, with a necklace of gold filigree around her neck. She was one of those tiny, compact people – rather like my mother, in fact – who made me feel about eight foot tall. I was suddenly aware of my elderly jeans and crumpled T-shirt. She looked from one to the other of us with a bird-bright, assessing gaze.

'*Oui?*'

I explained, in my rusty but serviceable French, that we were looking for Alice.

'I don't understand.' She switched immediately and fluently into English, and I tried not to feel offended that she hadn't thought me up to the task of carrying out the discussion in her language. 'No one of that name lives here.' I know now that this ignorance was feigned, but that my use of the name had alarmed her into the pretence.

'But . . .' Then I remembered: 'I think she might also be known as Célia.'

She looked at me curiously, and gave a shrug, as if implying it wasn't her problem if I were unhinged. 'All right. What is it that you want?'

I tried to remind myself that it was probably the fact that she was not speaking in her own tongue that made her sound so cold.

'It's rather difficult to explain.'

'Well, she isn't available at the moment.' I saw that she had a firm grip on the door, as if she were preparing to fling it shut in our faces.

'She lives here though?' This woman had already told me much more than she might have imagined. Alice was alive.

A curt nod. 'This is her house.' She began to close the door. 'I'm sorry, but I—'

'I need to speak to her.' I hadn't meant to raise my voice, but it was almost a shout. She raised her eyebrows, but her hand on the door stilled and I lowered my voice. 'I should introduce myself. My name is Kate.' I put out my hand, and she stared at it for a moment before taking it, reluctantly.

'Marguerite.'

'Would you . . . I don't mean to impose, but I know that . . . Célia will want to meet me. It's about something very important.' Then I added, as an afterthought, 'as important to her as it is to me, I think.'

Marguerite shifted in the doorway, apparently wrong-footed. I tried to peer past her down the length of the dark hallway, as though Alice might be waiting somewhere within, ready to receive me if I passed this first trial.

'Perhaps I could call on her later – or tomorrow?'

Marguerite looked puzzled, then turned and followed my gaze into the depths of the house. She shook her head and gave a funny sort of laugh. 'Oh no,' she said, 'no, she isn't here. Not in Paris.'

'I'm sorry . . . I don't follow. I understood this was her house.' The thought came to me then: perhaps she was dead, after all, and this woman was playing a nasty little game, to test the validity of my story. 'So where—'

'New York.'

'New York?' I echoed, faintly.

'She has a gallery there. One here, and one over there, in New York. This is still her house too, naturally. When she is away, I look after it.' She inclined her head. 'She spends more and more time there now.'

She smiled economically. 'So, you see, you will have to come some other time.' She waved a hand. 'A month, perhaps. I think she will return in November, for the opening of the new exhibition.'

'November? It can't wait until November—' I tried to calm myself. 'It's very important that I speak to her now.'

She looked unmoved. 'What can it be, that you need to see her so urgently?'

'I can't explain properly here . . .'

Marguerite shrugged, as though she didn't believe it would do any good, but couldn't summon the energy to argue the point with me. 'All right, you can come in.' She beckoned briskly, bidding us follow her into the house.

The corridor that led from the front door was lined with artwork. I tried to take stock of the pieces, but Marguerite moved too quickly, and glanced round a couple of times as if to see what was taking us so long. As we reached the end of the hallway, Oliver touched my arm and drew me back. It was all I could do to avoid remarking how my skin thrilled at the warmth of his touch.

'Look.'

It was an abstract: fierce squares of black and white, among which wandered bent humanoid figures. In one corner was a red cross, daubed in a quick, careless gesture, so that the paint had run from the lines to bleed down towards the bottom of the canvas. It was intriguing, certainly, but I couldn't understand why Oliver had drawn my attention to it.

'It's my grandfather's. One of his pieces on the war.'

Now I stared. It was so different from anything I had seen of Stafford's: so much more raw and violent.

'And there's another. One of his "Odalisques".'

I turned to see. A hugely fat woman, splayed on a sofa wearing nothing but a bath towel wrapped around her head, one hand dangling indolently – the fingers beautifully done. There was, despite her unhealthy size, something oddly arresting about her. A beauty that had been drawn out in the portrayal, in the delicate bluish pallor of her lolling breasts, the proud white meringue of her stomach.

It was curious, to say the least, that these two works should be in Alice's possession. Perhaps they had been presents. But then I saw that the Odalisque was dated 1962, and Stafford had told me that he had last seen Alice in the thirties. So, it seemed, Alice was a collector of his work. Did Stafford know? I felt sure that he would have mentioned it if he had.

Oliver had spotted another painting he recognized before Marguerite came out of the kitchen to check why we had been delayed. 'Is there a problem?'

'No,' said Oliver, apparently not inclined to say anything else. Then he changed his mind and added: 'Actually, I stopped to look at the art.'

Marguerite regarded us steadily, apparently trying to

decide whether we were pulling her leg or planning to steal one of the pieces. 'Oh yes?'

'Yes. I noticed' – Oliver gestured to them – 'a couple of works here I recognize. They're my grandfather's.'

'They are—' She stopped, wrong-footed. 'Your grandfather is Thomas Stafford?'

'Yes.'

She looked from one to the other of us, incredulous. 'But Célia is probably the largest collector of his work in the world.'

It was surreal, being in Alice's house without actually having come close to meeting her. Perhaps it was my imagination, but to me the air in the building felt rarefied, charged with some essence of the absent woman. There was the faintest savour of something smoky and exotic in the air that it seemed to rise up in a cloud from the cushions when we sat upon them.

We were at the back of the house. The light filtered green into the room from the small garden beyond the windows, and the topmost shoots of a white rosebush scratched against the glass with a tiny sound. A Burmese cat padded past on silent paws and slinked up the staircase, uninterested in our presence.

Oliver and I sat on a low, emerald-coloured ottoman with claws for feet, and Marguerite sat in a chair opposite, slightly elevated above us. I cradled my bowl of coffee in my lap, trying not to spill it. It felt like the start of an interrogation.

'So,' I said, to break the silence, 'how do you know Célia?'

Marguerite took her time answering. 'I've known her for a long while,' she said finally. 'Nearly all my life.'

'Ah.' No relation, then. I waited for an elaboration on this, but none was forthcoming.

'And how do you know her?' It was spoken like a challenge.

'Actually, I don't know her, not exactly.' She raised an eyebrow – perhaps wondering if she had made a mistake in admitting us. I hastened on: 'But, I'm . . . well, I'm her granddaughter. My mother was her daughter: June Darling.'

I had expected Marguerite's reaction to be one of incredulity, or worse, outrage. I read neither in her expression – if anything, it had softened.

'So you are Kate.' She studied me. 'Yes, you look like the photos I have seen of your mother. And a little like Célia, I think.'

'Thank you. But how—'

'Célia has known about you for a long time,' she said, answering before I could ask. 'I want to say that I'm sorry for your loss. Your mother was a wonderful dancer. I saw her, once, in *Swan Lake.*'

'Thank you,' I said, thrown by this compassion from a woman who had seemed so cold only moments before.

'When your mother died, Célia was nearly destroyed by grief. It was the great tragedy of her life, that she never knew her.'

320

'But she left her.' I failed to keep the censure from my voice.

Marguerite looked fierce. She leaned closer, until I worried she might be about to pour her coffee into my lap. 'Let me tell you something. I don't know exactly what happened – Célia has never told me – but she would not have left your mother unless she had no choice. That is not the sort of woman she is.'

She sat back, and regarded me with those bright black eyes. Perhaps she felt she hadn't gone far enough towards convincing me, because she went on, in a rush: 'I was so jealous of your mother. Of how much Célia wanted to make contact with her, how much she longed for her . . .' She stopped quickly, as though she had surprised herself with the confession. There was a weighted silence, punctuated only by the faraway retort of a car horn.

Suddenly Oliver spoke. 'Will you let Célia know that Kate will be coming to visit her? This week, if possible.'

'Oliver—' I turned to look at him, wondering what his game was, but he simply gazed back at me, impassively, as though it had all been planned in advance.

To my surprise, Marguerite was nodding her head. 'Yes,' she said. 'Yes, I think that would be best.'

Outside, in the street, Oliver seemed possessed of an unusual energy. 'We need to get there before they shut,' he said.

'Where?'

'The travel agents.' We walked back along the Rue

de Seine, and on to the grimy thoroughfare of the Boulevard St Germain. As soon as we found one, Oliver strode in and asked at the desk for a ticket to New York – and a flight back to London Heathrow. A stone of melancholy dropped through me at the thought of home – the place that now seemed so bound up with loneliness and grief. He hadn't suggested, I realized, that I might prefer to return to Paris.

Within minutes I was booked on the morning flight from Charles de Gaulle to JFK. I saw Oliver fish his wallet from his pocket, and suddenly realized what he meant to do. 'No,' I said, in alarm, as he took out his card. 'I can't let you.'

He turned to me. 'I want to,' he said, firmly. 'I told you before that I wanted to help – and it seems I've found a way to do so.'

'I know,' I said, 'but not like this – it's too much.' But as I looked at him I could see how adamant he was, for whatever reasons of his own, that he would do this thing. So, still wondering at it, I let him.

By the time we made it back to the apartment, dusk was falling, spilling its purplish shadow across the city. The streets were busy, the tables outside bars crowded with people. Oliver told me that only a few weeks ago many of the bars would have been shut, the city eerily quiet.

'I imagine you hardly ever see it like that,' I said, 'having always gone down to Corsica in the summer.'

'No, that's true. I'd never really known it until recently.'

'So you stayed here one summer?'

He made a kind of grimace, and I suddenly regretted asking him. 'Yes – for four years, actually. Isobel didn't like to travel a lot – well, not at all, to be honest. So we stayed here.'

'Ah.' I couldn't think of anything else to say. I had felt the name – *Isobel* – like a sting.

At the apartment I had a shower, hurrying from the bathroom to my room so I could avoid an awkward meeting with Oliver in the hallway. I changed my clothes – feeling the need for an outfit altogether more elegant than the jeans and T-shirt – now distinctly off-white – that I'd worn to travel in. I picked through my clothes indecisively, wishing I had something truly beautiful to wear. It was the city, I told myself, doing this to me.

I turned my bag upside down, prepared to be disappointed by what was in there. To my amazement, beneath the faded shorts and T-shirts stained with sun cream was my black crêpe de Chine dress: the one I had worn on my twenty-first birthday. I had not seen it since then. It must simply have been hidden in plain sight in my wardrobe, and I had somehow managed to sweep it up with my other things. I had certainly been distracted when I had packed for Corsica. Even so, I felt a thrill go through me.

It was perfect: cut high at the neck, sleeveless, close-fitting. I had forgotten how I felt transformed wearing it, several degrees more elegant. As I studied myself in the mirror I realized why I had always loved it so much. Because it made me look a little like her – like Mum.

I heard Oliver's footsteps then, approaching my door. 'Would you prefer to go out for supper?' he asked. 'Or we could eat here?'

I thought. I was dog-tired, but I hadn't been in Paris since I'd visited as a girl with Mum. Besides, a crowded restaurant would be infinitely preferable to an awkward supper *à deux* in this empty flat. I could not help but suspect that Oliver's cupboards would have nothing in them. I did not want him to have to humiliate himself by admitting it, to have to reveal to me how he had been living before he came to Corsica.

The restaurant was crammed with diners and dimly lit, clamorous with music and chatter. We were shown to a table in one of the shadowy alcoves that lined one brick wall. Its removal from the central chaos lent it a peculiar intimacy. It was a space intended for lovers, I realized.

While Oliver was speaking to our waiter I studied him. The candlelight acted upon his features: drenched the hollows in shadow, illuminated the sharp crests of cheekbone and brow. What was revealed was an almost terrible, unearthly beauty. Then he turned to me and gave a cautious smile – and became himself again. Still, I thought, how could I have been indifferent to such a face?

We asked for a bottle of wine, and drank it as we studied the menu. On my empty stomach the alcohol went to work quickly, and I began to feel a pleasant haziness descend. With each glass the restaurant around me became incrementally less real, fading gradually to an assemblage of light and noise and colour; of sensation and impression. Finally a waiter freed himself from the melee and came to take our orders.

'So,' Oliver said, when he had gone, 'New York.'

'Yes.' I felt my stomach twist with a sudden rush of apprehension.

'Have you been before?'

'Once,' I said. 'With Mum – though I can barely remember it. I was only a kid. Have you?'

'Yes,' he said. 'Only once.'

'When?'

'Oh,' he said, vaguely, 'quite recently. A couple of years ago.'

Immediately, I understood what this meant. He had been there with her. Perhaps the alcohol was to blame for my tactlessness, but suddenly, inevitably, I had to ask:

'Tell me about your wife. About Isobel.' Speaking her name felt like uttering an incantation – one that could wreak untold results.

'Oh,' he said, warily. 'You don't want to hear any of that.'

'Yes, I do.' I told him. 'I want to know.' Most of me didn't, most of me cringed from it. And, judging by his expression, I was certain that he didn't want to talk about her. Yet it seemed important now that I should hear it all.

Our food arrived then, and Oliver looked relieved. I wondered if he hoped it might distract me from the train of our conversation, but when the waiter had disappeared once more I waited for him to continue.

He took a long sip of his wine. 'She was one of the other students on my course. She was extremely talented, full of ideas – we all thought she would be the star graduate. I was mesmerized by her,' he said, '. . . at least to begin with.'

I tried not to hate her.

Isobel was manic depressive. Oliver didn't find out until they had moved in together after a few months, and he discovered her lithium hidden in an aspirin box.

'Before I lived with her, I think I only saw the "mania" – although she didn't seem manic, exactly, merely . . . alive, spontaneous. It was exciting. I'd never met anyone like her. I didn't see the bad times – though I did think it odd that sometimes she wouldn't surface for days.'

I thought of a student on my course whom I'd learned had the same condition. Because I hadn't known him well I too had only been aware of one side of things – the city-wide treasure hunts he organized, the all-night parties he held in disused warehouses. How could you not become infatuated by someone who seemed to radiate such vitality? Half the student body had been a little in love with him. Though there were also weeks when he wouldn't appear at a single class, and rumours of a failed suicide attempt.

Oliver took another long sip of wine, nearly draining the glass. Immediately the waiter hurried to top it up. 'Then her work started to suffer. She had all these ideas, all this imagination, but she couldn't channel it into her work. Architecture is creative, but it is also extremely practical, and she couldn't marry the two. She stopped taking her lithium because she thought it was stifling her. She became jealous – of my work, and of me, in general – who I was seeing, why I wasn't spending more time with her. I felt guilty when I wasn't with her too, because I knew she was fragile.' He paused. 'I thought – I thought that I would be able to help her, to make her better . . . I thought that loving her would be enough.' He stopped.

'It wasn't?' I ventured.

'No. There was one evening when I got home and I found her . . .' He swallowed. 'Anyway, they said it would never have been enough to kill her.'

With a shock I realized what he meant. Immediately, I remembered the picture he had painted, of a small boy discovering his lifeless mother.

'I started drinking too much,' he went on, 'in that last year. I wasn't sober often, in fact. I hoped it would make me care less – and it did, for a while. Ultimately, though, it made me hate myself more, for being so weak, for coping in the same way my mother had done.'

'Did you leave her?'

'No. In the end she left me. She'd been sleeping with a friend of her parents'. It caused quite a scandal when it all came out – he's a politician, and much older than her. I learned about it the same way everyone else did, in a French tabloid.' He plunged on, as if afraid of stopping. 'I got drunk. I drank so much that, looking back, I was lucky to wake up in the morning. The next day I got on a train and turned up in Corsica without any warning. Grand-père was wonderful about it.'

There was a long pause. Then I steeled myself to ask it: 'Are you still in love with her?'

He shook his head. 'No. I wonder now if I ever was – though I thought I loved her, in the beginning.' He sighed. 'In a way, when I found out that she'd been cheating . . . It sounds terrible, but I was relieved more than anything. She'd made the break that I'd been too scared to, because I'd been so worried about how it might affect her. She's getting married again, I heard.'

'To him – the politician?'

'Yes. Perhaps he'll be better for her than I was – maybe she needs someone older, someone stricter . . . I don't know.'

He looked drained for a second, as though the telling of all of it had cost him a great effort.

'So,' Oliver said, as we walked away from the restaurant, 'have you ever been in love?'

For a moment I considered it – recalling the only

two half-serious boyfriends I'd had: Charlie and the one other who came before him. 'No,' I said. 'I don't believe so. Sometimes . . .' I groped for the words, through the fug of wine, 'sometimes I think I never will . . . that I'll always be alone. I wonder if that's how I'm meant to be.'

Oliver gave a half-smile at this. 'Oh, Kate,' he said, quietly, 'I may have managed to make a disaster of it so far, but even I know that no one's meant to be alone. Least of all someone like you.'

As we wound our way through the dark streets a thought struck me.

'Are we near the river?'

'Not far. Why?'

I hesitated, feeling foolish. 'When I came here with my mother,' I explained, 'she took me down to the river to see how it looked at night, with all the lights.'

'OK,' he said, 'let's go there.' He was kind, I thought then. Coming to the house with me, booking the flight, and now this. It was so strange to think of how afraid I had been of him during those first few days in Corsica. Then again, he was different now – he, too, had undergone some sort of transformation.

We wandered through the old streets of the district, past the shadowy shops with their grilles pulled down and the odd bar bleeding music and talk into the night air. Then we were at the river.

It was as I had remembered: the black water, the

329

alchemical rush of gold beneath the surface. Across the river was the Left Bank, but before that was the glittering giant of the Île Saint-Louis. As a girl it had seemed an incredible place to me, an enchanted island that might at any moment uproot and sail downstream. Perhaps a little of that magic, unique to childhood, had faded, but as if in compensation, the lights were multiplied tenfold by a mist of tears.

'Thank you,' I said to Oliver.

He turned to look at me. 'Are you OK?'

'Yes,' I said, 'I'm fine.' He looked away, understanding.

'She sounds wonderful,' Oliver said, as we were making our way back to the apartment.

I nodded. 'I wish I could be more like her.'

'In what way?'

'She was so brave.'

'But I think you are, too. What you're doing, here in Paris: that is brave.' And then he said, 'I'm sure she had her flaws, too.'

At first, I was outraged. How dare he say that of her? Mum hadn't had any flaws. She had been more than a mother to me: she had been a best friend. Friends at school had told me how envious they were of this. She was chic in a way that other mothers weren't – and generous, too. On my sixteenth birthday she had rented a room at the Groucho Club, and we had sat at a candlelit table and eaten grown-up food – fillet steak and dauphinoise potatoes – and drunk champagne.

Then, in a flash, I thought of Mum missing Parents'

Evening, year after year, because it clashed with performance dates; and the time she'd forgotten to collect me
from my Geography field trip, because a rehearsal had
overrun. Those weren't flaws, though, surely – that was
simply being busy. Still – the strangest thing – some
part of me found it reassuring.

Back in the flat, Oliver asked if I wanted a *digestif*
before going to bed. I hesitated: I was tired, and more
than a little drunk, but also very awake. My mind was
alive with this somewhat altered image of Mum that
he had provoked: an image at once disturbing and,
strangely, comforting.

I sat down in his bare sitting room while he found
a bottle of wine and two glasses then came to sit beside
me – closer than he might have done, I suspected, had
he been completely sober.

'I've had too much to drink now,' he said, echoing
my thoughts, and paused, as though he were finding
his next words. 'But there's something I want to tell
you, Kate.' He'd been swaying slightly earlier as we
walked back, but his gaze now was intent, absolutely
focused.

'OK.' I suddenly felt quite sober.

'Well,' he said, 'I think you're great.'

'Oh – thank you.' It struck me that 'great' was possibly
the blandest epithet he could have used.

'No,' he said, as if realizing this, 'not *great* – I'm not
thinking properly. What I mean is that you're different.

In the best way,' he hastened to add. 'You're quiet, but you aren't shy . . . and you're watchful' – there it was, that word again – 'you see things differently, you understand them, in a way most people don't. Am I making any sense?'

'I think so,' I told him, though I wasn't entirely sure.

'What I mean,' he went on, enunciating carefully, 'is that I couldn't believe I'd told you – a stranger – all of those things, things I haven't even spoken to Grand-père about. I've been thinking about it . . . and I've come to the conclusion it's because of, well, how you are.'

'Oh,' I said again.

'I'm sorry I followed you to Paris,' he said.

'Is that what you were doing?' He nodded, and I felt a thrill go through me.

'Why did you?' I asked, as lightly as I could.

'I don't know.' He took a deep breath, let it out unsteadily. 'No, I do. I couldn't help myself. I sensed from the beginning that it was a bad idea to spend too much time near you.' He shrugged. 'Once I knew about your mother, I understood that you must be suffering – and I . . . well, you know now what a disaster my life has been. And yet I don't seem to be able to leave you alone.'

'Oh.'

'I think I knew,' he said, slowly, 'right from the start, when I picked you up at the airport.'

'No,' I told him. 'No, you didn't. You were horrible to me.'

'That's exactly it,' he said. 'It was the only thing I could do.'

He put down his glass, and I could feel his eyes on me. Possibility was there in the room with us now: thrilling, tangible – dangerous.

'Look at me, Kate,' he said, quietly. So I did, and found he was now very near to me. So close, in fact, that I saw for the first time a faint trail of freckles across his nose, and noticed the extraordinary length of the dark eyelashes that should have been feminine but were somehow absolutely not. His gaze dropped to my mouth, and I felt the pressure of it there upon my skin.

'I don't think,' I said, unsteadily, 'this is a good idea.' But even as I spoke I hoped he would prove me wrong.

Oliver nodded. 'I know,' he said, 'it's a terrible idea.' He didn't move any further away. 'And yet' – his gaze still on my mouth – 'I don't seem to be able to do anything about it.' The moment stretched to an unbearable tautness, and he moved even closer, the spice of the wine on his breath intoxicating as any drug.

Then something in me snapped. He had just told me about his divorce, for God's sake. We were surrounded by evidence of it: the misery symbolically present in the boxes of possessions that lined the hallway. With a great, wrenching effort of willpower, I put down my glass and stood up.

'I think I should say goodnight,' I said. 'But – thank you . . . for today.'

I walked unsteadily down the corridor to my bedroom,

moving with the slow, difficult steps of someone drugged. This was the only way it could be, I told myself, trying to think clearly. Anything else would be disastrous.

As I closed the door behind me, I heard his footsteps. Despite myself, I felt a leap of pure exhilaration in my chest. I opened the door a fraction and looked at him. He was lit from behind, his face in darkness. 'Kate,' he said, and his voice was hoarse. 'Please . . .'

Then he was pushing the door and his mouth was on mine. That first taste, so long in coming, was unutterably sweet. We fell back together into the room, and this time I knew there would be no stopping. I remember that I thought – rather matter-of-factly – *there's nothing to be done about it*. After that, I don't recall thinking much at all.

When I woke, Oliver was nowhere to be seen and neither was the pile of clothes that he had shed the night before – only my black dress, coiled there like a spilled slick of oil on the floorboards. For a moment I wondered if I had imagined it all. It seemed even stranger and less plausible in the light of day than it had in the small hours, as I had waited to fall asleep.

But no: I could make out the distinct imprint of where he had lain beside me. There was the way my body felt, too: the pleasurable ache, the faintest trace of his scent. There was even the faint pink reminder of his stubble against my collarbone, where he had kissed and gently bitten the skin there.

We ate breakfast together in the café beneath his apartment, and we were awkward with one another, overly polite – and then, when my taxi came, unsure of how to go about the business of saying goodbye.

I wasn't stupid. I think we both knew that it couldn't be easy between us; that there was no way of telling what would come of it. In many ways, what had happened was the exact thing I had feared, what I had been guarding myself against in the months since Mum's death. In my defence, it had taken me utterly by surprise, had ambushed me when I had been least expecting it.

This was what happened, I thought, when you let someone beyond the barrier you had set up: you opened up the possibility for pain. Yet, despite my fears, I could not make myself regret it. Because I had not felt that close to being happy in a long time.

PART THREE

A Girl with a Secret

32

Paris, September 1930

On the left bank of the Seine, not far from the shadow of the Panthéon, lives a young woman who is something of an enigma to those who have noticed her recent appearance here. She arrived one evening in August, smartly dressed if travel-worn, and asked for a room at Madame Fourrier's.

Fourrier's is, as many say, 'whatever you want it to be'. By day it is a café – a place to stop for breakfast or a morning *café crème*, a lunchtime *potage*, an afternoon snack. In the evening it is the most happening bar in the Quartier Latin.

The food is plentiful and cheap, a draw for those who can no longer afford to eat in the more expensive establishments. The crowd is a heterogeneous mix of professors and students from the nearby Sorbonne, writers, painters, elderly men and their mistresses, workmen and the occasional tourist, delighted by their authentic discovery.

People live here, too. The upper three floors of the building comprise the rooms where Madame Fourrier takes lodgers. The rooms are small and neatly, economically appointed – the topmost, the attic room, being the smallest of them all.

Madame Fourrier is as well known as her establishment: a big Belgesse with a broad, amiable face and a fringe of frizzy, reddish-blonde hair. She is loud and ardent, and often exacting of her hard-working staff, but those who know her well understand that this apparent fierceness conceals a heart of gold.

At first, Madame Fourrier wasn't sure what to make of the girl who turned up on her doorstep in search of a place to lodge. She was far too pretty for her own good, albeit on the scrawny side, and with an agitation to her that spoke of flight from some form of unpleasantness.

Madame F. is not one to turn away a young woman so evidently in need of a safe place to stay, but she has learned to be careful. Only last year she rented a room to another pretty young girl, only to discover that she was using her quarters – and the late-night clientele of the brasserie downstairs – for the most insalubrious activities. It was a shame, Madame F. thinks, that she had to ask the tart to leave. She always paid her rent so promptly.

The new lodger has been accepted on a short-term trial period. The landlady knew that she would be quicker this time at spotting anything untoward, but the new girl does not appear to have any friends, let alone acquaintances of the sort her predecessor did. She keeps her cards close to her chest, this one. Madame F. is curious about her and yet she knows, instinctively, not to probe too far. Unmistakably not French, though she has never said as much. Her accent is odd – Swiss, perhaps? – and she occupies that hinterland between competency and fluency, without the native's grasp of idiosyncrasy and slang. Alice – that is what she is called. Her name is all she is prepared to tell of herself. Despite this reticence, Madame F. can't help liking her. She is a mystery indeed.

On the second day, the girl came down and asked for a job. Had she any experience? A little, she said. To judge by her performance, this had been an exaggeration. She was a terrible waitress: didn't know the first thing about making coffee, pulling beer, or even arranging the linen cloths so that the creases met the corners of the tables evenly. Anyone would think that she had been brought up in a barn. She is a quick learner, though. Already she can carry three plates at once, one in each hand and the third held precariously in the crook of her arm. She only rarely drops a glass. She will never be an *excellent* waitress, but she may yet make a competent one. Besides, she is a draw, Madame F. has noticed, for some of the clientele. It is, perhaps, her strangeness that attracts them: the combination of those unusual looks, that odd accent, and the air of mystery that surrounds her.

She is clever, too. Not at waitressing, admittedly, but Madame F. has seen the way she stops to read the newspapers discarded by patrons – in French and, oddly enough, English. She'd read them from cover to cover if she were allowed to, Madame F. is certain. There are books as well: Madame F. saw them when she came up to show the girl how to boil an egg – honestly, *boil an egg!* – after seeing smoke pluming from beneath the door. She buys them from the bookshops with her meagre pay.

There was one other thing she saw, too. A beautiful drawing – a drawing of the girl herself, no less, tacked to the wall by her bed. With short hair and odd clothes – a rich woman's clothes, if Madame F. was not mistaken.

Yes, a girl with a secret, certainly.

33

I stayed in a hotel in the East Village, and hardly slept the first night, despite the jet lag. I lay there listening to the hooting of car horns, the laughter, shouts and music bleeding through from the street and the roar and rattle of the subway beneath me. Nothing could have been further removed from the blue quiet of those Corsican nights that had been punctuated only by the sound of the wind and the chirruping of crickets in the maquis.

When morning came I lounged in bed, feeling gritty-eyed and almost drunk with tiredness. My whole mission felt even more surreal now than it had done at the departure gate in Charles de Gaulle.

A toasted sandwich and a black coffee in an Italian

greasy spoon a couple of streets away went some way towards restoring me. I checked my reflection in the washroom there and combed my hair, rather pointlessly, as it quickly rearranged itself into its habitual tangle. For some reason it had suddenly become important that I should be looking my best. It bothered me that there were dark circles beneath my eyes, that any colour I had managed to pick up in Corsica seemed to have disappeared overnight. In the halogen light, my skin had the bluish tinge of skimmed milk.

I liked the East Village, I decided, making my way to the subway at Astor Place. It was raw and unformed back then – a creative's Mecca, not unlike modern-day Brooklyn. The phone boxes here weren't plastered with phone-sex ads but with flyers for exhibitions and ad hoc installations in flats, warehouses and vacant lots. Art was visible on the street, too: en route to the platform I saw a Keith Haring-like mural of nude commuters carrying briefcases.

New York then was a cheaper, rougher place than it is now, and the Village was almost unrecognizable from what it has become. At least, that's my experience. Travelling back recently, I saw bijou espresso bars and boutiques, sleek four-wheel drives, loft conversions. You could find the imprint of the old place, if you looked carefully. Or could you? Was, perhaps, the gritty appearance of the record shop I found on Bleecker Street merely clever, nostalgic ersatz? It was difficult to say.

It was also different to the city I had known when I

visited with Mum. She had been an honorary guest at a special Christmas exhibition by the New York Ballet, and we had stayed in the St Regis, a white-and-gilt wedding cake of a hotel on Fifth Avenue. The city had glittered with new-fallen snow: as deliriously unreal as the one that lived inside the snow-dome Mum had given me on the plane. We had come on one other occasion, in summer – though I had been too young to remember much of that. Now that Mum was gone, I found it hard to accept that there were memories like this, that would be for ever lost to me.

It seemed that I was bound to return to that world of old New York splendour. The apartment was in one of those huge blocks that soar into the sky on the east side of Central Park, and I was immediately intimidated, understanding that I was about to enter into a rarefied sphere. These buildings housed the inconceivably wealthy – the old, moneyed American families, scions of the dynasties that had built New York. I knew suddenly how Tom must have felt, walking up to the front door of Chebworth Manor. I recalled what Oliver had said about the townhouse in Paris: Alice had clearly returned to the life of privilege.

I thought the porter would look at me askance, but when I gave my name he smiled as though we knew one another and swept me inside with a bow. Inside, the building was even more awe-inspiring than without, and there was more marble, more gilt, more baroque splendour than I remembered at the St Regis.

I was taken up to her floor in one of those lifts in which you aren't allowed to press the buttons yourself: a liveried member of staff does it for you. When the doors pinged open at the top, a single door faced us beyond a carpeted antechamber.

'Is the way to the apartment through there?' I asked the attendant, bemused. 'Which number is it?'

'That is the door to the apartment. She has this floor and the next one up.'

'Oh.'

I pressed the doorbell and waited for so long that I was tempted to ring again. At last I heard quick footsteps behind the door and it swung open to reveal a tall woman in a tailored tweed suit.

She spoke before I could introduce myself. 'Hi, Kate. I'm Julie.' She was American. 'I'm Célia's housekeeper.'

Then a voice called from within, high and slightly quavering. 'Is it her, Julie?'

Julie smiled and beckoned me in. 'Would you like anything to drink?' she asked, as we passed through an elegant, sage-green anteroom. I opened my mouth, but was suddenly lost for words. Julie seemed to understand. 'Well,' she said, gently, 'I usually bring her coffee at eleven, in half an hour, so you could have something then.' As she spoke I noticed a picture hanging behind her – a charcoal sketch of a street scene that, judging by the unmistakable shape of the fire hydrant in the corner, had to be New York. The style was by now familiar to me: I recognized that sparseness of line, that

346

expert but restrained treatment of light and shadow. And there in the corner was the small hieroglyph I knew so well: those two linked initials.

We were moving through into open space, entering the great lofty sitting room of the apartment proper: high-ceilinged and airy, thanks to the huge windows that looked on to the park. Of the other three walls, only the smallest and most necessary of spaces remained between the artworks that had been hung upon them. The effect should have been one of chaos, and yet it was not. Or rather, it was the best sort of chaos: carni-valesque, a celebration of colour and human creativity.

A tiny figure perched in an armchair facing us, the light coming in behind her haloing her white head. Her smallness was, if anything, emphasized by the size and clamour of the room in which she sat.

'Hello, Kate,' she said.

My voice, when I spoke, sounded not at all like my own. 'Hello, Alice.' Perhaps I should have called her Célia. That was her new name: Alice was a person from the past. Yet that person, the one Thomas Stafford had loved, was the one I knew.

Julie moved across to her and plumped the cushion at her back, helping her to sit up in her chair. Alice was far frailer than Stafford, I saw. I couldn't imagine how it could be that she still travelled between New York and Paris; it was hard to believe that she ever left the chair for long. She was no longer slim, as Stafford had described her, she was skeletal: delicate as a bird's bone.

For all that, her expression was alert, her gaze upon me interested and alive. How I wish I had inherited those eyes. Mine are also grey, but to leave it there is to mislead: a comparison of lead with silver. Hers had a unique luminosity, like mother-of-pearl, their brilliance undimmed by age. She was dressed immaculately, and yet there was something bohemian about her appearance – in the bright splash of the blue silk scarf about her throat, the golden bangles that clattered up her arm as she reached towards me.

I moved closer and she grasped one of my hands in both of hers, half a handshake, half a caress. Her skin was cool, as thin and dry as tissue paper.

'So you are Kate,' she said. 'You are Kate, and you have come to see me, at last.' A pause. Her eyes were travelling my face, and I felt completely exposed to that silver gaze. I fought the urge to step back, to lower my head in case she found me wanting.

'You are like her, unmistakably, and yet I think, though it is a boast to say it, that you are even more like me. Or as I once was.'

I couldn't speak. I looked beyond her to the table beside her. On its surface sat a pair of reading glasses, a stack of books, and a photograph. It was my mother, performing in *Swan Lake*. She was Odette, in that moment when she emerges from the lake a woman for the first time, no longer a swan. Mum looked as beautiful and ethereal as I had ever seen her: hardly real. I hadn't seen that image for a long time, but it was a well-known shot. Alice must have found it somewhere and bought a print, I realized. The idea that this woman, surrounded by the otherwise richness of her life, had had to buy a photo of her own child was almost unbearable. But she had left her behind, I reminded myself. Whatever Marguerite had said, that fact was incontrovertible.

I looked back at Alice and she was studying me closely. 'I imagine you must have much to ask me,' she said.

'Yes. I . . .' In the end, I asked the only question that I could think of, even though it was probably too soon to ask it. It was the only question that seemed important. 'Why did you leave my mother?' I said. 'I mean . . . I know you were young, and . . .'

There was a long pause, and then Alice smiled, sadly. 'But, you see, I never did leave her.'

'I thought—'

'Or at least, not knowingly.'

'What do you mean?'

'I think, perhaps, that I have rather a lot to explain.'

Julie chose that moment to enter with a pot of coffee and wafer-thin almond-studded biscuits. She poured two cups, and left the room. As we drank the silence was punctuated only by the ring of our delicate china cups on their saucers. Then Alice finished her tiny biscuit and placed her coffee carefully down before her.

'You must understand,' she said, suddenly, 'I had always intended to bring her with me.'

'That was what Mr Stafford said.'

'Yes – because I told him as much.'

'So how did she get left behind?'

I'd anticipated excuses that I might, perhaps, be ready to forgive, knowing that she was so young and undoubtedly so afraid. She would not be the only woman to have acted as she did. But I could not have anticipated what came next.

'I did not know that I had left her – not in the way you think. You see, they told me that she had died.'

34

She remembers pain: a great deal of pain. Followed by a total absence of it, of any sensation, a drifting in shadows, a sinking through dark water.

It seemed years, centuries, aeons.

They tell her it was only a couple of days. They tell her that she lost a lot of blood, so much that she had nearly died. But the baby – where is it? She must try and rest, they say.

35

New York, September 1986

Alice spoke into the silence.

'The birth was difficult. There was a complication that the doctor hadn't foreseen. I was too narrow. They should have performed a Caesarean, but no one had realized, and once the labour had started it was too late.

'I lost a lot of blood, and I am sure that I was barely conscious for much of it. It was a few days, apparently, before I was able to understand anything anyone said. I was told that I had come close to losing my own life, and I do not think that was untrue. As for the baby . . . the air supply had been cut off for too long. The doctor had explained to my mother that the child had been unable to breathe, and had suffocated inside me.

'Perhaps, if I had been less weak, less confused, I might have asked more questions, though I'm not sure it would have done any good. They had the story sewn up, and I had no reason to doubt my mother. We had never got along, but I had no cause to suspect that she might try to do me harm.'

'But that's monstrous—'

'It was unforgivable. She wasn't evil, my mother, I want to make that clear. I'm certain that, terrible as it may appear, she didn't act out of a desire to cause me pain.'

'To do such a thing, though – to pretend – that *was* evil.'

'I think that, as she saw it, she was doing me a great service. She was protecting me from shame.'

36

Chebworth, July 1930

Lady Hexford sips her coffee and touches her blonde hair with an elegant white hand. She is looking particularly radiant today, astonishingly young. Her head and face are bathed in light from the long windows, and she survives the sun's exposing rays well: her forehead remains relatively unlined, her profile taut. From the right angle she still looks like a girl – not much older than the Sargent portrait of herself as a sixteen-year-old debutante that hangs in the drawing room.

Her daughter, by contrast, is a dismal sight: her skin blotched where it isn't sallow – the invalid's complexion. Her cheeks are gaunt, her hair lank. These things, of course, are eminently reversible, and Lady Hexford is keen to emphasize this.

Appraising her daughter, she says, 'Next week, I shall take you to have your hair cut in town. I can't understand this vogue for "shingling", but anything would be better than what you have at the moment, which is no style at all.'

Alice stares down at her egg. The bald, pink dome of the shell defeats her. She picks up a triangle of toast and eats it laboriously.

Lady Hexford watches her and gives a small sigh. 'It's time we returned to London. We need to have you seen. They all think you're recovering from glandular fever. Thank goodness dropped waists are still the thing – it will make our task rather easier.' No one, Lady Eversley explains, save for a select few members of staff, and she and Alice herself, know anything of what has taken place at Chebworth Manor. She sits back, good-naturedly, as her boiled egg is swept away and then replaced with some ceremony, its cap neatly excised, the yolk beginning to bleed its way through a fissure in the white. 'Any longer than it has been and I am sure people will start to talk. So we must have you seen at a function or two . . .'

They may talk of the Modern, Lady Eversley says. Girls now may drink as much as men. The clothes may have changed. But a bastard remains a bastard. An unmarried girl who has a baby is still ripe for ostracism: a social leper.

'Which was it?' Alice asks.

'I'm sorry, I don't understand.'

'A boy or a girl?'

'It was a girl.' Lady Hexford gives another small sigh. 'It will not do to be morbid about this, Alice. You must move on, return to what was always the proper path for you. We will treat this . . . this entire episode as a momentary aberration. A lucky escape, in fact. Such an outcome . . . don't you see? You have been given the chance to preserve your dignity, to begin anew. Think,' she says, as a passing shot, 'of your stepfather, of the damage this whole affair could have done, had it not gone thus. To speak of this to anyone would cause harm beyond what it would do to you. We must remember to be selfless.'

37

New York, September 1986

'So how did you find out about Mum?' I asked Alice. 'How did you discover that she didn't die, after all?'

'I went to see my mother when I learned that she was very unwell. She had suffered a gradual mental breakdown – no doubt brought on by the continuing shame over my stepfather's fall from grace. For someone with such a fear of scandal, I am sure she'd had rather a hard time of it. There was money, but the humiliation would have been terrible for her.

'I hadn't had any contact with her for twenty years. I read about her illness in a newspaper, if you can believe it. I'm not sure exactly why I decided I had to go, but I know I would not have forgiven myself if I hadn't.

'She was completely changed from the woman I had known. Meek, fearful – a rather pathetic figure. Perhaps it was a result of the illness, or simply of the scandal that had caused it in the first place, but it seemed that she now questioned all that she had been certain of before. But she was so altered that, when she told me, it was as though she were speaking of the actions of another. My anger with her felt thwarted. I knew then that I had to try to free myself from it, or I would carry it for life. I had learned that much from experience.

'I was forty-one years old when I learned the truth, and your mother was by then almost the same age as I'd been when I had her.'

Julie entered with a tray bearing lunch, and I was amazed to discover that more than two hours had slipped by without my noticing. The spread was almost preposterously British: the sandwiches were cucumber, the crusts neatly excised. It was a translation of English custom from across the water and from an earlier time, unweathered by exposure to the customs of modern Britain. There was lemonade, too, in a cut-glass pitcher. We were silent as we ate. I was too stunned by what Alice had told me to think of anything to say. Of all the things I had imagined I would never have expected that.

Alice picked her way through two tiny triangles, and

swallowed as much of the lemonade as a bird might drink of water from a leaf. When she was finished, she passed a hand in front of her eyes and seemed to sink further into the chair, as though the effort had sapped her last reserves of strength.

'I'll go,' I said, standing. 'I can see that you're exhausted.'

She made no attempt to deny it, but said, 'I am so lucky that you have come to find me, Kate. I have always hoped that, by some miracle, your mother might turn up at my door, and then, when you were born, that you would, too. That I might get that one chance to meet you. I never allowed myself to believe it would happen though.'

'I'm glad too,' I told her, conscious of a tightness in my chest, trying not to think about the fact that only half of her wish had come true.

'You'll come back?' she asked, a little querulously. 'Tomorrow?'

'Yes, of course.'

'Good. I will look forward to it so much,' she said. 'Thank you.'

'For what?'

'For not judging too harshly, when you didn't know the truth. For giving me the chance to redeem myself.'

I felt guilt then, sharp and sour, because I *had* judged her harshly, because I had been unable to stop myself from believing the worst.

359

'When you come tomorrow,' she said, 'I think we should go for a walk. What do you say?'

I couldn't help glancing down at her legs, which seemed frail and misshapen inside her loose trousers, but I nodded, all the same.

She gestured towards the park. 'Let's meet by the boating lake. Do you know the one?'

I started to shake my head, but something surfaced from the depths of memory: eating ice cream from a glass flute with a silver spoon, watching through the windows as the gliding triangles of colour moved like shapes dancing in a kaleidoscope. It wasn't the boating pond in Battersea Park, I knew, nor that one in the Tuileries where Mum and I had drunk hot chocolate together from Styrofoam cups. It must, I decided, have been Central Park, that first time we'd visited the city – the time I'd believed beyond memory. So I nodded. 'I think I do,' I said.

I wandered back to my hotel, trying to reconcile the person I had come to know via Stafford – that girl so full of youth and vigour – with the old woman I had met. Stafford's recollections had so captivated me that I had failed to consider the changes that the passing of time would have wrought, ageing her almost beyond recognition from that figure in the sketch. The sleek black hair faded to bone white, the supple lines of her frame diminished to brittleness.

To see her there in her chair, so small and frail, had been a great shock. Nevertheless, once she had started talking, this had lessened, because it was evident that there was immense strength in her still. Her voice was not an old woman's, weak and tremulous, but deep and clear – like those silver eyes, it had not aged with the rest of her.

38

Paris, November 1930

The new waitress at Bistro Fourrier is largely ignorant of the interest and speculation her arrival has caused. She is aware only of the peculiar delight of being mistress of her own destiny, answerable to no one but herself.

Alice likes the room in the attic, this low triangular space beneath the twin slopes of the roof. It is so far removed from the vast bedroom in London where she, like a blot of ink in that cavernous white expanse, craved privacy. A place, however small, truly hers: somewhere free from the intrusions of the maids, her mother, or even – God forbid – her stepbrother.

From the small bedroom window she can see for miles: across the slate roofs of the Latin Quarter in their variations of grey, lavender and mother-of-pearl green, past the dome of the Panthéon and the bluebell-shaped turret of St Étienne-du-Mont, as far even as Sacré-Cœur, gleaming a burnished silver above the city.

Sometimes, in the quiet of the early morning, Alice thinks of Tom, with the same tentative, gently self-destructive manner as someone probing a bruise. On several occasions she has picked up pen and paper to write to him, and her various attempts to explain her actions litter the small desk in the corner of the room. None, thus far, have been sent.

In the opposite corner from the desk is a washstand where Alice performs her morning toilette with the aid of one of her few extravagances – a small sliver of soap scented with Attar of Rose. Then she steps into her uniform: a fitted black dress, a plain serge apron. When she dresses in the mornings she thinks, sometimes, of Chebworth – of how those in uniform were like a different race, a separate species. How they would gawp to see her now, all of them.

At six o'clock, she makes her way carefully down the three flights of stairs, past the rooms occupied by the other lodgers. She enjoys the atmosphere of anonymous slumber. She even rather likes the peculiar smell of the place: creeping damp and cigarettes and the cheap perfume of strangers.

Downstairs in the bar, whilst the rest of the city sleeps, Madame Fourrier will make them each a short, dark coffee with a thick sediment in the bottom. Alice will sip hers gingerly, wincing even as she enjoys the strange bitter savour, whilst her employer tosses hers back with finessed nonchalance, slamming the cup into its saucer with a clatter.

Alice relishes these early hours before opening, the hush of the square outside, the sleeping buildings. The only sounds are within, it seems – their voices, occasionally, and the clang of cutlery landing in the metal bucket after Alice polishes it, the tick of the clock, the whine of the hot water in the pipes. It is a time for quiet, companionable industry.

She has grown fond of big, red, loud Madame Fourrier – which is not to say that she isn't slightly afraid of her. In her forthrightness, her undemonstrative kindness and her small eccentricities, the Belgian woman reminds her of Aunt Margaret. She is a woman who is proud of her aloneness, who draws from it strength and authority.

Some of the customers at Fourrier's are known to Alice by sight, if not by name. These are the regulars: people who come back almost daily to sample Madame Fourrier's brand of Belgian cooking – her eel stews and mussel broths, her superior hot chocolates, her waffles with their thick crust of caramelized sugar.

There is the professor of literature who comes for his baked eggs every morning before cycling off on his ancient bicycle, bound for the nearby Sorbonne. He stops Alice as she takes his order one day and tells her that he is becoming quite alarmed by the version of the language – 'polluted with Belgian horrors' – that she is imbibing from Madame F. 'You must read,' he tells her, 'it will fight against the infection.' The next morning he hands her a canvas bag, extraordinarily heavy, crammed with books. She lines them up on the shelf next to her bed, where, along with the volumes she has acquired herself, they provide the only real colour in the room. In such a small space they are luminous, jewel-bright in the low light.

Then there is the writer, an American, who lives in a flat across the square, but insists he has to remove himself from his apartment in order to work. 'The silence is deafening,' he told Alice once. 'In there, the work becomes all-important, and therefore impossible. Here, in the café, with the noise, it is merely another part of the scene – small, unexceptional . . . and hence achievable.' He writes, longhand, in notebooks, but often 'work' seems to consist of little more than staring out at the square, drawing greedily on a cigarette.

The writer, Madame Fourrier tells Alice, used to be part of a far larger scene here in Paris, but many of his former cronics have moved on now – back to America, to London, to Marrakech. 'They would take over one corner of the bar,' she tells her, 'for a whole day . . . long into the evening, until they'd got drunk and foolish and I had to tell them to leave. There were always some very attractive girls that dressed like boys.' She raises her gingery eyebrows expressively. 'Those English and American girls. So modern.'

One night, the American writer asks Alice to have a drink of pastis with him at his table. She watches in fascination as the water he pours into their glasses turns the spirit an exquisite bluish white. They speak in English because, despite having lived here for several years, his French is abominable.

'You fascinate me,' he tells her, with no preamble.

'In what way?'

'That accent. I may be a Yank, but I know that's not the way I'd expect a French waitress to talk, even if she's talking in English. You *are* English, aren't you?'

Alice smiles and takes a sip of her drink, but doesn't deny it.

'I knew it. Cut glass, that's what they call it, I believe. You speak like a duchess. Are you a duchess?'

Alice shakes her head and laughs, partly in an attempt to convince him of how far from the mark he is, and partly in secret recognition of how close he is to the truth.

'The way you hold yourself, your profile – there's something regal about it. I think I'll write about you, if you don't mind. The English aristocrat, slumming it as a Paris waitress. I like that.'

'Well, I'd be honoured. Even though you've got it all wrong.'

'You don't want to set me straight?'

'No. Surely it's better that way? It leaves you more room for the fiction.'

He chuckles and touches his glass to hers.

When she isn't needed for serving, Alice begins to work some evenings as an amanuensis for the writer. She uses his Corona, which they set up on one of the tables in the quietest corner of the bar. The going is slow at first – she has to ask him to repeat sentences and occasionally whole paragraphs, and the keys stick and the ribbon jams. But after a couple of weeks it becomes easier, and she realizes that she is able to type without thinking about it: to type better, in fact, if she lets her fingers move almost of their own accord.

The work isn't paid, but Alice earns enough from the waitressing to manage her rent. And the writer introduces her to Paris by night. They attend parties where men dance with men and women dressed in three-piece suits kiss one another openly. They watch the dancers flit and shimmy across the stage at the Bal Négresse to the beating of drums and the howling of the saxophone. They visit a nightclub called La Coupoule – where the writer's current lover works as a barman. Here they dance and drink until an egg-yolk dawn has broken on the horizon and spread pale gold along the Seine and the men who come to fish the water near the Île Saint-Louis have begun to unpack their kit and bed in for the morning's sport.

On these mornings, viewed through tired eyes, the city is at its most beautiful. At the same time it is, for Alice, tinged with melancholy. Why? Perhaps because the mad distractions of the night are over, because there are still several hours before she is needed at work . . .

leaving nothing for her to do but think. So it is now, more than any other time, that she remembers what, or specifically *who*, she has left behind. He who would appreciate this beauty even more than she – who would, no doubt, attempt to harness it for her.

Not for the first time, she wonders if she should write to him. But what to say? So difficult, with this lie between them. What would be the good in it? What would be the point of having started this new life? Of having left him free to find greatness? Because she knows that he will be great.

So she comforts herself by reading the papers, scouring the arts pages for any mention of his name. It is only a matter of time before it will appear, she is certain of that.

39

I looked up from my cappuccino. We sat in the café that I remembered, bathed in September sun and watching the gaudy boats glide and turn before us. Alice had come in an electric wheelchair: Julie had escorted her here and then left. 'I know I spoke of walking,' she said, 'but I'm afraid I meant it rather euphemistically. Still, one can pretend. It does much the same thing: the fresh air, the sights, the sense of being out in the world, exploring.' For all that she was dressed exquisitely, as before, and the Pucci scarf that she'd tied about her neck almost made up for the lack of colour in her complexion.

Alice seemed energized by the life about us: she watched

369

the couples in boats and the families chattering at nearby
tables with a kind of hungry delight. I, by contrast, had
slept badly again and felt I would have far preferred
the hush of her airy drawing room to the chaos of
Central Park on a Saturday. My mind had been too full
that night to switch off. I had been unable to prevent
myself from imagining various scenarios in which things
had turned out differently. Scenarios in which Alice's
mother hadn't committed her crime, or in which Evie's
conscience had forced her to tell my mother about the
letter.

'So you have met my Tom?' Alice asked me now.

'Yes.' I looked up. 'Mr Stafford was kind enough to
invite me to stay with him.

'How is he?'

'Very well.' I thought of his vigour and health, of
how much better he seemed to be faring in old age than
she.

She smiled. 'That is good to hear. And you managed
to contact him. I have learned from experience, you see,
that it is rather difficult these days.'

She said it lightly, but I wasn't fooled. I thought of
that postcard Stafford had kept so carefully, and never
found himself able to answer.

'Yes,' I said. 'I wrote to him, and I sent him the
drawing – the one of you by the lake.'

She brightened at this. 'You saw the drawing?'

'Yes.'

'Did she see it, too? June?'

370

'No, I'm afraid . . . no, she didn't.'

'So she never knew?'

The pain was so naked upon her face that I considered lying – considered whether, perhaps, I might say that when Mum had boarded that plane she knew that she had not, as a child, been cast aside. But I couldn't do that. I shook my head, then immediately felt compelled to add: 'But she was happy, you know. Content. It didn't make her a victim.'

'No, I can see that.' Alice sipped her coffee carefully. 'I was – am – so terribly proud of her. I wish I could have known her, or met her, just once. Perhaps it's selfish of me to feel that. Perhaps it was best that she never knew about me, that I never had the chance to explain. I wouldn't have wanted to jeopardize what she had with her stepmother.'

'It was wrong of Evie, not to tell her.'

She shook her head. 'I'd like to believe that, of course I would. But was it, really? Would I have acted differently, in her position? I wonder.'

We listened to the splashes and the screams of delighted children for several moments.

'Is he still working?' Alice asked, suddenly.

'Yes,' I told her. 'He's still painting, every day – I believe.'

'It is how I imagine him. On his wild isle, with his canvases, surrounded by the wind and water – it is exactly the sort of place where he would be happiest. You liked him? Did you get along?'

371

'Yes, very well.'

Alice seemed pleased by this. 'I thought you would. You're quite like him, in many ways. Funny, because I always thought expression, gesture, that sort of thing came from nurture, not nature. Perhaps they too are in the genes.'

This didn't make sense. 'You're speaking of us as if we're related.'

Alice looked at me, and there was the longest pause. Then she said: 'But, my dear, you are. Tom Stafford is your grandfather.'

I felt as if I'd fallen down the rabbit hole. 'No,' I said. 'No, he isn't.'

She gave a laugh then, more surprised than amused.

'My grandfather is the man you met in Venice – Julien.'

'That is what Tom believes – it's what I told him – but it was a lie. I never did have those sort of relations with Julien – though certainly he tried.' She sighed. 'So, you see, everything I told Tom that day in the garden was true . . . except the part that wasn't.'

'*Why?*' I asked, wildly. 'Why would you do that to him?' I saw the couple at the next table glance our way and managed, with an effort, to lower my voice. 'I think it broke his heart.' It sounded drastic, but I realized the truth of it even as I spoke.

'I know.' Her voice was small. 'It was a necessary cruelty . . . if you can believe such a thing. And if you can accept that, perhaps you can also understand that I did it for him. You've met Tom, Kate. You know what sort of man he is. He would have given it all up, everything he hoped for. He would have continued doing that job he detested in order to support us. I am sure that he would have resented me, in the end.'

'But what about afterwards, when you thought the baby had died?'

'Why make it his tragedy too? It would have been a needless cruelty. I want you to know something, Kate. It wasn't only his heart that was broken when I told that lie.'

I couldn't stop myself from going further. 'If you had kept her, my mum, if they hadn't taken her to the orphanage . . . would you have confessed to him eventually?'

'Yes, I think so. I wanted to leave him free to do the thing he loved. I'd planned to run away with the baby. I knew that we would go to Paris. Then, maybe, when Tom had had the chance to realize his hopes, perhaps I would have told him. Not in order to bind him to us, but because he deserved to hear the truth.'

'How did you know it would be Paris?'

'When I was sixteen years old, my aunt—'

'Lady Margaret,' I supplied.

She looked at me in surprise. 'Yes, Aunt Margaret took me to Paris, for a weekend. We went to her favourite café, near the Boulevard du Montparnasse. The place was full of interesting sorts, but there was one woman in particular. She was by herself, and she had ordered a coffee. There was a small dog sleeping at her feet, and she had a book, held up in her right hand, like this—' She mimed it. 'I thought to myself: "That is the person I want to be. Someone who can sit on her own in a café without being answerable to anyone."' She smiled. 'You can tell from that how naïve I was. She could have been someone's mistress. She could have been killing time while her husband worked. To me, however, she represented someone in charge of her own destiny. And I thought to myself in that moment, "Paris is where I could be that person."'

40

Paris, June 1934

It seems strange to Alice that her time in the city has been as short as four years. For it is home to her now: the centre of her own particular universe. She could walk the streets near her rooms with a blindfold tied over her eyes and know where she is at all times. If she ever thinks about all those years she lived in London it appals her to think that she never understood the city; never knew the fine arterial network of streets that connected those places she might have passed in the back seat of a car.

There are those who say that Paris is not what it was in the 1920s, when the city was awash with money and the sort of happy abandonment that accompanies a time of prosperity. There is no one interesting dining at the Ritz now, they claim. The arts are not what they were, now that so many of the great writers and painters have left in search of pastures new. Those big expatriate names: the Hemingways, the Fitzgeralds, the Joyces . . . all gone. Alice, never having known that Paris, cannot imagine a more exciting place than the one she inhabits now.

She has found herself another prospective job. It has come to her through Madame Fourrier, whose sister works as the housekeeper for a wealthy family in the 16th arrondissement.

'They're looking for a governess,' she told Alice. 'I told Bertrande you'd be perfect.'

'Why?'

'Come, my dear, it's easy to see that you are bright, even educated. I've seen you racing through those books you bring back. Besides – and you mustn't take this the wrong way – you clearly aren't meant to be a waitress.'

'It's been so long since I was at school . . .'

'You needn't worry about that. The children have a tutor for most subjects. He comes every day.'

'Then what am I needed for?'

'English. The parents want them to learn it, though goodness knows why people think English is of any use to anybody. They want someone who will teach them to speak it naturally – you know, as well as a British person might. They're good employers, Bertrande says. If you don't mind permitting their sort a bit of oddness.'

'What "sort"?'

'You know: Jews.'

Alice's first meeting with Madame De Rosier is something of a surprise. She had expected a great and lofty personage befitting of the house – a building of which her mother would approve, built to awe and intimidate. Sophie De Rosier, however, confounds her preconceptions. Alice is shown into the morning salon – a white temple of a room flooded with the green light of the garden beyond the windows. In this space, Madame De Rosier seems small, and very young. In fact, she appears barely older than Alice herself – in her late twenties, at the most. Her face is an almost perfect oval, with a small mouth and large dark eyes. It is a face that could be solemn, pious, even, were it not for the smile of welcome.

'So you are Alice.' She speaks in English, but nervously, as though unfamiliar with the feel of the language in her mouth. Alice nods.

'You speak French?'

'Yes.'

This is evidently a relief. Madame De Rosier moves gratefully into her mother tongue. 'Good. Let us sit.'

Alice takes the seat indicated, and for a moment her attention is caught by the painting behind Madame De Rosier's head. It is a study of an orchard: a work of green and light. White spaces of empty canvas show through the branches of the trees, but the result is not so much one of incompleteness as of a greater realism than had they been filled in with paint: the effect of a pale spring sun penetrating the canopy of new leaves.

Madame De Rosier catches Alice looking. 'Cézanne,' she says.

'I was wondering if it might be . . . I've seen some of his work in the Gallery Luxembourg.'

'My husband is a great follower of the arts. Both of us are, but he knows about the different movements, the new techniques and styles emerging . . . I only know what I like.' Madame De Rosier gives a shy smile.

'It's beautiful. One of the loveliest I've seen of his.'

'Thank you. It seems we share the same taste.'

It is Alice who feels she should introduce the purpose of this meeting, for Madame De Rosier appears in no hurry to do so. 'I understand you're looking for a governess.'

'Yes, we are. To the matter in hand, as my husband would say. You come with excellent recommendations . . .'

Alice shifts in her seat. She hasn't heard anything of these recommendations, though it wouldn't surprise her if this were Madame Fourrier's work.

Madame De Rosier seems to interpret her discomfort as modesty. 'If I am honest,' she says, sitting forward in her chair, 'the most important recommendation of all is that you are *actually* English.'

'I am, though I live here now – I think of Paris as my home.'

'But you could teach my children English ways and

customs – and teach them the proper English, not that of a foreigner, however fluent. Perhaps, if there is any time left after the children's lessons, you might instruct me, too?'

Alice is introduced to the children: Antoine – five, cripplingly shy, and barely able to look her in the eye for more than a few seconds, and the girl, Marguerite, with that peculiar self-possession especial to six-year-old girls.

'You don't look very old,' she tells Alice, challengingly.

'No, I suppose I'm not.'

'I thought all governesses had to be. Our tutor is. He's a fossil.'

On her way out, Alice's attention is caught by another beautiful object: an elaborate eight-armed candelabra, wrought in silver.

'It's exquisite,' she says.

Madame De Rosier is suddenly ill at ease. 'It's an heirloom, from my husband's family,' she says hurriedly, then adds, 'But, you know, we think of ourselves as French, first and foremost.'

Alice is nonplussed. 'Yes, of course.'

Several weeks on, Alice sits once more with her new employer.

'Why is it that you want your family to learn the language?' Alice asks. They speak in English now as often as possible. Sophie insists upon it; she must be pushed, she explains, or she will become lazy.

'It's a wonderful language.' Sophie takes a careful sip of her tisane and regards Alice over the fine rim of her cup as if trying to come to a decision. 'There is another reason though. Monsieur De Rosier and I . . . for some time now we have been considering a move to England.'

'Why?'

'Well, you know, things have been . . .' she hesitates 'more difficult for my husband of late.'

'In what way?'

'I realize it has been harder for everyone the last few years, and we have been lucky by most standards. For us, business is still good; you wouldn't think people would be buying fur in a Depression, but it seems French women consider it a necessity. There is, however, a certain . . . resentment towards those of our kind. Not that it hasn't always been there, to a degree. Of late, though, it has been more . . . shall we say . . . *energetic.*'

'You believe England will be better?' Alice thinks of her stepfather and his cronies.

'Perhaps, perhaps not. Monsieur De Rosier has family in London, and there is talk of moving the business – joining with them. A new start for us.'

'But you won't go soon?'

'Not right away. It will take some time to get our affairs in order. Besides, we won't go until we can speak the language like locals. Monsieur De Rosier doesn't believe that he needs any help with his English, but then it *is* true that, one way or another, he seems to be able to make himself understood wherever he goes.'

'Ah.'

'You are so good with the children,' Sophie says, 'we couldn't take them away from you so soon even if we wanted to – I am certain they wouldn't allow it.'

'Thank you,' Alice says, touched. She has become fond of them in return. The girl with her fierce intelligence, picking up whole phrases easily – almost greedily – and challenging Alice to explain quirks of grammar and pronunciation: 'Why did they decide to spell dove and move the same,' she demands, 'if they wanted them to sound so different?' And the boy, slower to understand than his sister – but still almost a baby really – who likes to sit with his small, warm arm curled around Alice's neck as she reads to him, his breath across her cheek sweet and vaguely milk-scented.

'I don't only mean the teaching, though,' Sophie says, with a smile. 'You have such a tender way with them. If it wouldn't put poor old Nanny Bisset out of a job, I'd have you looking after them all the time. I know they would prefer it, too.' She regards Alice, curiously. 'You must want to have children of your own, some day.'

Alice nods, mutely.

'I'm sorry,' Sophie says, quickly – sensing something amiss. 'That was too forward of me.'

Alice shakes her head. 'No,' she says. 'It's not. It's . . .' She takes a deep breath, hardly believing she is going to say it: 'There was one, a baby girl. She died.'

'Oh, Alice.' In one swift movement, Sophie has moved

381

to Alice's seat and put her arms around her. The suddenness of it causes something in Alice to yield, and she is surprised to feel a single hot wet tear slide down her cheek. She brushes it away and tries to remember the last time someone comforted her in this way. She finds, to her surprise, that she cannot.

A pattern is soon established. The children have their lesson first, for a couple of hours. Sophie's tutorial follows, but it doesn't seem formal enough to count as such. The two of them sit in the morning room and simply talk together, no topic out of bounds. Or rather, no topic save that of Tom. Alice has avoided mentioning him – not because she doesn't think Sophie would understand, far from it, but because she fears that doing so would be too painful.

Afterwards, Sophie almost always invites Alice to stay for lunch, sometimes with the children in the nursery and sometimes just the two of them in the airy breakfast room at the front of the house.

One day, walking back to Fourrier's, Alice understands for the first time her great relief at knowing that the De Rosiers' move to England is not imminent. It is not simply the prospect of losing the companionship of the children or the satisfaction of the work. It is that she appears to have found in Sophie De Rosier, unexpectedly, what she has not truly had since Tom. A friend.

The thoughts of Tom haven't left her, though. And

now it feels as if the tears shed earlier have caused some sort of transformation within her. She feels emboldened, even reckless. Has she allowed enough time to pass? She isn't sure, but she sits down to write to him, all the same. A secret part of her longs to tell him the truth, but she must not – the larger, more sensible part of her knows this to be so. Instead she tells him, with no small pride, of her new independence. She describes Madame De Rosier, the American writer, her room at Fourrier's, and she gives him the return address, care of Madame F. Does she secretly hope that, armed with this, he will board the first boat across the Channel and come in search of her? She will not allow herself to examine her feelings too closely.

It would, she knows, be an absurd hope. She tells herself this when a package arrives instead: smallish, card-backed. She opens it carefully and discovers a letter and a sketch wrapped in oilcloth, the ink already beginning to fade with age. There she is by the lake, sitting beneath the overarching boughs of those twin elderly willows. She remembers the languorous heat of the day. She recalls too how she felt Tom's eyes upon her as she removed her clothes and how she revelled in it, the awareness of her power over him. And the evening afterwards . . . Alice feels a pressure within her chest, almost as though she might be about to cry again. She turns quickly to the letter, in the hope of distraction.

1 September 1934

Dearest A,

What it is to hear from you, and to know that you are happy. You are often in my thoughts, so now I can picture you more accurately – writing your letter, looking out across the rooftops of the city. Pardon me for saying this, but I can't imagine you as a governess. Perhaps it is because it is such an indoor role, and I only ever seem to be able to imagine you outside. But I am glad you are enjoying it.

I should say first that I have some sad news. Last week, father took his own life. It was Ma who found him, and she is beside herself. And yet – though it is a terrible thing to say – I can't help feeling it has also come as a relief. He had been so much worse in recent years that caring for him had become a daily trial, and I'm not sure Ma could still see in him the man she married. Understandably, she no longer wishes to remain in the house in Putney. Tomorrow she will move to Islington to stay with Rosa and her family.

I left the job on Silk Street yesterday. It was making me dull and unimaginative – I had begun to realize how much it was affecting my painting, and it scared me. I managed to sell six pieces – would you believe it? – to a man your aunt Margaret put me in touch with. Incredibly, I made from this sale almost what I would earn in five months at Locke & Proudfoot.

So I am headed to New York. As I see it, there are two cities in the world where a would-be artist should want to be at the moment, and they are New York and Paris. I don't want to be another Englishman like Rupert Grant, travelling to France to try to copy Picasso. They say New York is the place now: where artists are moving beyond what they have learned from Europe.

I have enough from the paintings and my savings to pay for my passage, and, I hope, for a modest rent and living expenses for several months. It must seem unfeeling for me to be leaving so soon after my father's death, but Ma is positively encouraging me to go – I would never have gone without her full blessing. I'm putting most of my work into storage over here, but when I discovered this drawing of you I didn't want to consign it to some dry, dark place. I hope it will remind you of the fun we had together.

My ship leaves Southampton in a couple of days' time, and the crossing, weather permitting, should not take more than five or six days – incredible, when one thinks that not so long ago it might have taken as much time to get to Europe. For the first week or so I will be staying with an American fellow I knew at Oxford, Eddie Bloomberg. I can't recall if you ever met him – I doubt it. Eddie is far too charming for me to have risked the introduction if I had any sense.

After my time with Eddie I will try to find a place of my own, somewhere, ideally, right in the middle of it all. Eddie has offered to help me look, though I suspect his standards may be loftier than my budget will allow.

I shall write again when I have crossed the Atlantic. There – doesn't that sound like something?

Yours, T.

He sounds – what? – happy. Well, good. Alice is pleased for him. And yet she cannot do anything about the ache in her chest that forms at the thought of him moving yet further away from her, towards a new life. It is absurd, she knows – she was the one to enact the first separation, after all. But if Alice has learned anything from the previous few years it is that feelings are not rational, and cannot always be suppressed in the way one might like.

41

'What is it you do,' asks Sophie De Rosier, 'on the days you don't come here?'

'I type, sometimes, for a writer . . . but he can't pay me. I also waitress at the Bistro Fourrier, though I'm not particularly good at it.'

'That won't do,' Sophie tells her. 'You must be horribly bored – you're far too intelligent for waitressing. You should have somewhere interesting to work.'

Alice shrugs. 'It pays for my lodging – and there doesn't seem to be much else about.'

'Well,' says Sophie, 'that's just it. I've heard of something that might have opened up.'

And so, only a few days later, Alice begins a new job at the Dupré Musée d'Archéologie. It is owned by a friend of Sophie's late father – the two men having studied together at university. Jean Dupré is elderly even beyond his years now, made frail by almost-blindness and the blow of his wife's death. When he was young, fit and vigorous, Sophie tells Alice, he travelled the world as a self-made archaeologist, sourcing pieces for his collection. This was back in those days when a gentleman of leisure could still dabble in such a pastime as an amateur and hope to have some success.

Most of the items now housed in the museum were discovered on Dupré's travels, and many of them are intriguing curios rather than pieces of proper archaeological merit. All the same, they have the power to fascinate.

Alice's role used to be performed by Dupré's daughter, Lucille, who has recently left Paris to live in the South with her new husband and start a family. As a result of Dupré's incapacity, the de facto running of the museum has for several years been the work of his son, Étienne. Étienne is one of the tallest people Alice has ever seen – a good seven inches over six feet – and also one of the most gentle. He is thin and pigeon-chested, with a disobedient thatch of fairish hair – all of which lends him the appearance of an overgrown teenage boy.

Then there is Georgette, a student of Archaeology at the Sorbonne, who works as the museum's archivist to earn her 'going-out money'. As the daughter of intellectuals, Georgette takes her university education completely for granted. 'But think,' she says, 'what Papa would say if I decided to work in an atelier, or . . . oh, if I were to get married and do nothing but have babies. He'd be horrified! He'd disown me, most likely.'

Alice enjoys working with Étienne and Georgette – the one quiet and attentive, the other boisterous, wickedly bright, with a frequently bawdy turn of phrase and a string of inappropriate boyfriends, whose shortcomings she will describe in excruciating detail. But she also enjoys the times, usually first thing in the morning, when she is alone in the museum.

Early in the day, the air in the museum has a peculiar chill and stillness, hung with motes of dust that stir lazily as she moves through the rooms. Alice has wondered whether the temperature in the rooms is affected by the artefacts themselves – wondered if they carry with them some memory of the cold earth in which they were buried for so long.

There are the jewels, the earrings and the neckpieces, beautiful and probably once a sign of great wealth, but with a quaintness to them now, due to their hand-made lack of symmetry. There are the coins, hammered discs of real gold and bronze, some as large as jar-lids, others no bigger than a thumbnail. Alice loves to look at them: these objects that once represented such power, now valued for their status as relics, rather than anything they might purchase or control.

There is one skeleton in the museum. She lies in the centre of the last room within a glass cabinet. The remains date, according to the plaque, to the Norman era. She is the gallery's most precious exhibit. She was discovered in an unmarked grave near Caen – shallower than the norm, and at some distance from the nearest church. A worse burial than would have been accorded to the poorest serf. Yet the ring found on her finger – a piece of incredible delicacy, set with a precious stone – would suggest that she was once a noblewoman. The plaque that introduces her speculates that she might have brought disgrace upon her family, with some ignominious act that could not be forgiven: a child born out of wedlock, perhaps. Or that she ran away and died alone, far from her own people, and this burial was provided as an anonymous courtesy. Georgette doesn't like her and avoids going into the room, but Alice finds an odd sort of sanctuary here, alone in the early morning, and a strange sense of peace.

The next letter from Tom arrives about a week later.

9 September 1934

Dearest A,
And so I have arrived in New York. It's been a couple of days on dry land now, but it was a rough crossing and I still feel at times that the ground is listing beneath my feet.
I say New York, but this may be misleading. When you, as I, imagine New York, I suspect you

think of skyscrapers and statues. But I'm not in Manhattan, you see, but a place called Sand's Point.

Bloomberg's family is from Old American Money. The house is spectacular, if incongruously English in aspect: oddly like a Jacobean manor, with plenty of dark wood and leaded glass, and a slightly excessive number of columns and parapets. The important difference, I suppose, is that while it may look centuries old, the essentials (such as plumbing and electricity) are all absolutely state-of-the-art, which means that everything functions with almost disconcerting efficiency.

Eddie has two young sisters, Lou and Beatty: rather silly creatures who model themselves entirely, it seems, on the Talkie stars they so admire. When I arrived, in fact, Beattie was still reeling from a failed attempt to dye her dark hair Jean Harlow platinum. It had turned, instead, an unfortunate shade of tangerine. They're amusing enough together, like a comic double-act – only it's rather disconcerting when one remembers that all of their ridiculousness is not intentionally comical. Lou told me this morning that it was important I sketch her before I leave because 'a girl is nothing without a man wanting to take her likeness'. A photograph, she told me, would have been preferred, but she would make do with my meagre pen and ink.

For all the luxury of the house and the grounds, and my hosts' great generosity and kindness, I can't wait to get over the water to Manhattan. I can see it across the sound, the skyscrapers like a row of dark teeth against the sky. Tomorrow I am going across to look for lodgings, probably in a neighbourhood that would make poor Mrs Bloomberg faint with horror. Apparently, in this post-crash climate, it's easy enough to find short-let places on the cheap. I shan't give the return address here: I intend to be in my new place soon, if I can, and I'll write as soon as I am.

Yours, T.

As promised, the next letter arrives within a few days.

13 September 1934

Dearest A,

I have found the place! It's perfect for me, small but light, and not too smart, so that I don't worry as I perhaps should about getting paint on things. It's in a neighbourhood they call The Village, and I suppose it is rather like a village, as it seems to have an identity of its own separate from that of the city. And you should see the number of journals purely dedicated to the cultural output of this little enclave.

I live on a street called Bleecker, above an Italian bakery. I wake each morning to the scent of the new bread baking, and the fear that they will sell out of my favourite loaf gets me out of bed and downstairs far more effectively than any alarm clock. There is a German grocer further down, and a Polish barber beyond that, with his pole standing sentinel outside like a giant stick of confectionery. If you go the other way along the street, you meet with an Armenian launderette and a French bistro. So much of Europe is represented on a fifty-yard stretch of this street alone.

Everyone, it seems – everyone who still has the money to spend on anything other than basic necessities – wants to be seen as a patron of the arts. To be investing in culture, apparently, is a nobler endeavour than buying a racehorse, say, or a racing car – which would be unseemly at a time of such want.

To be an artist in this city, even an unknown like me, is therefore to carry a sort of passport that allows one to move within the social order as one might not otherwise be able to. I am invited to the most unexpected events and presented to people as 'the painter' – despite no one actually knowing my name. I find myself, of an evening, travelling from my modest lodgings to places like the nightclub they call the Elmo, where the wealthy and celebrated recline on zebra-skinned seats, and a single Tom Collins costs more than my neighbour the Polish barber is likely to make in a month.

For these people, the crash was nothing but an inconvenience – they carry on in much the same way as they did in 1928. Perhaps they order the 1922 vintage rather than the 1910 but probably more out of a desire not to seem extravagant than due to a genuine loss of funds. And nowadays, of course, they're mainly thankful that they can drink it legally.

Naturally, some of those dancing on Elmo's sacred floor are only pretending to be members of this rarefied group. I was first taken there by two Broadway chorus girls who were working as artists' models in the daytime to make ends meet. They wore their costumes into the club like some sort of uniform and kicked their legs about in a dance called the Lindy Hop. After this performance, they draped themselves over any specimens old and ugly enough to have millions in the bank.

Always, around every corner, you come face to face with someone who has lost everything. I think it may be something about the road system in New York, which is arranged like a grid. It means that you turn left off an elegant avenue of boutiques and cocktail bars and find yourself on a street where men lie on the sidewalk like so many broken umbrellas. I feel, walking down a street like this,

guilty for the shoes on my feet, the coat on my
back. I can't look these men in the eye when I
hand over my change, for the fear that they will
see a wastrel, a sponge: a man who gave up a
perfectly decent job to live a life of decadence and
irresponsibility.

When I see these men, I feel that I should be
using my art to make a statement, to deliver a
lesson on the wrongs of Capitalism as played out
in this city. Instead I am drawn to tell a story. I
want to show New York in all its wonder and evil,
its colour and darkness.

I am working better than I have ever worked,
here, and the pieces seem to take shape at an
astonishing rate. I wake each morning terrified
that it will have left me, this new surge of
productivity, that I will be wrung out, dried up.
But each day the miracle repeats itself. I don't
stop to question why, or where it has come
from. To look too closely at it might cause it to
flee.

The works are selling, too. If you can believe it,
in a week's time I will have a show of my own.
Yours, T.

42

We had made a circuit of one end of the park, tracing the edge of the reservoir that is now named after Jackie Kennedy Onassis, and were headed away from the Upper East Side towards Midtown – where Alice said she knew a good French restaurant for lunch.

The weather had turned grey and the water of the reservoir was a darker reflection of the sky, pinched and ruffled by the breeze. Alice manoeuvred her chair quickly, even impatiently, and I had to walk fast to keep up. I sensed that she had always done everything with great energy, and that she wasn't going to let old age and frailty get the better of her now. She was frail, though. I could see the blue-white of her scalp through the sparse white hair, the skeletal hunch of her shoulders beneath the enveloping swathe of scarf.

As we walked she asked about my life with Mum. Where had we lived? What had we liked to do at weekends? Did Mum read – who and what did she read? Did she like art? Music? Aside from the ache of loss, these questions provoked in me a sense of unease because, banal as they were, Alice asked them with such evident hunger.

'I've read all the interviews,' she told me, 'but, as I'm sure you understand, it isn't enough.'

I tried to convey as much as I could – both the big and the little things. I told her how Mum had always seemed to me just as graceful dancing in her slippers as she ever had en pointe. I told her about the times she took me swimming at Tooting Lido and for ice cream afterwards, about how for my fourteenth birthday she baked me a birthday cake, accidentally substituting salt for sugar, then let me drink a whole glass of champagne in compensation – which made Alice laugh. I spoke about the Barbara Morgan show and the darkroom she'd installed for me in the cellar.

None of it would be enough, though; I could see that. Knowing her favourite pastimes, the dishes she liked to cook . . . none of it could be a substitute for having known her, because without that the answers to the questions were all in the abstract.

As I was thinking this, wondering how she could be blind to the futility of it, Alice said, 'I hope you don't mind my prying, but I so enjoy hearing you talk about her. It is as much the way you speak of her, you see, as what you tell me about her. It helps me to understand how much she was loved.'

There was a long pause, the two of us moving together in companionable silence. Then: 'You were very lucky,' Alice told me, 'to have had that sort of friendship with your mother. Certainly, it may be the difference between generations, too, but I can tell you that that sort of bond is not guaranteed.'

She had knowledge of the fact first-hand, I thought. 'I know,' I said. 'I always thought of her as my best friend.'

I saw Alice nod. 'But of course,' she said softly, 'that must have made it all the more terrible, when you lost her.'

I couldn't quite find the words to answer her, and was glad in that moment that she couldn't see my face.

The restaurant was indeed very good – and very French. Inside it was difficult to believe in the American city without. The look of the place was Art Deco: gleaming dark wood and chrome, glass leaded in geometric patterns.

'The original owner left Paris in the thirties,' Alice told me, 'and the food is of that time. Perhaps superior, even, to anything I can remember eating there. Back then, though, I would never have been able to afford the better sort of restaurant.'

A waiter swept over and Alice ordered us each a cocktail called a French 75. 'There's nothing especially French about it,' she explained, 'except for the champagne. It's rather good though.' The drinks came immediately, twinly tall and pale and beautiful, with a waifish curl of lemon rind balanced expertly on the rim. I chose the confit of duck, because it seemed the right sort of thing to eat in a place like that, and Alice had poached trout and creamed spinach.

We ate in silence for a few moments and then Alice said, 'So, Kate. You have told me a great deal about your mother and you have already heard much – no doubt far too much – about me. But what about you? Tell me, please, about yourself.'

I looked at her expectant face, and felt something like despair. 'I'm not . . .' I shrugged, and laughed, rather desperately, 'I'm not especially interesting. Not like Mum.' It came out sounding like an apology, which I suppose in a way it was.

She put her glass down, and her expression was rather fierce. 'I shall pretend I didn't hear that,' she said. 'I don't have enough time left to listen to nonsense.'

'Well,' I gestured, helplessly, 'I have no great talent, like her.'

'What about your photography?'

I felt my face grow hot. 'How do you know about that?'

'It isn't difficult. Even had you not had the strap dangling from your bag' – I looked, and saw she was right – 'I do already know a bit about you. I have, shall we say, kept an eye on things.'

'What do you mean?'

'Well . . .' she paused, as though deciding whether or not to continue, 'I visited your degree show – at the Slade.'

I stared at her.

She smiled, almost sheepishly. 'I work in the art world, Kate – it is a small enough place. I found out about it relatively easily. And I should tell you . . . I do not come to London often. I didn't visit the city for a full two decades after I left for Paris.'

'But . . .' I was trying to make sense of it, 'only about fifty people came to the show.'

'I was one of them. Why should you have noticed me? I was a stranger.'

It was true, I thought. It was only upon closer acquaintance that one understood the ways in which Alice was exceptional. From a distance, she was just another elderly woman.

Then I thought of something else. 'The letters. You sent Mum one once a year, every year she performed.'

She nodded. 'Yes. Seeing her perform became . . . rather like a ritual for me – despite it often requiring travel to London. I only permitted myself one such excursion a year. It would have been wrong to do so more often – too much like an obsession. As it was, it became a way of being connected to her, I suppose.'

Then she changed the subject – perhaps because she

could not stand to see the pity on my face. 'Tell me,' she said, 'I want to hear more about your photography.'

'I don't know,' I said. 'I love it, but sometimes I wonder if I should give it up – get a proper job.'

Alice looked at me quizzically. 'What do you mean?'

'I mean a proper career . . . teaching, perhaps – or an office job.'

'Absolutely,' Alice said, 'if that is what you want. You should not be doing it out of fear though. I once knew a young artist who had exactly the same doubts as you – who had a first-class degree from Oxford, a promising career in Law. He, too, was fearful – and almost convinced – of failure.'

I nodded. 'He told me. He told me, too, that he wasn't particularly good when he started out.'

She seemed amused by this. 'Did he? Yes, I can imagine he might have done.' Her gaze, for a few seconds, grew vague, pensive. Then it snapped back to me. 'Where are you living, now?' she asked.

'I'm still in the house I grew up in, in Battersea – where Mum and I, and . . . ah, Evie, used to live.'

She digested this, frowning slightly. Then she said, 'I think that you should leave.'

'Excuse me?'

'I'm sorry,' she said. 'I seem to be getting terribly opinionated in my dotage. We hardly know each other – though to me it doesn't feel like that – and already I am trying to tell you what to do with your life.'

She smiled. 'The beauty of it, of course, is precisely

that it is your decision alone what you do with it. Even so . . . I cannot help feeling that a young woman of your age and talent should not be rattling around on her own in a big house full of memories.'

'I don't know where else I'd go.' It sounded particularly feeble, spoken aloud.

'A new city, perhaps? A new country. Is there anywhere you can see yourself living?'

Paris, I thought immediately, without quite knowing why. It was more a feeling – or rather a constellation of feelings – than anything specific. It was the discovery that, although there were memories there, they had not drained or oppressed me in the way that the memories in the house did. I thought of that vision of the lights on the water, at night, and how I had remembered seeing them with Mum and had – almost – been able to enjoy doing so, rather than finding myself disabled by grief.

But then I realized that it was where Oliver lived; that it would be impossible. I pushed it from my mind, and shook my head. 'I'll think about it,' I told Alice.

The waiter returned to clear away our plates, then swept back with a dessert menu.

'I could imagine staying here all day,' I told Alice, somewhat eager to shift the attention from myself.

Alice nodded. 'I have done, before. When I sit in here,' she told me, 'I can almost imagine that I am back there – not so much in Paris, because I am there often, but in that time: when everyone was so unsuspecting, still, of what was to come. Naïve, you could say. People thought, with the first war, and then, with the crash, that we'd weathered the worst that could happen.'

'Were you happy?'

'Oh, ever so. I had begun to feel very much at home in the city, and I was busy. For the first time in my life I felt useful. You know the play, *Three Sisters*?'

I nodded; only because it had been on the O level syllabus at school.

'Much fun is made of the sister Irina, of her fanciful idea that work will give her life meaning, but I think she is on to something. I have always thought it rather unfair, how disappointed she is by life in the end. Because, if the nature of the work is right, there is great reward to be found. The feeling that one has a place in the world, that one is useful in some small way, is not to be underrated. Perhaps my only regret was in not having someone to share my new happiness with. However there was no one I wanted to share it with, apart from Tom, and I had altered things irrevocably there, I thought.'

'You must have been happy for him, finding success in New York.'

'Yes, I was – I was thrilled. It was the beginning of everything he had hoped for, back when I knew him in 1929. That first exhibition, small as it was, put him on the map. And it is such an extraordinary thing, to witness someone's dream becoming a reality.'

That must have been how it was for Evie, I thought then, when Mum had her first successes. It was hard to imagine Mum not being the star she became but just another hopeful. An even stranger thought struck me then – and I couldn't believe I hadn't considered it before. If it weren't for Evie, would Mum have found that path? Perhaps not. In fact, *probably* not. I wondered if Alice had ever thought of that.

'I wished I could have been there to see it,' Alice continued. 'Reading about it in his letters – and increasingly, in the newspapers – made it all feel so far away, hardly real. Once they even printed a photograph of him, and I wished I hadn't seen it. I don't know whether it was the haziness of the newsprint, but I felt almost as though I were looking at a stranger.'

43

Almost three years have passed since he first left for New York. It seems that the name Thomas Stafford now has some currency in the art world; Alice hears it mentioned in the same breath as Hopper and Bellows. When she does, she feels a strange sense of estrangement, as though this Thomas Stafford cannot really be the one she knows.

Apparently, a couple of big collectors have taken a serious interest in his work. One of his pieces, *Bowery Morning*, sold to an American hotelier for an eye-watering five thousand dollars.

Stafford, people say, is one of the few English artists not caught up in aping Picasso or Matisse. Aunt Margaret's advice about originality found its mark. Every so often Alice sees his name appear in one of the British newspapers she buys from the *tabac* at an eye-watering premium. She cuts out these mentions and keeps them in the drawer of her bedside table.

Her stepfather's name also appears in the papers with increasing frequency: 'BUF rally in Kensington: Mosley and Hexford speak', 'Hexford talks at the Cambridge Union', 'Lord and Lady Hexford entertain the Führer'. Photos, too, of her mother, frostily beautiful in a white mink tippet, stepping from Goebbels' gleaming Mercedes-Benz. Her stepfather wearing that black shirt and those ridiculous riding breeches, addressing a crowd of admirers. These pictures Alice does not cut out.

Paris, August 1939

The news from Europe is bad. Sophie De Rosier has cousins in Bohemia, and she has not heard from them for some time – since March, in fact, when German troops moved in from the Sudetenland and took control.

'Why,' she asks Alice, 'is no one doing anything? The French and British governments . . . why are they allowing this to happen?'

Alice thinks of Archie, and of Tom's father – poor Mr Stafford, for all those years effectively a prisoner of war – if only within his own mind. 'I think it's fear,' she says. 'They don't want another war – people remember the first one too clearly.'

Sophie nods in understanding. She too lost a brother – her eldest. 'But if they don't act,' she says, 'then it will surely continue. It could be France or England, before too long.'

Cycling home later, Alice tries to imagine the city, balmy and almost eerily quiet on this day in high summer, invaded by a hostile force. It is impossible. She is so intent on her thoughts that she does not see the glass in the road in front of her until it is too late and the tyres have passed over it with an ominous hissing. It is a broken bottle – a drunk's, probably, that has rolled from the pavement and smashed. She looks at the damage and curses quietly under her breath. Twin punctures, decisive ones at that – so that all of the air has completely left both tyres. She wheels her bike back to the De Rosiers' house, and leaves it there – too tired to think about how to mend it now. For once she decides she will take the Metro instead.

As she waits for her train, a poster on the opposite platform catches her eye. It depicts a bright, abstract painting of a street scene – unknown to Alice, but something about it tugs at her, demands her attention. Someone stands in front of it, so that she can't quite be sure what it says. She moves in agitation, trying to see. The train is coming in now: she should get on, but she has to know what it says. The carriages slow to a halt, obscuring the other side from view. People pour off and on. At last, in a grinding of gears and with a mechanical hiss the train lumbers away, rattling off into the dark tunnel. The opposite platform is revealed. The woman has disappeared, and Alice can finally see it properly. Though she has to read it more than once, to be sure.

- EXHIBITION -
Thomas Stafford: The Lights of New York

At the gallery entrance Alice hesitates, unsure of herself suddenly, of whether she has done the right thing in coming here. There is a press of people inside and a pall of cigarette smoke hangs several feet from the ceiling. She fights her way through the throng, torn between stopping and taking a look at the works hung along the walls and searching the room for his face. A couple of times she thinks she sees him and starts forward, only to be disappointed. Every so often she is stopped by someone she knows and forced to make small talk before she is able to escape. 'Have you heard?' someone mutters, nearby. 'Gertrude Stein is here.' Sure enough, there she is, in the corner of the room, surrounded by an admiring crowd. Slightly smaller and older than Alice had imagined, but at the same time magnificent, wrapped about in a jewel-coloured shawl, her hair, steel grey, cropped close to her head like Joan of Arc's.

But where is *Tom*? Alice is beginning to wonder whether he hasn't attended his own exhibition. She has done a full circuit of the two rooms now, pushing her way past the same groups of people, making a nuisance of herself. Then she sees something: the back of a head, the particular tapering of the hair at the nape of the neck that gives her pause. She had noticed before and dismissed it. On second glance, though . . . No, it can't be. The shoulders are too broad, the posture too . . . different, the hair a shade darker than she remembers. And yet it is him, unmistakably. His head bows as someone leans in close to say something. She is diminutive and Nordic blonde, this person, and Alice is sure, even from this distance, that she is beautiful. She feels a shock of jealousy go through her, that – unreasonable though it is – she doesn't quite know how to quash.

She cannot believe the change in him. When she remembers Tom, it is always as he was that last time she saw him: tall, but with the lankiness of youth – a stretched quality, like a spruce that had shot upwards without finding the time to put branches out. His face was still that of a boy. Now she is confronted with the fact of that near decade that has passed. Those years have done their work indeed, and the changes they have wrought fascinate her. His frame is broader and his face has coarsened, but the change suits him – his prettiness has evolved into a more masculine register of beauty. He has kept his high colouring, the almost feminine flush of his cheeks, but it is tempered now by the shadow of stubble upon his chin, the more resolute shape of brow and jaw.

He is taller than any of those who have gathered about him. One of them says something to him that causes him to raise his head and look about the room, and his gaze, suddenly, rests upon her. And stays there. Unnerved, she feels the need to acknowledge this strange moment. She raises her hand, feeling the small tremor that runs through it, and gives a tentative wave.

The blonde woman has seen her too, now and she watches Alice with the unwavering, blue-eyed regard of a Siamese cat. She is exquisite. The modern, polished beauty of a Hollywood starlet, neatly voluptuous in her close-fitting grey suit: Schiaparelli, undoubtedly. A little white hand lifts a cigarette to her lips, and another man from the group steps in quickly to light it for her, retreating with a look of absurd pleasure upon his face. *She*, however, only has eyes for Tom, and the other hand finds its way to rest upon his forearm. Suddenly, with a lurch, Alice knows who this woman reminds her of. Her mother.

Alice turns and heads for the exit, almost breaking into a run in her eagerness to be outside in the anonymous street, where she can merge with the crowd and slip away. A hand brushes her arm and she wheels about – thinking it might be . . . No – it's . . . ah, a friend of the American writer. She smiles, nods, and excuses herself. She realizes, as she gains the cool air without, that she can't remember a word of what the man said to her.

It was a mistake to come. If Tom had wanted her here, he would have written to invite her. She should have been content with his letters.

It is past nine o'clock, and Alice is thankful for the concealing twilight. She is halfway down the street when she hears her name called and a smatter of quick foot-steps.

'Alice?'

He stands before her, tall and flushed, breathing hard. 'I knew it was you. I couldn't get away . . .' He stares, fascinated. 'You've changed so much.'

'I know. So have you.'

'I was going to surprise you, tomorrow. We weren't meant to meet like this.'

'You didn't want to tell me about the exhibition?' Alice realizes as she says it how hurt she is by the slight.

'I didn't want us to meet like that, with all those people. I wanted to come and find you first.'

'But *of course* I would want to be there. Tom, those pieces . . . they're so different: such energy and colour. You've done so well.'

Tom shifts from one foot to the other. 'Thank you, but . . . I don't know. It all seems . . . not quite real. I keep feeling that I'll do or say something wrong, something that gives me away as a phoney.' He grins. 'Shall we escape?'

'You can't leave your own exhibition!'

He shrugs. 'They'll do just as well without me in there. I'm not sure I was needed, to be honest. Most people there have better-informed opinions on my work than I do. I doubt they'll notice.' He takes her arm again and tucks it under his. She feels the thrill of his nearness: this person so familiar and yet so wonderfully strange.

Alice can't help herself. 'Your friend might. She seemed particularly interested in what you had to say.'

He looks at her in bemusement and she feels her face grow hot. She has *no right* to be jealous.

'What do you mean?'

'The woman you were talking to in there, the blonde.'

'Grace?'

'Is that her name? Yes, I suppose it does suit her. She's very lovely.'

'Grace is a friend.'

'Ah.' But I am your 'friend' too, she thinks, and look how little that says about what has been between us.

'She's the wife of one of my patrons: they paid for my passage here. In all honesty, I find her rather hard work, but it would not do to be rude.'

'Ah, yes.' Alice tries not to betray her relief. Tom gives her a quick dart of a look, a tiny smile. She feels him draw her slightly closer to him with his linked arm.

The light is fading. They walk along the quiet Boulevard des Invalides, past the long shape of a flower stall, its canvas covering snickering in the breeze. Alice points out the Lycée Victor Duruy, vast and silent – a sleeping giant. 'Matisse teaches there.' They peer up together at the dark windows as though they might glimpse that bearded face through one of them like an apparition.

'Did you know,' Tom says, 'Matisse was supposed to be a lawyer, too.'

Alice is astonished. 'Then thank goodness you both saw sense!'

She is only aware of how far they have wandered when the lights of the Boulevard du Montparnasse appear ahead of them. There are sounds: music, shrieks, laughter, the hum of idling engines. The night-time revelries start early in this part of town. As they turn the corner on to the thoroughfare, Tom's eyes widen at the spectacle, and Alice feels a thrill of pride that this, her city, is able to fascinate him – one who has lived a decade in the American metropolis.

'All right,' she says, matter of fact. 'What do you want to do?'

'I'd like to try a dish of oysters – I've never eaten them.'

'Not even in New York?'

'Never.'

She grins. 'Neither have I.'

'I thought that was all people ate in Paris. Oysters
. . . and plenty of champagne to wash them down with,
naturally.'

Alice laughs. 'Some people, perhaps. Not me – that
isn't the sort of life I have here. My salary doesn't stretch
to many oysters.'

'Well, we definitely have to try them. My treat. After
that, I'd like us to get extremely drunk. Do you
remember that party, by the lake?'

She nods.

'I'd like to do that: drink too much and then sit
together, talking until dawn. The champagne will keep
us warm.'

'All right.'

The oysters, quavering on their bed of briny ice, are
a strange thing. After the first, Alice isn't sure she
wants another. Her mouth seems to taste of salt and
metal.

'They aren't quite what I expected.'

'No, nor I.'

'They don't taste of much, do they?'

'Of the sea, I suppose.'

'And the texture: slippery, cold. Slimy, you might say.'

'Hm. Perhaps if we tried each one with the champagne straight afterwards? You know, sluice them down
with it?'

By the time the bottle is finished, oysters are Alice's
favourite thing in the world.

'They merely take a bit of understanding,' she tells Tom earnestly. 'They're very subtle.'

When the waiter comes with their bill, Tom insists on paying for everything. 'I told you,' he says, batting her away, 'I have money now.' He says this with such incredulity, so like the Tom she remembers, that on an impulse she reaches across the table for his hand and presses it against her lips. He goes quite still and watches his fingers there, resting against her mouth. Suddenly self-conscious, Alice lets his hand drop.

He buys them absinthe in the next bar. 'This is what everyone drinks here, surely? Besides champagne, I mean.'

'No – in fact I'm not even sure if it's strictly legal.'

'How odd. Such a harmless little drink. Surely nothing tasting of sweets could be truly bad for you.'

They watch, captivated, as their waiter goes through the elaborate performance of preparing their drinks: the delicate perforated silver spoon, the steeped sugar cube, the peculiar alchemy that occurs when the water meets the jewel-coloured liquid and turns it cloudy white.

Afterwards, they dance in La Coupoule. They move with the intense concentration of people more than two-thirds drunk, and with each new piece of music they press closer together. Alice feels the strength of Tom's supporting forearm behind her back and his breath, faintly liquorice-scented, on her cheek. After an hour or two they break for air and make for the riverbank, where they find a bench to sit upon. The water seeps below them like a flow of black treacle, reflecting, wetly, the lights from both banks.

'I can see why you love it here,' Tom says, his words ever so slightly slurred.

'I don't go dancing every night, you know.'

'You should – you do it so well. That time I saw you by the lake. You moved like . . . like water. You could *be* a dancer.'

She laughs and swats his arm. 'You flatterer!'

'No, I mean it.'

He turns to look at her. His face is flushed and his eyes bright. She reaches up to feel her own hot cheeks with the backs of her hands. Then she does the same to him. She senses the pressure of his gaze intent upon her face, but she can't quite look up at him. To do so in this moment, she feels, would be like staring directly at the sun. As if of their own accord, her fingers trace their way lower, until she is touching his lips. She has always loved the shape of them: the curve of the top lip perfect – a drawn bow – the full lower lip.

'I'm so glad you came.' She strains to keep her voice light, but knows it has come out rougher than she intended. The words are like an incantation for both of them. She reaches up with her hands, cups his head and draws him down towards her so their lips can meet. He is gentle, at first, but she forces him not to be, and his arms go around her and pull her almost into his lap.

He is hard beneath her, and the rush of longing that she experiences in this moment is almost frightening – though not enough to make her stop.

'I think you should come back to my room.'

'Alice, are you sure?' His eyes are unfocused, his breathing erratic. She can feel her own breath catching, and her heartbeat resounding through her whole body. She doesn't answer, but pulls him up after her, looking away, embarrassed and aroused, as he shrugs off his jacket to hold it in front of himself.

It isn't far to her apartment from here, but it takes them far longer than it should – they keep having to stop along the way. They are both bemused and thrilled by this thing that has happened to them again, and each new kiss is a reaffirmation, a further avoidance of doubt.

Alice falls back upon the bed and Tom follows her down, his mouth on her forehead – almost chaste – then the side of her neck, the hollow above her collarbone. She unbuttons her blouse for him and he sits back to stare at her. She laughs and tries to pull him down but then she realizes what he is doing, making it real for himself, fixing the details in his memory.

When they are both naked they become desperate, fumbling, urgent. Not particularly gentle, or graceful – but it is just as she would have wanted it, somehow.

In the morning, Tom manages to get the stovetop coffee pot to produce two bitter black cups that they drink in bed with the sunlight swimming across them, spilling over the discarded pile of clothes on the floor. They don't say much to one another – deliciously tired from the night before, content with silence. Then, suddenly finding themselves ravenous after the meagre supper of the night before, they venture downstairs for breakfast, taking one of the ironwork tables outside. The air still holds the coolness of early morning, but the sky is an undisturbed Wedgwood blue – the sign of another hot day to come. Madame Fourrier emerges from the kitchen, eyeing Tom censoriously. He struggles manfully through the interrogation that follows in his schoolboy French.

Later, they find themselves retracing their steps – back to the Boulevard du Montparnasse, past the entrance to La Coupoule. In the new light, the entrance to the club appears slightly shabby and subdued, like one of its own partygoers stumbling into the sun, ruing the excesses of the night before. They sit down by the Seine again, on the same bench.

'Why don't you come with me?' Tom covers her hand with his – his touch questioning, tentative, not yet quite sure of itself.

'Where to?'

'To Corsica.'

'Why there?'

'A friend of mine – a collector, actually – has lent me his place. To paint. Before I left for New York I saw an exhibition at the National, a series of works by a Victorian artist – I forget the name. Not my style, there's too much realism, but they've stayed with me – the quality of the light, the wildness of the landscape . . . a town hewn out of a mountainside. I thought then: I want to see that place for myself, capture it, if I can. I've had enough of cities for the time being.' He begins to stroke her wrist with his calloused thumb, up to her forearm, down across the sensitive skin on the back of her hand. Alice shivers. 'Will you come?' he presses.

She takes a deep breath and stirs her coffee with her free hand to focus her mind on his words, not on the delicious friction of his skin upon hers. 'When do you go?

'In the morning. I have a train ticket to Marseilles.'

Alice thinks. The De Rosier family is holidaying in Provence: they will be there for the whole of August, as is their tradition. The museum is quieter than ever in this empty season, and there is no question that Étienne, Georgette and old Monsieur Dupré will survive without her. The American writer is visiting with friends in Marrakech. Then she thinks of her conversation with Madame De Rosier the previous morning: the feeling of vague, unspecific dread that she had carried with her for the rest of the day. She is struck by the thought that she must not let this chance pass her by.

'All right.'

He looks so astonished by this that she laughs. 'You thought I wouldn't say yes?'

'Not exactly. I hadn't quite dared hope that you would.'

The train south is an exercise in self-control. They sit with their knees touching as the carriage grows ever more crowded with passengers, rather than emptying as might be hoped. Alice tries to focus on the newspaper she bought at the kiosk in Paris but realizes that though she has looked at every page she has not read a single word.

Corsica is sun and dirt and herbs. It takes a few minutes, stepping queasily off the boat from Marseilles, for Alice to appreciate it fully, this vertebra of rock protruding from the placid green wash of the Mediterranean.

The cottage is a former peasant's dwelling. Two rooms: an upstairs and a downstairs, not much larger than Alice's room at Bistro Fourrier, but it is sufficient for their needs. The view of the sea, which is almost limitless, more than compensates for any lack of space.

On that first day they go immediately to the beach, picking their way along the coastal path that skirts the cliffs and then plunges down between them to sea level. The sand is hot underfoot and coarse, reflecting the midday sun with a dull mineral glimmer. There is a small patch of shade in the lee of the rocks where they choose to sit. It is only the two of them and the loud silence of the surrounding beach; the slap and swell of the water, the delicate vibration of the wind.

In the evening they have supper in a small town outside Bonifacio. The place appears utterly unchanged by the twentieth century: no motor vehicles in sight and fishermen setting out for the night-time catch, oil lamps burning to attract the creatures out of the black depths. Tom sits and sketches the scene, while Alice imagines that the furthermost lights are in fact pirate ships, off to plunder and pillage.

They eat in the only restaurant available; an unusual meal of sea urchins, surprisingly creamy and delicious, hidden among buttery strands of pasta. All eyes are upon them: the foreigners with the city clothes, but Alice is unaware of anything but the miracle of his face before her, and the secret knowledge of what further pleasures the night will bring. She feels that they are, briefly, outside time, that they have carved out a space for themselves in which they are protected from it. The past – and her lie – the present drama in Europe, the future – and all that it may bring.

The next day they hire a fishing boat with a peeling green hull that seems barely seaworthy on dry land but sits reassuringly high in the water. The flimsy awning slaps and screeches in a stiff new breeze that has rushed in over the sea without warning. The sea is a deep purple-blue now, stippled with tiny waves.

Alice relishes the respite from the heat. She sits on the

421

wooden seat near the bow, and between her feet is their lunch basket: bread, boiled eggs and cheese, matter-of-fact Corsican red wine. She licks her top lip and finds a thin crust of salt. Tom sits opposite her, grinning into the wind. Alice explores him secretly with her eyes: she has still not had her fill of looking. The changed shape of him, the sun on his brown hair turning it to gold. He catches her looking and smiles a different sort of smile.

When they reach the place they haul the boat up the sand behind them to where it will be safe from the swell. The beach is sheltered by two arms of rock on either side and the heat immediately has them in its grip again. They discard their clothes and run into the pale shallows, where shoals of silver fish scatter and re-form.

Tom doesn't take his eyes from her, and she feels doubly naked and doubly warmed, his gaze like a second sun. 'Remember that day, by the lake?' he says, with an odd urgency.

'Of course I do.'

'When you came out of the water . . . I'd never seen anything so beautiful—'

'Tom . . .' She is embarrassed by his fervency.

'—but it pained me, too, because I knew that no matter how I tried I could never have captured you as you were, not properly.'

They return to the cottage in the evening gritty with sand: burned and buffeted by the day spent outside, deliciously tired. They roast a fish whole and watch the smoke rise up and mingle with the purple dusk. In the distance are the lights of Bonifacio, the dark headland. Gradually the light fades further into velvet blackness and the stars begin to show themselves. It is a clear sky and they appear so bright that the man-made lights of the city seem like their dull, imperfect reflection.

'We could live here,' Tom says. 'One day, when we're old.'

'Perhaps.' She doesn't want to say yes, though, suddenly, she knows that she wants it desperately. To agree, she feels, might be to alert the Fates. But perhaps it could happen, she thinks. It might.

Overnight, with no warning, the wind grows. They lie in bed listening to it begin to gnaw about them, hearing its eerie exhalation down the chimney. After a while Tom falls asleep, but Alice lies awake in the crook of his arm, breathing in the scent of his skin that is unique to him, and so beloved to her. She does not say it aloud, but the wind unnerves her. It is the inevitability of it, perhaps, that makes her think of those other inarguable forces: fate, time. Try as she might, she cannot help but read some sort of message in it. It has discovered them in what she thought was their safe, separate place. Nothing stays still, it says: not air, not sand, not one moment stretched greedily between two lovers. Life is movement and violence.

By dawn the wind is howling in from the sea, whistling through the roof tiles, drumming against the windowpanes. It is astonishing, this violence of thin air. They say the Mistral can send you mad. It is not wise to venture out when it blows. And yet some brave souls do, hunched against the onslaught, driving themselves blindly forwards.

Alice and Tom are content to stay inside. They spend almost the whole day in bed, lost to everything but each other – the novel and yet familiar delight of each other's bodies. Tom explores her with his hands and mouth, but it is his gaze that feels warmest of all upon her skin. At one point, almost unnerved by the intensity of his concentration upon her, she laughs. He raises his head and gives a slow smile. 'I need to prove to myself that you're real, that it's not simply another dream.'

In turn she learns the changed landscape of his body: the coarse new hair upon his chest and those faint freckles along the ridge of his collarbone that seem to her like tiny particles of fallen rust. They must be new, she decides: she cannot see how she could have failed to notice something so distracting before.

His stubble leaves a pinkish rash across her breasts and the secret blue-white skin of her inner thighs and as even she watches it fade Alice wishes that it would remain like a brand. The strangest thing, but even as he moves inside her, even as she almost completely forgets herself in pleasure, the dread of impending loss follows close behind. It is irrational: he is here with her now, yet it is as though some part of her beyond thinking, a deeper sort of knowing, understands it cannot last.

They make a simple meal that they eat with their fingers, half-clothed. Alice asks Tom about New York. He tells her more about his life there, speaks of the glamorous excesses of the nightclubs and restaurants he has known, the famous names he has encountered. And he talks about that other side of the city that is rough and dirty and desperate. The streetwalkers who patrol the streets near his flat with runs in their stockings and broken heels. The Brooklyn neighbourhood he visited where he saw a family rummaging through the contents of the rubbish bins, the children climbing over the refuse like stray cats. It is, as they say, a jungle, a melting pot. Infuriating at times, and exhausting, but the energy of the place is addictive, like no other place on earth. 'Not even Paris?' she asks, rather jealously.

'I haven't spent long enough in Paris to say,' he says prudently.

The next morning they wake to a peculiar hush. As quickly as it appeared, the wind is gone. They lie in bed and listen to the silence, their legs tangled together beneath the sheets. Tom brushes the skin of Alice's back with his fingertips – lightly – up, down, in widening circles. She presses her face deeper into the pillow and revels in the sensation of his touch.

'Come back with me, Alice.'

She had expected the question, and dreaded it. 'I can't,' she says, knowing it to be true but wishing there were some way to soften the blow for both of them. 'Not yet, anyway. I have a life in Paris, and there are ties I can't break quickly. I am needed there, and I like it, Tom – I like being needed.'

'But I need you,' he says, almost peevishly.

She tries to smile. 'Not like that. I mean that I am useful – I have a purpose.'

'So when could you come?'

'In a year, maybe.'

'A year!' He is appalled.

'It's not such a long time.'

'But what if you *have* to?'

'What do you mean?'

'If war does break out. If France is threatened.'

'It wouldn't make me leave.' It is only as she says it aloud that she realizes the truth of it.

He is exasperated by this. He can't see the logic in it.

'You'd stay in America, if there was a war?'

She can see that this has defeated him. He shrugs. 'No. I wouldn't want to be so far away, but it's—'

'Precisely. You'd want to be at home, so that you could do your part, if it were needed. Paris is my home, Tom.'

He throws up his hands in surrender. 'You're

infuriatingly stubborn, but part of me can't help loving you for it.'

That *word* – spoken so lightly. And yes, like a powerful, yet subtle, incantation, it has worked its inevitable magic, caused everything to shift.

44

New York, September 1986

'It must sound,' said Alice, 'as though we were very naïve. That we had no idea of what was around the corner. We understood that the machinery was in motion, that something was coming, even if we didn't know exactly what . . . though I knew that the De Rosiers had felt it more than most. And yet . . .' she smiled, 'and yet knowing, in some interior, cleverer part of yourself, isn't the same as acknowledging it. It's a sort of arrogance, I suppose. Not believing that it is going to affect you. We could talk about the possibility of war, Tom and I, but we didn't actually think it would come to us. Because when the war is somewhere else, however much you might try to prepare for its arrival, it isn't real. There's something Martha Gellhorn said: "War happens to people, one by one." That's exactly it, you see. Until it happens to you, you have no way of understanding it, let alone imagining it. Until then, it is simply a monster under the bed.

'So Tom went back to his life in New York, and I carried on in Paris, certain that I would join him, in the end. I was addicted to the city, to my life there, but I knew that for him I would go anywhere. I only needed some time to say goodbye to it all.'

'But you stayed,' I said, realizing in that moment that that must be the case. 'You never left.'

'Yes, I stayed. You see, when it came to it, I couldn't leave.'

'Were you trapped?'

'No, not exactly. I could have escaped, with all the others that left – before they arrived. But I had already made the decision to stay if it came to it – just as I'd told Tom. Tom liked to tell me that I was brave, but I wasn't. I'd run away from everything once before. I wasn't going to run away again.

'If I had known then what it would mean for us, in the end, would I have acted differently? Perhaps, in staying, I was acting not out of courage but from that same arrogance, that belief in one's own invulnerability. Believing, blindly, that everything would work out all right.'

Alice cocked her head to one side and regarded me. Then her eyes slid to the waiter moving silently between the tables at the far end of the room. 'The wine is lovely, in its way, but I think for the next part I have to tell you we could benefit from something stronger.' She gave a quick, conspirator's smile. 'Tell me, my dear. Have you ever tried absinthe?'

45

'When do you leave?'

'As soon as we have finished packing. In the next couple of weeks, hopefully.' Sophie makes a twist of her mouth. 'We had been planning to leave at some point, but I hadn't thought it would be quite so . . . so like rats escaping from a sinking ship. It feels horrible, to be running away. But with the children, you know, I think one cannot be too careful.' She grimaces. 'I have family in Czechoslovakia, and it has been very bad there. The Führer does not like us, you see.'

Sophie's children have already left the city in the company of some of the De Rosiers' expat friends. Monsieur De Rosier has insisted on staying on for another month. 'He wanted to tie things up properly,' Sophie explained. 'He was loath to leave his employees in the lurch. You know, if he hadn't seen with his own eyes all those poor people flooding in from the Ardennes, he might never have been persuaded to go.' Because Monsieur De Rosier, like most other Frenchmen, didn't believe it would happen. Until the Maginot Line turned out to be as unbreachable as the *Titanic* was unsinkable.

Monsieur and Madame De Rosier will go south in the hope of catching a boat from Spain to England. In doing so they will join the line of Parisians and northerners that has straggled out of the city for the last few weeks: a maundering procession of men, women, children, animals – cars, bicycles, horse riders and those on foot, pushing wheelbarrows or prams laden with possessions.

Anything Sophie cannot take with her, she gives to Alice. Flanders linen that was once part of her bridal trousseau, a library of books – some of them first editions.

In return, Alice hands over her most valuable possession: a sketch of a woman sitting by a lake: an early Thomas Stafford.

'I will come and collect it from you,' Alice tells her, 'when all of this is over. Look after it for me in the meantime, will you? I'd like to know that it's safe.'

Sophie studies the drawing closely, and then looks up at Alice with a curious smile. 'You never cease to surprise me,' she says. 'One day, you know, I'm going to force you to tell me all about the real Alice.'

'The problem is, Sophie, I'm so far now from the

person I was before that none of it seems real. It would be like telling a fairy tale.'

Sophie shakes her head. 'I disagree. I think we carry all of our past selves with us, in tight layers. Somewhere within you is *that* girl, however many other, new selves you may have grown in the years since. She's what holds you together, at the very centre.'

46

Alice had been tired when I left her at the apartment. She had tried to insist that I stay longer, but the concern in Julie's expression had told me that there had been enough talking for the day.

When I returned to the East Village there was a message at reception for me from Oliver, which the desk clerk had transcribed for me: *Kate, I hope all is going well. I am thinking of you. O.* It wasn't much, and it had the inevitable dislocation of any message sent via a third party – like a card written in a florist's hand – but it was enough to lift my spirits. Surely, I thought, this meant that he did not regret what had happened.

I had planned to stay at the hotel and while away

434

the rest of the afternoon, but the silence and smallness of my room oppressed me. I wandered out on to the street and then along Broadway, hardly aware of where I was headed but enjoying for the first time the noise and chaos of the city, the purposeful – if directionless – sense of moving forward through the fray.

At one point I looked about me and realized I was completely lost – though I was strangely unworried by it. I would keep going, I decided, and something must eventually reveal itself to me: I didn't feel like turning back, anyhow. I came to a huge roundabout, followed it round, and kept walking.

Suddenly, I glanced to my left and saw, across the lanes of traffic, a building I recognized. The lofty, graceful arches that formed the front; the windows with their geometrical leading: these were as images remembered from a dream. I had a fleeting impression of snow falling thick and silent from the night sky – thicker than I had ever seen it in England – and a white carpet already formed on the pavement, squeaking beneath my booted feet. A memory of light blazing through those tall windows as though a giant fire had been lit within. And I saw Mum, her dark hair drawn back into a chignon and a soft grey shawl wrapped about her. As I drew this image towards me I could even detect the perfume she wore: rich, powdery, enigmatic. It was a scent that I would forever associate with Mum's 'evening' self, clad in one of her many black simple dresses, poised and delicately beautiful, but not without a particular emanation of strength. I grasped for the tail of the memory, tried to force it to reveal itself. Then I saw a sign that had been strung up, and I understood.

It was the Metropolitan Opera. The night I recalled was the first evening of the Royal Ballet tour – a series of short, radically experimental different parts that Mum had choreographed. Now I could remember her apprehension and excitement: she had been uncharacteristically nervy and breathless, almost childlike. It was a big gig for her, and – I have heard it suggested – the one that cemented her reputation as more than just an exceptional dancer.

At the time I had been too young to recognize it, but now I understood how much courage it must have taken. Mum could quite easily have rested on her laurels: she had made more money in her years as Prima, she had said once, than was 'quite sensible'. Then I thought of Alice, remaining in Paris despite all that called her away. Alice's was a different manifestation of bravery, certainly: a more momentous, newsworthy sort. Nevertheless, it was of the same stock. I knew, innately, that Mum would have stayed too. I saw in that instant how like one another they were: how steadfast in their ways – even to a fault. Would I have stayed? I did not want to examine it too closely.

On the far side of the road stood a mother and her small daughter, looking up, like me, at the building. I blinked at them stupidly, wondering if this too was an illusion borne from memory. But no, this was real. They were part of a crowd of people, in truth, but they were the only ones I saw. The child spoke and the mother bent down to hear. As surreptitiously as I could, I took my camera from my bag and framed the shot.

47

Paris, June 1940

Paris is a changed place: a ghost town.

Georgette says that she is staying put, as are her parents, even though they have been living with friends since a rare night-time visit from the Luftwaffe destroyed one wing of their house. The damage included Georgette's own room. 'I was out with my boyfriend Jean when it fell,' she says. 'My parents think he's a no-hoper, but even they couldn't argue that it was a good thing I went out with him that evening.'

Étienne, too, will remain. He would never leave the museum – Alice sees that. It is as much his as his father's, if not more so – a part of him. He worries, though, about the exhibits: ever since the raids started he has been carrying the most precious pieces down into the basement. 'Like a squirrel,' laughs Georgette to Alice, rather unkindly, 'rushing about with his tuft of hair bobbing, his arms full of goodies.'

Madame Fourrier is staying, though this comes as no surprise – she is as permanent a fixture on the Left Bank as the Panthéon itself. But leaving Fourrier's each day, Alice finds fewer people on the pavements, less bread in the bakery – and in the *épicerie* where she gets her groceries the few vegetables are spotted with age. Cats and dogs that have been left behind forage in packs, yowling in the evenings. Two days ago a herd of cows was seen grazing on the marigolds in the Tuileries, having wandered in from some deserted outlying farm.

One evening, on her way back from the museum, Alice passes a salon from which the music of a gramophone bleeds out into the empty street; inside, the coiffeur and his clients banter and gossip as though nothing were amiss. Alice has cut her hair herself for a decade, but she is so encouraged by the normality of the scene that she goes in and asks for a trim, an excuse to be surrounded by the laughter and the companionship.

---

12 June 1940

Dearest A STOP Back in London STOP Staying with Rosa in Islington STOP Signing up tomorrow STOP I love you Alice

---

439

The telegram reaches her just in time, before the silence falls.

At first she decides to keep it with all of her other treasured things, in the drawer with the newspaper cuttings. Then she changes her mind: she will keep it with her, like a talisman.

They say that they are but a day or so away. Tall plumes of smoke seep into the sky from the factories, ablaze, on the outskirts of the city. This waiting is the worst part. The silence in the streets is even more profound now, with a new intensity to it: the potent quiet of an indrawn breath.

They will come, perhaps this evening, perhaps tomorrow, first thing. Alice imagines that she can sense them there, circling the city like wolves surrounding a cottage, misting the windows and breathing through the letterbox.

And then they arrive. Alice, Étienne, and Georgette hear the rumbling of the tanks from the museum, and head to the Champs-Élysées to watch. They hear too the incoherent trumpet of a man's voice, amplified by a loudspeaker. This sudden hubbub is all the more marked in comparison to the hush that has descended over the rest of the city, like a child shouting in an empty playground. When they reach the Champs-Élysées they see the crowds. They throng along either side of the road in two thick ribbons, watching as the tanks and foot soldiers move past them in weird pageantry. They look, at first, like spectators at a bicycle race. Only there are no cheers here, merely that great, collectively held breath and, every once in a while, a hastily stifled sob. All except for one woman, who, forgetting where she is, begins to clap, then remembers herself and looks about in apologetic mortification.

It is almost a relief that the moment has finally come. For weeks, and especially the last few days, the city has waited, crouching, fearful, for the next turn of the screw. Now the thing they have feared is before them. And it is strange, because the German soldiers don't look like men of war. Most of them look like boys: sunburned, flushed with excitement; the wolves of Alice's imagining were far more terrible. Some of them even behave like performers in a pageant, smiling down as they pass by – giving the occasional wave. 'Like school-children on a trip,' Georgette mutters. Somehow these soldiers are far worse to behold than those who scowl. Alice feels outraged by these smirking boys, gliding past as they survey their new home. It is robbery, in broad daylight. It isn't their city. It is hers, and Georgette's and Étienne's; it is Sophie's and her family's. How can something like this be permitted to happen? 'It can't be allowed,' she thinks, before realizing that she has spoken it: a whisper, but audible to Georgette, who turns and looks at her.

It is two weeks before Alice sees Georgette again. Georgette has never been away from the museum for so long before, but things are different in war – people do not keep to their usual itineraries. Nonetheless, Alice is relieved when Georgette does eventually appear at the museum, flushed from riding her bicycle.

'The pigs,' she fumes, throwing down her bag. 'As if it weren't enough to sit in our cafés and steal our petrol and food, they seem to think it's all right to whistle at you as you cycle past. I nearly stopped and thumped him.'

'Thank goodness you came to your senses before you could.'

'Part of me regrets that I didn't. By the way, have you heard?' she says, disgustedly. 'They've only gone and draped the bloody tower itself with swastikas.' She laughs, drily. 'Though at least they had to work for it. The lifts were blocked off, so they had to climb up the sides. Wish they'd fallen off.' She looks around to check they are alone, and drops her voice. 'What was it you said, the other day? "It can't be allowed."'

'Yes . . . but I didn't intend to say it aloud.'

'Did you mean it? Did you say it for . . . oh, something to say? Or did you mean you want to do something about it?'

'Both, I think. I would want to act if I were able—'

Georgette cuts her off. 'What if you could?'

'Well, certainly, but I don't see . . .' Alice stops to watch Georgette rummaging furiously in her bag. She pulls out a notepad, tears off a leaf and scribbles something on it before handing it to Alice. 'Read that.'

Alice does. It is the name of a bookshop, an address, a date and time.

'Do you know the place?'

'I've never been there, but I know the street.'

'Can you remember this address?'

'Yes.'

'Good.' Georgette plucks the piece of paper back. She draws a box of matches from her bag and, with something of the theatrical, sets it alight, letting the flakes of ash fall to the floor. 'I'll see you there.'

'I don't—'

'Just come along.'

It is strange, thinks Alice, the way a smell stirs the memory far more powerfully than an image, or a sound. Sitting in the dimly lit basement of an antiquarian bookshop in the Quartier Latin early one evening, she is transported to the library at Winnard Cove. It is the smell of old leather and paper, of accumulating dust. Oddly enough, to Alice this is the scent of the summer, of childhood. She was too young to read properly then, but she could sit and look at the pictures in Lord Eversley's books – of ships and continents and shelves of ice – while her father worked.

She remembers the sound of the breaking water outside and the screeching of the gulls sounding so faintly through the old stone and glass that they could have been portents of another reality. Alice's mother never entered the library. She claimed that the dust made her cough and wheeze, but Alice wondered, thinking on it later, whether it was because the place reminded her of her well-hidden ignorance.

Sometimes, Archie would join them, picking up a volume, leafing his way quickly through. But he seemed to find the air, the very fact of being inside, stifling. After quarter of an hour he'd throw down the book, almost as though it had offended him in some way, and stride from the room. He could never be still for long. How strange to think of him forever stilled, enclosed in a tomb of Flanders mud.

The atmosphere in this basement, of course, is utterly unlike the quiet and repose of the Eversley library. The air feels charged with the tightly coiled expectation of its occupants. Most of those gathered here are students, in their early twenties, and it is with a shock that Alice realizes that she is no longer young herself, but some undefined, in-between age. Georgette and Étienne – he too has been persuaded along – sit nearby. Her eyes move from them to the new faces. There is a handsome young man, his hair slicked against his skull with grease, as is the current fashion among the students. 'Anton,' murmurs Georgette, following Alice's gaze. The marked indifference of her tone is a clear sign of her special interest in him. Next to him sit a couple of girls of around the same age, leaning forward on their seats – apparently impatient to begin. They, like Georgette, wear almost identical, thick-lensed glasses that do nothing to mask the freshness of their complexions. 'Danielle and Berthe,' Georgette clarifies. 'I don't know him' – this directed at a quiet-looking man in a trenchcoat – 'or her.' Georgette gestures at perhaps the most surprising attendee: a middle-aged woman sitting on her own. She wears a suit of pale tweed and clutches a finely made handbag to her chest, as though afraid to set it on the dusty floor. She looks rather 'Right Bank' – and absolutely out of place.

Before Alice can consider her further, the man in the trenchcoat stands up and introduces himself. His name is Yves, he tells them. He is small and extremely slight, and the outsized coat is aged, possibly old army-issue. He can be no older than forty, but his dishwater-brown hair is thinning severely across the pate and the skin sags tiredly beneath his eyes. He speaks, though, with a quiet confidence – a natural assumption of authority – and it is apparent that they are to consider him their leader. He looks at each of them in turn, assessing. He has, he says, the greatest confidence in them. He believes they will do their part for France. He is modest about his own experience, though it is clear that it is extensive. The Parti Communiste Français; activities for the Front Populaire; communications with Russian revolutionaries. He has been, he tells them with quiet pride, an activist his entire adult life.

At the next meeting their roles begin to crystallize. Yves has arranged for some false papers to be made up.

Alice receives hers and sees that her backstory has been cleverly chosen, that the details to a large extent match her own, while differing in the essentials. Her name is Célia, an anagram of her own name but different enough, her surname is Mertenat, and she grew up in Martinique, which accounts for any oddities of accent. When her parents died, she came to France and then to Paris to look for work as a governess, but her previous employers left the country after war was declared, necessitating her move to the museum. The quality of the documents impresses her too – they are indistinguishable from the real thing as far as her inexpert eye can establish.

'Why do we need false documents?' Georgette asks. 'It isn't as though most of us are wanted men and women.'

'They are for your own protection – and that of those you hold dear. If they were to catch you, and discovered details of a mother, father, sister . . . they could use your love for them against you. You understand?'

Georgette nods.

'The best agents are those with no family, with nothing to lose. So we must approximate that as closely as we can with fictional relations . . . those who can never be harmed.'

Shortly, Yves moves on to the leaflets the group has been distributing, which consist of anti-German propaganda, articles, advice for the occupied Parisians.

'Georgette has done a good job so far,' he tells them.

446

'But we need to think in terms of greater reach. We have to produce at least a hundred times the number we have been circulating to have any real impact.'

'We should look for someone to type the articles,' says Georgette. 'There isn't time to write them all out by hand, and after a while your hand gets so tired you can't manage anything but a scrawl that no one can read.'

'I can type.' Even as she says it, Alice wonders whether she will regret having spoken. She hasn't decided for certain whether she wants to be a part of this. Certainly, she dislikes the fact of the occupation as much as anyone here, but she isn't one of *them*, she isn't a Communist. She didn't put all her faith in the Front Populaire, has never felt that the answer to the country's ills lies in looking towards the Soviet Union, as Yves does. Alice doesn't believe in anything as rigidly defined as socialism. She believes simply in liberty. Yet perhaps all that is important is that they have at least that one common end: the expulsion of the Nazis.

Georgette grows animated as she thinks it through. 'Yes – Alice can type them at home, and we can copy them in the museum. There's a mimeograph machine in the basement. I can find out how to operate it.'

Alice turns to her. 'But Étienne? He's almost always in the museum. He'd notice something.'

Georgette raises an eyebrow. 'You think so? I reckon I could shimmy in there wearing Josephine Baker's bananas and it would go unremarked.'

Alice thinks of the silent intensity with which Étienne watches Georgette's every move and suspects otherwise. 'I don't know, Georgette. He sees more than you think.'

'Fine. Then we'll bring him in on it.'

Alice is wary. She can't imagine Étienne wanting anything other than a quiet life. It isn't that he appears cowardly, exactly, more that he is so gentle, so sanguine. Georgette, however, seems determined on her course.

The next morning she beards Étienne in his den, striding straight into his office and closing the door, coming out triumphantly an hour later. 'He's in. He even wants to help. He says he'll come to the next meeting with us.'

The typewriter they find Alice is an ancient Remington, and the keys feel odd to her – stiffer, less sensitive than those of the Corona. The 'e' key sticks, so that she has to strike it with extra force, and sometimes, even then, it doesn't register. She practises first on paper, with typewriter ink. Then comes the precious mulberry paper to make the stencils, with its thin curd of wax. The typewriter ribbon is removed so the bare metal of the keys can strike the paper directly, punching the letter-shaped holes that the ink will occupy.

Alice sits late into the night at the Remington, the pile of handwritten articles next to her. She has become adept at recognizing the different hands, the different styles. Some are more politicized than others, exhorting the reader to look to Russia, to embrace the revolutionary cause. Others, such as one pamphlet called *33 Conseils à l'occupé*, speak of the shame of living in one's own country as a second-class citizen, of having to defer to the authority of the occupying power. They ask the French people to resist in the small ways that are available to them. Not disobedience, but not cooperation either. Refusing to smile at the German soldiers, giving vague or misleading directions when asked. Treating them, in the shops and restaurants, with civility but never friendliness or deference.

She works with squares of black paper stuck to the windowpanes. The bombing raids are no more, but the night-time curfew is strictly enforced, and a light in the early hours of the morning, however dim, could draw the wrong sort of attention. She lives on three or four hours of sleep, now, but the museum is so quiet these days that there is often time for a half-hour's rest in the elderly armchair in Étienne's office. In the mirror above the washstand each morning she appears tired and wan, but determined, too. It is undoubtedly the work of her imagination, but her features seem more resolute, the face of someone with a purpose, with a secret of great power.

At twilight – that time of day when things can slip more easily beneath notice, Alice and Georgette do their rounds of the city. They put leaflets through doors, in bus shelters, on the benches in the Metro stations. Their movements are sure and practised – both can now boast a sleight of hand to rival any pickpocket's. They are masters of the moment, the snatched opportunity. Alice has learned to arrange her features into an expert pretence of studying a timetable, or examining one of the new German notices as she ferrets the papers from her bag and scatters them in plain sight.

People do get caught, though. No one from their particular group, but Alice has seen it happen. She's seen a teenage boy beaten to the ground with a truncheon, papers spraying from his hands like so much confetti, and hauled into a waiting car. Driven away to no one knows where – but there are rumours of hostages, of prison camps, of daylight murder.

Étienne has become an invaluable addition to their team – bringing to his role the same quiet focus that he applies to everything. He stays late into the night in the museum basement, intent upon his work. By morning, neat stacks of mimeographed pamphlets line the walls.

Georgette laughs at him. 'Étienne . . . how will we get rid of all of these? There are more here than there are people left in Paris!'

Étienne shrugs, and a hot flush creeps across his pale cheeks. Georgette always seems to have this effect upon him.

Alice jumps in, to save him. 'What she means is that

this is fantastic – more than anything we could have hoped for.'

Étienne smiles, weakly.

The group meets once a week now, down in the bowels of the bookshop, to report on progress and discuss new ideas.

At the third meeting, Alice manages to speak to Madame Beauclerc, the wearer of the pale suit and pearls who had appeared so out of place at the initial gathering. Anyone less like a political rebel – except Étienne, perhaps – would be difficult to conceive. Hélène Beauclerc is from one of Paris's oldest families. Her father was the city's mayor, her late husband a bishop. She does indeed live on the Right Bank; in one of the soaring stucco mansions of the leafy 16th arrondissement.

'Why are you here?' Alice asks, unable to stem her curiosity.

At first, Hélène is defensive. 'For the same reason as everyone else,' she says, shortly. Alice nods. Then the other woman gives a sigh of defeat. 'There's something else too . . . My son, he's a prisoner of war, in some godforsaken prison camp in Germany.'

'I'm sorry.'

The sympathy seems almost too much for Hélène, who grips the ever-present handbag yet tighter, until her knuckles show white on the handle. She speaks fiercely, eyes fixed on the floor in front of her. 'He's no soldier,

451

Philippe. He's a bright, happy boy – and gentle. I see those boys, those Boches – the same age, falling out of our bars, treating Paris like their playground and it makes me *sick*. I'll do anything, if it helps get them out.' She looks up at Alice, steely.

48

It was early evening, and beyond the glass a purplish haze had bled into the blue of the sky nearest the horizon, above the tops of the tallest trees in the park. We were entering that time of year, and the time of day, in which I've always felt the light is at its richest. Some recompense from nature, perhaps, before the impending plunge into night and winter.

Alice had made us our drinks herself – insisting to Julie that she had done enough for the day. They were a deep and luminous orange-red and very strong. They were Negronis: the drink Alice had discovered as a girl in Venice.

'Do you like it?' she asked, watching me take my first sip.

'I . . . don't know.' The sweetness was cut by a cough-remedy bitterness, and the gin bit at my throat. Yet it intrigued me, too, and made me take another draught.

Alice looked pleased by my answer. 'Then you will come to love it. If you don't detest it from the off it will have its chance to grow on you.'

'Is that a good thing?'

'In moderation, yes.' She smiled. I was beginning to know that smile: slow, thoughtful, heavy-lidded. 'I hope it isn't a disappointment. I wasn't one of those girls who jumped from planes in the middle of the night, or carried secret messages in their knickers, but, in my defence, I think it's fair to say that what we were doing was arguably as useful to the cause – and perhaps as dangerous – as all of that. We were showing people that hope was not lost: that someone was fighting for them. That is a potent thing. The way the Boches' – she favoured this word, rather than 'Nazis' or 'Germans' – 'reacted shows that they recognized that fact.'

She took out a tin then, and opened it to reveal a row of slim white cigarettes, snugly packed; some foreign brand. 'Would you like one?' I realized I hadn't known that she smoked. 'A habit from the war,' she said, by way of explanation. 'A filthy one, too, but I find that it relaxes one so efficiently.'

Alice lit one for me, then another for herself. She smoked thoughtfully – not hungrily, as many people do. She made it look almost like a form of meditation.

'I think it was the feeling of doing something,' she

said. 'It was the same for Hélène. She'd never had a job, she confided in me. She'd never been anything much, besides a wife and mother. Yet it turned out that she was useful, despite her doubts. She had a natural way with words, and she was good at writing pieces for the leaflets, pieces that might incite ordinary French people to action, not just those that were already politicized. She was also extremely brave: right up until the end.

'Hélène and I were the only two who weren't political. Nearly everyone else in that room was a Communist, had been part of the Popular Front – even Georgette, who had been involved in some student movements. The situation we were in, I felt the important thing was to be joined in the cause, if not in precisely the same ideology. Do you understand?'

I said that I did.

'Before I joined them,' she said, 'I liked to think of myself as brave. But, when I thought back on it, I'd run away from everything I was afraid of: my mother, my stepfather, what had happened . . . even love. I've since learned that to overcome fear one must confront it. It might sound like a tired platitude – and perhaps it is – but it's the way I've tried to live my life ever since.'

49

It is at the fourth meeting that she sees him. Julien. A decade has passed, and yet he has hardly changed. The hair is liberally streaked with grey, but the blue pirate's eyes are the same. Beside him sits a young blonde, who looks up at him every few seconds with a gaze of total adoration.

Yves introduces him to the room as a hero, a veteran of the Spanish Civil War, a long-standing member of the PCF. Julien sits and smiles modestly, looking about him at his audience. Alice has evidently changed more than he in the time that has passed, because he doesn't recognize her. Or perhaps it is the context, the strangeness of her being here, that throws him. Eventually, however, his eyes return to her and he frowns. She sees him struggle to place her, and then she sees recognition.

Julien stands to deliver some rousing words on his experiences in Spain, of the guerrilla tactics that were vital to the Resistance there. Oh yes, thinks Alice – I remember that voice. Then he introduces the blonde young woman next to him. 'This is Marcelette,' he tells them. 'She will be joining our efforts.' Alice looks at her again, incredulous. She cannot be more than sixteen or seventeen, though the full cheeks and large round eyes make her look even younger. She is beautiful yes, but in the way a child is beautiful.

'He must be joking,' Georgette murmurs. 'She's a schoolgirl.'

Julien, it seems, has overheard. He flashes Georgette a quick smile. 'I am completely serious. Marcelette may be young, but do not doubt her bravery, her dedication to the cause. She is to be our secret weapon.' He smiles down at her. 'Who could suspect such a face?'

He has a point, Alice thinks. Looking at her, it would be almost impossible to believe Marcelette capable of guile.

He comes to find her afterwards. 'Alice?'

'Julien.' Alice can see the girl – Marcelette – watching them from the corner of the room.

'I couldn't believe it . . .' He smiles, but she can see he is unnerved. She remembers, all in a rush, the last time she saw him.

'Neither could I.'

'Yes, but—' he gestures '—this is my city; it's where I was born. You . . . in Paris?'

'I've been here for ten years.'

He laughs. 'I don't understand. Last time I saw you, you were an English schoolgirl . . .'

She shrugs. 'I've changed.' She does not choose to explain more, and he apparently knows not to ask.

'Come for supper with me?'

'I'm not sure.'

'Please. It's so good to see you after all this time.'

'Fine.' What harm can it do? 'Will you bring Marcelette?'

He frowns. 'Why would I?'

'But she's your . . .' she pauses to let him give the answer and then, when nothing is forthcoming, supplies it herself: '. . . daughter?'

He laughs and shakes his head. 'No. Not my daughter. A friend.'

He takes her to an anonymous bistro a few streets away from the bookshop. During the meal – an approximation of a cassoulet, indifferent in the way that all food in the city is now – she becomes aware of something. He has no power for her, any more. As he talks of his heroism in the Spanish Civil War, his promotion in the PCF, his charm separates, like soured milk, into its constituent parts. He is not a bad person – indeed, if even half of what he says of Spain is true, he is an extremely courageous one – but he is egotistical, self-interested.

Alice congratulates her younger self: she might not have escaped his lure at first, but at least she did not give into him completely.

A pattern has been established. Less frequently now, but every few weeks, Georgette, Alice and Étienne meet with the rest of the cell. Yves, Julien, Marcelette and several of the others are involved in different work. Something that requires them to be away for weeks at a time. From the little that she has been able to glean, Alice's suspicion is that it involves travel to the Free Zone. She has heard rumours of people being helped out of the country this way – and some, a smaller number, helped *into* it. In the Free Zone the Vichy authorities have a reputation for being less stringent in their attitudes to border control. All the same, getting people there and managing to help them across the border must be treacherous work indeed.

Compared to something of such scale and inherent risk, the task of producing pamphlets seems like child's play. But no, Georgette reminds Alice, in many ways their work is as dangerous. The importance of propaganda to the Nazis can be seen on every street, where grinning, horribly caricatured Jews prey on cowering head-scarfed women, where British planes rain fiery death on unsuspecting French villages.

By day the museum functions as normal – though it is quiet enough that one or sometimes two of them can leave for an hour or so to distribute leaflets through the city. In the evenings, Alice goes home and works at her typewriter. Étienne and Georgette remain in the museum, copying those pieces that have already been typed up, working into the small hours. The three of them might be betrayed by their pallor and the blue smudges beneath their eyes, were it not for the fact that most Parisians – tired and malnourished, worn down by the daily struggle – share the same appearance.

Alice is accustomed to letting herself into the museum in the morning to a sleeping silence, knowing that Georgette and Étienne have probably snatched a few hours of rest from their work in the basement. Every day, she creeps downstairs to make a pot of strong coffee that they will drink together when the others wake. The morning Alice makes her discovery she does just this, lifting the trapdoor concealed beneath a thin rug, making her way carefully down to the musty warmth below.

There are two armchairs in the cellar. In the usual scheme of things, Étienne will take one, Georgette the other. On this particular morning, however, this is not the case. It takes Alice a moment to comprehend the scene before her. One of the armchairs is empty. In the other are two bodies. Curled about each other, so still that Alice begins to panic, until she sees Georgette's exposed shoulder blade move, ever so slightly, with an indrawn breath. Georgette is nude from the waist up: her pale skin bluish in the weak electric light. A small white breast is visible in the crook of Étienne's arm, which is thrown tightly about her. Georgette's red curls spill over his shoulder, and one hand has found a resting place in the hollow beneath his throat. Her face is pressed into his chest. Étienne faces outwards, towards Alice. Even in sleep, he appears to be smiling.

Alice retreats as soundlessly as she can, clutching the coffee pot to her chest. She lowers the trapdoor, cringing as it sighs home. She makes her way to the front desk and sits, trying to collect her thoughts. Her whole body is shaking. She feels what – exactly? Joy, certainly . . . but undercut by something that feels rather like envy. She is worried for them, too. At a time like this, can such a thing have a future?

Over the next few weeks, Alice sees everything that must have slipped beneath her notice in the past. The looks they exchange when they think they're un-observed, which belie their careful civility with each other in public. She still finds it hard to believe: Georgette with her beauty and confidence, Étienne so quiet and awkward. Observing more closely now, she sees how tender they are with one another. In Georgette's presence, Étienne speaks and laughs more – is, at times, even witty – and in return her sharpness is softened by his gentleness.

One morning, they come to her – and she sees that they are holding hands.

'We wanted you to be the first to know,' says Georgette.

Étienne nods, and clears his throat. 'We're getting married.'

Alice's surprise is only in part feigned. She had never quite imagined that it could come to this. Perhaps there is hope for the world after all.

The ceremony is small and cheap. Alice is the only person attending who is not related to the bride or groom. She sits beside old Monsieur Dupré, who sleeps through most of the proceedings. He wakes just in time for the final blessing and applauds loudly, as though he is at the theatre. Georgette's mother, an austere professor of mathematics, surprises everyone by bursting into noisy tears.

Later, Alice will cling to this day – the joy and hope, the normality. She will invoke it as proof that there is something beyond the new truth of her situation. It will be the last day of her old life.

50

It comes in the middle of the night. The hum of an engine in the square, the raised voices downstairs. She hears Madame Fourrier, indignant, and can imagine her in her nightcap and gown, facing them down. She hears them, too; voices carrying the authority of those for whom no place, whatever the hour, is out of bounds. She hears the door slam, another, weaker cry of protest from the land-lady, and then the old steps ringing with quick, heavy footsteps. The whole house will be awake now, of that Alice is certain. Waiting to see who it will be.

It is for her, of course it is. She had known it would be. All she can do is wait. They are taking their time, banging on each and every door. Madame Fourrier has evidently not helped them as far as she might have done. She does not need to look about her room to check that there is nothing to give her away here, at least not without an extremely thorough search. The Remington is as well hidden as it can be, in the secret cavity in the wall behind the chest of drawers. She has set a match to any wasted stencils each night over the sink, washing away the blackened evidence. She is grateful now for all the wine Monsieur Dupré produced after the ceremony, the wine that made her too clumsy and stupid to think about typing that night. Otherwise there would be the usual fresh sheaf of stencils on her desk.

Finally – and it is almost a strange relief – the knock comes. Alice doesn't answer at first. She will pretend that she has only just been woken by the commotion, from the deep, uninterrupted sleep of someone with nothing to hide. It comes again, louder. Then a thud, lower down – a boot, perhaps. She throws herself from the bed. She won't have them breaking in: an act that would, in itself, seem to criminalize her. She goes to the door and turns the key, flings it back as the man in front goes to strike it again. He falls forward into the room and swears in German, just stopping himself from losing his balance. He is small but powerfully built, this first one. The man behind him is tall and palely blond, and Alice is unnerved by his passing resemblance to Étienne. They wear the black uniform of the Gestapo.

'Alice Eversley?' the stockier man asks. As he says it he smiles, and Alice realizes that he is enjoying himself. He lets his eyes run over her body, insubstantially concealed by her thin nightgown. But she is Célia, now, she thinks. She is no longer Alice Eversley. Should she deny it? Claim that she is an innocent woman, with no knowledge of this other person?

Before she can decide, the taller man speaks in French, pre-empting her. His voice is surprisingly soft, his accent good, but his eyes, as he studies her, are cold. 'There's no use pretending,' he tells her. 'I'm afraid, my dear' – *ma chérie* – 'that we know both of your names – Alice, Célia . . . quite clever. One of your friends has given us all we need.'

Who? She knows that it can't be Étienne or Georgette. She prays they will be safe, the one night neither of them is at home. The tall man shakes his head, as though reading her thoughts. 'We have them, too,' he says, almost regretfully. 'They'd tried to fool us, I think, by checking into a hotel. We found them easily enough.'

The hotel had been booked for their wedding night. It was probably easier for the Gestapo to find them there than anywhere else, Alice thinks. The hotels, especially the better ones, are all packed with Nazis these days.

The taller man searches the room, riffling through drawers, flicking through her books, feeling under the bed, while the other takes her arm in a firm grip, far tighter than it needs to be. They don't produce anything – it would take a far more imaginative, extensive search to discover the Remington. The man's disappointment is palpable, despite the pains he takes not to show it. It would earn him extra credit, undoubtedly, to have unearthed some new piece of evidence.

They escort Alice downstairs, and she can sense the other tenants listening, curious and relieved. At the bottom of the stairs she glimpses something odd, a black shape protruding through the doorway that leads to the restaurant. Then she realizes what it is. A foot. As they move past, she sees the fallen form of Madame Fourrier spread-eagled on the tiles.

Alice stalls, hoping for some small movement that might indicate the landlady is alive, but the men haul her on, out into the black wet street to the waiting car. They drive her through the silent city, along the Boulevard du Montparnasse. When they pass the entrance to La Coupoule, Alice looks away.

The men observe her closely: she feels their gaze upon her. She understands, instinctively, that it is important not to show anything by her expression. She knows she must prevent herself from asking about Georgette and Étienne, about whoever it is that has given them all away. To do so might be to accidentally reveal something they don't already know.

51

'They took me to one of Paris's oldest prisons,' Alice told me, 'a place called Fresnes. It was either that or the Cherche-Midi.'

'I've heard of it,' I told her. 'They tortured people there.'

'Yes,' said Alice, 'and perhaps I was lucky in that I had so little to reveal. Fortunate – if it can be described as such – in that my questioner, an older man, was clearly experienced in the art of interrogation. I think he had seen enough to know when someone had something to hide, and he had no qualms about showing me that I was a waste of his time. Others who knew more – like Yves, the leader of our cell – they didn't fare so well.'

'They let you go?'

She shook her head. 'No, that wasn't how it worked. I didn't know it at the time, but I was essentially a hostage, one of hundreds. We were being held, all of us, as collateral. There was a sort of mathematics to it. A ratio, I think, of about one to fifty. If one Boche life was taken in a Resistance attack, fifty French prisoners would be executed.'

52

The room is less than a room, slightly more than a cupboard, far taller than it is wide. It is almost completely dark, but there is a letterbox-sized hole near the bottom of the door through which a dusty ray falls to illuminate a small rectangle of floor and the mattress, loosely stuffed with straw.

Alice's watch has been taken from her, but she is able to mark the passing of the days by the occasional interruption of a meal. The food is always the same: a thin, bitter broth. What it contains is difficult to distinguish. Not much that is edible, certainly. Alice found it hard to swallow, at first, but now she longs for it – more as an interruption to the long hours than as sustenance.

It is pushed through the opening in the door, often with some force so that a quantity spills over the top of the bowl. One day, Alice was so hungry that she was tempted to lick up this spilt portion, but managed to stop herself with the knowledge of how ill – and therefore how weak – it might make her.

In the dark and the silence, thoughts grow loud. There are the good thoughts, those that remove her from her surroundings. These should be encouraged, and Alice forces them into being by invoking that party by the lake, the night she was reunited with Tom. If she focuses carefully enough, she can almost see the white mist that settled upon the surface of the water, and the way it bloomed pink in the new light of day.

Occasionally she travels back to that time in the boathouse when she first realized Tom's talent, or to that afternoon tearing down country roads in Aunt Margaret's motor car, the trees scorched by autumn, the clouds racing above them.

Every once in a while she allows herself to think of Corsica, or of that morning in her attic room with the sunlight falling through to wake them, the sheets tangled around their feet, his thigh thrown over hers, warm and heavy. She must treat these memories lightly so as not to sully or bruise them, like all delicate things that are damaged with too much handling.

There are the bleak thoughts too, thoughts that make Alice believe that she will be there for ever, that she will never escape, that she will die in darkness upon this very floor without seeing anyone she loves again, without being able to say goodbye.

It is vital not to let these thoughts take hold. Alice understands that these are the thoughts that could destroy a person more efficiently, more integrally, than anything her captors might do.

Ten meals have passed before Alice hears it. At first, she assumes that it is inside her head: a projection of her own longing for company. But the more she listens, the more she becomes convinced that it is a real voice. Not just one voice, in fact – another has joined it. And there is a peculiar sound, a scrape and a thump – clumsy, percussive. And in rhythm, she realizes, with the song. And she recognizes the melody, though her thoughts seem slow, and it takes her several bars to name it. They are singing 'The Marseillaise'.

53

New York, September 1986

'They sang it every week,' Alice told me. 'It was the most hope-inspiring sound I have ever heard. Those thin voices in unison, the thump of palms against doors, litter pails, bed boards – anything that could be struck. The guards hated it because they were powerless to stop it. Yes, they could mete out punishment at random or single out those seen as inciters, and they could – and did – punish us all. But when everything has been taken from you, everything except hope, it gives you a strange sort of strength. For us, hope could be found in singing that song.

'I learned, too, that there was a means of communication

between the cells. I hadn't been aware of it until I heard a whisper, high above my head. I looked up through the gloom, and I could see then that there was a metal grille there. I had to dismantle my bed, fold the mattress in on itself and stand on top, and even then it wasn't quite high enough. Still, I could hear the words faintly: a woman's voice.' Alice smiled. 'Do you know, it was at once the most mundane and the most wonderful conversation I have had in my life. It was the sort of conversation you might start up with a stranger on a train. "What's your name?" she asked me, and "How did you come to be here?" The sort of questions that would pass for inanities elsewhere. But in there, to have a conversation, a normal conversation, was a miraculous thing indeed.

'Her name was Madeleine. She was a simple farm girl from the Cévennes, but she had been involved in brave work, helping to receive parachute-drops of supplies . . . and sometimes people. One night it had all gone wrong. She said it wasn't even a particularly important drop: some fairly basic supplies, a small quantity of dynamite. They'd got to her before she had time to take her cyanide capsule, the one that had been given to her by the SOE. Her brother had managed to take his though.' Alice shook her head. 'Can you guess how old she was?'

I shook my head.

'Seventeen. She had barely any education, and no real knowledge of the world outside her small sphere, simply an instinctive understanding of what was right, of her duty.'

54

Alice has an image in her mind of what Madeleine looks like, though the girl has never given any indication of her appearance. She imagines solemn dark eyes; a thick, practical braid of hair – a farm girl's hair – slung over one shoulder. A capable solidity to her, strong arms and thick legs. Perhaps a sheen of prettiness too, or maybe something more profound, drawn from that deep well of character and vigour.

She hears the tap of a fingernail against the grille: the signal they have chosen to indicate that they have something to say. There is no sense in wasting breath if the other is asleep, or otherwise insensible. Their voices, rendered weak in this place, are precious commodities. Alice clambers her way up.

'I'm here, Madeleine.'

'I thought I'd ask if you wanted me to send a message.'

'To who?'

'To someone inside – in one of the other cells.'

Of course. For one delirious moment, Alice had imagined she might be able to send a message to Tom.

The cells are created alike – each with the same small perforated air vent near the ceiling. Briefly, ridiculous though it is, Alice feels a prickle of jealousy that Madeleine – her Madeleine – is in contact with others besides herself. She has long ago discovered that she must be at the end of a line of cells, because there is no grille in the other wall, no sound from the other side.

'Yes,' she whispers back, suddenly struck by inspiration. 'I would like to. I'd like to ask a question, actually, if that's possible.'

'What is it?'

'I'd like to know whether my friends are here – Georgette, and Étienne.' She uses their real names so that they will know it is from her. 'I want to know if they're here, and if they're well.'

It takes a few hours for the reply to come. 'Yes,' Madeleine tells her, 'both here. Both well . . . or as well as can be expected in this place.'

Good news and bad. So they were found, after all. But they are alive, too, and that counts for something.

'Oh, and Alice . . .?'

'Yes?'

'Georgette wanted you to know that this isn't quite how she saw married life turning out.'

55

Fresnes Prison, November 1942

They are led outside, into the yard, a hundred or so of them. It is a grey, dreary day, but they have lived in darkness for weeks – some of them months – and the light sears their eyes. To Alice it seems as though a layer of her skin has been removed, and she feels every breath of wind like an abrasion. She has become a different animal – subterranean, dark-dwelling – some helpless, naked thing. She looks about her at her fellow prisoners, grey-skinned and hollow-eyed, who seem like another species from the guards who flank them. For the first time, Alice sees Madeleine, and she understands that Madeleine would, indeed, once have been that pretty, plump farm girl of her imagination. Not any more though.

Finally, she glimpses her friends on the opposite side of the yard: Georgette, Étienne – even Madame Beauclerc. Étienne looks like a consumptive. Georgette has lost three stone, at least. As for Hélène Beauclerc: they must have decided she had something to tell them. Or perhaps her interrogator was more than usually sadistic. Alice can hardly bring herself to look at her. There is a thin trail of dried black blood at the corner of her mouth, and her nail-less hands hang limp and purple at her sides like ruined fruit.

Georgette looks up and catches sight of Alice. She gives an involuntary start, and Alice realizes that she, too, has changed almost beyond recognition. At least Georgette does recognize her, and she smiles.

'What's going on?' Alice hears the man behind her murmur to another prisoner. They are being herded into the centre of the yard and then divided into two groups. A small, uniformed woman is in charge. She makes quick annotations on a clipboard as each prisoner steps into place.

'I don't know,' the other mutters back, 'the camps, perhaps.'

'*Halt dein Maul!*' Without further warning, a guard steps forward and cracks the second man over the back of the head. He gives a moan and crumples to the ground. The speed, the quietness of it, makes the whole spectacle more shocking. People look, and try not to. Is he dead, or merely unconscious? He is not moving, and there is a wet, blackish stain beneath his head. The other prisoners must step over him to move towards the centre.

Alice sees Étienne, Hélène and Georgette in front of her. She watches as Étienne and Hélène are sent to one huddle of prisoners, and Georgette to the other. Then it is her turn. The woman looks her over, briefly, and orders her to the first group.

A shout rings out. At first, Alice isn't certain where the noise has come from. She turns, and realizes it is one of the prisoners in the other group, one who has suddenly found her voice. The noise cuts though the silence of the yard. 'My husband!' she calls. 'Let me go with him. Please.' Alice realizes with horror that the woman is Georgette. She waits, hardly daring to look, for a guard to step in and knock her to the ground. But no one moves. The guards seem too taken aback by the outburst to know how to act. 'Please.' All watch as Georgette sinks to her knees in supplication. The woman with the clipboard regards her, and looks back towards the other group, to where Étienne stands, his eyes filling with tears.

The woman shrugs. 'Fine.'

She moves to stand before Alice and Étienne's group, and looks carefully along the front row. She stops at Alice, and runs her eyes over her once more, assessing her according to some unknown criteria. Again, she shrugs, apparently not quite satisfied by what she sees, but not concerned enough to worry overly about it. 'You,' she says. 'Swap.'

56

'What most of us had assumed,' Alice said, 'was that we were being moved on to the camps. That the two groups signified two different locations. Only it wasn't that. One group was being moved on: the group I was swapped into. We were the 'fitter' consignment – those who would be better suited to labour. I was deemed unfit at first, but I was obviously near enough to be swapped with Georgette. It is a matter of small degrees, you understand, among people who have been starved and locked inside for weeks.'

'What about the other group?'

'They were taken to be shot, in a wood outside Paris.'

*

I could not stop thinking about the expression on Alice's face when she told me of her friends' fate. In fact, I had hardly been able to bring myself to look at her. The grief and guilt was etched on her face, even after all these years, and in some dilute way it became a grief I now shared – for I had begun to feel I knew them too, through her.

At the same time I was aware of Alice's strength. She might still carry that pain, just as she carried the pain of twice losing her daughter, but she had not allowed it to destroy her. I remembered my instinct, after Mum died, to stop up my life and let the dust settle over me. I had almost achieved it – would perhaps have done so had Evie not made her revelation. Alice had found it in herself to keep living.

It got me thinking, too: had I ever had a friend I truly loved, as Alice did Étienne and Georgette? There was Mum, of course – I had always thought of her as my best friend – but discounting this, the answer was probably no. I'd had friends, though, and I saw now how much I had enjoyed those afternoons in the Goodge Street pub, listening to the big talkers in the group and laughing at or with them, feeling a warmth spread through me that had to be due to more than the wine.

I had liked to tell myself that they had given me up quickly, when Mum died and I stopped coming, but that wasn't strictly true. Like someone surfacing from a trance, I could now recall the voicemails left un-answered, the envelopes unopened and filed away. They had tried – and they had persisted longer than I had expected. Eventually I had found myself alone: exactly as I had planned. Now the feeling rose inside me, demanding to be acknowledged. I didn't want to be alone any longer.

57

This is the place, the place that makes her understand that hers is to be a sentence of death, as certain as any more traditional mode of execution. It will merely be a slower perishing, strung out in this wasteland. She will be buried in this frozen black earth.

There are women of all nationalities here, it seems, including German. Some of them are, like Alice, political prisoners. There are other varieties of criminal here too. In Alice's quarters there are two murderers, one prostitute and a thief. It is best to avoid drawing attention to yourself. It is important, too, to keep hold of your possessions, meagre as they are. Never to let your shoes or toothbrush stray from your sight, however broken and useless they may appear. Alice's shoes might once have been a pair of clogs: now only the soles remain, and a piece of rough cloth has been nailed to each to keep them in place. Still, she sleeps with them clasped to her chest, because to be without shoes here is to invite a slow rotting of the flesh through frostbite and gangrene.

This place operates according to its own set of rules or, rather, according to its own particular variety of chaos. Some of the seemingly healthiest women – though all things are relative – are the first to succumb to the cold, to the lack of food, to one of the many epidemics. While there are those who look as if they should no longer be able to stand or speak, and yet they manage by some miracle to survive the long hours required of them in the freezing fields.

They are housed in a barracks of cramped, dingy bungalows – 'more like pig huts in a field,' says the prostitute, whose name is Berthe, 'than a place where human beings might be expected to sleep.' Berthe is small and fierce, with a filthy turn of phrase. The other Frenchwomen are wary of her brash manner, but Alice discovers that she rather likes it. To retain your fierceness here is no mean feat: a clinging to life. And there is something about Berthe – the brilliant dark eyes, perhaps, the quick-witted turn of phrase – that reminds Alice of Georgette.

She thinks of Georgette often, and Étienne. She hopes that they have managed to stay together. Being with the person you love must make it easier to bear it all – the dirt and cold, the many greater and lesser indignities; must make it easier, in fact, to keep a hold on your humanity.

Alice thinks of Tom, too. She finds that if she focuses on the details – the scent of his skin; the hard warm plane of his chest beneath her cheek; his irises blue as the Corsican water; those long, clever, artist's fingers – she can invoke him more effectively than if she tries to conjure him complete, all at once.

There isn't time to invoke him when she crawls into her bunk, because she is always so exhausted that sleep crashes over her in a black wave, instantaneously, never mind the hunger. But she thinks of him when she stands in the frozen field at the morning line-up. Every morning, several women fall where they stand, never to rise again. When she feels the cold beginning to permeate to her core, Alice draws upon her memory of those days on sun-warmed beaches, the feel of Tom's skin against hers.

'You must have someone,' Berthe whispers to her early one morning when they sit facing each other on the bunk having been shocked awake by the roar of Allied bombers above. 'To conjure.'

Alice understands. 'Who's yours?'

'My little girl, Thais.'

'Where is she?'

For the first time, Alice sees Berthe unsure of herself. 'I don't know. I told her to go straight to the nearest church if there was trouble.'

'I'm sure she would have done it,' Alice says, for reassurance. Then, because she has been wondering: 'Why are you here?'

Berthe gives a humourless smile. 'A man came to see me. He asked me to do something that I don't do, so I told him it wasn't on the menu. Then he tried to make me do it, so I bit him, here.' She taps her cheekbone. 'There was a lot of blood,' she adds, with unmistakable relish. 'It turned out he was SS – an Oberführer – and the next day they came to pick me up. I never had a chance to check on Thais, because they came for me at work.' Her eyes are black in the low light, unblinking.

'I'm sure she will be all right,' Alice tells her, as confidently as she can. She tries a smile, but the muscles of her face seem to have forgotten the expression. 'Especially if she's like her mother.'

Alice and Berthe work side by side. Their task is to clear the land of the rocks and stones that pervade the poor soil, preparing it for future propagation. The idea that anything might be expected to grow here is ludicrous. As Berthe says, they must be getting desperate. They work with broken spades and shovels, wheelbarrows with no wheels.

Every day, another handful of women will survive the torturous roll call only to be ground out several hours later in the frozen earth. Apparently, it could be worse. There are rumours of processing plants where the fumes cause slow blindness; of munitions factories in salt mines, where the chemicals eat into the skin and weather it away in layers, leaving weeping sores that refuse to heal. Perhaps it is preferable to die in the air, in nature, beneath this endless sky? Or perhaps it is all the same, in the end.

They are ordered to work in complete silence, and contraventions are punishable by a day cleaning the latrines, or the floor of the infirmary, which, even more surely than anything else here, equals death. Yet they have become skilled at the art of communicating without detection. It is worth the risk. Alice does not know how she would survive the day without conversation.

When the nearest guard to them has made his progress along the line to the furthest point away from them that he can get, Berthe whispers, 'Who's yours?'

'What do you mean?'

'You know, like Thais is mine.'

'Oh.' Alice, suddenly, isn't sure that she wants to say. She feels, irrationally, that to mention his name aloud in this stinging air might taint those memories of him that are so precious. But she must. Berthe, after all, has offered up her daughter.

'His name is Tom.'

'Your lover? I know that he can't be your husband.'

'Why?'

'Because of the way you say his name. I've never met a woman yet who speaks of her husband with such a tremor in her voice.'

'All right. Yes, he was. And my friend.'

They fall silent as the uniformed figure makes his way back down the line. Later, Berthe revisits the subject.

'Tell me about him, then, your Tom.'

'It's complicated.'

Berthe nods. 'I can understand complicated.' She gives an odd smile. 'I wasn't always a whore, you know.'

Alice looks at her, deciding. Berthe *will* understand, she realizes. She is aware, too, that this may be her only chance to tell anyone. 'I don't think I'd ever loved anyone before him,' she says. 'I mean any sort of love. My father and my brother, perhaps, but they died when I was a child. I know, if I get out of this place, that Tom's the person I want to spend my life with.'

'So what was the problem?'

'There was a child . . .'

'Ah,' Berthe says, knowingly. 'He didn't want you to have it?'

'No, nothing like that. He didn't know that it was his.'

Berthe seems unconvinced. Alice can almost read her thoughts: there's not knowing, and then there's *choosing* not to know. She is quick to explain. 'I told him it was someone else's.'

'Even though you were almost sure it was his?'

'Even though I knew it had to be his. He was the only one.'

'Why? You were scared of how he would react?'

'Yes, I suppose so – though not in the way you might

think. If I'd told him the truth, he would have given up everything – all his hopes and ambitions – in order to provide for us. I could never have forgiven myself.'

'Sounds like a saint.'

'Not a saint, no. Just a very good man. Then the baby died, so there was even less reason to tell him. Or so I thought. But having that secret from him . . . it has made it difficult to imagine a future for us.'

'You have to tell him, you know,' Berthe says. 'Can't go keeping things like that from the person you love.'

'I know.' I will, thinks Alice. If I survive this, I will tell him. Then we'll start anew.

58

Poland, November 1943

Every few weeks, a new consignment of women arrives at the camp. Usually, enough prisoners have died in the interim for there to be space to accommodate the influx. The new ones are easy to identify. They may have become underweight and unkempt wherever they have been before, but they are never as malnourished, as grey-skinned, as ridden with sores as the women who have been here for several weeks.

Alice watches the new arrivals being marched through the gates. Something about one of the women gives her pause. It is the tug of familiarity, she realizes, looking closer. Then she understands. It is Marcelette, the beautiful child. She is quite changed, now. 'Marcelette?' Alice calls, incredulous.

The girl starts, seeing her, and hangs her greasy head. Alice moves a little closer, making certain. 'Marcelette – is it you?' She tries to make eye contact, but Marcelette refuses to look up. Alice goes to her. She takes hold of the thin shoulders and feels that the girl is trembling like an animal caught in a trap.

'Marcelette, please! Talk to me. Are you ill?' All the time, she is thinking: is it a fever? She has heard talk of a cholera outbreak. She presses her palm to the girl's forehead, expecting to find it livid with heat, and is surprised by its coolness. So, not a fever after all. Yet the girl's trembling is getting worse. Then a terrible sound – a howl – rips from her. It isn't just a sound, though: Alice hears words too, incoherent though they may be.

'I don't understand,' Alice says, as calmly as she is able. 'What is it that you're trying to tell me?'

Marcelette's voice drops to something less than a whisper. Alice strains to hear, and this time the words are unmistakable: *It was me.*

'What was . . .?' Alice looks at the girl again, and suddenly understands.

The story spills from her – terrible, inevitable. 'It was Julien,' she says. 'They came to me – they found me out. They told me that they had him, but they said if I could give them names . . .' She trails off.

'What, what did they say?'

'They promised that they would let him go. They'd

arrange for us both to travel to the Free Zone, to help us to leave France.'

Alice stares at her, in pity and fury. 'And you believed them, Marcelette? You actually thought they would do that?'

The girl gives a miserable shrug. 'I loved him,' she says, simply. 'I would have done anything.'

59

'I don't want to talk much more about that place. I lost three years of my life to it,' Alice said. 'It isn't that I'm not able to, you understand. It's the fact that, with the worst things, merely to speak of them is to allow some of their taint to seep back into the world. Do you see?'

I nodded.

'Good.'

'But . . . one last thing, if you don't mind my asking. How did you survive?'

'There wasn't anything noble about it,' she said. 'I wasn't any braver or any stronger than those who died. I was luckier, perhaps. That my sores didn't spread and fester as some did. That I didn't get properly ill until

495

the end, as we were about to be liberated. It was what they call lockjaw.' I must have looked blank, so she explained: 'Tetanus.'

'But that's fatal, I thought.'

'Often, yes – if it is allowed to progress. Again, I was fortunate. We were already with the Polish Red Cross when I started showing symptoms. The doctors knew what it was straight away. They'd seen enough cases in men at the front.'

The camp had been liberated in January but Alice hadn't been fit to travel until May. When she was out of danger, she had been taken with a group of others to recover on a farm in Sweden. 'We stayed with an elderly couple. They fed us cream and eggs and fish . . . things that had been difficult to come by, even when we were free. Back in that place, I had tormented myself dreaming of such food – but when it came to it, it seemed so rich that I almost couldn't stomach it. They were so kind, our hosts, but all I wanted was to go and find him.'

60

London, March 1946

Alice makes her way along Upper Street. She is aware of the strange figure she cuts. She has not yet regained a healthy weight, and her form floats in the too-large dress and coat – donations from her Swedish hosts. Her skin is greyish, her hair thin and lank. She has never been vain, but she avoids the reflections of shop windows all the same.

All about her is the evidence of the bombing. Yawning craters expel powdered mortar on to the wind. They are building sites now, and men crawl over the rubble, working busily with picks and shovels. Alice hurries her step. She cannot allow herself to entertain the possibility that Tom's home may, at this moment, be spilling on to the street in a mess of masonry and glass.

It is Rosa who answers the door. She is unmistakable: the wide-set blue eyes, the chin with its unusual dimple and even the seraphic dark-gold hair are unaltered since childhood. Forgetting how she herself has changed, Alice waits for some sign of answering recognition from her. None comes.

'Can I help you?' Rosa asks.

'Is . . . Thomas Stafford here?'

Rosa shakes her head. 'No, he isn't, I'm afraid. He's in Corsica. What is it about?'

Alice can't be sure exactly why she does it. Perhaps it is the humiliation of not being recognized, of realizing how much she must have changed. Or perhaps it is that she doesn't feel like Alice Eversley any more – as though the last vestiges of the person she was were sloughed away in that place.

'My name is Célia,' she says. 'I'm a friend of Tom's. I wanted to ask . . .' She stalls. What is it, exactly, that she wants to know? 'I wanted to ask . . . is he well?'

Alice can feel Rosa's curious gaze upon her. 'Would you like to come inside for a cup of tea?'

When they are both sitting at the kitchen table Rosa, who has been studying Alice's face with new scrutiny, says, 'I'm sorry . . . but what did you say your name was?'

'Célia.'

'Because, you know, looking at you again I could have sworn . . .' She shakes her head. 'It must simply be a likeness. You remind me of someone I knew ever so long ago. Look,' she places a sponge cake on the table between them. 'Can I offer you a slice? I hope you don't mind me saying, but it seems you could do with it.'

Alice looks down at herself. It is still a shock to her, when she glances down and sees this frail, stranger's form: the wasted limbs and flattened chest; the body, to all intents and purposes, of an elderly woman. 'Yes,' she says, 'I've been unwell.'

'So you've come about Tom.' Rosa takes a bite of her cake. As she chews, Alice sees the dimple in her round cheek show itself, exactly as it had when she was a child. It had fascinated Alice at the time, this small detail. Rosa had always had an expressive face, and the mark had seemed to Alice like much-needed punctuation for the capricious play of emotion across her features.

'Yes,' she remembers to say, as Rosa looks up and catches her staring.

'How did you say you know him?'

Alice thinks quickly. 'From . . . New York. We met in New York.'

'Ah. He's all right, which is a relief. He got some shrapnel from a shell in his leg – in the shin, but he's recovered well. But he wasn't quite himself when he came back from France.' Rosa lowers her voice. 'My father had some . . . trouble, after the Great War, so we feared the worst.'

Alice strains to maintain an expression of friendly concern – the sort that an acquaintance should feel – without letting her real anxiety for Tom show through.

'Still, it all seems to have worked itself out now. He took himself off to Corsica – I think he'd spent some time there before the war.'

Alice is already reaching for her coat and bag. Corsica. She should have known he would return there.

'And,' says Rosa, blithely, 'he seems to have got himself married, of all things. Ma was hurt that we weren't invited, but in the circumstances I suppose—' She breaks off and stares at Alice. 'But my dear woman . . . is something the matter?'

61

New York, September 1986

'I don't know what made me lie,' Alice told me. 'Whether it was some instinct of self-preservation, some idea of what I might discover . . . I'm not certain. I was glad that I hadn't told the truth, when it came to it.

'So you see, I had a rather bad time of it in London, in the end.' She said it lightly, but I could only imagine how eviscerating it would have been, to discover that the man you loved had given himself to someone else.

Should I tell her that he had come looking for her? I wasn't sure. Before I could decide she had continued, and the opportunity was lost.

'My next visit,' she said, 'was to the address in Hampstead that Sophie had given me for her friends.

When I arrived there, I discovered that the De Rosiers had never arrived. I'd spent the war imagining them safe in England, but they had never left France.

'With hindsight, it is easy to see that they were cutting it too fine. They hadn't the right papers, which would always have caused problems, but they were unlucky, too. The last telegram that Sophie's cousin had from them said that they'd stopped at a hotel in Montoire overnight. As they slept, all of the fuel was stolen from the tank of their car, so they would have to continue on foot.

'That telegram was the last anyone heard from them.'

'That's awful.' Even as I spoke the words, I was hopelessly aware of how inadequate they sounded. 'What happened to the children?'

'They had got to England, thank goodness, thanks to Sophie's foresight in sending them on ahead. I was so happy to see them that I wept. Marguerite has told me since that they didn't recognize me at first – emaciated and altered as I was – so it must have made an alarming sight.'

'Marguerite?'

'Ah, but you've met Marguerite – I forget. She's Sophie's daughter. She resembles her mother so closely that at times I find it hard to believe it isn't Sophie I'm looking at, even though she's older now than her mother was when I knew her.

'When Aunt Margaret died, not long after the war, she left me rather a sum. I didn't want to take it at first, you understand. I had been happiest in my life when I had been at my poorest. I didn't see how money could improve my lot in any way. But then I realized what I could do with it. I could afford to support Marguerite and her brother Antoine – and so I became their guardian. I already loved them almost as my own.

'So we returned to Paris, the three of us. We didn't know anywhere else to be – it was our home. Besides, we had to go back: because otherwise it would have been as though they had taken that from us, too.'

Alice smiled, and I could see how tired she was, though undoubtedly unwitting to admit it. I began to make my excuses.

'You will come to the gallery tomorrow?'

'Yes, I'd like that.'

'Good.' She seemed very pleased by this.

On my way back to the subway, I couldn't stop thinking about that ill-fated trip she had made to Islington, only to find out that the man she loved was lost to her for good. And then to Hampstead . . . I felt – it's difficult to explain – *infected* by her grief, as though it had got right underneath my skin. I wanted to call Oliver, to talk to him about it. I hesitated outside a payphone, doing the calculations. It would be the small hours of the morning in France, I realized, so I carried on my way.

Back in my hotel room, I thought about Oliver, realizing that I hadn't heard anything more from him since that last short message. Was he, now that we were apart, realizing that it was too soon for him after all? Was he beginning to have doubts? I don't, I said to myself, twisting the pillow in my hands. I don't have any doubt. But is that enough?

62

New York, September 1986

The gallery was off East 64th Street. I don't know exactly what I was expecting, but the building was far grander than I could have imagined. My first thought was that it was like some great, white, secular temple. Beautiful, and stirring, in its starkness.

Alice was waiting for me in the foyer, a lofty, sunlit atrium. She wore one of her characteristic brightly patterned silk scarves, and her white hair seemed almost to reflect its colours. She was pleased, I thought, but there was something else too. It was with some astonishment that I realized she seemed nervous.

Within the atrium the light had an incredible quality, as though it were being filtered through the spray of a waterfall, and I realized that the effect came from the great glass panels that surrounded it. They were like no stained-glass windows I had ever seen, the pattern an abstract of green and blue leaf-like shapes.

Alice followed my gaze. 'There is a chapel, in a town called Vence, in southern France. The Chapelle du Rosaire. Matisse designed it with windows similar to these. When I visited, I thought it was the most peaceful place I had ever been. I wanted something like that here. I wanted people to come in from the busy, dirty street, and find sanctuary. A cleansing, if you like, of their daily concerns, before they go on to see the art. So I asked Matisse to make me these. I think it works, no?'

I nodded. 'It does.' Matisse, I thought. Henri Matisse had made them for her.

We made our way up to the next level. There were no stairs, just a circular walkway that gradually ascended. It was a weekday morning, but the gallery was already quite busy, and many of the visitors seemed to be students, sitting and sketching, taking notes.

Alice gestured to a long row of benches along one wall: 'I had those put in, so that people could sit and draw, or simply look. There are never enough places to sit in galleries, I find, to relax and look. I don't want people having to temper their enjoyment of the pieces with backache.'

As we moved past the pieces she reeled off names:

'Epstein, Stafford, O'Keeffe, Miller, Stafford, Newman, Still, Stafford, Stafford . . .' She turned to smile back at me. 'Do you see something of a pattern forming?' She hadn't lowered her voice, and some of the students looked up as she passed with expressions from amusement to irritation. 'They think I'm some mad old lady,' she said, gleefully.

I craned for a look at each piece by Stafford. There were several of the New York night-time scenes he had spoken of: the colours slightly blurred as though viewed through rain. Scenes of Corsica from the Maison du Vent, scenes I knew so well and that, I realized, Alice would never necessarily have known first-hand. That thought gave me pause.

Alice was urging me on. 'We'll go to my office, so that we can talk properly.'

It was less like an office than another elegantly appointed drawing room, and there was no desk in sight: merely a vast glass table in the centre, strewn with books and attended by two armchairs. More books were stacked upon shelves that spanned the length and breadth of one wall. The windows of the exterior wall were the same stained blue and green glass as the atrium. The remaining two walls were covered with artworks.

They were, by and large, simple monochrome studies in pencil, ink and charcoal. All Stafford's. Some were of New York, but many were from an earlier period, as proven by the handwritten dates.

'They're all his.' I moved along the wall, studying

each in turn. One stood out because it was done in watercolours: a view of the Grain de Sable, foregrounded by the white dart of a yacht's sail. *Bonifacio, 1939*, I read, and understood why it was that she had kept this one here. This was a view she had been there to see.

'Almost,' Alice said, 'but not quite.' I followed her gaze and, suddenly, I saw it, right in the middle where it had somehow been previously invisible to me. I had to look twice to be absolutely sure.

'That's one of mine,' I said. It was one of the series I had taken of Mum – barefoot, electric with movement – for my final show.

She nodded. 'It was my favourite. I could not have left London without it.'

All these years, I thought – all of these years of our not knowing anything – and something of Mum and I had been here with Alice after all.

Next I found a series of a young woman I now recognized instantly: sitting on a Corsican beach, at a quayside restaurant, at the stern of a small boat. 'These are all of you.'

'Yes, I suppose they are. I'm selfish to keep these here with me. One day I know that they must be shared, but some of them feel . . . almost too intimate for unknown eyes – at least while I am alive. When I am gone, which cannot be long now . . . then, I think, the time might be right.' She said it philosophically, as though she had given it considered thought. 'For the time being I keep them here to remind me of her, the girl that I was. Sometimes it's easy to forget that she and I are one and the same person. For all her faults – for all the selfishness, the naïveté, I still want to remember her.' Alice laughed. 'But you must think I'm talking nonsense,' she said. 'Perhaps I am a mad old woman, after all.'

'No,' I said. 'Stafford – Tom – said something similar. That he couldn't believe sometimes that he had been that young man once . . . the person who painted these. And then, at other times, that he could not understand how he was no longer him – how he had suddenly grown so old.'

She looked up at me, and I had to glance down, discomfited, because her eyes had filled with tears.

'I'm sorry,' she said. 'I've embarrassed you. It's that . . . well, to me he will always be that young man. I imagine it is the same for him . . .

'Do you like it?' she said, suddenly.

'What?' I asked, confused by the leap.

'The gallery.'

'I do – it's . . .' I gestured, 'far more than I had imagined.'

'I was very lucky, to be able to do this.'

'How did you?' I said, thinking of how much the building alone must have cost.

She smiled. 'Aunt Margaret. She left me a good deal of her fortune when she died. The other half went to her favourite projects – those artists who had not yet made a living from their work. The art world went into mourning at the loss of her. A number of prominent figures wrote about the influence she'd had on their career. Tom, as you might guess, was one of them.'

There was a give in her voice as she spoke his name.

'It seemed right to invest the money she left me in art – I felt she would have approved. The gallery in Paris came first. I bought the old Dupré Museum. Old Monsieur Dupré, thank goodness, had made his way to his daughter in the countryside after Georgette and Étienne were taken. The Germans had gone into the museum and destroyed or ransacked everything. Anything of value, they took. The rest was broken and smashed or burnt.

'At first the memories were so painful, I wasn't sure whether I would be able to go through with it. I am unable, even after all these years, to go down into that basement and not see them asleep there in one another's arms. In the end, though, it seemed the right thing; the only thing. I like to think that they would have been pleased with what I have done.

'The first piece I hung there was the drawing I sent you. I discovered it in a warehouse, full of pieces that had been looted by the Boches. One of so many things they took from Sophie.'

The next thing Alice said came as a surprise: 'I was never going to love anyone again, not in the way that I did Tom,' she told me, 'but that is not to say I didn't take lovers in the years that followed – many of whom were to become good friends for life. All great men, in their way, even if they were not that person they could never have replaced.'

I must have seemed taken aback by this, because she smiled and said, quite gently, 'I do not say this to embarrass you. It is that I don't want you to see me as a victim, someone who stopped living when I lost the person I loved. To do so, when I had survived something that had claimed so many, would have been a terrible, selfish thing. In many ways, my life has been rather like a record of the lost and found. Perhaps all lives are like that. Lost: love; found: independence. Lost: a daughter; found: a granddaughter.' I felt something expand inside me at this, almost a pain – but of the best sort.

'I made some sort of choice in 1939,' she said, 'even if I could not have known then what the consequences would be. If I had gone with him, after that weekend in Corsica, I know that my life would have been very different. It is difficult, of course it is, not to dwell on what could have been – and I have had to struggle against that.' She paused. 'That is not to say that I haven't thought of him every day since. Collecting his work has been my way to remain connected.'

I asked something that had been intriguing me: 'Did you keep your new name, so that he wouldn't know it was you?'

'It was convenient – though that wasn't the main reason. So much had happened that there was no question of returning to Alice Eversley. Célia was my way of starting a new life . . . a means of survival, you could say. I knew from the start that the gallery would not be in my name: old or new. It would be the Galerie De Rosier.'

This time I couldn't stop myself from asking it. 'Did you know that Tom came to find you, after the war? That he met Madame Fourrier, and she thought you were dead?'

She shook her head. 'She did say something, but it was already too late – he was married.'

'You didn't . . .' I knew that I was out of line, but some demon was in me, forcing me on. 'You didn't think of going to Corsica, to find him?'

Her silver gaze was unwavering. 'I was too late. Perhaps I knew that even before I saw Rosa. Perhaps even before the war, when I chose to stay in Paris. In another life, things might have been different. Or if I'd been a different person, I'd have gone with Tom when he asked me to. I'd have left France when there was still time.

'But I wasn't that other person, I was me.' She smiled at me. 'I can tell what it is you want, Kate. You want a love story. But, you see, I've given you a love story. It just doesn't all work out the way one might have written it. You could say ours was not a generation blessed with many happy endings.'

Postscript, 2015

Alice lived for another year. She died in the autumn of 1987. Julie said that it had started as a cold that had taken root and wouldn't let go, eventually turning itself into something lethal. She refused to be moved into a hospital, even at the end, and insisted on being taken to the gallery each day until she was too ill to leave her bed.

You could say that the grief I felt was disproportionate to the short time I had known her, but I don't think so. After all, it wasn't as if we were really strangers before I met her that first time – even before I first heard about her from Stafford. There were so many ways – her strength of character, her beauty, her bravery – in which she was like my mother. And I hope that in some ways she was also a little like me.

She left me almost everything she owned of Stafford's work – including those pieces that she had kept in private, at her study in the gallery. At first, I didn't know what to do. But then I remembered what she had said about hoping, one day, to be able to share them with the world. Several of them now hang in the National Portrait Gallery in London, though the De Rosier Gallery has the lion's share.

There was also the study Stafford had made of me. He showed the finished work to me when I next went to visit, and I understood then what it was he had seen that first time we met. Looking at it made my heart ache, for it seemed that I found two other faces there besides my own, both so dear to me. When Stafford asked if he could keep hold of it for a while, I agreed. After all, I never felt that it was really mine to keep.

The strangest thing is that it was found in Alice's apartment after she died, hanging beside the photograph I had sent her of Mum. Yet something stopped me from questioning Stafford about it. A few months later, when we were re-framing the picture for display, I discovered an envelope tucked between the parchment and backing: an odd place to keep such a thing. It was addressed, care of the museum, to Miss Alice Eversley. The letter that must have come with it was never found. It is almost as though Alice took it with her when she went.

Stafford is gone now too. Though whenever Oliver and I visit the Maison du Vent, which we do often, I always feel that he is there, somewhere out of sight.

Down at the cove, perhaps, or taking a swim in the freshwater pool. The floor and walls of the studio are still splattered with colours of every hue, and in certain lights the paint gleams as though newly wet, and it makes me smile.

Epilogue

The two drawings hang together now. If you were passing quickly you might assume that they depict the same woman. On closer inspection, it is clear that this is not the case. There is a resemblance between the two faces, but it is familial rather than identical. It is the expressions that are so uncannily alike. Both women wear a look of slight incredulity, as though uncomfortable with the idea of themselves as muses. Their gaze enquires, too, demands something from those who look upon them. Not for them the quiet and patient passivity of so many subjects. One feels that their attention may be snatched away at any moment, lost to some more immediate and enticing thing beyond the realm of the paper.

516

Oddly enough, most onlookers are apt to see all of this before they notice the great gulf of years between the two dates: 1929 and 1986. Almost a lifetime.

Acknowledgements

I would like to express my huge gratitude to everyone who encouraged me in the writing of *The Book of Lost and Found* and helped to get it out into the world. Without the following people this book would undoubtedly have remained a poorly-formatted Word document on my laptop. So thank you to:

Cathryn Summerhayes, for your agenting genius, unfailing support and for being such fun to work with. I am so lucky to have you on my team.

Dorian Karchmar, Annemarie Blumenhagen, Siobhan O'Neill and Ashley Fox – for all your wisdom, advice, patience and brilliance.

Kim Young: thank you for loving and understanding *Lost and Found* from the very beginning . . . and for still claiming to love it on the fifth reading! And to Laura Tisdel and Jennifer Lambert, for, with Kim, forming an incredible triumvirate of international editorial wisdom, working tirelessly (and ever tactfully!) to make the book stronger.

The team at HarperCollins: Ann Bissell – star publicist (and modesty-defender!), Charlotte Brabbin, Sarah Benton, Claire Palmer, Heike Schuessler (the incredible creative talent behind the cover), Katie Sadler, Charlotte Dolan and Thalia Suzuma.

The team at Little, Brown: Terry Adams (thank you for falling in love with Corsica!), Fiona Brown, Miriam Parker, Reagan Arthur and Carina Guiterman.

The team at HarperCollins Canada: Iris Tupholme, Cory Beatty, Michael Guy-Haddock, Rob Firing and Colleen Clarke.

Sherise Hobbs and Clare Foss for wonderful confidence-boosting lunches and invaluable insiders' advice.

Mark Lucas, for being a mentor extraordinaire.

Richard Charkin, for telling me I should try writing all those years ago – I haven't forgotten!

Anna Hogarty and Emily Kitchin for being the best friends and advisors a girl could hope for.

My beloved parents, Sue and Patrick Foley, for twenty-eight years – and counting – of love and encouragement. You have always made me feel that I could do anything I set my sights on. To Kate and Robbie, for making life so much fun (and for providing inspiration for the games Alice and Tom play on the beach!). To the whole family (Foleys, Colleys, Simmonds, Allens, O'Flynns and Crofts!) for all your support.

My darling Alex, without whose patience and wisdom this book would never have been finished, let alone sent out into the world. Thank you for putting up with me through all those long Sundays together in cafés while I worried over plot holes and sentence construction. Thank you, proofreader, cheerleader, chief strategist. I love you.

Read on for
Reading Group questions
and inspiration behind

The Book of
Lost & Found

A Q&A with
lucy foley

The Book of Lost and Found is your brilliant debut novel. Have you always aspired to write?

It was something I'd always wanted to try, though I wasn't sure whether I'd be any good at it, or whether I could find an idea that would sustain my – or, more importantly, the reader's – interest for the length of a novel. So it was exciting when that idea began to take shape.

You wrote this novel when you were still in your job as an editor at a book publishers – was there something in reading other authors' manuscripts that sparked a feeling of, 'This could be me'? Were there family tree-type doodles and potential plot notes all over your desk?

I definitely think that working with books at every stage of the production process definitely gave me the confidence to try writing something myself. It taught me that even manuscripts by some of the most talented authors often take some polishing, and that every sentence didn't have to be perfect straight away.

The book is laced with wonderful historical detail and various exotic and contrasting settings – has the story you've chosen to tell been influenced by a love for history and travel?

It certainly has. I enjoy the research phase almost as much as I do the writing phase – I've always been particularly interested by personal histories and how they interact with world events. And if I could I'd spend all my time travelling – especially now that I can call it work. I recently went to the Italian Riviera, Madrid, Morocco and New York for research for my second novel.

Do you identify with any of the characters? Or have any of them been inspired by people close to you?

I think there are inevitably elements of myself in the characters, in their views and experiences. And perhaps there are elements of who I'd want to be, too: I'd love something of Alice's bravery or Tom's compassion (or talent!). Aunt Margaret was in large part inspired by my beloved grandmother – also called Margaret – who recently passed away at the age of ninety-four. They both shared the same rebel's confidence – and a fantastic sense of style.

You could say that Alice is a woman ahead of her time: she's adventurous, spirited and non-conformist, and we sense that she feels stifled by her mother's impositions and the expectations dictated on her behaviour by society. Was this something that you wanted to consciously write into her character?

Absolutely, though I wouldn't necessarily say Alice is ahead of her time so much as very much of it, one of the many women at the time who were pushing the agenda: trying to take charge of their own destinies, demanding more from life. Alice shares this questing spirit with her one-time suffragette aunt, Lady Margaret. Alice's mother, meanwhile, is very much in the Victorian/Edwardian mould of the 'angel in the house': decorous and seemingly passive.

From Kate's photography to Stafford's paintings, there's an 'art' theme running through the book. Are you an artist yourself?

In a very amateurish way! I do love painting and drawing, though – and it's something I'd love to start devoting more time to. I have a huge box of materials – oils, acrylics, pastels, charcoals – but I don't use them as much as I'd like. What is it that they say? All the gear and no idea . . .?

Kate sets off on a very personal voyage of discovery when she seeks out Thomas Stafford. Is family history something that you find particularly interesting?

It is – and increasingly so as I get older, though I always loved listening to my grandparents' stories. I think there are novel-worthy elements in every family history. I'm sure most people can think of an ancestor who was notably brave, unique or controversial in some way; or of incidents or actions in the past that changed the shape of things for years to come.

At the novel's heart is a beautiful, bittersweet love story – in this respect was it difficult to tie up the narrative in the way that you did?

Yes, although I knew that it was the only way the novel could end. Above all I wanted it to feel real – true to the characters and how they would have behaved.

What would you say is the hardest part of the writing process?

The editing process! It's so difficult picking back over your work, realising that what you got down on the page wasn't quite what you thought it was, trying to coax it into a more pleasing form. Sometimes it can be almost like re-reading a diary – slightly embarrassing . . .

Can you tell us a little bit about your next book or any other exciting ideas that you have?

My next book is set in the 1950s, in the Golden Age of film and – a nice writerly challenge this! – largely takes place aboard a yacht sailing along the Italian Riviera towards the Cannes film festival. There is also an interwoven narrative set in 1930s Spain, during the Spanish Civil War. There is a love story at its heart, too, though with a slightly darker twist . . .

Finally, and perhaps quite predictably, what would your Desert Island book have to be?

A very difficult question, but I think I'd choose a collection of short stories by one of my favourite authors, James Salter. Each work is a complete, tangible world in itself, and these are stories that bear re-reading – there is something new to discover each time.

READING GROUP QUESTIONS

- Alice and Tom meet when they are young, adventurous – and slightly mischievous – children. Did you think this part of their story helps us to fully appreciate the deep-seated history and special bond between them? Would their love story be a little less captivating without this knowledge?

- After returning from Venice, Alice retreats and ends up lying to Tom. Do you think this was the best way of protecting him?

- Do you think Tom would have been able to forgive Alice for not telling him about their daughter?

- Discuss Tom's decision to go against family tradition and pursue a career as an artist.

- Does Lady Eversley have any redeeming qualities? Did she love Alice in her own way?

- Discuss the relationship between Kate and Oliver. Were you rooting for them to get together?

- After all she had been through, was Célia still the girl by the lake at heart?

- Towards the end of the novel, Alice says, 'I can tell what it is you want, Kate. You want a love story. But, you see, I've given you a love story. It just doesn't all work out the way one might have written it.' Would you write Alice and Tom's story in any other way?

- What do you think the message about family history and identity is?

- How did you feel after reading the novel? What would you say when you pressed it into someone else's hands?

A NOTE ON INSPIRATION FROM LUCY

As you might have noticed, this book is dedicated to my grandmothers. I grew up influenced by these fearless unconventional women, and sought inspiration from them when I came to write the female characters in the book. I wanted Alice to be like them: to be brave and often selfless in the decisions that she makes. And I wanted Kate to be inspired by Alice and her choices in the way that my mother, sister and I have been by the older generation.

My father's mother, Margaret – 'Mama' – died recently at the age of ninety-four. I still find it hard to believe that I won't hear her recount another memory from her incredibly varied life. I still worry that there are tales I hadn't yet heard. Most recently, she told me how, as a medical student in the Second World War, she was sent at midnight into the dark gardens of a stately-home-turned-hospital, to collect blood for transfusions from the gardening shed. This was to be added to other tales of hers I had from that time – brushing incendiary bombs from the roof of King's College hospital, lifting survivors from the bombing of the Sunpat factory next door over the adjoining fence. She was barely twenty at the time.

Mama was married three times, and had two great loves: my grandfather John Foley, a dashing, brilliant surgeon who took her dancing in the Café de Paris for their first date and with her hosted legendary parties at their house in the country; and Gary O'Flynn, a kind, artistic doctor with whom she travelled the world. These were real-life tales of passion, tragedy and devotion – and I never tired of hearing them. To the day she died, Mama was the picture of elegance and intellect: with one of her many silk scarves tied about her neck (I never saw her wearing the same thing twice), and an open book always beside her.

Mama (Margaret O'Flynn) as I will always remember her, looking incredibly elegant and thoughtful. When I was little, she'd let me try on her jewellery, and pose in front of the mirror at her dressing table. I thought I looked the bee's knees.

My mother's mother, Bubbles – Granny, to me – is vitality itself. She cycles everywhere, and plays tennis several times a week. I really believe that she may have found the secret to eternal youth, because every time I see her she looks a little younger. Her present for her eightieth birthday last year? A new bicycle, which she rode around the marquee in front of her assembled guests. Granny is also the best letter writer I know, and my favourite person to go to the theatre with.

My love of storytelling is inherited from Granny. Whenever we went for a walk in the local woods, she would point out the evidence of trolls and tree sprites in the foliage, and, as often as not, our bedtime story would be one from her own rich imagination. But she is also a voracious reader, with a wonderful library. When I stayed at my grandparent's house, I would have my pick of the vast collection of children's books there: Enid Blyton, C.S. Lewis, Roald Dahl, Beatrix Potter alongside many lesser-known names.

At one stage, Granny had an antiques shop, and I know that one of the things that fascinated her most about the items she bought and sold were the stories behind them. So Granny's influence on me has been twofold: I was inspired by her verve and capacity for love – all traits I wanted to imbue Alice and Kate with – and I was encouraged by her to try my own hand at storytelling. When, at the launch party of the book, she told me she was proud of me, it was the highlight of my short writing career so far. After all, I wrote the book with my grandmothers, my mother and sister in mind: as motivation, as inspiration, as readers.

Granny (Bubbles Simmonds) a great beauty, and the picture of life and energy. Granny and Grandfather lived near the sea, and my childhood memories are full of long, salt-and-sand days on the beach with them, followed by suppers in their sunlit garden and bedtime stories.

Lucy's Guide to Corsica

1. Have supper in Bonifacio Old Town, watching the sea change colour far beneath you as the light fades. Even better, go during the Bastille Day celebrations, and watch the spectacular firework display.

2. Hire a boat (the older the better – preferably one of those ancient ones with a precarious canvas awning) and visit the inlets only accessible by water, as these are some of the best beaches on the island.

3. Go swimming in the clear green waters of the mountain rock pools. There are many of these, so avoid the larger, more populated spots and carry on until you discover one you can make your own.

4. Taste some Corsican wine. A perfect rainy-day activity (being an island, the weather can change suddenly). See if you can, indeed, taste the salt and herbs of the island.

5. Hike the GR20 (not for the faint-hearted). This is a route that runs from one end of the island to the other, over the mountainous spine, and takes about two weeks. It's notorious as one of the most challenging marked hiking routes in Europe. I have to confess to not having done it yet, but it has been on my list for a while!

Photographs ©Shutterstock.com